W9-AKS-502

WHERE DEAD MEN MEET

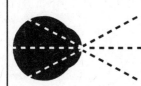

This Large Print Book carries the
Seal of Approval of N.A.V.H.

WHERE DEAD MEN MEET

MARK MILLS

THORNDIKE PRESS
A part of Gale, a Cengage Company

Farmington Hills, Mich • San Francisco • New York • Waterville, Maine
Meriden, Conn • Mason, Ohio • Chicago

LIBRARY OF CONGRESS CATALOGING-IN-PUBLICATION DATA

Names: Mills, Mark, 1963– author.
Title: Where dead men meet / by Mark Mills.
Description: Large print edition. | Waterville, Maine : Thorndike Press, 2017. |
  Series: Thorndike Press large print historical fiction
Identifiers: LCCN 2017022397| ISBN 9781432842345 (hardcover) | ISBN 143284234X
  (hardcover)
Subjects: LCSH: Intelligence officers—Great Britain—Fiction. | Paris
  (France)—Fiction. | Large type books. | GSAFD: Suspense fiction.
Classification: LCC PS3613.I569 W47 2017 | DDC 813/.6—dc23
LC record available at https://lccn.loc.gov/2017022397

Published in 2017 by arrangement with Blackstone Audio, Inc.

Printed in the United States of America
1 2 3 4 5 6 7 21 20 19 18 17

"Yet meet we shall, and part,
and meet again
Where dead men meet,
on lips of living men."
— SAMUEL BUTLER

■ ■ ■ ■

ENGLAND

■ ■ ■ ■

CHAPTER ONE

Had Sister Agnes been less devout, she would have lived to celebrate her forty-eighth birthday.

Not that celebrating such milestones had ever come naturally to her. She had no difficulties with Easter, steeping herself in Christ's selfless Passion, living His suffering as best she could; but even His birthday seemed trivial by comparison, never mind her own. If she played along, it was purely for the sake of the children, whose small faces lit up like beacons whenever Sister Beatrice produced from the orphanage's ancient oven one of her chocolate cakes, its sponge as dense as brick (and almost as tasteless).

There had been no birthday cakes at the Carthusian nunnery where Agnes took her sacred vows at the age of nineteen. No, there had been seemingly endless hours of prayer and silent meditation within the confines of her tiny cell and meals handed out through a hatch to limit the distraction of human contact. The devotional rigors of the order had ultimately proved too much for her, and despite the passage of the years, and the gratifying sense of purpose that three decades at St. Theresa's Orphanage had brought her, she had never quite been able to shake off the feeling that she had somehow fallen short in the eyes of the Lord.

This was the reason she still rose dutifully from her bed at midnight, as she had back at the nunnery, to offer a prayer to Our Lady. It was also the reason she heard the dim but distinct sound of breaking glass — a bright tinkle, not unlike the Angelus bell — cutting through the silence of the sleeping building.

Nearing the foot of the main staircase, she paused, straining her ears, wondering if perhaps she had imagined the sound, somehow brought it into being. No. Another noise, different from the first — a vague sort of shuffling. Someone was definitely at large on the ground floor. One of the children, up to no good? It certainly wouldn't be the first time.

The light leaking beneath the door to

Mother Hilda's study lay like a silver thread in the deep darkness of the corridor. The floorboards groaned beneath her feet as she approached and pressed her ear to the door. Silence. She thought about knocking, but she had never known Mother Hilda to be up at this hour, so she entered unannounced.

She had time just to take in the filing cabinet that had been forced open, and the scattering of gray folders in the tight pool of light thrown by the desk lamp, when a hand clamped around her mouth.

The man must have heard her coming and taken up a position behind the door. *"Sssh-hhh,"* he soothed, his lips close to her ear. "Don't make a noise. I don't want to hurt you. Do you understand?"

Trembling, she nodded. The door closed behind her, and she found herself being forced toward the overstuffed armchair near the fireplace. "Sit down," said the man, removing his rough hand from her mouth. She looked up at him only after she had drawn the woolen shawl around her shoulders, against the draft from the broken window.

He was short, with a thin, eager face and lank, sandy-colored hair receding at the temples. She had seen a pistol before — her grandfather's service revolver from his time in the Crimea, the one with which he claimed to have dispatched eight Russians in a single afternoon — but she had never had one pointed at her.

Scared before, she now felt strangely calm, unthreatened. She was under the protection of someone infinitely more powerful than this desperate little man in a gabardine overcoat.

"If it's money you're after, you've come to the wrong place. We barely have enough to feed ourselves."

"How long have you been here?"

"Excuse me?"

"The orphanage. How long?"

She detected something in his accent now — a faint foreign clip that she might have been able to identify had she traveled the world more widely.

"Almost thirty years."

"That's good," he replied. "A boy was left here in 1912. A baby, left on the steps."

Her heart gave a sudden lurch. "So many of them come to us that way." The lie tripped off her tongue with an ease that surprised her.

"It was winter. January."

"If you say so."

She remembered. How could she not? She

was the one who had heard the urgent knocking and hurried to the entrance door. There had been a shallow blanket of snow on the ground, and the tracks in it had led her eye to a tall, shadowy figure standing some distance away in the twilit gloom of the driveway. Only when the man turned on his heel and disappeared into the darkness did she notice the small bundle at her feet: her own little Moses, swaddled in a crocheted blanket — asleep, peaceful, and untroubled, even then. His gift to her.

"I need a name," said the man.

"Do you have any idea how many children pass through our hands?"

"I also need to know where he is."

She saw the many letters from Luke neatly bundled in the box beneath her bed, and her curiosity finally got the better of her. "Why?"

The man hesitated. "I have a message from the person who left him here."

There was a shared acknowledgment in the look they traded: that a message carried by a man who came skulking in the night, gun in hand, was not a message worth receiving.

"Leave it with me," she replied. "I'll see what I can do."

The man grunted, then tucked the pistol

away in the pocket of his overcoat, and for a moment she thought she had worn him down with her dignified resistance.

"I'm sorry, but I don't have much time."

He produced an object from his other pocket. Shaped like a policeman's truncheon, it appeared to be made of leather.

She would have been less afraid if she had seen some malicious intent in his eyes, but all she detected was an emptiness that spoke of weary resignation, even boredom.

Her last thought before it began was that this was a test, a kind of penance, and that she would show herself equal to the suffering He had endured.

■ ■ ■ ■ ■

FRANCE

■ ■ ■ ■ ■

CHAPTER TWO

"Luke! Where's that coffee?" came the cry through the closed door separating their offices.

"Coming, sir."

Luke flicked a switch on the intercom console and lowered his voice. "Diana, coffee for His Highness, and don't spare the horses . . . I forgot to say before."

"Tut-tut."

"I'll make it up to you."

"Don't feel you have to," came back her lazy drawl of a reply.

Diana appeared in his office a few minutes later, carrying a tray. Today, she had her hair pinned back behind her ears, which, like everything else about her, were petite and perfectly formed. She knew what he thought of her ears. There was a time not so long ago when he had been allowed to tell her such things.

"Shall I do the honors?" she asked.

"No, I'll take it through. I need to go over some papers with him."

Diana placed the tray on his desk. There was a letter propped between the coffeepot and the sugar bowl. "This just came for you."

He was surprised to see his father's crabbed handwriting: *Luke Hamilton, the British Embassy, Rue du Faubourg Saint-Honoré, Paris.*

"Everything all right?"

"Yes." He tilted his head at the tray. "And thank you."

He waited for her to leave before tearing open the envelope.

My dear Luke,

It is with a heavy heart that I'm writing to you so soon after my last letter, and I'm very sorry to say that you will find nothing dreary or rambling about this one . . .

Luke knew he was walking, but the ground felt dull beneath his feet, as though the paving stones were made of India rubber. The other pedestrians seemed to flit around him like phantasms.

Not just dead . . . murdered . . . bludgeoned to death. How was it possible? How

18

could anyone . . . ? Sister Agnes, of all people. And for what? Some candlesticks and a handful of other near-worthless trinkets?

Grief and impotent rage scrambled his thoughts. The first person he had ever known, ever loved — his mentor and guide for the first seven years of his life. She had taught him to read and write, taught him the names of the trees and the birds, taught him right from wrong, scolding him when he strayed and praising him when he excelled. She had wiped blood from his knees, snot from his nose, tears from his eyes; and when the influenza tried to take him, she had sat at his bedside in the sanatorium and laid cold compresses on his burning body to keep him from slipping away.

Where was the logic? Where was the justice? Where, he asked himself, was her God when she needed him? He knew what she would have replied: that the book was already written, and even if we could not see our place in the story, we could be sure that it was a good book with a very fine ending.

Not such a fine ending for her, though. And very nearly a rotten one for Luke, too, when crossing Avenue George V.

Lost in a somber trance, he looked the

wrong way as he stepped off the pavement, and was almost struck by a speeding lorry. Shaken by the close call, he found a vacant bench in some welcome shade and fumbled a cigarette between his lips.

A moment of distraction . . . a blur of hurtling steel . . . certain death mere inches from the tip of his nose. What unsettled him most, though, was that for a split second, it wouldn't have mattered.

Paris had been moving to the beat of the Exposition Internationale since the beginning of the year, when the first pavilions had begun to spring up along the banks of the Seine. The site of the World Fair (as most people called it) lay at the heart of the city, straddling the lazy bend in the river between the Pont de la Concorde and the Pont de Grenelle.

This was Luke's third visit. His first had been in late May, to attend the official opening of the British pavilion, a fashionably cuboid building that looked like a large packing case dropped beside the Pont d'Iéna by a passing giant. After the interminable speeches, they had strolled around the exhibits, champagne flutes in hand, cooing politely to those involved while privately pondering the scale of the disaster.

This was supposed to be a showcase for the very best that Great Britain had to offer the world in 1937, and yet, the first display to greet visitors was a selection of suitable clothing to be worn while out shooting. Next came a baffling array of squash rackets and cricket bats. And so it continued. There was almost no nod to the country's rich industrial and technological heritage. Anyone who didn't know better would have thought that forty million Britons frittered away their time in sport and country pursuits. Bizarrely, and unlike many of the other pavilions, it had no garden — the very thing for which the British were known (and affectionately mocked) by their continental cousins.

"It's a national bloody disgrace," was Wing Commander Wyeth's muttered verdict, and for once Luke had found himself agreeing with his boss. "I mean, what kind of message are they trying to send to our friends over the way?"

He meant the Germans and the Soviets, whose pavilions stood on the other side of the bridge, facing one another across the wide avenue running down to the river from the Palais de Chaillot. No stumpy packing cases for them, but two soaring testaments to self-belief. There was a rumor doing the rounds that Albert Speer, the architect of the German scheme, had somehow laid his hands on the Soviets' plans, thereby ensuring that the German pavilion stood taller by a good margin, topped by a giant Nazi eagle unfurling its wings. The Soviets had responded by crowning their pavilion with a monumental sculpture of a worker and a peasant woman brandishing a hammer and sickle at their neighbors over the road.

The visual confrontation of National Socialism and Stalinist Communism wasn't lost on anyone; and when viewed from the Palais de Chaillot, with the Eiffel Tower looming behind, the impression was of two bullies squaring off in the school playground while the teacher looked on helplessly. It was a sight to bring a smile to your lips, even as it sent a chill down your spine.

During his second visit to the Fair a few weeks ago, Luke had made a tour of both pavilions and been pleasantly surprised to find nothing more ominous on show than a shared message of peaceful progress through the happy marriage of science and art. According to Diana, the same couldn't be said of the Spanish pavilion — recently opened, almost two months late — where she and a friend had dropped in over the weekend. "Prepare yourself for something a little different," she had warned him as he was leaving the embassy earlier.

He had glimpsed the building on his last visit: a flimsy glass-and-steel structure that looked as though it wouldn't fare too well in a high wind. Tucked away behind the German pavilion, it had been crawling with workmen racing to put the finishing touches to the place. These now included, Luke could see, a large photographic mural high on the facade, showing some troops drawn up in serried ranks. Below it was a stark declaration in French that ended with these words: WE ARE FIGHTING FOR THE INDEPENDENCE OF OUR HOMELAND AND FOR THE RIGHT OF THE SPANISH PEOPLE TO DETERMINE THEIR OWN DESTINY.

An attractive couple leaving the pavilion passed in front of him, their young son at their heels, absorbedly picking his nose.

"Disappointing," was the man's verdict. "Not at all in the spirit of the Fair."

The woman pushed a wayward lock of hair from her face. "Darling, they *are* at war with each other."

"Do *you* want to be reminded of that? Because *I* certainly don't."

The civil war in Spain was raging more fiercely than ever, with General Franco's nationalist troops now holding half the country and moving with increasing brutality against anyone who resisted the military coup. The future of Spain was trembling in the balance, and the republican government clearly saw the Fair as a showcase for highlighting the deadly serious problems at home.

Luke had some idea what to expect as he stepped inside the building, because he had skimmed a French newspaper's snooty review of the vast painting that occupied almost an entire wall of the ground-floor entrance area: "Mr. Picasso's trademark trickery is not just on full display, it has attained whole new heights of self-importance . . ."

He stood and stared, unable to think straight, although he knew immediately that the art critic was a fool. It wasn't simply the painting's enormous size, twice the height of a man and well over twenty feet long; he had never seen another work of art like it. In fact, he had never seen *anything* quite like it. There was nothing for the eye to settle on more than momentarily — no obvious structure, no shape that allowed you the comfort of recognition. Even the horse's head wasn't a horse's head; it was a howl of pain with some sort of obscene pointed object protruding from the mouth.

The subject was Guernica, the Basque town bombed to rubble by General Franco back in April. Luke knew the grim details more intimately than most, for it went with the job. He had scoured the intelligence, pored over the reports from the embassy in Madrid (strangely nonjudgmental in their tone). However, the painting had almost nothing in common with the photos he had flipped through of the blasted buildings and the bodies heaped up in the streets and the lucky living standing around in sorry clumps.

This wasn't the stilled storm of the aftermath; it was the moment of devastation itself: forms fragmented into facets, shattered then scattered across the canvas in dull monochrome shades of black, white, and gray — willfully unvivid, which somehow served to heighten the horror. It was hell on earth, a man-made hell that seemed to reach beyond its subject, embracing all of man's inhumanity to man.

He couldn't drag himself away, and it was a good few minutes before he realized why this was. She was on the left-hand side of the painting, just below the bull's head, her own head thrown back toward the heavens in a broken-toothed, screaming plea for mercy.

She had a ponytail, as did Sister Agnes.

"It's coming."

Luke glanced to his right, realizing only then that the comment had been addressed to him. "Excuse me?"

The man had a full head of stiff silver hair, cropped close at the sides, and his kind, lucid eyes shone with a youthful vigor despite his advanced years. "For all of us," he continued in French. "This is our future."

"You think?"

"You don't?" The man turned his attention back to the painting. "German and Italian planes doing Franco's dirty work? The fascists are uniting, and they have started practicing on women and children. You think they can stop themselves now?"

"Are you a Communist?"

It was a stupid question, glib and lazy, but the man smiled, amused by the notion. "I've had dealings with both, and I can tell you they are not as different from each other as they would like to think." He paused before adding, "Beware the man who tells you he knows what's best for you; he usually starts by stealing your rights."

"Who said that?"

"I did."

I doubt it, thought Luke.

The man offered his hand. "Bernard Fautrier."

With tensions rising across the continent, and with Italy and Germany effectively lost to dictators, Paris had become the clearing house of Europe, the place where the real business was done. The city was swarming with agents of all kinds, and the currency of the moment was information. They had received firm instructions at the embassy to rebuff then report any approaches made, but Luke was in a restless, contrary mood.

"Luke Hamilton," he replied.

"Not French?"

"English."

The man released Luke's hand and switched languages effortlessly. "Your French is impeccable. So is the accent."

"Madame Vallet will be thrilled to hear it."

"Madame Vallet?"

"My teacher. And we both know my accent is atrocious."

The man ignored this challenge. "You don't look English. You are too . . ."

"Dark?" Luke offered.

"Yes, and the mouth is too strong. Where are you really from?"

Maybe it was the ghostly presence of Sister Agnes, both in his thoughts and on the giant painting before them, but when Luke finally replied, it was with the sort of honesty one reserved for total strangers. "I don't know. I'm an orphan. I was brought up by nuns."

The man looked shaken by this news. "Your parents?" he asked tentatively before raising his hand. "No, don't tell me. You never knew them."

"No."

"You were a baby and it was 1912."

Luke had had enough; the game had gone too far. "Bravo," he said tersely. "You've done your research."

"It was a question."

"Listen, nothing I know is worth buying."

"I'm not buying."

"Neither am I," Luke replied. "So let's just call it a day, shall we?"

He turned and left, skirting the strange iron fountain that flowed with mercury rather than water. He hadn't noticed before, but the coins tossed in by visitors were floating on the silvered surface of the round pool.

CHAPTER THREE

Borodin was a cautious man. He had learned his lesson young, just shy of his nineteenth birthday, on a wet and wind-blown night in Ragusa. The scars that had decorated his midriff ever since were an unsightly reminder of the dangers of dropping one's guard, even for a moment, even when you thought you knew exactly where you stood with people.

He had learned another lesson a few months after the attack: that he drew no satisfaction from the act of vengeance. The thrill lay in the hunt, in the slow decipherment of motives, of shadowy ambitions and betrayals. Watching a man die by your own hand was an altogether different experience. He wasn't a natural. That first time, he had emptied the contents of his stomach onto the floor beside the cooling corpse, feeling better for it only because his revulsion suggested he wasn't a soulless psychopath, but simply a pragmatist looking to stretch out his life as long as possible.

Well, that pragmatism had managed to add another forty-odd years to that life, and he saw no reason to let up now. It was the reason he poked his head into the concierge's front room, as he always did when returning to his building on Rue Brochant.

"Good evening, Thierry. Did anyone call for me while I was out?"

Thierry's fat fingers were fiddling with the brass guts of a door lock. "One day I'll say yes, Monsieur Fautrier."

Maybe, but only if prompted. The concierge was about as quick-witted as a packhorse. It amused Borodin to know that Thierry thought of him as a sad, lonely, deluded old man. He caught the odor of Isabelle's cooking. "Smells like pork tonight."

"Belly. Straight from the plate to here." Thierry patted his paunch and laughed.

It was a long climb to Borodin's apartment, and it seemed to have gotten longer over the year he'd been living here. Really? Another floor? There was no mistaking when you arrived, because there was nowhere else to go, only left to his apartment or right to the Chavigniers'. Their young son, Emile, was usually to be found at this time of the evening playing on the landing, because its terrazzo floor offered a perfectly smooth surface for the boy's marbles. Borodin enjoyed his brief exchanges with Emile. It felt like practice for the grandson he might one day meet, although not if his daughter had anything to do with it.

Emile's absence sharpened his senses, but he relaxed when he spotted the small shard of paper, barely visible, tucked low down between the jamb and the door. It told him that no one had entered his apartment while he was away.

Closing the door behind him, he dropped his keys into the chipped porcelain bowl on the console table.

"If you even flinch I'll kill you," came a voice at his shoulder. Far too close to risk making a move, not even for the gun so tantalizingly within reach, taped to the underside of the console table.

A hand searched him — a knowing hand that went straight for the stiletto he always wore in a scabbard above his right ankle. That one small act was enough to narrow the field down to his very closest associates, his own people. The hand also discovered the Browning pocket pistol tucked into the back of his waistband. He didn't draw much comfort from the fact that he wasn't dead already — it only meant they wanted answers first — but at least it offered him a slender lifeline, a chance to stall and confuse the man now propelling him toward the sofa with a firm shove between the shoulder blades.

He must have come in through one of the windows, via the roof. Unless, of course . . .

Stay focused on the immediate danger, he told himself. There'll be time enough to figure out the mechanics later.

The man remained standing behind the sofa. An unseen enemy. "Put your hands on your knees. Move them and I'll shoot."

"Do that and they'll hear it next door. You should know, he's a big man with a bad temper."

"Was he?"

Borodin felt his shoulders sag under the weight of the past tense. "The boy?" he asked, dreading the reply.

"The boy put up more of a fight than his father."

Little Emile, with his ready smile and jug ears, snuffed out before he had a chance to show what he was really made of.

"You didn't need to do that."

"Yes, I did," came the voice. "You're obviously getting soft in your old age."

"If you're lucky to live as long as I have in this game, you may find yourself going the same way."

"I'm not falling for that. I was warned about your tricks."

"Oh? By whom?"

"It doesn't matter. What matters is you've had three days to finish the job."

"I made contact today."

"I know. I saw you with him."

And Borodin recalled the three "tourists" who had piqued his suspicions in the Spanish pavilion earlier. The slim, nervy woman in the *eau de Nil* dress could be dismissed, but he was fairly certain that one or the other of the men in question was now standing at his shoulder. The younger and taller of the two, he guessed — the one in the fawn twill jacket and the panama hat, who had been examining Picasso's painting of Guernica with an air of almost theatrical indifference.

"Make contact, win his confidence, wait for instructions. Those were my orders." He was pleased with the response, even though it earned him a sharp clip on the back of his head with a pistol butt.

"Lies," the man hissed.

Borodin rubbed his head. More than anything, it was to test just how strict the rules were about the hands remaining on the knees. "We're obviously speaking to different people. I assumed you were here with the instructions."

"My instructions are to find out why you haven't finished the job, and then to finish it myself." He didn't need to add what this meant for Borodin.

"Kill him? That's absurd. Do you have any idea who he is?"

"Who cares?"

"Think of the two people you fear most in the world, because that's who cares; that's who I answer to. The only people . . . always directly."

"Lies."

True, but there was a new note of uncertainty in the man's voice, and no accompanying blow to the head this time. Borodin pressed home his advantage. "Listen, my friend, I don't know what's going on here, but I'm pretty sure you're on the wrong side of it. And believe me, that's not a place you want to be."

Casting them both as victims of some grander intrigue seemed to have the desired effect. He could almost hear the information being digested, tested.

"He said you'd try and mess with my head."

"Let me guess . . . Petrovic."

There was no guesswork involved. If nothing else, Petrovic was the only person within the organization who knew where he lived.

"No."

Not convincing. A feeble effort to throw him off course. He could have challenged it, playing for more time, but he had a sudden vision of Emile, his skinny arm swinging like a metronome as he lined up a shot on the landing.

"Then do what you've come to do," he said. "But at least allow me to look you in the eye when you do it." Turning slowly, resignedly, he plucked the silenced pistol from its hiding place beneath the sofa cushion and shot the man once in the throat.

There was a time when he would have leaped over the back of the sofa, but his arthritic hip had long since put paid to such acrobatics. Rounding the sofa, he gathered up the handgun and crouched beside the man. He lay flat on his back, gurgling and twitching grotesquely, both hands clutching his throat, heels drumming against the wooden floor. The panama hat lay a little distance away.

Borodin recovered his Browning and the stiletto from the man's jacket pocket. "That was your life," he said. "And this is for Emile."

As he eased the tip of the blade between the man's ribs, it struck him for the first time in his long career that revenge could, in fact, taste very sweet indeed.

He didn't linger. Once the body was still, he made straight for the windows, taking care not to place himself in view of anyone who might have the apartment under observation. He had always made a point of checking the window locks before going out, and all were still intact. Moving on, he found no signs of forced entry in any of the other rooms. This suggested an accomplice, someone on the outside to reset his crude little paper alarm once the front door lock had been picked.

The bedroom offered the best view of the street below, and he finally spotted her at the café on the corner. Not all of her, just a pale ankle and the hem of her *eau de Nil* dress, barely visible beneath the edge of the awning that, from this angle, masked most of the tables out front.

The leather holdall was ready and waiting behind the false back he had built to the cupboard beside the kitchen sink. It contained everything he required for a swift getaway: a change of clothes, a pair of shoes, a washbag, a substantial quantity of cash in various currencies, along with three passports in different names (impeccably forged by an old Armenian who ran an antiquarian bookshop on the Île Saint-Louis). He gathered together the various weapons he kept secreted around the apartment, and then stripped the dead man of his trousers and jacket. His last act before leaving was to pack the novel and the reading spectacles lying on his bedside table.

It was a long while since he had thought of anywhere as home, and he felt little sense of sorrow as he pulled the front door shut behind him. Besides, he had only himself to blame. Petrovic had instructed him to kill the Englishman, and he had hesitated, detecting something in Luke Hamilton's face, his bearing, that chimed with dim, disturbing memories from long ago. Answering to curiosity, he had then broken the cardinal rule and made contact with the target.

That Petrovic had taken out insurance against such a possibility reeked of more than his reputation for efficiency. There were other factors at play, shadows shifting at the back of the stage. If Petrovic had known the truth about Hamilton's identity, he would never have assigned Borodin to the job in the first place. No, a mistake had been made, had been recognized as such, and now was being rectified. The order to kill him could have come from only one place: the top.

He felt a cold hand clutch at his heart. He might have cheated death upstairs just now, but he was as good as dead, destined to see out his days glancing over his shoulder. He pictured a simple life of honest toil on his cousin's sheep station in Australia . . . and saw a car approaching in the shimmering distance, throwing up a plume of dust in its wake. No, they would hunt him down, search him out. It would be a point of both pride and principle for the Karaman brothers, men known for never leaving a loose end.

The solution came to him as he was crossing the darkened courtyard, and it stopped him momentarily in his tracks. He saw what he had to do, saw with absolute certainty that Luke Hamilton, alive and well, was the only bargaining chip available to him. There might even be some money in it — a lot of money if he played his hand correctly. The plan taking shape in his head left no place for the nostalgic sentiments that had given him pause before and almost gotten him killed just now.

"Eating out, Monsieur Fautrier?"

Thierry stepped jauntily from the shadows, swinging a bunch of keys in his hand.

Borodin would have replied in the affirmative if it weren't for the leather holdall he was carrying. "Dropping some old clothes off with a friend who needs them more than I do."

Thierry frowned. "Is that blood on your jacket?"

Borodin couldn't resist leaving the concierge with a line he could dine out on for the rest of his days. "Not my jacket — the jacket of the man I just killed."

Thierry laughed. "Oh, dear, I suppose I should call the cops."

The speed and wit of the response surprised Borodin. Maybe he had underestimated Thierry all this time. "Tell them it was self-defense."

"Don't you worry, Monsieur Fautrier, I'll even stand as a character witness at your trial."

"There isn't going to be a trial. I'm fleeing the country."

Thierry was still laughing as Borodin heaved open the wooden door and stepped outside onto the pavement.

He thought about pulling the brim of the panama hat down over his eyes, but the night had drawn in enough by now that it wasn't necessary. Judging from the reaction of the woman seated at the table in front of the Café Metropole, she took his appearance at face value: the hat, the jacket, the gray flannel trousers, discernible in the gloaming, but only just.

Nodding for her to follow him, he set off at a brisk pace toward Square des Batignolles. A quick glance saw the woman settling her account with Gustave, the cadaverous waiter who served Borodin his coffee and croissant most mornings. Another glance established that she was in pursuit and had him firmly in her sights as he entered the small park at the end of the street.

The timing was ideal. The dog walkers were long gone, driven off by the thickening dusk, and it would be a good while yet before the drinkers, lovers, and other reprobates began to make an appearance. He picked a hiding spot beside the graveled pathway, and when she finally appeared — slowing to a hesitant walk and hissing a name he couldn't quite make out — he stepped silently from the bushes and punched her in the side of the head.

Not too hard. Just enough to knock the fight out of her. He needed to know exactly who and what he was up against.

CHAPTER FOUR

Luke had heard the anecdote before, and it had changed with every telling, shifting shape under Fernando's embellishments. Improbably, a rabbi had now been added to the cast of characters.

Fernando claimed to have gotten the story straight from the horse's mouth: a society lady who was woken one night in her bed by the intimate kisses of a man. She knew it couldn't be her husband, because he was away in Lyon on business, but she wasn't sure at first just which of her many lovers it might be. She soon rejected the Romanian sculptor. Where was the rasp of his thick stubble between her thighs? As for the young Polish composer, well, it wasn't impossible, but he had always been a bit squeamish about that sort of thing. And the rabbi (who wasn't at all squeamish about that sort of thing) seemed an unlikely candidate, what with it being a Saturday night. Stumped, she was about to slide her hands beneath the covers in search of clues, but it was so good, so very good, that in the end she just lay there and allowed herself to be transported to a place she had never been before. When she finally awoke, she was alone, and none the wiser.

The next morning, after breakfast, she telephoned each of her lovers in turn and established in discreet, roundabout ways that none of them had been the mysterious visitor. This left the only other two people present in the apartment at the time: her seventeen-year-old stepson and the maid. Cornering the stepson in his bedroom, she asked, "Did you enjoy yourself last night?"

The boy blushed with embarrassment before finally blurting out, "You won't tell Father, will you?"

"Of course not," she replied.

"I've never done it before."

"You don't expect me to believe that, do you?"

"I promise. It's the first time I've slipped out at night, and I was back before sunrise."

Amélie gave a loud gasp. "It was the *maid*?"

Fernando spread his hands. "Who else? The boy was out on the town, living it up." He caught their elderly waiter's eye and signaled for another bottle of wine.

"What did your friend do?"

"She fired the maid, of course."

"Fired her?"

"She's a respectable lady."

The big laugh from the two girls was swallowed up in the lively buzz filling the restaurant. L'Hirondelle attracted a mixed crowd, everything from ancient widows with painted faces to skinny young men with beards, chasing the bohemian dream. Its lofty stuccoed ceilings, crystal chandeliers, and plum-colored velvet banquettes oozed a shabby fin de siècle grandeur that flew in the face of its more modish rivals in the *quartier*. A five-minute stroll from Luke's apartment, it had effectively become his canteen over the past few months.

"It doesn't seem fair," said Amélie's friend. She had a resolutely cheery countenance and a name he had made a point of remembering. He was fairly certain it began with a *V.*

"Don't worry about the maid," said Fernando. "She now lives in an apartment in Montparnasse, all expenses paid." He threw in a stage pause. "And once or twice a week, she receives a visitor."

More laughter, then a challenge from Amélie's friend. "I don't believe you."

"It's as true as those sweet little dimples in your cheeks, my dear Véronique. Ask Luke. He'll tell you."

"I've never known Fernando to lie. Cheat, deceive, betray, yes, but never lie."

It was another of Fernando's setups, although by this stage of the evening Luke usually knew which of the girls his friend had set his sights on. He had assumed it was Amélie, but the compliment paid to Véronique's dimples had thrown the field wide open again. Seen from the other side, the truth was the same as always: both girls wanted Fernando; Luke was the consolation prize. He didn't mind. Who could blame them? How many men combined the brooding good looks of a young Valentino with intelligence, wit, a ribald sense of fun, and a genuine devotion to women?

"The truth is, I much prefer women to men," Fernando had once told him. "If they ruled the world, I would happily serve under them." He hadn't intended it as a joke.

"Maybe they will one day."

"Not in our lifetimes. But we can help them get there."

The money and the status didn't count against Fernando. Born into a family of wealthy landowners who had backed General Trujillo in his bid for the presidency, he

44

now held down some hazy diplomatic post at the embassy of the Dominican Republic. Luke had heard from a shifty little attaché at the American embassy that Fernando was making a small fortune peddling immigration visas to Jews looking to relocate from Chancellor Hitler's new Germany. To Luke, it sounded like money made in a good cause — certainly if the stories coming out of Germany were anything to go by. Jews were being obliged to hand over their businesses to the government for a fraction of their real worth. Cut and run? Why not? And why not the Dominican Republic? There were far worse places to start over than the Caribbean.

No, it wasn't the sort of thing Luke could get exercised about. Besides, Fernando was the best friend ever: attentive, energetic, and loyal — so much so that one might have felt almost oppressed by such devotion if he weren't just as quick with his ridicule. It was only four months since they had first met, through a mutual acquaintance at a mediocre production of Molière's *Le Malade Imaginaire*, but Luke already sensed that Fernando would drop everything for him should the situation ever demand it. He also knew that the reverse was true, even if he couldn't conceive of a scenario in which Fernando would require his assistance. For all the clowning and frivolity, Fernando had a shrewd and hard-nosed quality that brought to mind something Luke's mother had once said of her flamboyant and dissolute older brother, Uncle Leo: "Don't be fooled. Peacocks have claws, too."

Well, right now this peacock was fanning his tail feathers at the two Belgian girls he had met at an embassy function earlier in the week, and Luke was wishing he felt more in the mood. He wanted it for himself, to help him forget. Thoughts of Sister Agnes had been haunting him all day.

At almost this exact hour tomorrow evening, he would be pulling out of the Gare du Nord on the boat train to London. The funeral was on Friday. He could picture the yew-trimmed graveyard beside the orphanage chapel, the resting place of nuns and children. And he could see the hole in the ground, the soil heaped up around it — the same soil that already held Michael's bones. Michael, his protector, three years his elder, ungainly and rough-hewn even as a young boy, unwanted by the couples who had trooped through the place in search of other people's children. Michael, carried off by scarlet fever a month before Luke was plucked out of the crowd by the Hamiltons. It was the one consolation: Michael had never lived to witness it.

He forced himself back to the present and topped up his wineglass. Self-restraint clearly wasn't working, so maybe excess was the way to go. It had worked well enough in the past.

Fernando sensed the shift in him and asked, "Changed your mind? Want to come with us to the Bal Tabarin?"

"Why not?"

Fernanado turned to the girls. "I told you, he's not as innocent as he looks."

"Oh, I don't think he looks innocent at all," said Amélie. "I don't think either of you do."

"I can't speak for myself, but I can tell you that Luke is anything but."

"Not now, Fernando," groaned Luke, guessing what was coming.

Fernando held up his hands in a gesture of surrender. "Okay," he conceded.

"You have to tell us now!"

"You can't not tell us now!"

"No, no," came Fernando's grave reply. "If Luke doesn't want you to know about the affair he had with a fellow officer's wife in India, then who am I to go against his wishes?"

47

"You didn't!"

"Did you?"

"He's lucky to have a job."

Luke caught the look in Fernando's eye. It said, *Trust me, this is the way to play it with these two.*

"What was she like?"

"Did you love her?"

Luke had to smile. Whenever the subject came up in male company, the first question tended to be, *How did you get found out?* He replied to each of them in turn. "She was unhappy. And yes, I did love her."

A slight frown corrugated Fernando's brow. "You never told me that before."

"Well, maybe I didn't want the whole of Paris to hear it."

The girls laughed, then begged for more details.

"That's all you're getting. Anyway, there's not much to tell. It didn't end well."

Inevitably, they extracted the story from him. It wasn't in his nature to share the details of a scandalous incident that cast him in a shameful light, but Fernando was right: Amélie and Véronique lapped it up. He sensed them warming to him, especially Véronique, who held him fast in her large, dark eyes until she and Amélie excused themselves to go and powder their noses.

48

Fernando lit a cigarette and smiled.

"Enjoy yourself. It's your last night. They won't even be here when you get back from England."

Luke didn't need persuading. He could muddle his way through work tomorrow, dressing up his exhaustion as grief, and then sleep on the train.

"Just so you know, Amélie is already taken."

"Says who?" demanded Luke.

"She does." Fernando fired a smoke ring into the air. "Her hand has been on my thigh for the last ten minutes."

Luke was refilling their glasses when Pascal, the maître d', appeared at his elbow and handed him a folded note. "A message for you, Monsieur Hamilton."

"From whom?"

"The gentleman over there." Pascal swiveled toward the bar and frowned. "Well, he was there just a moment ago."

The note was in English, handwritten in capitals:

DO NOT REACT. DO NOT SHOW THIS TO YOUR FRIENDS. TWO MEN IN THIS ROOM HAVE BEEN ORDERED TO KILL YOU. I AM ONE OF THEM. THE OTHER ONE IS READING A BOOK AT THE TABLE NEAR

49

THE DOOR TO THE KITCHEN. DO NOT
LOOK AT HIM. IF YOU WANT TO LIVE,
MAKE AN EXCUSE AND MEET ME OUT-
SIDE.

GUERNICA

"A billet-doux from your boyfriend?"
enquired Fernando.

Luke almost passed the note straight over.
It was utterly preposterous, and yet, some
small splinter of doubt stayed his hand.
"How did you guess?"

"Come on, what is it?"

"Nothing."

"So why have you turned white?"

Under the guise of reaching for his wineglass, Fernando lunged and snatched the
note away. His look of amused triumph
quickly faded. "Who is Guernica?" he asked.

"The man I told you about. Fautrier. The
one at the Spanish pavilion."

"The spy?"

"I don't know if he was a spy."

"Not just a spy. A hired assassin, too."

"You believe him?" Luke asked.

Fernando gave a dismissive snort. "Oh,
for God's sake, don't be ridiculous. Can you
think of one person who wants you dead?"

"No." He remembered the drunken threat
spat out for all to hear by Alice's husband

50

in the officers' mess in Risalpur. "Yes."

"Rubbish. Someone's messing with you. Here, I'll prove it to you."

Before Luke could react, Fernando was on his feet, heading for the back of the restaurant, leaving him little choice but to follow.

The man eating alone and reading a book looked like an accountant, though not quite as threatening. His lank brown hair was parted at the side, and the mustache served only to point up his weak mouth. He looked mildly startled when Fernando deposited himself in the chair opposite.

"Good evening, sir. My apologies for the intrusion. You do speak French, don't you?"

"Yes," replied the man timidly, removing his spectacles.

"And several other languages, too, I imagine, given your line of work."

"Excuse me?"

"My friend here has a question for you. He's curious to know why you would want to kill him. He can't think of a single reason why."

The man glanced up at Luke. "I don't understand."

"Oh, I think you do." Fernando placed his elbows on the table and leaned closer. "You see, my good fellow, the cat is well and truly

51

out of the bag. We know everything."

Fernando's persistence was verging on cruelty, and Luke was about to speak up when the man struck like a snake: a flashing fist that caught Fernando hard on the jaw, snapping his head around.

Had he been more of a fighter by instinct, Luke would have exacted swift revenge while the man was still seated, at a disadvantage. Instead, he found himself reaching to catch Fernando as he slumped from the chair toward the floor.

Time seemed suddenly to slow, then shatter, reduced to a series of snatched impressions: the man rising to his feet . . . reaching inside his jacket . . . a glimpse of leather shoulder holster . . . the silver finish of the gun being brought to bear on him . . . the cold intent in the man's eyes . . .

The end? Really? Like this? Why?

There was a deafening report, and a spray of red mist erupted from the side of the man's head. He swayed for a moment, as if drunk; then his legs went out from under him and he crashed to the floor, toppling the table as he fell.

The screams were muted by the ringing in Luke's ears left over from the gunshot. On his knees, awkwardly cradling his unconscious friend, he stared blankly at the detritus and the destruction. Was that blood pooled beside the man's head, or wine from the broken carafe?

A firm hand gripped his arm. "Come with me." He recognized the voice before he turned and found himself looking up at Fautrier. "He's not alone. Come now if you want to live." Luke allowed himself to be hauled to his feet and steered toward the entrance.

Diners and waiters cowered as Fautrier swept the room with his pistol, searching for an enemy. Luke's jacket was snatched from the back of his chair and thrust into his hands. It wasn't the last thing he registered before Fautrier ushered him through the main door. He glimpsed Amélie and Véronique in the narrow corridor leading to the toilets, pinned to the wall in wide-eyed terror.

Only once they were outside did Fautrier finally release his iron grip on Luke's arm. "This way," he said, casting a glance over his shoulder and making off down the boulevard. "Don't run. Walk. And don't talk. Just breathe deeply. You're in shock."

It was a balmy night, and a young man wearing khaki trousers and a short-sleeved shirt was strolling toward them, hands in his pockets. Fautrier picked up the pace, leveling his pistol directly at the man's head. "On the ground! Face down!" he ordered in French.

The young man spread-eagled himself on the pavement. Fautrier pinned him in place with a knee and searched him for a weapon, all the while keeping an eye out for anyone else drawing close. Satisfied, he finally stood up. "Go," he ordered.

The young man took off like a rabbit in the direction of L'Hirondelle, where a small crowd of wary diners was beginning to gather out front.

The car was parked on a side street off the boulevard. Fautrier instructed Luke to lie on the floor in the back and stay out of sight. Then he fired the engine and pulled away.

"Where's your passport?"

"P-passport?" It was the first word Luke had spoken since Fernando sat himself down at the stranger's table in the restaurant.

"Where is it?"

"At work. At the embassy."

"That's good — they'll have someone at your apartment."

"Who are 'they'? In fact, who the bloody hell are *you*?" he added, on a tide of fear-fueled indignation.

"I'm the man who just saved your life. Now, shut up. I need to know if we're being followed." A few moments later, something hard landed on Luke's thigh. "I don't think we are, but just in case." It was a revolver, and it offered little comfort.

Another minute or so passed before Fautrier spoke again — a single word muttered in a language Luke didn't recognize, although it sounded like an expletive. "I was wrong. There is a car following us."

"Are you sure?"

"Yes, I'm sure," came the irritated reply.

They didn't accelerate; if anything, they slowed down. From where Luke was lying, he could see Fautrier checking the rearview mirror every so often.

"What's happening?"

"He's trying to decide if I know he's there." Fautrier pulled a packet of cigarettes from his pocket and lit one.

"You're smoking?"

"Someone who is being followed doesn't have time to." Fautrier exhaled. "One man. Small. That is good."

"Small is good?"

"Small is bad; small is dangerous. But one small man is better than two."

Luke gave a nervous snort of laugh.

"Listen to me, Luke Hamilton. If anything

happens to me, you must disappear. You must go far away and you must never come back. Never. Do you understand?"

"Yes."

"No, you don't. You must change your name, change everything. If you don't, they will find you and they will kill you. Nothing can protect you — not your family, not the police, not your government. Go to Buenos Aires, Cape Town, Malacca . . . Go anywhere far away. Make a new life. Don't ever return."

"Why? What have I done?"

The reply didn't come immediately. "Nothing. They think you are someone else."

"That's all this is — a bloody mistake?"

"People have died for less," replied Fautrier. He glanced once more in the rearview mirror. "Keep coming, my little friend; we're almost there."

"Where?"

"Les Jardins du Luxembourg." The car took a left turn. "The park is in front of us, at the end of the street. It's a good place for you to disappear if this goes wrong."

"If what goes wrong?"

"This."

The car slammed to halt. Wrenching the gearshift into reverse, Fautrier twisted in his seat to peer over his shoulder and floored the accelerator. The engine screamed in protest.

Luke guessed what was coming, and braced himself against the impact, but he still cracked his head hard against the back of the footwell. Dazed, he was reaching for the door handle when the first shot rang out. Three more quickly followed. Revolver at the ready, he stumbled from the car to see steam rising from the crumpled bonnet of the small black car behind. A man was sprawled over the steering wheel.

Fautrier lowered his pistol. "Get the bag from the front seat."

They were on a narrow residential street wide enough for one vehicle — possibly chosen by Fautrier for that very reason, so their pursuer couldn't swerve around them. He had tried, and you didn't need to be a mechanic to know that the angle of impact had crippled their own car. One of the rear wheels was skewed way out of alignment.

"Is everything okay?"

The voice came from a woman peering down on them from a second-floor window.

"There's been an accident," Fautrier shouted up at her. "Call the police."

More shutters were being thrown open now. Someone speculated that he had heard gunshots; someone else agreed; and with the discussion crisscrossing above their heads, Luke and Fautrier made off down the street toward the Luxembourg Gardens.

"Did you really have to kill him?"

"He fired first," said Fautrier.

The road fronting the park was spotted with puddles of light thrown by the street-lamps. Looking for the safety of a crowd, Fautrier bore left toward the bars and restaurants clustered near a roundabout.

"Wait," said Luke.

A woman in a cocktail dress was emerging from a smart apartment building off to the right. A tall man, also in evening wear, accompanied her across the pavement toward a car. It was a long, sleek sedan, and the woman was just settling into the passenger seat when they appeared.

"We need your car," said Fautrier in a low voice.

The man seemed remarkably undaunted by the sight of Fautrier's pistol pointing at his midriff. He peered down his long nose at it with amused disdain. "Well, you can't have it."

"Which leg would you like me to shoot her in? You choose."

"Lucien . . ." pleaded the woman, not nearly as sanguine as her companion about having a pistol pointed at her.

The man fired a foul look at the two of them, then helped the woman out of the car. "Do you have any idea who I am?"

"It's not personal," Fautrier replied, holding out his hand for the key.

"I'm a government minister. And it has just become personal."

Fautrier didn't bother to reply; he simply handed the key to Luke.

"Drive."

CHAPTER FIVE

Luke savored the feel of the steering wheel in his hands. After the blind panic of the past half hour, it felt good to be in control of something, even if it happened to be only a car passing through the streets of Paris. The sensation vanished when Fautrier folded back his jacket and examined his side.

"Is that blood?" asked Luke.

"I told you, small is dangerous."

"You've been shot?"

"It's nothing."

It was bad enough for Fautrier to pull a shirt from the holdall at his feet and press it against the wound.

"We have to get you to a hospital."

"No hospitals. I know a man."

"Where? Tell me where."

"It can wait. Your passport can't."

Fautrier thought it unlikely, but there was a chance the embassy building was already being watched. It was a risk they would just have to take. "Unless there's someone who can get your passport for you."

Luke thought on it. "I know someone who can help. And she won't ask questions."

"Your *passport*?" said Diana. "Why? And why can't you fetch it yourself?"

She had just gotten home from the cinema, and Luke could picture her standing in the hallway in her bare feet. On the two occasions he had spent the night there, she had made him remove his shoes, too, because the elderly woman in the apartment below was obsessed with the noise of people walking around above her head. Even when they had made love, Diana had warned him not to be too vigorous, in case the feet of her bed scraped against the parquet floor.

"I really need you to do this for me, Diana."

"Are you all right?"

"Honestly, I'm about as far from all right as I've ever been in my life."

"Okay," she said. "I'll do it."

He told her to take a taxi to the embassy. He told her where to find the key to his desk, where in the desk to find his passport, and where to bring it once she had it. He was about to hang up when he remembered what Fautrier had said.

"Oh, and I need a suitcase."

"You don't have one?"

"Not one I can put my hands on right now."

There was a brief silence at the other end of the line. "I can't wait to hear what this is about."

"I'll explain when I see you. And, Diana . . ."

"Don't go all gooey on me, or I'll change my mind."

"You're a brick."

She gave a soft chuckle. "I should have known better."

Luke slipped the barman a couple of francs for the call. His generosity earned him a top-up on the house. He swirled the cognac around the glass. It was filthy stuff, but it was hitting the spot. Fautrier was still in the loo, tending to the wound in his side, and Luke was struck by a sudden impulse to slide off the bar stool and walk out of the place.

Yes, he had just fled the scenes of two murders in the killer's company, but he was an innocent man caught up in a situation not of his own making. How hard would it be to convince the police of that? Fernando would testify to the mysterious note delivered to their table at L'Hirondelle, as would Pascal, the maître d'. Moreover, there was the hard evidence of the note itself, which at this very moment was probably being examined by some detective or other.

He needed to stop the situation in its tracks before it escalated further, and throwing himself on the mercy of the authorities was the obvious way to go. Only one thing slowed the onrush of these thoughts: Fautrier's stark warning that no police force could protect him from the people who wanted him dead. Why should he doubt the word of a man who had saved his life twice in the past hour, in the process taking a bullet for his trouble?

He wished his mother were here, not only for her comforting presence, but also for the clear, calm logic of her thinking. Women were supposed to be emotional, instinctive, even irrational, but these were traits far more evident in his father than in her. How many times had he seen her pick apart a complex dilemma, methodically unraveling the arguments until she got to the nub of the thing?

"Don't believe Keats," she had once told him. "Beauty isn't truth, and truth isn't beauty. Leave that romantic nonsense to your father and his friends. Beauty declares itself to the world, whereas truth prefers to lurk in the shadows. You have to coax it into the light, and it comes blinking like a bear out of hibernation. That's how you recognize it."

His father liked to joke that she was a chip off the old block, the old block being a no-nonsense Scotsman who had recently retired from a physics professorship at Cambridge University. Where else had she picked up her Newtonian approach to life? For her, human beings were simply objects in motion, continually exerting influences on each other; and the force of intellect, if properly applied, could decipher the cat's cradle of cause and effect.

Luke knew from his father that she hadn't always thought of the world in such mechanistic terms. It was the crutch she had reached for after Douglas' death. Her way of coping with the unthinkable: that the son she brought into the world had been vaporized in a blaze of high explosive on a hillside near Béthune — reduced to a bloody pulp in the sucking mud. Luke sometimes wondered if she replayed the scene in her head, toying with the vectors that had determined the parabola of the German shell: the length and elevation of the barrel, the gravitational acceleration, the strength of the crosswind.

There were other considerations to be factored in, such as Douglas' friendship with Roland, the fellow officer he had gone to assist when the shell struck, obliterating them both. A myriad of variables, and if each of them could be explained, then maybe so could Douglas' death.

If these were the kind of calculations that plagued his mother in her private moments, she never shared them with Luke. He had never been made to feel that the ghost of Douglas stalked the corridors of the big house, or that they had adopted Luke as some kind of stand-in for their thwarted affections. Though they talked freely about Douglas, he was never idolized. The silver-framed photograph on the grand piano in the drawing room was the only image of him on display in the whole house, and when they marked the anniversary of his death each year, they did so openly, without awkwardness. If anything, Luke was the one with a tear in his eye, at the thought of the older brother he would never meet, snatched away by the Fates well before his time.

This was the sort of language his father employed: the ill winds of fate, the fickle wheel of fortune — phrases his wife would have dismissed as twaddle while recognizing her own part in their usage. She had swung one way, her husband the other. It was Newton's Third Law of Motion: for every action there is an equal and opposite reaction.

By nature, Luke leaned toward his father's more whimsical take on the world. What he needed right now, though, was a strong shot of his mother's inductive reasoning.

A case of mistaken identity? she would have asked. Who do they think you are? Could it be that the man they're really after is known to you, even involved in misdirecting them? Is he sacrificing you to protect himself?

"I didn't expect to find you still here."

Luke swiveled on his stool. There was a clamminess to Fautrier's face that one might have ascribed to the close heat of the bar, if it hadn't been for the accompanying pallor.

"I thought about it," said Luke.

"You were right to stay. What did she say?"

"She'll do it."

"Good."

"She lives nearby. She won't be long."

They took their glasses to a table at the back of the bar. It was an unprepossessing place, small and shabby, its painted walls stained yellow with decades of cigarette smoke, but it fit the two criteria Fautrier

66

demanded: it was just around the corner from the British embassy, and neither of them had ever frequented it before.

"How is it?" Luke asked, meaning the wound.

"Worse than I thought. The bullet is still in there, but I'll be okay."

"And if you're not?"

"Then remember what I said before. Disappear."

Luke took a moment to digest the line. "Who do they think I am?"

Fautrier savored a sip of brandy. "A German agent."

"That's ridiculous."

"I happen to agree with you."

"Why?" Luke demanded. "You said in your note you'd been ordered to kill me. What changed your mind?"

Fautrier hesitated, as if questioning the motive himself. "It was *Guernica,* Picasso's painting . . . the look in your eyes . . . the disgust. You're not working for the fascists."

"I'm sorry, but that doesn't sound very plausible."

Fautrier dabbed at his sweat-beaded brow with the back of his hand. "Twenty years ago I would have done it, taken my money. You got me at a good moment."

"A killer with a conscience?" said Luke,

ladling on the skepticism.

"No," came Fautrier's terse reply. "A killer who questioned his orders, only for them to send someone to kill him." He paused. "That's right, I was lucky."

Luke stared at his drink, suddenly chastened. There was no denying the evidence of his own eyes: the deceptively meek-looking man at L'Hirondelle had been on the point of putting a bullet in him when Fautrier intervened.

"I would tell you more if I knew it. The best I can do is try and convince them they've got the wrong person — not just for you, for me, too. Until then, you do what I say if you want to stay out of their way."

"Who are they?"

"I only know who I get my orders from, but that means nothing. He deals with anybody, as long as they pay."

Again, it didn't ring entirely true, but what else could he do?

"Why the passport? Where are we going?"

"I'm not; you are," said Fautrier. "Konstanz."

"Germany?"

"Only just. The border with Switzerland runs through the town." He made Luke memorize a name and an address, testing him on both until he was satisfied.

"And who is this Pippi Keller?"

"Someone I know. Someone they don't know. You'll be safe with her."

Fautrier drained the last of his cognac, then announced he was going to make himself scarce before Diana turned up, in case she had company.

"I told you, I trust her."

"That is your choice." Fautrier grimaced as he levered himself to his feet. "Don't tell her more than you have to."

Luke watched him leave the bar, impressed that there was nothing in the way he moved to suggest he was carrying a lump of lead in his side. His back was straight, his head held high.

When Diana appeared fifteen minutes later, she had something of the same composed dignity about her, even though the suitcase she was carrying made her look like a refugee. Luke rose to greet her and was rewarded with a perfunctory kiss on the cheek.

"This better be good."

He already had a glass of red wine waiting for her. She took a sip. "Brouilly. You remember."

"It wasn't so long ago."

She produced his passport from her jacket pocket and handed it over.

"Thank you."

"I'm waiting," she said.

He held her gaze for a moment. "You wouldn't believe me if I told you."

"I'll be the judge of that."

She was going to hear it soon enough anyway. The news would rip through the embassy tomorrow morning.

"Someone just tried to kill me at L'Hirondelle." Diana was acquainted with the restaurant; they had dined there together several times before strolling back to his apartment. "Another man stepped in and shot him — shot him in the head."

"Not funny," she said.

"There's more. Another killing." He told her about the showdown near the Luxembourg Gardens, and the hijacking of the government minister's car.

"Luke . . ." she pleaded feebly, still wanting to believe he was pulling her leg.

"It's true. It'll be all over the embassy tomorrow."

"Oh, God," she muttered.

"I've got nothing to do with it, I promise you. It's a mistake. They think I'm some kind of spy."

"Are you? I've sometimes wondered. I even hoped . . ." She glanced off, embarrassed by the admission.

"What?"

"Oh, you know, something exotic to tell my grandchildren."

"Diana, I'm a nobody, Wyeth's lackey, his boy Friday."

"I thought that might be a front. You're so much smarter than he is."

"Well I'm sorry to disappoint you. Listen, you have to stay out of this, keep your mouth well shut, for your own sake."

"That might be difficult. Tweedledum was very surprised to see me just now."

It was their nickname for one of the two portly guards who shared the gate detail at the embassy. "Pity it wasn't Tweedledee," observed Luke. "Still, he's not the sharpest knife in the drawer; he may not put two and two together. If he does, you'd better have a story ready." He thought on it for a moment. "Tell them I decided to head back to England a day early for Agnes' funeral — yes. But I realized too late that my passport was at work and I'd miss the train if I went and got it, so I asked you to grab it and meet me at the Gare du Nord."

"It's not very convincing."

"It doesn't have to be. I asked you to run an errand. I *am* your boss, remember?"

"Whatever gave you that idea?"

Outside on the pavement, Luke hailed a

passing taxi. Diana planted a kiss on his cheek, her body pressed close enough to stir memories. "Where are you going to go?" she asked.

"You know I can't tell you."

She looked downcast. "I wish I could help."

"You've done enough already." He was about to close the taxi door on her, then paused. "Actually, there's one more thing you can do for me. Call my parents and say I'll be in touch as soon as I can."

She nodded.

"And tell them I love them."

For a worrying moment, Luke thought Fautrier was dead. He sat stooped, head hanging, in the passenger seat of the stolen sedan. He was, in fact, counting out bills on his lap. Luke slid the suitcase onto the backseat and got behind the wheel.

"She is beautiful," said Fautrier.

"Yes, she is."

"You are lovers?"

"Were. Briefly."

"Why did she end it?"

Judging from the faint smile, the presumption was intended in jest.

"She had never felt such desire before. It was so overwhelming it scared her."

Fautrier laughed, then winced. "Poor girl."

"It petered out. The spark wasn't there. We both knew it."

Fautrier handed Luke a bundle of cash. "Reichsmarks and some dollars. Now, drive."

"Where?"

"The Gare de l'Est."

They parked near the church on Rue Saint-Laurent, just south of the station. Fautrier rummaged in the holdall at his feet and produced a semiautomatic pistol fitted with a silencer. "Do you need me to show you how it works?"

"No."

"There are six rounds in the magazine."

"I thought a Browning took seven."

"I used one at my apartment."

The briefing then began in earnest. It was as thorough as any Luke had received during all his years in the Royal Air Force. Fautrier spoke fluently, concisely, backtracking every so often to check that some instruction or other had been properly logged.

They parted company at the end of the road. "I'll see you safely onto the train. Don't look for me. I'll be there. If you hear a gunshot, it is a warning. Run, and keep running. Find another way to get to Konstanz. There is a café in Zurich, in the old town, in Hirschenplatz — Café Glück. I'll meet you there next Tuesday at four o'clock. If you can't make it, I'll be there at the same time every day after that. What is the name of the café?"

"Glück," said Luke. "Luck."

"Easy to remember, because you have had a lot of it today."

"It doesn't feel that way."

"You will need more of it before this is finished." Fautrier offered Luke his hand. "Be careful. It is good to trust others, but better not to."

"Does that go for you, too?"

Fautrier smiled. "You're learning."

CHAPTER SIX

"It's me."

"Is it done?"

"No."

Petrovic was left hanging with only the crackle of the telephone line for company. The voice, when it finally came, was laced with menace. "Was it Borodin?"

"Yes."

"How many dead?"

"Two for certain, probably four."

More silence. "He knows."

"How can he know?" asked Petrovic.

"If he didn't before, he does now."

"And if you'd told me before, I would never have put him on the job."

"Since when do you dictate what we do and don't share with you?"

"I'm just saying —"

"I know what you're saying, Petrovic."

"Best not to use my name over the telephone."

"Best not to show your face around here until you have some better news." There was a note of apology in the weary sigh. "I should have killed that old fox years ago."

"Don't worry, I'll take care of him — both of them. They can't stay hidden forever."

"Oh, they won't. I have a feeling you'll be hearing from Borodin before too long."

"You think?"

"He knows what he has in his hands, he knows its value, and for the right money, he'll part with it."

"He'll never get to spend the money."

"I doubt he assumes we intend to let him," came the dry reply. "Never underestimate an old fox. It's not by chance that they live as long as they do."

CHAPTER SEVEN

"What's in the syringe?" asked Borodin.

"Nirvanin. It's an anesthetic."

"Don't bother."

"The bullet is lodged deep in your external oblique muscle."

"That means nothing to me."

"It will when I start digging around in there."

"I'll take my chances," said Borodin.

He was stretched out on the examination table, propped up on his elbows. Zanotic laid the syringe aside in a metal tray on the trolley beside him. "Listen to me. Our friendship ends tonight, and we both know it. But I don't want my last memory to be of you mistrusting me."

"It's not about trust."

"No, it's about living or dying. There's material from your jacket and shirt in the wound. It'll become infected if it isn't properly cleaned out."

"So clean it out properly and stitch me up. I'll be on my way and you'll have earned a month's salary in an hour."

"I don't want your money. I don't even want to know what happened to you tonight. It's nothing I haven't suspected about you."

They conversed in the Dalmatian dialect they had both grown up with, not that they had known each other back in the old country. It was quite possible they had passed each other in the streets of Ragusa, or even caroused in the same bars, but they'd had to wait more than twenty years before their lives finally collided on the far side of the continent — two displaced Croatians thrown together in a humble restaurant in Pigalle by a shared craving for the food of their homeland.

Borodin had been dining alone, Zanotic at the next table with his French wife, Lucille — petite, coldly attractive, and wary enough of her husband's past to have played almost no part in the relationship that sprang up between the two men after that first encounter. They would meet not quite in secret, sometimes for lunch, more often for drinks, trading memories and stories and debating the plight of the nation both had abandoned, with that mix of vehemence and doe-eyed sentimentality peculiar to exiles the world over.

Zanotic had happily agreed to become Borodin's doctor, which until tonight had involved little more than the odd checkup and the prescription of a mild opiate whenever Borodin's troublesome hip flared up.

"Maybe I want to feel the pain," said Borodin. "Maybe this old man needs to sharpen his mind and his resolve."

"And maybe this younger man doesn't need his wife and two daughters woken by your screams." Zanotic's eyes flicked toward the ceiling.

"*That's* what you're really worried about?"

"Of course. I couldn't care less if you live or die."

Borodin smiled. "Nirvanin, you say?"

"A local anesthetic. You won't feel a thing. You can even watch the maestro at work."

This wasn't an idle boast. Zanotic probably knew as much about gunshot wounds as any man alive. Qualified as a doctor just at the outbreak of war in 1914, he had found himself, like many Croatians, drafted into the Austro-Hungarian army against his wishes. He was assigned as a medical officer to the Slovenian front, where the Italians were trying to punch their way eastward into the heart of the empire. The brutal standoff across the milky waters of the Soca River lasted two and a half years and cost half a million young men their lives.

Zanotic once joked to Borodin that the experience had literally left its mark on him. The deep lines scoring his face were the chasms, rifts, and gorges of the Julian Alps, as if the place had laid itself across his features like some crude veil, a reminder of the hell he had known.

"Okay," Borodin conceded. "Stab me with that thing and let's see how good you really are."

He didn't watch — didn't have the stomach for it. Lying on his back, motionless for the first time since swinging his legs out of bed this morning, he felt strangely restful despite the dull prod and probe of the instruments.

He hadn't consciously cultivated the friendship with this moment in mind, but he wondered whether a shady second self hadn't somehow known that one day he might have to call on Zanotic's surgical expertise. He set great store by that kind of instinct. Other animals lived by their intuition, so why shouldn't man? Although there was nothing in science to support it, he was convinced that the sensation of being observed was both real and palpable for those attuned to it — a defense mechanism buried away by nature in everyone. Admittedly, his own had let him down earlier in the day, but that was hardly surprising under the circumstances.

From the moment he had started tailing Hamilton at the gates of the British embassy, he had been so distracted by the wild theory taking shape in his head, he failed to register that he, too, was being stalked. He had almost paid the full price for this lapse, and he would have been a lot tougher on himself if he were wrong about Hamilton's true identity. Their exchange in the Spanish pavilion, however, had only confirmed his suspicions.

Again, instincts. No hard-and-fast evidence, just vague whispers from another time and place: something of his mother in the slant of his large dark eyes; the same long, stooping stride as his father's; the deep timbre of his voice, just like his grandfather's.

"It's out," said Zanotic. "Do you want to see it?"

"No."

Borodin heard the hard clatter of lead on tin.

Why had they come for Hamilton now, having already spared him twenty-five years ago? What possible threat could a person ignorant of his true place in the world pose to them after a quarter of a century? And why had they not simply allowed him to live on in ignorance? It didn't make sense.

"There's a fair amount of damage. You're not going to heal overnight, not at your age."

"Just do your best."

He knew that the answers were out there, just as he knew that he should put them from his mind and concentrate on the serious business of staying alive while securing a fat nest egg for himself. Now was not the time to let curiosity prevail over common sense.

"It's quite something."

"What?" asked Zanotic.

"How I came to be shot."

"I don't want to hear it."

"That's a pity. The story would appeal to you. It's right up your street."

"Don't think you can hook me with your abstruse replies."

"I know you far too well to even try," Borodin replied. He let the silence stretch out. "Imagine not knowing who you are."

"Everyone knows who they are."

"Not if you were abducted, say."

"Abducted?"

"As a baby. Kidnapped, then transported

82

from one end of Europe to the other and left with people who knew nothing of where you came from."

Zanotic kept fiddling away, cleaning the wound. "Why was the boy kidnapped?"

"Revenge."

"For what?"

"I thought you weren't interested."

Zanotic ceased his bloody ministrations and peered at Borodin over the top of his spectacles.

"I'll hear your nonsense out if it makes you feel better."

Borodin smiled up at his old friend. "I'm going to miss you, Nikola."

"Yes, yes. Just tell me the story before you croak."

■ ■ ■ ■

GERMANY

■ ■ ■ ■

CHAPTER EIGHT

Cordell Oaks was a big man, both tall and well fed, but there was a curious delicacy about him. He sat upright and almost perfectly still in his seat, his large hands folded on his lap, picking his words carefully before delivering them in a high, fluting voice.

They had struck up a conversation as the train was pulling out of Strasbourg station — two foreigners thrown together in a first-class compartment and recognizing each other for what they were. Luke had made the first overture, eager for the distraction — anything to take his mind off the imminent border controls and the pistol. At Fautrier's instruction, he had wiped it clean of fingerprints and hidden it at the bottom of the bin under the washstand in the toilet down the corridor.

The border crossing proved to be a surprisingly straightforward affair. Two uniformed German officials sporting swastika armbands made a cursory examination of their passports before politely inquiring in perfect English about the purpose of their visit: tourism for Luke, business for the big American. Recent talk of a British rapprochement with Hitler, at the expense of Mussolini, may well have contributed to the guards' contained courtesy, but even if they had chosen to search Luke's suitcase, they would have found nothing to contradict his story. It was now neatly packed with clothes and other accoutrements befitting a gentleman traveler: everything from semiformal evening wear to a French edition of Baedeker's guide to Germany. There was even a Zeiss Ikonta camera and half a dozen rolls of 120 film. All had been bought this morning in Strasbourg — again, according to Fautrier's thorough instructions.

The sleeper from Paris had pulled into Strasbourg shortly before seven o'clock in the morning, and Luke had killed an hour at a café in the station, with a copy of *Le Petit Parisien,* waiting for the city to stir, before taking a short tram ride into the center. The purchases made barely a dent in the Reichsmarks that Fautrier had furnished him with. Fully equipped, he had then returned to the station in time to catch the 10:20 to Konstanz, his head by now thick with exhaustion.

Despite the privacy and luxury of his own sleeper compartment, he had hardly slept a wink the night before. Even the double cognac he had ordered from the porter around midnight hadn't been enough to nudge him over the edge. Instead, he had lain on his back in the darkness, immune to the hypnotic rattle of the steel wheels, trying to make sense of the cataclysm that had so abruptly torn his existence apart.

All he could say for certain was that Fautrier had saved his life before giving him a pistol and a considerable sum of money and sending him on his way. These were the bald facts as known and witnessed by him. Everything else was conjecture, and he had spent seven interminable hours wrestling with the bedclothes and searching for some kind of logic or pattern to the chaos that engulfed him.

The letter from his father informing him of Sister Agnes' death had landed on his desk like a curse, a contagion, infecting his life with the same savagery by which Agnes had met her end. He had tried to tease out a connection between the two events — a bungled burglary in England and a failed assassination in France — but nothing even remotely plausible had presented itself.

Agnes and he had only ever been bound together by good things. She had treated him from the very first with a sort of tender hauteur, both mocking and affectionate — her way, he now suspected, of preparing them both for the inevitable wrench of separation, for when he finally left St. Theresa's. Fortunately for them both, his new parents, Lorna and Ramsay, had seen immediately that the nun and their new son held a special place in each other's hearts, and they had gone out of their way to foster the friendship over the years. Agnes, a regular guest at the house, had attended Luke's university graduation as well as his passing-out parade at Cranwell RAF College, weeping at both and hating herself for the cracks those tears had revealed in her usually cast-iron composure.

No, there was nothing in the intertwining of their lives to suggest a common cause for the violence recently visited on them both. Besides, Fautrier's talk of mistaken identity made considerably more sense, even if it did stir up a hornets' nest of further questions: Who had they mistaken him for? And how could they have gotten it so wrong?

It was true that his job in air intelligence involved a certain degree of subterfuge —

the Germans weren't exactly going to hand over details of the Luftwaffe's first-line strength — but Luke was a minor cog in the machine. Not even. More like a lubricating squirt of oil. Most of his time was spent gathering and collating data from various sources about the rapid acceleration in aircraft production taking place in Germany. It was Wing Commander Wyeth, in his capacity as air attaché, who drew the conclusions and shaped the reports that were then enciphered and dispatched to the Air Intelligence Directorate in London.

The notion that he had been mistaken for a German agent seemed utterly absurd. If anything, he was far warier about Hitler's true intentions than Wyeth, who blithely believed that air parity with the British was a Nazi pipe dream. Any data contradicting this private intuition was given short shrift in his reports.

It was at this point, in the early hours of the morning, that the idea had lodged itself in Luke's head. What if he had been mistaken for Wyeth? Wyeth, the anchor dragging in the sand, forever calling into question the intelligence, or dismissing it as irrelevant to their brief. One incident in particular stood out. Earlier in the year, two Royal Air Force officers on holiday in

Germany had somehow talked a friendly Lutwaffe squadron into letting them pilot a Junkers 88 bomber. Hurley and Atcherdy's account of the aircraft's capabilities had never found its way into the hands of the bigwigs back at Whitehall, because Wyeth had deemed it immaterial to the more pertinent matter of aircraft numbers, on which the two airmen had been unable to furnish any worthwhile information.

Gross ineptitude on Wyeth's part, or subtle sabotage? In his eagerness for an answer, Luke had found himself leaning toward the latter, recalling further examples of Wyeth's obstructiveness, which now began to look like rank treachery. Then again, it was a theory rooted in what Fautrier had told him, and he wasn't convinced that everything Bernard Fautrier said should be taken on trust. He hadn't answered Luke's questions so much as parried them away with a string of vague and cursory explanations that didn't stand up to scrutiny now that the immediate danger, the quaking terror, had passed.

Was it really possible that a professional assassin would question his orders based on a brief conversation about fascism while standing in front of a painting? And why had Fautrier's momentary hesitation brought the wrath of his own people down on his head? Was that the way things really worked in his business: do or die, like an officer summarily executing a foot soldier for refusing to go over the top in the trenches?

These were some of the questions that had swirled through Luke's head, robbing him of sleep, and they hovered there now at the fringes of his thoughts as he listened to Cordell Oaks hold forth on the challenges of large-scale milk production in the modern age.

The American was attending the World Dairy Congress in Berlin next week as one of twelve delegates from the United States — an honor he had earned as head of the dairy division at the New York State Agricultural Experiment Station. He was going to be presenting a paper on thermoduric bacteria in pasteurized dairy products, but he was keen to point out that his real fields of expertise lay in butter aroma and the various treatments to alter the viscosity of pasteurized cream. A few years ago, he and a colleague had patented a new procedure for the production of cream cheese, and something coy in his manner suggested that they'd both done rather well out of it.

Like all the best bores, Cordell Oaks had

absolutely no idea just how dull he was. He asked a question from time to time, but it was generally an excuse to forge ahead with his favorite subject. ("What do you make of the new trend for foil bottle tops?") This was fine with Luke. All he had to offer in return was a bunch of lies, and he didn't feel like lying to Cordell Oaks, who seemed to be a good man, genuinely devoted to his family and the cause of feeding the masses while keeping them safe at the same time.

Who could possibly have foreseen a few days ago that Luke would be winding his way through the Black Mountains while being lectured on the antipathogenic benefits of high-temperature, short-hold pasteurization over low-temperature, long-hold? His life, neatly stacked like a deck of cards, had been hurled high into the air and scattered to the four winds. This thought gave him pause, for there was something in it that appealed to the person he used to be.

For as long as he could remember, right back to those early days at the orphanage, he had dreamed of adventure. The wild fantasizing probably sprang from the fact that most of the other children knew something of their stories, their origins, whereas he had landed from nowhere, abandoned by a stranger, both his name and his birthday assigned to him by the nuns.

This had counted against him at St. Theresa's, where even among the ranks of the unwanted there was a clear hierarchy. Bastard. By-blow. Son of a whore. Then there was his coloring: the black hair and the olive complexion. Coon. Nigger. Gypsy. Pickaninny. The nuns had tried their best, but what could they really do once they'd taken to their beds at night? In the darkened dormitories, at the end of every day, a new regime held sway, and you quickly learned to find your place in it, picking your friends and your battles with care. He had also learned that the best refuge was to be found in his thoughts, where he was free to travel off and explore new worlds, trying them on for size.

Even after the Hamiltons took him into their lives, he had continued, a little guiltily, to plug the yawning hole in his past with fanciful speculations, and to build a future brimming with madcap possibilities. Lorna and Ramsay had sensed the dreamer in him, yet had done nothing to curb this tendency — quite the reverse, in fact. Ramsay had filled his eager young ears with the stories of Aeneas and Odysseus; of Hannibal's crossing of the Alps and Marco Polo's epic journey to the palace of Kublai Khan; of

Columbus, Magellan, Cook, Drake, and Raleigh; of Vasco da Gama, Cortés, and Pizarro. And then there were the ones who never quite made it into the history books: men like Nikolaus Federmann, Anthony Knivet, John Chilton, and Samuel White.

Never one to let the truth stand in the way of a good yarn, Ramsay had spiced his tales with pirates and buccaneers and mythical creatures and monsters of the deep and cannibal tribes and half a hundred other ways to die.

Luke couldn't say exactly when it happened — somewhere around the age of ten, perhaps — but he had found himself turning his eyes to the high skies of the flat Cambridgeshire Fens that were now his home.

Flight.

It was all around him, in the flocks of geese and ducks that winged in from foreign parts every year when the rivers jumped their banks, brightening the low pastures. And when it came time for them to move on, to head south, he always felt a stab of sadness that he couldn't be going with them, because south, he had learned by then, was where people who looked like him came from.

He saw now that the seeds had been sown

in him long ago, quietly putting down roots with the passage of the years. It was almost inevitable that he would sign up for the University Air Squadron. Flight. *Just the one time,* he had told himself, *to see what it's like. Well, maybe once more. Okay, this really is the last time.*

The addiction was immediate. To finally soar way above the world and survey it like a map was the most exhilarating sensation, alien yet oddly familiar, not so different from being on the ground, on the outside looking in, never quite belonging. Maybe that was why he had excelled and found himself being courted by the RAF.

Professor Soames, his history tutor at Trinity, had been dismayed when Luke announced he was going to forgo a doctorate in favor of flying airplanes.

"What makes you think for a moment that there's a future in those infernal contraptions?"

His parents, as in all things, had supported his decision, but only once they established that he was not looking to fill the boots of their dead son by taking up a career in the armed forces. They were less happy when Luke had found himself posted almost immediately to the North-West Frontier with his squadron.

They needn't have worried. Engine failure was the only real danger one faced when bombing villages and strafing tribesmen. That was where the dream had died, in the jagged foothills of the Hindu Kush, in a miasma of self-disgust and insubordination. When the drink no longer dulled the pain, he had reached for a stronger opiate: Alice, sleek and self-possessed, all that fire so cleverly concealed beneath ice. The discovery of their affair had done for him, and almost for her marriage. He was lucky not to have been drummed out of the RAF there and then. The only reason he hadn't been was because her brute of a husband was an army officer and, therefore, an enemy as well as an ally in the eyes of Luke's superiors. He suspected that Squadron Commander Braithwaite had rather enjoyed the whole sordid debacle for the opportunity it presented to get one over "the other half," as he referred to the army regiments garrisoned alongside them at Risalpur.

The desk job in Paris was Luke's penance, and for the first few months it hadn't seemed too high a price to pay. The city's many charms had carried him through. When it came down to it, though, his wings had been clipped, and only the looming threat of war offered any prospect that he might once more find himself in a cockpit, soaring with the birds.

This was no reason to wish for another conflict so soon after the last. He knew that, just as he knew that the perilous predicament in which he now found himself appealed to something deep inside him, some stratum of his soul laid down long ago.

The invitation came out of the blue as the train was pulling into Konstanz: dinner at the American's hotel, a grand lakeside establishment that had just passed by outside the window when the offer was made.

Cordell Oaks seemed slightly shocked by his own impulsiveness. "Your friend is welcome, too, of course."

The "friend" was a fictitious acquaintance of Luke's from university days, now an English teacher at a school in Konstanz.

"I think he might already have made plans for us tonight."

"Well, if he hasn't, the offer stands. I promise not to mention milk, in any of its countless forms."

Luke struggled to suppress a smile. Cordell Oaks looked bashful.

"My wife and children keep me in check, so when they're not around I do tend to go on a bit."

They parted company with a handshake in front of the station building, the American then folding his bulky frame into the back of a taxi. Luke waved goodbye and strolled to the small port tucked beside the station. He lit a cigarette, enjoying the caress of the sun on his tired face, taking stock of his reduced circumstances: a foreign town, a name and an address, a suitcase, and a pistol tucked into the back of his waistband.

An attractive young woman with a wavy blond bob passed by in front of him pushing a stroller, making for one of the white ferryboats docked at the long jetty, and it seemed for a moment that she had been sent by some higher power to taunt him with the certitude of her carefree existence. He finished his cigarette, picked up his suitcase, and made his way back across the train tracks.

Konstanz was not much more than a name to him, a town set near the head of the Bodensee, the vast lake whose shores were shared by Germany, Switzerland, and Austria. But you sensed immediately the air of easy and ancient prosperity about the place. The buildings were tall, some five or six stories, with stone-trimmed windows and doorways. Their stuccoed facades were painted a medley of colors, everything from soft ochers to pale greens and blues: a gentle palette that stood in marked contrast to the harsh red, white, and black of the Nazi flags littering the main square. Most buildings seemed to have one draped from a window or hanging from a wall-mounted flagstaff.

It was almost one o'clock, and the tables in front of the restaurants and cafés on Markstatte were crowded with diners. It was also Friday, so the smell of grilled fish carried on the light breeze — an aching reminder that he hadn't had a square meal in over twenty-four hours. He was tempted to wrestle himself a table in the shade and enjoy a lazy lunch while watching the world pass by, but his appetite lost out to nerves when a group of uniformed young men, handsome and hard-eyed, sauntered into the square. They wore jackboots and khaki shirts and swastika armbands, and they moved with the lolling superiority of prefects policing a school playground.

Fautrier had told him that Pippi Keller lived near the cathedral, and he pushed on, guided by the tip of the spire poking above the tiled rooftops. The cathedral was set on a rise at the heart of the old town. Constructed of the same gray stone as the station building, it was an austere temple to Protestantism, its clean, hard lines stripped of all frivolous detailing. A leafy square abutted its southern side, and it was from here that Hohenhausgasse dropped away.

Number Twenty-Three presented a haggard face to the cobbled street. Its faded yellow stucco had crumbled away in patches to reveal the brickwork beneath, and the large wooden doors closing off the stone archway were cracked and dried like driftwood. In them was set a smaller door. It had no handle, just a keyhole, so he reached for the bellpull.

The distant tinkle was followed by a creaking sound above his head. He looked up in time to see the window being pulled shut again. He waited, knowing that his presence had been registered, and before long he heard footsteps, followed by the rasp of a heavy steel bolt. The door swung open to reveal a woman. She was near enough his own age, midtwenties, tall and strikingly attractive, with auburn hair worn modishly long.

"Yes?" she asked. Not exactly cold, but close.

His German, like his French, was halting but competent. "I'm looking for Pippi Keller."

"Pippi Keller? She doesn't live here any-more."

"Can you tell me where I can find her?"

"Who wants to know?"

"My name is Luke Hamilton. I'm a friend of a friend of hers."

"Oh? Who?"

"Bernard Fautrier. He's French."

It was almost nothing, just a faint flicker in her large green eyes. "Wait here. I'll see if my aunt knows anything." She closed the door in his face.

He thought about lighting a cigarette, decided against it, then went ahead anyway. It was half smoked by the time the door finally swung open again.

"Come in," said the woman.

Beyond the deep archway lay a cobbled yard with an old, dusty sedan parked in it. A door was set in the wall to the right.

"Follow me."

A wooden staircase climbed steeply to a narrow landing. Reaching for a door handle, she turned and delivered a disarmingly warm smile.

"I should warn you, she's a bit deaf."

She led the way into the room. Luke just had time to register a table laid for three — a meal abandoned — when the frozen tableau shattered into a kaleidoscope of colors and then went black.

CHAPTER NINE

He knew he was coming to, because he heard a female voice say in German, "He's waking up."

His chin seemed glued to his chest, and the searing pain burned a path from the back of his skull to the tips of toes. He was seated in a chair. No, not just seated, bound to it by the ankles and wrists. It took a superhuman effort to raise his head and force open his eyelids. It took him a little while longer to focus.

The woman was regarding him impassively from a chair opposite his. A tall, rangy man stood at her shoulder, smoking a cigarette. He had lank hair the color of straw, and the lazy, heavy-lidded eyes of a born cynic.

Luke retched suddenly, violently. Almost nothing came up, just a bit of bile that he was able to keep back. It was a good job he had skipped lunch.

"Who are you?" asked the woman.

"I told you: Luke Hamilton."

She held up his passport. "This means nothing. I have three of these. And you don't look British." She tossed the passport onto a side table, where the cash that Fautrier had given him was neatly piled next to the pistol and the camera he had bought in Strasbourg. She picked up the Browning and turned it in her hands.

"Did you come here to steal or to kill? Or both?"

"Neither."

Only when he received a stinging slap on the cheek did he realize someone was standing behind him. "Answer her!" snapped a male voice.

"Neither."

Another slap, the other cheek this time, followed by a weary reprimand from the woman: "Erwin, that's enough."

"Pippi, he's lying."

So, Pippi Keller was a consummate actress, the deaf aunt no more than a convenient fiction to put him at ease as she lured him into the trap.

"Why did Fautrier send you here?"

"He said you could help me."

"Help you? What does he look like?"

Luke described Fautrier as best he could.

"It's definitely him," came the voice at Luke's shoulder.

"His real name is Borodin," said Pippi. "He's not French. He's Croatian. And he's no friend of ours."

"No," growled the man at her side.

"So what are you *really* doing here?"

"It's a long story."

"We have time," she replied. "Say it in English if you want."

"You speak English?"

She ignored the question, her eyes flicking to the man standing behind him. "Get him a glass of water." And then, more forcefully: "Just do it, Erwin."

Erwin was younger than the other two, though not by much — closer to twenty than to twenty-five. He filled a glass from the jug on the table and roughly forced the rim between Luke's lips, banging it against his teeth.

"You should know that Borodin was responsible for the death of a friend of ours," said Pippi.

"A good friend," added the tall man.

A shadow of something in Pippi's eyes, and a hardening in her voice. "So be careful what you say."

"I can only tell you what I know."

"In English if you want."

He started at the beginning, with Fautrier's approach at the Spanish pavilion, but as he continued with his account of the past twenty-four hours, he grew increasingly uneasy. Hearing it from his own lips made him realize how utterly far-fetched it all sounded. It didn't help that every so often, Pippi would silence him so that she could bring the other two up to speed in German. Their skepticism was palpable, in both their faces and their comments. "Oh, really?" . . . "That's ridiculous!" . . . "Does he take us for complete idiots?"

He quickly figured out that he had only one thing going for him: anyone looking to do them harm would have to be a fool of the first order to come calling with such a preposterous story. It was scant solace. There was no avoiding the fact that Fautrier — who wasn't Fautrier at all, it now seemed, but a Croatian named Borodin — had knowingly delivered Luke into the hands of his enemies.

When he had finished his account, Pippi rose to her feet and told the others to follow her. They filed into the kitchen, like jurors retiring to consider their verdict, leaving the accused to stew in the dock.

Outside, the cathedral bell tolled three o'clock. Had he really been dead to the world for almost two hours? Probably. He could tell that the blood on the back of his neck had dried to a crusted track. He glanced at his suitcase lying open and empty on the floor, the new clothes he had bought this morning scattered all around.

Voices filtered in from behind the kitchen door: male voices, muffled but insistent; then Pippi's, firm and assertive, bringing the men to order. If he hadn't been sure of it before, there was little doubt now who ran the show, whatever that was. Something not entirely aboveboard, not if they'd had dealings with Borodin, during the course of which someone had lost their life.

The heated debate taking place in the kitchen reached a new pitch. Voices rose in anger. Pippi had the last word before entering the room alone. She pulled the door closed behind her and drifted to the window, peering outside.

"If Borodin were sitting there, I would shoot him."

They were the first English words she had spoken, and her accent held almost no hint of the guttural undertones one would expect of a German.

"I sympathize," said Luke.

She turned to face him. "You said he saved your life."

"Twice. But look at me now."

"Out of the frying pan, into the fire," she replied absently. "Isn't that what you say in English?"

"It is."

She came and stood before him. "We don't believe you."

"It's the truth, I swear it. You must know someone in Paris. Call them. If it's not in the papers by now, it will be tomorrow. A shooting at the restaurant — L'Hirondelle — and another near the Luxembourg Gardens. I'm probably named."

She weighed his words. "He was told to kill you, then changed his mind? I know Borodin, and that's not him."

"I'm not saying I understand. I'm as confused as you are."

"You think?"

"I don't know what else to say."

"Then listen," she said. "Borodin kills two men in Paris to protect you. Even if it's true, is it going to stop there? No. This is the beginning of something bad. You think we want to be part of it?"

It was a fair point. "So let me go. You'll never see me again."

"Too late for that."

"You have my word."

"It was too late the moment you rang the

bell." Raising her voice, she called: "Otto."

The rangy man with the lazy gaze appeared from the kitchen, exchanged a complicit nod with her, then made for the dresser against the wall behind Luke.

"I'm sorry," said Pippi. "It's the only way."

Luke tried desperately to see what was going on behind his back, but all he got was the barest glimpse of Otto busying himself at the dresser.

"Don't worry," said Pippi. "He knows what he's doing. He's a medical student."

Luke's head snapped back to her. "I had nothing to do with your friend's death. I swear to God I didn't even know Borodin before yesterday. Please, you're making a big mistake."

"It's just a precaution. We're not going to kill you."

Otto had closed in silently from behind. "Not yet," he said into Luke's ear. "Not here." He seized Luke's hair and yanked his head back.

Luke's first thought was of a knife being dragged across his windpipe. The second, as a rag was clamped over his mouth and nose, was of a straightforward smothering. No mess, no noise, just the silent snuffing-out of a life.

He struggled, fighting for breath, which

came in small sips, sweet and acrid. He felt himself falling . . . the darkness drawing tight around him, swaddling him in its black cloak.

CHAPTER TEN

Luke stood squinting at the edge of the airfield, watching as the caravan drew closer through the white heat and the wind-whipped dust. They crept toward him like a column of ants — men, women, children, camels — making for the hills and the homes they had left behind many weeks before.

The camp's political agent had assured them all that they were Afghans, nomads, harmless traders who journeyed south, deep into India, to sell their carpets and other wares. From the look of them, though, they could just as well have been Waziris, the enemy. Either way, friend or foe, they were Pathans, betrayed by the blue-green eyes that shone like jewels in their bronzed faces. The men walked with long, lazy strides, proud and erect, rifles slung from their shoulders. Not all the women were in purdah; those who were rode on the camels, bobbing about on big bundles tied with rope.

He was expecting them to slow and try to sell him something. They usually did. Not today. They filed past without so much as a glance his way. But then one of their number — a tall man, his long beard as black as his turban — turned and caught his eye and swung his arm in a looping arc: come with us. Another man behind made the same gesture. An elderly woman repeated it. So did a young boy leading a baby black bear by a tether made from colorful twisted cloth.

"Where to?" he called in English. "Where are you going?"

The boy shrugged as he walked on by, not understanding the question, or, if he did, unable to offer an answer.

He heard the familiar crackle of an aircraft engine coming to life. Turning, he saw one of the squadron's Hawker Harts taxiing to the end of the landing strip. Was the bloody fool really shaping up to take off downwind? He waved his arms and gesticulated wildly at the windsock. It made no difference. The biplane came tearing down the strip, and as it shot past him, he saw the number on the tail fin: K-2063.

It wasn't possible.

K-2063 had gone down in a dust storm

near Peshawar. He knew this for a fact, because he had visited the crash site. He had seen the charred and crumpled wreckage in the field beside the Swat River. Billy Taplin and his gunner, Oates, had bailed out blind before the impact, and their broken bodies had been found nearby, their parachutes half opened.

The Hart cleared the pepper trees at the end of the airfield by a matter of feet, fighting for height, sunlight flashing off its silver wings as it banked left, making a tight turn back on itself, lining up with the caravan, approaching from the rear.

What was it up to? If it kept coming, it would cause panic and havoc, scattering the camels. Maybe that was the plan. Or maybe, he thought with a sudden lurch of horror, the pilot had other ideas.

He spun back to see that even the stragglers had passed him by now, and he set off after them at a sprint. "Run!" he yelled. "He's going to open fire! Run!"

No one turned. Why couldn't they hear him?

"Run! Get away!"

A reaction at last. The woman seated atop the last camel turned to look at him, and even at a distance he recognized the smile.

It was Sister Agnes.

With a scoop of her arm, she signaled him to follow. Only he couldn't, because now he found himself sinking up to his knees in the sucking sand. It was like wading through molasses. He could only look on helplessly as they pulled away.

That was when it suddenly dawned on him. He didn't need to worry. Nothing could happen to them, because they were already dead. It wasn't a caravan; it was a procession of dead souls in limbo. Taplin and Oates were simply joining their own kind, searching for a resting place.

The sound of the Hart closing from behind rose to a deafening pitch, filling his skull.

Luke snapped awake with a buzzing in his left ear.

The high-pitched whine of a hungry mosquito searching for a meal.

He tried to swat it away but found he couldn't move his hands. It took him a few moments to get his bearings. Darkness, though not total. He was on his back on a large bed, bound by the wrists and ankles to its four corners, spread-eagled as though for sacrifice. His trousers, shoes, and socks had been removed, but they had left him with his undershorts and shirt, which was lacquered to his chest by sweat.

He strained against his bonds until he felt the rope beginning to strip the skin from his wrists. He lay back, panting from the exertion. Then he began to shout for help.

Before long, the door swung open and the room was flooded with light from a kerosene lamp.

"No one can hear you," said Pippi.

"You can."

"Not if I put a cloth in your mouth. It's your choice."

She dragged a chair to the bedside and placed the lamp on the floor. She sat in silence, brooding, studying him. "I think I know why Borodin sent you," she said eventually.

"Why?"

"It's just a theory. It needs to be tested."

"So you believe me?"

"I didn't say that."

She drew some cigarettes from the pocket of her skirt and lit one. "The money you had with you, the money you say he gave you — it is the same amount he stole from us."

"You're saying he sent me to make amends?"

"Nothing can make amends for what happened," she replied darkly.

"Who died?"

She looked at him askance, deciding whether to reply. "His name was Johan." She didn't need to say any more; the rest was written in her face.

"I'm sorry."

"Why? You didn't know him," she replied flatly.

"I lost a good friend recently."

"Who?"

"Her name was Agnes."

It seemed for a moment that she would quiz him further, but she gathered up the lamp and replaced the chair against the wall.

"I need the toilet."

She turned at the door. "Otto and Erwin don't know about my theory."

"Meaning?"

"Don't give them a reason to hurt you. They would like to, especially Otto." She paused. "He and Johan were like brothers."

He wasn't alone for long. The two men appeared, untied him wordlessly, and led him at gunpoint down the stairs and out into the night. It was only then that he realized he'd been moved while knocked out by the chloroform. They were in a clearing deep in the woods, with tall trees walling them in on all sides. The building was some kind of farmhouse, dwarfed by the large barn beside it. The outhouse stood a short distance away, on a grassy slope. He smelled it before he saw it, and when he pulled open the door, the odor was so rank that the need to relieve himself almost deserted him.

Pippi had prepared a snack for him in his absence: cheese, a hunk of old bread, a couple of tomatoes, sliced and salted. He ate it at the plank table in the kitchen, under the mistrustful gaze of his three captors. Pippi reached for a pitcher and splashed some red wine into a glass. This earned her a sharp look from Otto.

"What if he's innocent?" she asked.

"What if he isn't?" retorted Otto.

"Even a condemned man is entitled to a last meal."

Something in her fleeting look told him not to take her words too seriously. As he reached for the glass, Otto snatched up a knife and buried the tip in the tabletop, inches from his hand.

"Where is Borodin?" he demanded.

Luke looked up at him. "I said. Paris. He was shot."

"When is he coming here?"

"I don't know. He could be dead."

Otto sneered and shook his head. "Pippi, he's lying."

"We don't know that," she replied.

"You seriously think Borodin left it at that? 'Here's the address of my friend Pippi Keller. Good luck. See you in another life.' "

Erwin gave a skeptical snort. Pippi's eyes turned enquiringly to Luke.

"He said I'd be safe here. He said he'd be in touch."

No need to mention Zurich, not yet. It was the only card he had left to play.

CHAPTER ELEVEN

"You're late," said Petrovic.

Borodin settled himself down on the wooden bench. "I needed to be sure."

"I came alone, like you said."

"I doubt it. But wherever they are, they're well hidden."

It was a glorious morning, just the odd cloudlet drifting across a powder-blue sky, and the gardens were already filling with visitors eager to beat the noonday heat.

Petrovic tapped the ash from the end of his cigarette and cast an appreciative eye around him. "I'm surprised I've never heard of this place."

The Parc de Bagatelle was a secret well kept by those in the know: a manicured oasis, a walled-off world tucked away in the wilds of the Bois de Boulogne.

"Well, keep it under your hat," replied Borodin.

"Since when do you walk with a stick?"

"Since you tried to have me killed."

"Just a flesh wound?"

"Kind of you to ask. Nothing too serious."

Petrovic smiled. "The order came from the top."

"Via you."

"You know how these things work. You crossed the line. Don't blame me."

"I don't. It's just business. Speaking of which, is that my money?" He meant the leather attaché case resting on Petrovic's lap.

"Yes."

"How much?"

"As we discussed: half now, the rest on delivery. I'm assuming you didn't bring him with you."

"Open it so I can see."

Petrovic raised the lid of the case to reveal some bundles of notes tied with rubber bands. "It's all there. High-denomination notes, like you said."

"Flip through them. Slowly."

Petrovic did as requested.

"Put them on the bench between us."

Petrovic removed the money and closed the lid, snapping the latches shut. An elderly couple, impeccably dressed, were approaching along the graveled path, arm in arm. Borodin took off his hat and laid it on the money. "Good morning," the woman said from beneath her lace-trimmed parasol, a relic of the past century. They both returned the greeting, then watched as the stooped pair shuffled off in their button boots, toward the orangery.

"I'm curious," said Petrovic. "How did you know?"

"The eyes. His mother's eyes. A beautiful woman. Before your time."

"Have you told him who he is?"

Borodin had been expecting the question. "No, I spun him a yarn."

"And are you spinning me one now?"

He turned and looked Petrovic hard in the eye. "He doesn't know. He doesn't need to. But I do. What went wrong twenty-five years ago?"

Petrovic drew on his cigarette and exhaled slowly. "That wasn't part of the deal."

"Didn't I mention it on the telephone?"

"No."

"My mistake."

Petrovic gave a mirthless smile. "Why do you care?"

"You know me. I don't like . . . gaps."

He could see Petrovic's mind at work behind the small, pale eyes, deciding what to reveal and what to hold back. "Someone let the side down," he finally offered.

"Who?"

"Do you remember Gotal?"

"Gotal?" How could he forget? The intellectual with the face of a thug — a member of the inner sanctum from the earliest days, when politics still counted for something and Borodin was a young man searching for a role within the organization's ranks. "What did he do?"

"It's what he *didn't* do."

Borodin took a moment to process the response. He remembered the rumors at the time: that the family had refused to meet the ransom demand; that they had paid up but the child had not been returned; even that the child had been killed in a bungled operation by the Venetian Carabinieri and the whole sorry affair had been covered up by the authorities. Only one thing was certain: nothing more had been heard of the kidnappers or the baby boy.

"Gotal was supposed to kill the boy? Why? Wasn't the money paid?"

"It wasn't just about the money," Petrovic replied. "You know that."

No, it was about bad blood between two families; it was about vengeance. But it was also about a man with the face of a boxer, whose conscience had gotten the better of him.

"Why England?"

"Who knows. Gotal was told to lie low for a few weeks afterward. It seems he went traveling instead."

Maybe England was the farthest place Gotal could picture in his mind — the safest place for an innocent child to start a new life.

"What did he do with the boy?" Borodin had a pretty good idea, because Hamilton had mentioned being brought up by nuns.

"So many questions."

"I'm almost done."

Petrovic dropped his cigarette on the gravel and crushed it underfoot. "An orphanage . . . Catholic . . . in the middle of nowhere. God knows how he found it."

"Why now? After twenty-five years?"

"Because that's how long Gotal sat on his secret. He died a few weeks ago. It was quick. So was the village priest who took his final confession."

"The priest ran straight to the Karamans?"

"Even priests know which side of their bread is buttered." Petrovic paused briefly before adding, "And who are we to take the moral high ground?"

Their dealings over the years had never been anything other than purely professional, but that didn't prevent a strange kind of complicity, even fondness, from springing up between them. Borodin found himself appealing to it now.

"I'm sorry it's come to this, Tibor. These aren't our battles."

Petrovic stared off into the distance. "Not if you keep your side of the bargain."

So be it, thought Borodin, tucking the cash into his jacket pockets.

"Where's Hamilton?" Petrovic demanded.

"I don't know, but I know where he's going to be."

Petrovic seized him by the elbow.

"Don't worry," said Borodin. "It's a lot of money, but not enough to retire on. You'll get your man."

Petrovic released his grip. Borodin pocketed the rest of the money, then eased himself to his feet with the aid of the walking stick. "Do you see those trees over there?"

Petrovic turned to take in the dense stand of trees and shrubs off to their right. "Yes."

"What you can't see is the man with a rifle aimed at your head."

"Oh?" There was a note of amused skepticism in Petrovic's voice.

"If you make any kind of move or signal in the next five minutes, you'll never know I wasn't lying. Five minutes. After that, I suggest you take a tour of the rose garden. They have hundreds of different varieties."

"I don't care for roses," said Petrovic.

"So why do you have three of them on your balcony?" He paused to let the words sink in. "Two white, one red. I've even watched you water them of an evening."

He could see Petrovic struggling to contain himself at this revelation.

"If anyone tries to follow me, don't ever go home, Tibor."

Petrovic's face was set in a plastered smile, but his eyes burned with impotent hatred.

"Dust off your passport. I'll see you in Switzerland in a few days."

"Switzerland?"

"I'll call and tell you where exactly."

Borodin tipped his hat, turned, and set off across the broad sweep of lawn behind the bench. He was tempted to glance over his shoulder, but he knew that their best chance of abducting him (before torturing the information out of him) wasn't here in the open, with witnesses all around; it was in the car park at the entrance to the gardens. They had probably watched him pull up in the sedan that he and Hamilton hijacked from the government minister two nights ago, and they were probably all set to bundle him into the back of their own vehicle and make off at speed before anyone could intercede.

They weren't to know that he had no intention of returning to the motor car, or that he had arranged meetings here before and had in his possession a key to one of the doors in the high stone wall that ringed the park. He hadn't just checked the lock late last night; he had oiled it for good measure. He had done this after parking the stolen van in a leafy lane off the Allée de Longchamp, just beyond the perimeter wall, and had then walked through the woods to Porte Dauphine, where he flagged down a taxi back to his hotel.

The van had been there less than an hour ago — he had checked on his way to the meeting — and it was still there now. He approached it circuitously, just to be sure, stepping silently through the sun-dappled undergrowth. Satisfied, he pulled on the blue workman's overalls and the peaked cap. Then, with his pistol resting in his lap, he set off south, making for the Pont de Suresnes. Only once he was over the bridge and there was still nothing in the side mirrors to cause concern did he finally begin to relax. He even permitted himself a smile.

Phase One completed without a hitch. His

hesitation yesterday had almost gotten him killed, but it had now made him a rich man, richer than he had ever been. And there was more to come. He reached inside the overalls, took one of the bundles of cash from his jacket pocket, and riffled the end of it with his thumb.

He had expected excuses, stalling tactics, but Petrovic had evidently been instructed to settle the matter swiftly. It was odd to think of the two Karaman brothers running scared, but he could see why they might be. There had been suspicions, but nothing concrete to connect them to the kidnapping all those years ago.

No one had believed that a ragtag bunch of Croatian crooks based in Spalato would even dare to attempt such a thing in Venice. Within the organization there had been a blanket denial of any involvement. Yes, the coffers seemed suddenly to have swelled, but this boost in financial fortunes had been ascribed at the time to a bank heist in Zagreb. The wagging tongues, knowing what was best for them, had gradually fallen silent; and a few years later, the tide of war had engulfed Europe in a flood of misery, death, and destruction that touched everybody's lives, drowning out the story of a baby boy snatched from a pram while his nanny's back was turned.

Borodin checked the mirrors once more, and as he headed north toward Puteaux, an image flashed into his skull unbidden: Gotal's big hands reaching down and scooping up the child from its pram. Had Gotal known what was expected of him even then, or had the order to kill the infant come later? Had anyone else been involved? If so, what had happened to him — or her? Had a boat been waiting to whisk them away from Venice to the mainland?

Imponderables. And besides, the speculation was beginning to make him feel distinctly uneasy because Gotal's actions shined a harsh and unforgiving light on his own. He told himself that none of this was of his making, that ultimately Gotal was to blame for not carrying his secret with him to the grave, and that by rights Hamilton should be dead by now — *would* be dead if Borodin hadn't stepped in to alter the outcome at the restaurant.

When that didn't work, he told himself that he wasn't doing it solely for himself; he also had his family's interests at heart. The consolation didn't last long. He saw his daughter flatly refusing to accept the money he offered her, however much she needed it, and he saw the grandson he had never met, kicking his pudgy feet in a crib.

He also saw a stranger's hands reaching down to carry the little chap off.

CHAPTER TWELVE

It was better than being lashed to a bed, though not by much. His hands were tied behind his back and attached to a rope slung over a high beam in the barn.

He was only just able to sit on the ground, and when walking around, his freedom was limited to a circle some fifteen feet across. This struck him as an inverted kind of justice for past misdeeds. As boys, they had begged netted plovers off the fenmen, tied fishing line to their legs, and watched them fly in circles before hauling them in and handing them back.

The barn housed a sawmill. There were hoists and winches and a long steel rail for wheeling the tree trunks toward the giant circular blade, which lay still and menacing like a sleeping beast in its lair. The wooden racks against one wall were stacked with planks, and the scent of wood resin filled the air. Scattered around the place were any number of implements and tools that could have freed him in a moment had they only lain within his reach, but all he had to work with was the rusty nail he had found buried in the blanket of sawdust at his feet soon after he had heard the car leave.

An hour of picking away blind at his bonds had left him with cramps in both forearms, and the nail kept slipping from his feeble fingers. He was groping around for it behind his back when the barn doors were thrown open.

The sight of Otto and Erwin came with a splash of fear. It must have been Pippi he had heard leaving in the car earlier, which meant that the two men were free to do whatever they wished with him in her absence.

"Where's Pippi?" he asked.

Otto produced a knife from his pocket and released the spring-loaded stiletto blade. "Get up."

Luke rose awkwardly to his feet, eyes on the knife.

"I have some questions for you."

"I've told you all I know."

"We'll see." Otto spun him around and cut the rope running to the beam. "Outside." He shoved him toward the doors.

"Can I have some water?"

Otto laughed. "How did you guess?"

The stone trough was tucked in beside a large bush at the corner of the farmhouse. It was fed via a rusted downpipe with rainwater from the roof, and it took both men to force his head beneath the surface.

He tried to remain calm, figuring that the best tactic was to start struggling long before his breath ran out. This worked well enough at first, but they seemed to sense he was playacting, and soon began holding him down longer, in between the bouts of questioning. "Why are you here?" . . . "What are you planning?" . . . "Where's Borodin?" . . . "When is he coming?"

Otto grew increasingly frustrated, but when Erwin, the reluctant accomplice, suddenly delivered a stinging slap across his face, Luke began to worry for his life. They weren't just developing a taste for torture; they were working each other into a wild-eyed frenzy. There was no playacting on his part when they next dragged him from the trough. The fit of coughing was to clear the water from his nose and throat.

"When is Borodin coming here?" Otto yelled into his blinking eyes.

Only one thing held him back from telling them about Zurich: it would mean they'd been right all along, and in their current state there was no saying what they would do when they discovered he'd been holding out on them.

"I don't know," he sputtered.

He hadn't been under for more than about thirty seconds when, strangely, they released him. Thinking it a ruse, he surfaced to sneak a quick breath and heard shouting. Pippi had returned, and she was screaming blue murder as she ran over from the car.

He remained kneeling, too spent to stand, in the mud puddle that had formed in front of the trough. He managed to gather the general gist of the heated exchange, though. Pippi had been in contact with someone in Paris who confirmed Luke's account of events. The story of the two shootings had indeed hit the Parisian papers. Luke was named and being sought by the police.

Otto mumbled some lame excuse, which earned him a tirade of abuse. Erwin cowered under Pippi's glare, a boy once more. She came and stood before Luke.

"Are you all right?"

"Better for seeing you."

"I'm sorry, I didn't think they . . ." She turned to Erwin. "Put him back in the barn," she ordered.

It was after one o'clock when Pippi looked

in on him, which was why she found him kneeling on the ground, head bowed in prayer. In England, it was just past midday.

"You don't need to pray for your life."

He looked up slowly. "My friend . . . the one I told you about . . . the one who was murdered . . . she's being buried right now."

"You didn't say she was murdered."

"I should be there. I was meant to be there. Not here."

He hadn't just pictured the deep ring of mourners at the graveside; he had tried to transport himself into their midst, to insert himself between his mother and his father, to clasp their hands and feel their love flowing through him as the coffin was lowered into the ground. It had come to him clearly then: he wanted to go home, and he no longer cared what it took to get him there.

"I'll come back later," said Pippi.

"I can give you Borodin," he called after her.

She turned back. "Oh?"

"He's going to be in Zurich on Tuesday."

"Zurich?"

"I need your word that you'll let me go."

She hesitated for a moment. "You have it."

"Why should I believe you?"

"I could ask you the same."

He was in no position to negotiate, nor was he in the mood. He just wanted out.

"I'm supposed to meet him at a bar in the old town — Café Glück."

"When?"

"Four o'clock." Pippi walked over from the doors and crouched down in front of him. "It's true," he said.

"I believe you." She reached out a hand and gently brushed away some wood shavings stuck to his forehead. "Let's get you cleaned up; then I'll drive you back to Konstanz."

Was it really that straightforward? A simple trade? His freedom in exchange for a bit of information? Not even an hour ago, her two colleagues had been drowning him in a water trough.

He began to believe it only when she set about untying the rope at his wrists.

Neither Otto nor Erwin shook hands with him when he appeared in the kitchen with his suitcase, but they both muttered apologies (demanded of them by Pippi, he suspected, while he was getting himself together upstairs).

They didn't come outside to wave him off.

He placed his suitcase in the boot of the car, then dropped into the passenger seat.

"I won't be recommending this hotel to my friends," he said.

Pippi smiled and started the engine.

For the first five minutes, they drove along a stony road through dense woodland. They didn't see another dwelling or another soul, and they didn't speak.

"Tell me about your friend Agnes," said Pippi, soon after the trees had given way to rolling pastures, as if the sweeping view demanded that they also be more expansive in their conversation.

"She was the first person I knew. A nun."

"A nun?"

"I'm a foundling."

Pippi frowned, her eyes fixed on the road ahead. "I don't know that word."

With high hedgerows whipping past on both sides, he told her of his abandonment and his early years at St. Theresa's, and of Sister Agnes' role in getting him ready for the world. Pippi didn't have to prompt him. The story poured out of him, a steady stream that dried to a trickle only when the subject turned to Agnes' violent death at the hands of a housebreaker.

"I can't help thinking she must have known him, recognized him. I mean, why else would he . . . could he . . . Sister Agnes, of all people?" He felt the pressure build suddenly in his chest. "Maybe he'd been at the orphanage himself," he added, aware of the waver in his voice.

"Maybe," said Pippi. "When did this happen?"

"A week ago."

There was something ominous in her brooding silence, but then she turned to him and asked brightly, "Are you hungry?"

It was a small country inn set in an orchard of ancient apple trees near a remote crossroads. Pippi knew the owner, Uta, a stout woman with a mad mop of silver hair. She looked Luke over with the wary eyes of a protective parent before showing them to a table on the terrace out back. Two tall cold beers arrived promptly. Luke savored a sip.

"Good?" Pippi asked.

"Better than rainwater."

He offered her a cigarette, lighting it for her, and then his own.

"Stay," she said.

Had he heard her right? "Excuse me?"

"You're free to go, but I'm asking you to stay."

"Why?"

"Because I don't want Borodin. I want the man who really betrayed us." She allowed him a moment to take in her words.

"It's why he sent you, and the money. It was a message, a warning, his way of telling me he didn't do it. It was someone else."

"Who?"

"Otto or Erwin. Maybe both, but I don't think so." She paused. "If you help me, you can have the money back and I'll deliver you to Zurich."

He smiled at the expression. "Like a letter?"

"Didn't Borodin say? It's what we do."

"Deliver people to Switzerland?"

"Not just people."

"You're smugglers?"

She looked affronted by his use of the word. "We help people get out of Germany with as much as they can take."

"Jews?"

"Yes. Not always."

His mind turned to Fernando and the rumors about him doing a brisk business selling immigration visas to the Dominican Republic. "Is the money good?"

Her green eyes hardened. "Everyone needs to live. And you've seen how we live. We don't do it for the money. Johan was Jewish."

They had met at Freiburg University, where she was studying languages and he medicine. When the Nuremberg Laws were passed a couple of years ago, stripping Jews of German citizenship and banning "cross-racial" marriages, they both gave up their studies in protest. It was Johan's idea that they begin assisting Jews and other opponents of the Nazis to leave the country while they could.

"This is only the beginning," she said. "There is worse to come."

"You think?"

She cast a wary glance around her. It was late, and the only other diners on the terrace were a young family of four, tricked out in traditional dress — dirndls for the mother and daughter, lederhosen for the father and son — like something off a picture postcard. Pippi still lowered her voice, though.

"Do you know what is really happening here? Two weeks ago, I was in the bakery. There was a woman in the queue, a widow, Frau Pfeiffer. She said something about our dear Führer getting too big for his Austrian boots. No one has seen her since. I heard the other day that she has been taken away for 'reeducation.' Think about that. When people start denouncing each other, it is all over. Opposition is dead. He has even stolen the minds of our children." A glance at the perfect German family. "I have a niece the same age as that girl. How old is she? Six? Seven?"

Luke looked over. "Something like that."

"Lisl talks about *Rasse* — race. They learn it at school. I asked her if she even knew what a race was. *'Arisch oder nicht,'* she said — Aryan or not. Six years old. She cried when I told her my boyfriend was Jewish."

Luke watched her run the tip of her forefinger down the beaded sweat of her beer glass.

"Johan used to say that every person we help is a life saved. I believe him now."

"What happened to Johan?"

Pippi was about to reply when their food arrived: grilled cutlets of lamb fanned out on a wooden platter, along with fried potatoes and a green salad. She waited for Uta to retire with the tray before answering.

They had dealt with Borodin before and had no reason to believe the exchange wouldn't go off as smoothly as the previous ones, especially since no people were to be trafficked this time, just some paintings. These they planned to spirit across the lake into Switzerland in the dead of night. Borodin sometimes used an intermediary, but on this occasion he made the delivery in person. The rendezvous was a remote fishing community near Friedrichshafen, a hamlet of houses set on a small cove. They had used it before, and as before, the handover took place away from the dwellings, on a wooded promontory nearby.

The paintings were precious enough to be packed individually in wooden crates, and once they'd been unloaded from the back of Borodin's van, Johan checked and pocketed their fee for the transport. Borodin then disappeared into the night. Ten minutes later, while they were still loading the paintings into the boat, four men materialized from nowhere with flashlights and machine pistols.

They were forced at gunpoint to lug the paintings back through the trees to a couple of waiting cars. Even Johan, hot-headed by nature, understood that there was nothing to be done — they were outgunned — but when the leader of the gang also demanded that they hand over the money they'd just been paid, he resisted and was clubbed to the ground with the butt of a gun. As he struggled to his feet, the leader kicked him hard in the head, and kept kicking.

Johan never regained consciousness. His breathing had weakened almost to nothing by the time they got him back to Konstanz, and he died a few hours later in the hospital.

Pippi hung her head at the memory, poking at her food.

"They were dressed like civilians, but I think they were military. The leader gave orders like an officer."

"Wehrmacht?"

"Or Abwehr." The feared German secret service.

"It doesn't make sense. They would have arrested you."

"Not if they were in it for themselves. They had what they wanted. It was enough."

"Maybe you're wrong. Maybe Borodin *was* behind it."

"Then why did he not hand the paintings straight over to them?"

It was a good point. "You didn't ask yourself that at the time?"

"Of course." She had assumed Borodin was just going through the motions to distance himself from the deceit. Besides, the idea that Otto or Erwin was behind the betrayal had been unthinkable at the time. "I'm glad, in a way, it wasn't him. I have always liked him."

"I'm not sure I'd trust him any further than I could throw him."

"I need your help," said Pippi. There was nothing imploring in her gaze, just a steady

144

certainty that he would do the right thing by her.

"What you need is to get out of this game before it's too late."

"Soon," she said. "Just one more job."

"Where are you from?"

"Munich."

"Go home, Pippi. That's what I plan to do."

"You can't go home."

"It's a misunderstanding, a mistake. I'll lie low, sit it out."

"Listen to me," she said forcefully. "The people Borodin works for don't make mistakes." They were, she explained, a Croatian crime outfit with a presence throughout Europe. The situation in Germany was just another lucrative opportunity for them to exploit. Vast sums of money were up for grabs as the systematic dispossession of the Jewish population gathered pace, but they had fingers in all kinds of other pies, from extortion to assassination and espionage.

Luke laid his knife and fork on his plate. "I'm telling you, they've got the wrong man. I've done nothing."

"Don't you see? It's not what you've done, it's who you are."

"Who I am?"

"Were. Before you became Luke Hamilton."

"That's ridiculous," he scoffed.

"Is it?" Pippi planted her elbows on the table and leaned toward him. "Your friend Sister Agnes is killed, and a few days later someone tries to kill you. Coincidence? You think? Because I don't."

Could she possibly be right? Had she teased out the connection he had failed to find? What if Agnes had simply been a stepping-stone toward him? What if the attempt on his life had not, in fact, been a case of mistaken identity? A part of him wanted to reject her theory out of hand, although he couldn't say why exactly.

"And you've worked this all out in the last, what, twenty minutes?" he said, heavy on the skepticism.

"I have a quick brain."

"And a remarkable lack of modesty."

She shrugged. "I can see why you don't want to believe it."

"Oh?"

"Because she died for you — because of you."

That cut deep, right down to the anger flaring inside him. "Thanks for that."

"If you want the truth, you have to be ready to hear it."

146

"And if you're trying to get me to stay, it's not going to work."

"Then go," she said, pulling a key from her skirt pocket and sliding it across the table. "Take the car. There's some money under the seat, enough to get you home. Leave it at the station in Konstanz."

His head ordered him to his feet, but his body refused to obey.

"I need to think."

Pippi turned her attention back to her food. He had noted it before but not examined it. A curious formality about the manner in which she ate: erect in her chair, straight-backed, elbows pressed close to her sides — details that spoke of a childhood ruled by a rigid code of manners.

She was the first to break the lengthy silence. "I could be wrong," she conceded, taking the linen napkin from her lap and dabbing at her mouth.

"Let's say you're not. What then?"

"Then Borodin lied to you. He helped you, yes, but he also lied to you."

"And if he lied to me, he knows who I am."

"Probably."

Luke reached for his beer. So here he was once more, back in that place he had sworn never to return to. The first half of his life

147

had been spent plagued by questions and aching for answers. How many times had he forced Sister Agnes to tell him the story of that night, of the snow on the ground, and the tracks leading through it to the shadowy man standing beyond the pool of light thrown by the porch lantern . . . and of the hand he had raised and held aloft until she returned the gesture . . . and how he had then turned up the collar of his overcoat and set off down the driveway?

A few years ago, shortly before Luke joined the RAF, Agnes had unburdened herself to him during a visit to Ely Cathedral.

"I could have followed him. I should have, but then I looked down and I saw you, and in my mind I urged him to keep walking. And when I heard the car drive off, I told myself I would never have caught up with him in time anyway. It's not true, though. I could have. I could have talked to him, maybe even . . ." She couldn't finish the sentence. "I'm so sorry, Luke."

"He drove through a snowstorm at night. I doubt he had any intention of taking me back."

"But he might have."

Luke banished the memory and set his beer glass back down on the table.

"If you're right, then Borodin also knows who killed Agnes."

"I can't say. But I'm sure of this: you need me with you in Zurich."

"But only if I help you first."

Pippi shrugged. "One good turn deserves another."

"Where did you learn your English?"

"I told you, I studied it at university."

"No. It's too colloquial. And your accent . . ."

She offered her hand across the table. "Do we have a deal?"

"I have to be in Zurich on Tuesday."

"It's happening tomorrow night."

Her hand hovered — a fine, elegant hand, with the long fingers of a pianist.

"Not until I know what 'it' is. So you can put that away for now."

But he knew already they would end up shaking on it. How could he not have her at his side in Zurich? She had a steely competence about her, a quality lacking in him — except, maybe, when he was seated in the cockpit of an airplane.

CHAPTER THIRTEEN

Neither Otto nor Erwin made any attempt to mask their displeasure on seeing Luke clamber out of the car back at the farmhouse, and Pippi's explanation did little to appease them.

"There's been a change of plan. We need another pair of hands. We're bringing his family out, too."

The man in question was a scientist, a Jewish physicist. Many had already left Germany for Britain and America; others had remained in the hope that the situation at home would improve. It hadn't, and whereas Hitler had once been happy to see the scientific establishment purged of Jews, he was now beginning to understand the true cost of the policy: he had handed some of his finest brains to countries that might well stand as enemies against him if war came. For Pippi, there was no "if"; it was only a question of time. And for Professor

Weintraub, time was in extremely short supply. The British had been courting him for more than a year, but only recently had he accepted their offer to spirit him away to England, via Switzerland.

News that the professor's family would now be traveling with him had come to Pippi's ears this morning, when she had called her British contact from Konstanz. She had sat on the information until now, while she figured how best to use it to her advantage, and against the possible traitor in their midst.

"We need to find another boat," said Erwin. "Something bigger."

Professor Weintraub was a widower, but his three children would be accompanied by their nanny, to say nothing of the extra luggage.

"This is nonsense," Otto growled. "Unacceptable."

"What else are we to do?" Erwin replied.

"I mean *him.*" Otto shot Luke a sour look. "You trust him?"

"I do," said Pippi. "Luke will help us get them into Switzerland, and then he'll hand himself over to his own people."

It was one of a number of lies they had hatched at the restaurant and during the drive back.

"I'm still against it," said Otto, flexing his jaw.

"Then we'll just have to make do without you."

"You would choose him over me?"

"I'm just trying to think like Johan. He would want us to do what's best for the professor and his family." She glanced at Luke. "And if I'm wrong about him, I'll be the first to correct my mistake."

"No," said Otto. "I'll be the first."

When Otto and Erwin drove off in search of a bigger boat, Pippi set Luke to splitting logs for the range. The reward for his labors would be a roast chicken for dinner, and enough hot water for a shallow bath in the tin tub in the corner of the kitchen. Alone in the woodshed beside the barn, he felt a strange calm descend on him. There was something comforting in the repetitive rise and fall of the ax, in the rhythmic thuds resonating off the planked walls. The systematic reduction of the logs to a pile of fresh stove wood suggested method, order, and purpose — qualities that could now be applied to his own situation when viewed through the prism of Pippi's hypothesis.

He wasn't entirely persuaded by it, but after the fear and confusion of the past forty-eight hours he at least had something firm to fix on, to aim at. He thought of Sister Agnes, buried now, sunk deep in the soil at St. Theresa's. A distressing vision of the last moments of her life came to him. He tried to repel it, but it caught him in its coils. He saw her resisting in order to protect him, and he saw the blows raining down on her. He couldn't form a face for her assailant, but if Pippi was right, there was every chance Borodin knew the man's identity and even where to find him. When he next swung the ax, it was with such force that the steel bit sheared clean through the log and buried itself deep in the chopping block.

Once they had got the fire going in the range, they went in search of their supper. The chicken coop was a walk-in affair beside the barn. As they peered through the wire mesh, selecting a bird for the pot, Luke sensed a hesitancy on Pippi's part.

"You want me to do it?" he asked.

"You have done it before?"

"Yes."

He entered the coop and gathered up the chicken with as little fuss as possible so as not to agitate it. Holding it close to his chest, he stroked it and soothed it with words, but once they had rounded the corner of the barn and were out of sight of the other birds, he didn't dally. Holding the chicken upside down by its feet, he gripped the back of its head in the cleft between the forefinger and middle finger of his other hand and extended his arm toward the ground, stretching out the neck and snapping it with a twist of the wrist. Pippi gave a sharp gasp as the wings flapped wildly.

"Don't worry," he said. "It's already dead."

The bird finally fell still. Pippi produced some twine, and Luke hung it by its feet from the beam over the kitchen sink, allowing the blood to drain into the neck.

"Where did you learn to do that?" They were the first words she had spoken in a while.

"A man called Solomon Finch."

In truth, chickens weren't really Solomon's thing, although he kept and bred a handful of them for eggs. This demanded the occasional culling of unwanted roosters, which was how Luke had learned at an early age how to dispatch a bird by hand.

His first glimpse of the mysterious figure who lived alone in the tiny thatched cottage on the far side of Wicken Fen had come a few weeks into his new life with the Hamiltons. He was down at the end of the garden, exploring the boundaries of the big house that was now his home, when he saw through the trees, silhouetted against the lowering sun, a tall man standing in his punt, slowly poling his way one-handed across the fen. Poised in his other hand was a long spear with a three-pronged head, like Neptune's trident. It flashed into the water and reemerged with a giant fish skewered on the end of it, writhing madly. Terrified but exhilarated by what he'd just witnessed, Luke turned and hightailed it back to the house as fast as his skinny legs would carry him.

It wasn't until autumn that they were finally introduced. The rains had come hard and early that year, and with them the floods that topped up the fens and turned the pastures into glistening meres. Luke was out walking this new water world with his father when they stumbled upon Solomon, heading home beside the swollen lode. He had a shotgun slung over one shoulder, a goose over the other.

"I seen the young pup around," said Solomon. "An' he's seen me. First time was when I darted that big pike, right?"

Luke nodded shyly up at the craggy face, with its side-whiskers and high cheekbones and sweep of long, lank hair.

"What Solomon doesn't know about birds and fish isn't worth knowing," said his father.

"An' much of what I does know ain't worth it, neither."

As far as eight-year-old Luke was concerned, their friendship was sealed right there and then with the little wink that Solomon fired at him.

Solomon was a true fen tiger, a sixth-generation wildfowler and fisherman who supplemented his income as his forebears had: by digging peat and cutting sedge during the kinder months. He was also one of the last punt-gunners operating in the Ely area. The gun, a muzzle-loading monster some eight feet long, hung on leather straps from the wall of Solomon's living room. He claimed to have once knocked forty-eight ducks out of the air with a single shot — half mallards, half wigeons. This might have sounded like a tall tale if, during that first winter, Luke hadn't been with him in the punt one bitterly cold morning when he bagged thirty-seven birds with one shot.

Like many fenmen, Solomon was tough as wire nails, stubbornly independent, and suspicious of strangers, but he didn't live alone by choice. He had lost his wife to cancer, his daughter to an itinerant lay preacher, and his son to the Great War. Luke learned all this from his parents; Solomon never spoke of the family he once had, although one time he did mention them in passing.

"It's six years now you been itching to ask about 'em."

"Who's that?" Luke replied, knowing full well.

"You're a sly 'un. I ain't going to get drawn by you."

"You brought it up."

"Only so's to say you done right to keep that trap of yours shut. Wouldn't be sitting here now otherwise."

"You mean sitting here mending your nets for free?"

Solomon gave a sudden loud bellow of a laugh. "Damn fool you is. Shoulda blabbed right on."

The knowledge that Solomon imparted was payment enough for Luke's help around the place. He taught him how to shoot a bird on the wing, dart a fish, and net a river. Luke learned to weave eel grigs from osier wands, and Solomon showed him where in the waterways to lay the long, funnel-shaped traps. In early spring, he gathered basket loads of plovers' eggs, peddling them door-to-door in the nearby villages; and he set horsehair nooses for linnets and goldfinches, which could then be sold to bird fanciers in Cambridge. He didn't just make good pocket money from everything Solomon had taught him; he also had the satisfaction of putting food on the family table: a brace of teal or a fat gold-sided tench.

By now, the chicken was plucked, ready to gut, and Luke realized he was still prattling on about Solomon, heedless of Pippi's interest or, rather, lack of it.

She dismissed his apology and pushed up the sleeves of her cotton blouse. "Show me what Solomon showed you."

He handed her the cleaver.

"Head and feet first."

Otto and Erwin returned shortly before dinner, dejected after failing to find a motor launch both large enough for their requirements and, more importantly, fast enough to outrun the German boats that patrolled the unmarked border running down the middle of the lake. They still had a couple of leads to follow up, but the clock was ticking and tensions ran high during dinner in the kitchen — not helped, Luke suspected, by his presence. There was little in Otto's and Erwin's behavior to suggest that they had reconciled themselves, over the course of the afternoon, to his involvement in the mission.

Pippi ran through the plan, as finalized with the British earlier in the day. They were to pick up their passengers from Friedrichshafen, which lay about twenty kilometers east of Konstanz, on the north shore. The weather was set fair for tomorrow, and what with it being a Sunday, the town would be packed with visitors, its port and surrounding waters teeming with all kinds of pleasure craft. They should have no trouble blending right in. Professor Weintraub was due to arrive by train in the late afternoon. He would check into his hotel and wait there until just before six o'clock, when he would tell the concierge he was going for a stroll before dinner.

He would then make his way straight to the port. All being well, at seven o'clock sharp, his children would arrive at the port in a car driven by the nanny. After loading the luggage, they would cast off and head south to the mouth of the Schussen River. There they would shelter up, waiting for darkness to descend, which it definitely would — not by chance, there was a new moon tomorrow night. Pippi figured it would take twenty minutes at most to make the run across the lake to Romanshorn on the Swiss side, where the British would be waiting for them in a field. The Swiss authorities had been alerted to their arrival and were ready to turn a blind eye.

Otto and Erwin expressed some concerns, which Pippi did her best to allay. A bottle of schnapps was opened. Glasses were raised three times in toast: to the success of the mission, to the boat they had yet to find, and to Johan. The alcohol worked its slow magic. Otto and Erwin began to unwind, with Erwin growing almost garrulous as the conversation turned to their escapades. The reminiscences were tinged with nostalgia, for they all knew that the drama was drawing to a close and the curtain would soon fall on the adventure they had embarked on together two years ago.

It was a different world back then. The German people still traveled, the land borders were still porous, and the crossing guards were still happy to look the other way for a few cases of wine or a quarter side of beef. As in all things, Johan had been the first to detect the subtle shift in policy, the slow sealing-off of the country by the National Socialists. Hitler and his henchmen had once been happy to drive their opponents abroad (while picking their pockets all the way to the border). No longer. Now they sought a reckoning at home with anyone foolish enough to challenge them: journalists, authors, artists, and other undesirables. And as for the Jews, well, they had to understand that personal freedom meant forfeiting all they'd accumulated over the years through their systematic exploitation of the *herrenvolk*, the master race.

The days of bribes and kickbacks were gone; officials at every level of the regime feared for themselves; and the Bodensee, with its watery frontier, had become the last feasible route for those looking to flee into Switzerland with their belongings. But how long would it remain passable? Erwin, emboldened by the drink and beginning to slur his words, declared that he intended to fight on — if not here, then elsewhere.

Relations with Erwin and Otto thawed still further when it emerged that Luke was not only a pilot but had seen active duty in northern India. These credentials seemed to elevate him to the same warrior class they imagined themselves belonging to. Otto even made a stab at a joke, suggesting that if they couldn't find a bigger boat, they could always steal a plane at the airfield in Friedrichshafen and have Luke fly them to Switzerland.

When it finally came time to turn in for

the night, Luke snatched a private moment with Pippi at the kitchen sink.

"How much of what you told us about tomorrow was true?" he asked.

"Most of it."

"Anything I should know?"

Her eyes flicked to the beamed and boarded ceiling. They could hear Otto and Erwin moving about upstairs. "Not now," she said, handing him a plate to dry. "In the morning."

He kept his voice low, too. "I know what you're doing, Pippi."

"Oh?"

"You're hoping the man who killed Johan shows up again."

"Am I?"

"Revenge clouds the judgment."

"Not mine."

"We'll see about that."

"Not mine," she repeated tartly.

"Good, because now there are children involved."

She looked shocked by the intimation. "I would never . . ."

"And I would never let you."

Lying in the same bed he had been bound to last night, he didn't even try to make sense of the day's bizarre events. It brought to mind the summer haze that would spring

162

up over the plain south of Miranshah, the strange miasma of heat and dust that thickened suddenly to a soup until you found yourself flying blind, reliant on your instruments. That was all he could do now: stay focused on what lay directly in front of his nose, get through tomorrow, and then get himself to Zurich.

He knew that tomorrow would not be without its dangers and its surprises. Pippi was running a couple of potentially conflicting agendas in parallel. She wanted the traitor whose betrayal had led to Johan's death, and she also wanted the man who had actually taken her boyfriend's life. It remained to be seen exactly how she intended to achieve both objectives while safely extracting Professor Weintraub and his family, but Luke was beginning to understand why she had worked so hard to convince him to stay on. She couldn't reasonably hope to pull it off without an accomplice.

That thought gave him pause.

Could it be that Pippi was playing him for her own purposes? That she had thrown together her theory linking the attempt on his life to Agnes' death just to persuade him to stick around? He wouldn't put it past her. She was a skilled dissembler. There had been nothing in her conduct over dinner to hint at the suspicions she harbored about Otto and Erwin. She had fed them and laughed away with them, while no doubt searching for signs and clues in their behavior. He had done the same, imagining at first that it must be Otto, with his streak of ruthlessness and his gaunt good looks, before leaning more toward young, overstrung, impressionable Erwin. It was odd to think that by this time tomorrow, he would know the answer.

As sleep closed in on him, he found himself groping for stray scraps of knowledge about Croatia. It was the place where all roads seemed to lead: Borodin, a Croat based in Paris, instructed by his Croatian crime bosses to snuff out the life of an Englishman whose complexion and coloring were far from English.

He knew that Croatia faced Italy across the Adriatic, that it was renowned for the beauty of its coastline, that the Venetian Republic had once had some sort of presence there, and that after the last war, the country had banded together with Serbia and Slovenia to form what was now called the Kingdom of Yugoslavia. He also recalled that a few years ago, King Alexander of Yugoslavia had been assassinated in Marseille.

A foreigner murdered on French soil by his own people.

It was beginning to look as though Luke himself had narrowly avoided the same fate.

CHAPTER FOURTEEN

Damp with sweat, Borodin lay on his back and stared at the ceiling fan's valiant efforts to generate a downdraft.

It was a miserable room — poky, filthy, and poorly furnished — and yet it seemed somehow appropriate. He had spent his first ever night in Paris in such a place. Why not his last? It lent a satisfying circularity to his twelve-year sojourn in the French capital.

He hadn't been ordered to move to Paris, but Budapest had become too hot to hold him, and when a vacancy popped up after the brutal murder of Malovic, he had put his name forward for the posting. A firm hand was required to restore the organization's interests following the takeover of its smuggling operation by a rival Portuguese gang. This had come about, Borodin soon discovered, from the collaboration of two detectives in the Sûreté — Malovic perishing in a hail of bullets while supposedly resisting arrest.

Borodin did what he had always done: he stayed in the shadows, and when he struck, he did so swiftly, without relish or ceremony. The detectives were the first to die, on the direct orders of the Karaman brothers. Impressively, the Portuguese didn't panic after losing their protection — not until Borodin began picking them off one by one. He saved their leader, Farinha, until last, and only then did he show his face, contriving a meeting in one of the Breton bars around Rue du Dragon — an apparently chance encounter between two strangers. The ultimatum, when he finally presented it to the wiry scrap of a man with pomaded hair, was both succinct and reasonable: if he received a postcard from Lisbon within the next two weeks, the matter would be considered closed.

The following night, at the vacant house he had already scouted in a quiet quarter near Sèvres (the same house whose address he had dropped to Farinha), he calmly took the lives of the two thugs sent to take his. Foolishly, Farinha was waiting in a car nearby. They drove to the Forêt de Meudon. Farinha pleaded for mercy, a second chance, but Borodin finished the business and torched the body in the car.

It was a job well done, and he had hoped for more in the way of gratitude from the Karamans. Instead, they had dispatched Petrovic to Paris to fill Malovic's shoes. Borodin knew better than to grumble. To the brothers, dissent was tantamount to treason. He could name several men within the organization who had failed to grasp this fact, and he had no plans to follow them to hell before his time. He quietly accepted his lot: that of an old warhorse put out to pasture but still expected to pull its weight from time to time. He did unquestioningly whatever was asked of him. He stole or hijacked a truck; he leaned on those who owed them money; and as the operation expanded under Petrovic's ambitious program, he scouted new warehouses around the country, hiring fresh personnel in the process.

He had heard it said that every man had two countries: his own and France. And he'd learned the truth of this through travel — getting to know the various cities and their histories, the regional cuisines and wines, and the many peoples united in their simple love of living properly. He lingered as long as he could whenever he was away from Paris, and he threw himself into the language, turning to books, to literature, for the first time in his life and working away at his accent until he almost began to think of himself as his alter ego, Bernard Fautrier.

With Hitler's rise to power in 1933, the German front offered new opportunities. Tyranny was always good for business, for it walked hand in hand with fear and flight. A drunken evening with a Jewish lawyer in a bar in Metz had led him to Johan and Pippi. They burned with a youthful zeal that he mistrusted by instinct, but he was taken with Pippi from the first. She lacked Johan's intensity; she didn't bristle with the same fierce indignation at the injustices being perpetrated by the Nazis. Or if she did, she also knew that he, Borodin, was not moved by such concerns and that Johan's impassioned tirades washed right over him.

He thought about Pippi now, privileged and damaged and looking to patch up old wounds of her own, and reminded himself why he had released Hamilton into her charge. Given the debacle with the paintings that had resulted in Johan's death, it was the last place the Karamans would think of looking for him. It was also Borodin's way of letting Pippi know that he was not to blame for the unfortunate events of that night, and that the danger lay in her own backyard. Had she been smart enough to work this out, or had he overestimated her? Worryingly, both she and Hamilton had disappeared off the map in Konstanz.

Whup . . . whup . . . whup went the ceiling fan, and a hand alighted on his stomach as gently as a falling leaf.

"Do you want to do it again?" came her drowsy voice from beside him.

"At my age?"

He sensed her smiling. "You might surprise yourself."

They had met in the bar downstairs. Every whore had a sob story up her sleeve, but as someone who had spent much of his life fabricating tales about himself, he had sensed a sizable grain of truth in hers. She was Italian, lured to Paris by the false promises of a Frenchman she had met in her native Naples.

"How much will it cost me?" he asked.

"How much do you have?"

"Three hundred thousand francs."

She laughed. She wasn't to know that the cash was hidden beneath a loose floorboard near the washstand in the corner.

"Breakfast will do," she said.

It hadn't been his intention to bring her to his bed, but little about the evening had gone to plan. He had at least set out to do the sensible thing. He knew that Petrovic would have put the word out, hoping for a chance sighting of him or a snatch of gossip. It was the reason he had installed himself in the Nineteenth Arrondissement, an area of the city he had almost no association with. It was also the reason he had bought a ticket for the film showing at the small picture house around the corner from his hotel.

He had lasted about half an hour, not that the film was to blame. He would happily have spent more time in the company of Pépel, Jean Gabin's quick-witted thief caught between his greed and his good intentions. But a sudden reckless impulse had driven him to his feet. Did he really wish to cower in the darkness like a terrified animal when the city was out there waiting to be savored one last time?

He had roamed the streets, his senses alert, absorbing the impressions and filing them away for future reflection: a shower of sparks from the overhead cable of an electric tram clattering along Avenue Jean-Jaurès, the passengers boxed and lit like specimens on display . . . the faint but unmistakable odor of the slaughterhouses up the road at La Villette . . . an old clochard dancing in laceless boots for loose change by the Métro station on Place du Rhin . . . the toy-town houses of Mouzaïa, a poor quarter where the men wore caps rather than hats . . . the languid strains of *jazz manouche* wafting up from a basement club, when not so long ago the gypsy musicians were to be found only on street corners . . . the Parc des Buttes Chaumont, somber and silent, a dark island in the city it brooded over from its hillside perch, the gypsum quarries of old now a fairy-tale kingdom of cliffs and rocky outcrops and shrouded pathways that wound past waterfalls and alpine grottoes.

He had made a loop through the park, the stars lighting his way, the moon a mere fingernail cutting. He had taken the high suspension bridge to the island in the middle of the lake: a soaring, craggy mass, like a mountain peak that had been lopped off and transported to the city. Its bluffs plunged vertically down to the inky waters, and it was crowned by a Grecian temple that offered a sweeping view across Paris, all the way to the Sacré-Coeur, lit up and blazing, wedding-cake white atop Montmartre. He had stopped to smoke a cigarette in the temple, then gone in search of a brasserie to serve him his last supper.

Strangely, it hadn't struck him at the time, but it did now: the vertiginous landscape of the park rang a note of home, his first home, Vrlika, with its cliff and its ruined castle looming over it. He pictured the damp, cramped farmhouse where he had grown up, when things were still good, before the crops failed several years running and his father turned to drink. The youngest of three brothers, he bore the brunt of the beatings, soon learning that to cry out only fueled his father's rage. And when he finally judged himself strong enough to retaliate, he waited a while longer, just to be sure.

The canvas knapsack he used for school was already packed when his father stumbled home from the bar that Saturday night. The boy knew what was coming, and the moment it began, he struck back with a sudden wild fury that surprised even him. His brothers were away, searching for work in Zadar, and he might well have finished the job if his mother hadn't intervened, crying and begging him to stop. He didn't say goodbye to her. He looked into the wet, red eyes of the woman who had never once raised a hand to protect him, and headed out into the night.

He recalled with shame some of the things he had done while on the move in those early years: the thieving from men who had offered him shelter and work and placed their trust in him; the girls he had loved and then left without so much as a farewell. No binding ties for him, the wanderer, the drifter, the man of the road. When he finally settled in Ragusa, it was for the anonymity that a big city offered, although the rich pickings to be had down at the docks were what had held him there for almost a decade. Real money in his pocket at last, and then a young wife and a small child — a daughter, Simona. It should have been enough, but Edvina's endless badgering about earning an honest wage for once had worn him down and brought on the old itch.

Young and new to the smuggling game, he'd had only cursory dealings with the Karaman brothers, so the invitation to go and work for them in Spalato had taken him by surprise. He leaped at the offer, driving his marriage into the ground before walking out for good. He already knew that the Karamans were ambitious (and ruthless when necessary), but it soon became clear that they were also smart. They understood the power of politics and political protection, and in the years before the Great War, the sands were shifting, presenting new opportunities to those prepared to seize them.

The coastal province of Dalmatia had always been a divided society. Tensions between the wealthy Italian minority and the largely uneducated Croat majority had been simmering away for as long as anyone alive could remember. Now, though, the Habsburg masters back in Vienna were turning up the heat with their policy of systematically disempowering the Italians. The last thing they wanted for the empire was an influential elite in a far-flung province dreaming of their homeland and a possible reannexation.

Italian schools were closed down, legislation was introduced to limit the use of Italian as an official language, and votes were rigged to keep Italians from political office. One of Borodin's first jobs for the Karamans was registering the dead in order to swing elections.

Before long, the tensions in Spalato boiled over into violence, much of it orchestrated by the Karamans, who were looking to cement their role as the unofficial muscle of the new hardliners. Italian businesses were targeted, their windows broken. Insults were freely and publicly hurled, and whenever things came to blows, the police invariably sided with their own kind, arresting any Italians who dared to stand up for themselves. Toward the end of Borodin's first summer in Spalato, two Italian longshoremen were assaulted by a group of Croats as they left a bar down at the port. Being dockworkers, they knew how to handle themselves in a fight, and they were still standing when reinforcements arrived in the form of their colleagues working the night shift at Albrizzi Marittima. The brawl quickly escalated into a pitched battle, which the police struggled to break up. Once they had, though, they knew better than to try taking a bunch of burly dockers into custody. Besides, Albrizzi was a name to be reckoned with.

The Karamans were less respectful. Sensing an opportunity, they decided to put the Albrizzis' authority to the test. The next evening, they gathered together a gang of young Croats and set off across town. A mob on the move was a dangerous monster. Numbers quickly swelled, and feelings were running high by the time they reached the Albrizzis' residence.

Borodin closed his eyes and summoned up the memory of that night, whose true significance was only now clear to him. He saw the large house set some distance back from the street, the iron gates chained and padlocked in anticipation of trouble. As the mob grew more vocal, Vittorio Albrizzi appeared from the house. A few members of his family joined him on the front steps, but when he set off down the driveway to confront the crowd, he was on his own. Arriving at the gates, he stood and waited calmly for the shower of abuse to abate. When it finally did, he opened with a joke.

"It is my father's birthday today. As some of you know, his mind is going. He thinks you have come to celebrate it with him."

Encouraged by the sound of laughter, Albrizzi's wife came to join him, slipping her arm through her husband's as he made a heartfelt plea for peace and unity. Were they not Dalmatians, all of them, first and foremost? And had not Dalamtia been in existence far longer than the empire that currently held sway over it — the same empire that sought to rule them by dividing them? They owed it to each other to overcome the dangerous passions being aroused in them by forces from afar. Dalmatia would still be here long after the Austro-Hungarians had left. Albrizzi proposed that all grievances be placed on hold for the night. Tomorrow they would meet again, at a place of their choosing, and talk things through in a cool-headed manner. He pledged to pay all medical bills and cover all loss of earnings resulting from injuries sustained in the fracas last night, for Croat and Italian alike.

He had us, thought Borodin. And then

someone threw the rock.

How many lives had been reshaped by that one rock? Hamilton's, for sure, even though, in the summer of 1909, he had yet to be born. Borodin's own? Undoubtedly. He wouldn't be lying here now next to an Italian prostitute in this grimy little room. How many other lives? Hundreds? More? He pictured the effects multiplying, proliferating, like the boughs, branches, and twigs of a towering oak tree. And not forgetting the roots quietly spreading beneath the soil — the unseen and unknown consequences. All because of a single, tiny acorn.

That was the way of it, though. The best-laid plans could carry you only so far. One's destiny turned on the smallest things.

"One rock," he muttered.

"What?"

"Nothing."

She was lying on her side, facing the wall, and he noticed for the first time the bruises on her back. *Breakfast will do.* The poor creature, fearful of returning home to her husband, evidently wanted a bed for the night. She had told Borodin earlier that all she hoped for was to earn enough money to buy a ticket back to Naples.

"What's your real name?"

She didn't reply immediately. "Rosaria."

He reached past her and turned off the bedside light.

"Do you want to do it again?" she said once more.

He planted a light kiss on her cheek and lay back in the darkness. "No. Sleep, Rosaria, and dream of breakfast. We'll go somewhere special."

And maybe over breakfast he would squeeze her a little to see if her story stood up. And if it did, well, maybe he would surprise her. Then again, his sentimental mood might well have dissipated by then, like a low-lying mist burned off by the heat of the new day.

CHAPTER FIFTEEN

Pippi appeared in Luke's room as he was packing his suitcase. She handed him the Browning pistol that Borodin had given him in Paris.

"Don't let Otto and Erwin see it."

"Am I going to need it?"

She hesitated. "No."

He released the magazine and thumbed a cartridge into the palm of his hand. "Can I hear what you've really got planned for later?"

"Nothing if they can't find a boat."

It was ten o'clock, and Otto and Erwin had been gone for almost two hours. The strain was beginning to show in Pippi's face.

"I can't help if you don't take me into your trust," he said.

Pippi settled on the bed. "It's not going to happen in Friedrichshafen. We're picking them up from Meersburg."

"Why Meersburg?"

"It's closer, just across the lake."

"Go on."

While she talked, he moved about the room, listening carefully and letting her spell out her plan with no interruptions. It was clever, bold, ambitious. Too ambitious. And flawed in parts. He was tempted to tell her straight, but opted for a more diplomatic approach.

"There are a lot of variables."

"There always are," she replied defensively.

"Do you even know how long it takes to drive from Friedrichshafen to Meersburg at speed?"

"Yes. I did it last week, to see."

He began feeding the bullets back into the magazine. "It's like baiting a hook to catch a fish, then hoping a bigger fish comes along and swallows the first."

"It can work."

"It can also go badly wrong," he countered. "Either way, you have to leave. You know that, don't you? You can't come back."

"I know."

"Maybe never."

"I know."

Of course she had thought it through. Who wouldn't have in her situation?

"And your family?"

"My family?"

"Will they suffer because of your actions?"

She seemed surprised by the question. "No. They are near the middle of what is happening here. Everyone knows there is a daughter who is a problem, an embarrassment."

"You'll be much more than an embarrassment if you pull this off."

"You don't know them," Pippi replied. "Let me tell you what they will do. They will empty my room and burn my things, everything, and they will make sure that people from the Party are there to see it. And my father will tell them all I am not his daughter anymore, and no one will ever speak my name again in the house, not even Margaret . . ." She trailed off, pensive.

"Who's Margaret?"

"Margaret is safe. I made sure. So I have nothing to worry about."

Luke slipped the magazine home and racked the slide. A cartridge was ejected from the chamber and bounced off the boards at his feet. "I'm sorry," he said, "but it's not good enough."

"What do you mean?"

"I mean no plan ever is." He had flown enough missions to know the truth of that. There was always scope for improvement, for more safeguards against the unexpected. "Talk me through it again, but this time we punish it, okay? We do our best to trip it up."

Pippi nodded. "Okay."

They were downstairs in the kitchen, still picking away at the details, when they heard the car. There was something triumphal in the three horn blasts that proclaimed Otto and Erwin's return. Sure enough, the news was good.

It was a large Swedish-built motor launch, with seating and storage to spare. Better still, the engine, recently serviced, could do almost twenty-five knots at full throttle. Otto and Erwin knew this for a fact because they'd taken the thing for a spin around the lake with the owner, who had wanted reassurance that the people looking to hire his boat for a couple of days were capable of handling such a craft. Erwin had done them all proud at the wheel, apparently. Being local, he was known to the harbormaster at Dingelsdorf, who had also vouched for his good character.

"If he only knew what we really have planned for it," joked Otto.

There was a nervous edge to their laughter. What they were about to embark on was anything but a pleasant jaunt around the Bodensee.

Luke loaded his suitcase into the boot of the car. Buried away inside it now was a buff envelope stuffed with cash and a leather handbag of Pippi's. Aside from the clothes on her back, it contained everything she would be leaving her homeland with: some articles of jewelry and a bundle of photos, as well as other curios and keepsakes. They were about to leave when Erwin remembered the chickens. The birds must be cared for — it was a condition his uncle had insisted on before allowing Erwin use of the place while he was away.

It was a twenty-minute drive to Dingelsdorf, a small community that drowsed beside the lake, stirred from its slumber every so often by the arrival of a ferryboat. These came and went from the end of a long wooden jetty that pointed like an accusatory finger at the distant shore across the placid waters. The motor launch was tied up near the ferry station, and they cast an appreciative eye over its low, sleek lines before going in search of lunch.

They ate lake perch under the front awning of the lone hotel on the promenade, washing it down with a crisp local white wine. The conversation was awkward, fractured, and when Pippi disappeared inside to make a telephone call, it almost died out completely before Erwin raised the subject of football. The German national side was well on its way to qualifying for the World Cup next year in Paris, and Erwin was curious to know why England had once again refused to participate in the competition. Did they really think the other teams so inferior, so far beneath them?

"Face it," drawled Otto. "We have never beaten them."

"How can we, if they don't let us try?" said Erwin.

"You tried two years ago," Luke observed drily, twisting the knife.

"Three–nil is nothing."

"Without their best players?" Otto asked, enjoying his friend's indignation. "It could have been ten."

Erwin had worked himself up into a right old lather by the time Pippi returned. Her voice dropped almost to a whisper as she broke the news: the British had just informed her that the plans had changed again. Her irritation at this turn of events was convincing.

Otto's anger was both sudden and unexpected. "What are they playing at?" he hissed. "First the children, now this?"

185

"It's a small change: Meersburg for Friedrichshafen."

"Why?"

"They didn't say. And everything else remains the same."

Luke forced himself back into character. "Where's Meersburg?"

Erwin pointed south, across the lake. "You can almost see it from here."

"So what's the problem?"

"There isn't one," said Pippi, looking to Otto for confirmation.

He glowered at her and lit a cigarette. "I don't like it. I don't like it one bit."

The vehemence of his reaction to the sudden shift of venue offered grounds for suspicion, but Erwin's quiet compliance could also be that of a man calmly processing the information and deciding how best to proceed. Either way, the hook was baited. If Pippi's instincts were sound, if another betrayal was indeed in the offing, then one or the other of them had to find a telephone and alert the people waiting to pounce in Friedrichshafen that the action had just moved twenty kilometers up the shoreline to Meersburg.

They didn't linger once the bill had been settled. Meersburg offered far more in the way of attractions than Dingelsdorf, and as

Pippi pointed out, it made sense to get there early and settle in before their six o'clock rendezvous.

Otto's black mood seemed to pass once they had boarded the big launch and were skimming across the lake. Even at a distance, it was clear that Meersburg was a place of great charm. A turreted castle lorded it over the upper town, which straggled along a high bluff set a short distance back from the lakeshore, where a run of imposing buildings with steeply pitched roofs stood neatly ranged like soldiers on parade. Drawing closer, they could make out the Sunday trippers crowding the tree-lined promenade of the lower town.

Erwin eased back the throttle, and the launch came off the plane, bellying low in the water. They waited for a ferry to leave the port before slipping past the jetty and tying up at the quayside. Pippi shot Luke a fleeting look. He knew what it meant. The game was now properly afoot. There could be no mistakes.

"Wait here," she said. "I have to make another call."

Not true. She was going to make contact with Professor Weintraub at his hotel. He had been in Meersburg since late last night.

"*Another* call?" Erwin groaned.

"To say we're in place."

"To see if they have any more surprises for us," Otto grumbled as she wandered off.

The sun beat down, and in the windless enclave of the port, the searing heat seemed to build by the second. They all lit cigarettes.

"A beautiful place," said Luke. "What is the wine like?" The slope stretching off to the south just back from the port was a cascade of vines.

"Excellent," replied Erwin. "You can try it for yourself. There's a bar I know in the Schlossplatz." He nodded toward the upper town. "We have time."

Not quite as much time as he imagined. The professor's children and their nanny would be arriving by car in two hours — at five o'clock rather than six, as Otto and Erwin had been led to believe.

Pippi returned with a manufactured spring in her step. Everything was on course. "The professor should be checking into the Schöngarten any moment now." A phantom booking at a different hotel, the wrong hotel, had been one of Luke's contributions to the stratagem. This was the call that Pippi had made during lunch in Dingelsdorf.

She said she was happy to stay with the boat while they took a stroll around town — a chance for Otto and Erwin to show

Luke some of the sights.

"We can try out that bar of yours in the Schlossplatz," said Luke — a line intended for Pippi's ears.

The lower town had a single main street, closed at the northern end by an immense tower with an arched gateway. Tourists, decked out in their Sunday best, thronged the deep pavements, window-shopping for antiques and gifts or idling at the tables scattered in front of the many cafés. As in Konstanz, the pleasing scene was tarnished only by the Nazi flags that fluttered from a few of the gaily painted buildings. When they passed the Schöngarten Hotel, a short distance from the port on the left, neither Otto nor Erwin appeared to register it. Across the street, some fifty yards farther on, stood the Hotel Walserhof, with raw rock face and the castle ramparts rising sheer behind it. It was a grander establishment, detached, and it was here that Professor Weintraub, at this very moment, waited patiently in his room.

Beyond the tower at the end of the street, the lower town suddenly ended, giving way to a paved road that climbed steeply toward the upper. Luke pictured Pippi at the wheel of the motor launch as it nosed its way out of the port. Or maybe she was already in

189

open water and tearing toward the real rendezvous just south of town: the timbered inn beside the lake, with its rickety landing stage and the square stone tower set amid the vines on the hillside across the road. Luke had insisted she describe the location to him in detail, in case the plan fell apart and he was forced to find his own way there later.

For the moment, there was no danger of that happening, just as long as he stuck to his immediate task: preventing his two companions from making a telephone call for the next forty-five minutes or so, until Pippi reappeared to help him police the situation. A tour of the castle seemed as good a way as any of eating up the time. Otto and Erwin weren't exactly overjoyed at the prospect, but neither of them had ever actually been inside, and they were happy to humor him. The grim stone fortress had a history reaching back to the seventh century, according to their guide, a fey young man bursting with enthusiasm. For all his best efforts to bring the world of Dagobert, King of the Franks, to some kind of meaningful life, the place was a soulless labyrinth of darkened chambers and tight stone staircases that corkscrewed between the floors.

The heat, the blinding glare, even the weary hordes tramping the pinched streets, felt like a welcome relief after the claustrophobic gloom of the castle. It was a short stroll to the Schlossplatz, where they found a table in front of Erwin's favorite bar. He ordered a flask of chilled white wine.

Their waitress had barely poured it when Pippi came hurrying toward them across the cobbles, looking suitably agitated. She took a seat and trotted out the well-rehearsed lie — another of Luke's contributions. A couple of men had come snooping around the boat, asking questions, and the encounter had so rattled her that she moved it north of town.

"Where exactly?" asked Otto.

It had all the appearance of a casual inquiry.

"The first jetty you come across. It's about a kilometer away. It's why I'm sweating."

She had indeed just hurried through the heat, but from the south, not the north.

"What do we do about the professor?" Otto asked. Walking from his hotel to the port was one thing, a kilometer of open road quite another.

"We'll get word to him," said Pippi. "And he has a car. We can drive out there with him." As for the nanny and the children, they were coming from the north by car, along the lake. "All we have to do is flag them down as they're arriving."

It was good to see the lies they'd concocted earlier that day brought to life so convincingly. They certainly seemed to satisfy Otto. Erwin, who had been observing the exchange with an air of casual disinterest, drained his glass and announced that he was going to stretch his legs, maybe buy a bottle or two from the winery.

"I'd like to see the winery," said Luke.

"If you want," Erwin replied grudgingly.

It stood on the fringes of the upper town, a large warehouselike building faced in mustard-yellow stucco. An ancient wooden winepress held center stage in the entrance area, and beyond was a run of brick-vaulted rooms, the first of which served as the shop. To the right was a restaurant, as well as a wide corridor that, according to the sign on the wall, led to the toilets and the terrace.

"I have to go to the toilet," said Luke.

"I'll see you in the shop."

Luke carried on past the toilets to the terrace, where a number of diners sat beneath sunshades, stretching out their Sunday lunch. He slipped between the tables and headed through some double doors into the restaurant.

"May I help you, sir?" asked a waitress.

"I'm looking for a friend."

He worked his way toward the front of the restaurant, searching for the fictitious friend as he went. The main doors were a colorful art nouveau confection of lead and stained glass. There was no peering through them into the entrance area of the winery, so he eased them open a touch.

Erwin was standing at the reception desk, speaking on a telephone and keeping a nervous eye on the corridor that Luke had taken to the toilets.

A glimpse was all he needed. The fish had taken the bait. *Erwin.* Luke's anger was tempered by a quiver of trepidation. All of Pippi's predictions had come to pass, which meant that events were about to start moving rapidly, and in ways that could no longer be controlled. He glanced at his wristwatch: 4:41. They had twenty-five minutes, maybe a bit more, to execute the final phase of the plan.

His first priority was to chivvy Erwin along and get him back to the bar as soon as possible. Cutting across the terrace, he was stopped momentarily in his tracks by the extraordinary view stretching off into the distance, with the Alps a jagged backdrop far to the south, where the water ended. Everything that was about to unfold, good or bad, was spread out before him like a map: the lake they would flee across, the gently rising ground of Switzerland beyond the western shoreline, and Zurich, unseen but there, close.

When they returned to the bar, all it took was a look and a slight nod from Luke for Pippi to understand. He saw a spark of fury in her eyes, quickly mastered, and she waited no more than a minute before setting the wheels in motion.

"Don't look," she said. "The two men I told you about are sitting at the café across the square."

"Are you sure?" asked Otto.

"Yes, I'm sure. It's them." Turning to Luke, she said with undisguised menace, "If you have anything to do with this . . ." Another rehearsed line.

"I don't. I swear."

Otto glared at Luke. "What do we do?"

"We split up. We'll meet at the port in ten minutes. You come with me," she said to Luke. "One of them is wearing a raffia hat, the other dark trousers and a fawn jacket. If they follow us, forget the port; we'll see you at the boat at six o'clock."

Rising to leave, Luke glimpsed the two

men fitting Pippi's description, seated in front of the café, innocent as lambs.

"Nicely done," he said under his breath as they made off across the square.

"You know it is Erwin?"

"He made a phone call. I doubt it was to his mother."

Pippi muttered some German words that he'd never heard before. "When?" she asked.

He checked his watch. "Thirteen minutes ago."

"Then we have to hurry."

As soon as they were out of sight around the corner, they broke into a run.

Professor Weintraub was a thin, bespectacled man with a kindly face and receding hair brushed back off a broad forehead. His nervousness was palpable, in both his darting gaze and the clammy hand he offered Luke when Pippi introduced them. His room at the Hotel Walserhof was on the first floor at the front of the building. Pippi took up position at the window, checking the street below, waiting for Otto and Erwin to pass by on their way to the port. It wouldn't do for them to see the professor emerge from a hotel other than the Schöngarten; Erwin would know immediately that he'd been lied to.

"Is something wrong?" the professor asked.

"I'm just a cautious person," Pippi replied. "Any news from Ilse?" Ilse, the nanny, was under instructions to call the hotel only if there was a problem of some kind.

"No."

"Good." Pippi checked her watch. "That means they'll be at the boat by now. You'll be seeing them very soon."

The professor paced around, took a seat, paced some more. He was dabbing the sweat from his brow with a handkerchief when Pippi announced, "Okay, let's go." Luke gathered up the professor's suitcase. "Luke and I will leave first. Follow us in thirty seconds. We'll be in your car. Get into the backseat. Key?"

The professor produced the car key from a jacket pocket and dropped it into her hand.

The bland black sedan was parked directly in front of the hotel. Pippi unlocked the boot and Luke slid the professor's suitcase inside. She handed Luke the key.

"Do you mind?"

The engine fired on the third attempt, as the professor was making his way down the front steps of the hotel. He deposited himself on the seat behind them and they pulled away, crawling toward the port at the far end of the street.

Pippi turned to the professor. "You are about to meet two men who have helped us. We trust them, but that doesn't mean we've shared all the details with them. If you hear something that doesn't make sense to you, you must say nothing. It is very important. Do you understand?"

"Yes."

Otto and Erwin were waiting on the quayside, smoking. Pippi lowered her window and signaled them over. "Get in the back." They slid in on either side of the professor, quickly figuring who he must be.

"What's going on?" asked Erwin.

"We're not taking any chances."

"But they didn't follow you, or us," said Erwin. "We checked."

"It's true," Otto added.

"Who?" asked the professor, forgetting the promise he had made to Pippi just moments ago. "Who's following you?"

"It's probably nothing," she reassured him.

As they skirted the port, Erwin leaned forward in his seat. "I thought you said the boat was north. Why are we going south?"

"Only for a bit," said Pippi. "We'll head inland and work our way back to it."

Beyond the port, the town quickly petered out, giving way to open countryside. The road snaked along at the base of the vine-clad slopes, the lake lying just to their right, glimpsed every so often through the trees. When they hit a straight stretch, Luke accelerated, though not enough to alarm anyone. They had entered the gray area where every minute counted and anything could happen.

A moment later, a car came barreling around the bend up ahead, careering toward them.

"Police!" said Pippi. "Everybody down! Now! Get down!" She, too, ducked out of sight.

The oncoming sedan roared past them, offering Luke a brief glimpse of its driver, a lantern-jawed man with a pencil mustache and a Prussian haircut, close-cropped almost to stubble — details that fitted Pippi's description of the man who kicked Johan to death. Two other suited men were in the car, and he prayed he wouldn't see brake lights come on as the vehicle receded in the rearview mirror. He didn't.

"For God's sake!" exclaimed Otto. "Now you're being paranoid!"

"You're right," Pippi conceded. "I need to calm down. I need to get some air."

Good girl, thought Luke. It was a better excuse than the one they'd come up with earlier, and less likely to put Erwin on his guard, which was their most pressing concern right now.

"Here, pull in." Pippi pointed to the right. Beyond a screen of poplars stood the inn, tall and timber-framed, just as she had described it to him. The graveled parking area was bordered by a dirt track that ran down to the lakeside and a wooden dock. He saw the motor launch moored beyond a couple of sailboats, but only because he knew it would be there, and was looking for it. He was also expecting to see a woman and three children waiting in it. There was no sign of them. *Variables.* He and Pippi had thought the thing through from every imaginable angle, but they'd made no allowance for the possibility that the professor's family wouldn't show.

Pippi reached for the door handle. As she did, the muzzle of a pistol came to rest at the base of her skull.

The professor panicked, recoiling from Erwin. "My God . . . !"

"Shut up!" Erwin snapped.

"What are you doing!" Otto gasped. Awkwardly sandwiched between the professor and the door, he fumbled for something in his pocket.

"Don't bother," said Erwin. "I removed the bullets." He jabbed the pistol hard into the back of Pippi's neck. "Put your hands on the dashboard." She did as she was instructed. "Start the car and drive back to Meersburg," he ordered Luke.

It came to Luke suddenly, out of nowhere. "Are you sure that's a good idea?"

Erwin turned the gun on him. "Just do it."

"I'm on your side, you idiot. Haven't you worked that out by now?"

"Shut up and drive."

"Why do you think I'm here? Because Borodin sent me."

"Borodin?"

"Who else? He knew Pippi didn't trust you after the last time. I'm the insurance."

It was just enough to give Erwin pause. "Kapitän Wilke didn't say anything."

"Wilke?" scoffed Luke. "You think it stops with Wilke? He is nothing."

"You bastard!" Pippi spat, launching herself at Luke, claws bared like a wildcat. For a moment, he feared she had fallen for it, too, but he felt her hand groping for the gun tucked into the back of his waistband, and he knew they stood a chance.

Erwin was out of his depth, bellowing

futile threats at Pippi while trying to separate them. As soon as Pippi had a good grip on the gun, they spun around as one, Luke lunging for Erwin's wrist, pinning it and the pistol to the roof of the car with both hands. Pippi shoved the Browning in Erwin's face, then changed her mind and jammed the muzzle into his crotch.

"Is this what you want, Erwin? I'll do it. You know I will!"

The prospect of parting company with his privates loosened Erwin's grip on the pistol enough for Luke to pry it from his fingers.

"Does somebody want to tell me what the hell is going on?" said Otto.

"He betrayed us. The last time, too. It wasn't Borodin; it was him."

There was a strange moment of stillness within the confined space; then Otto launched himself over the professor and landed a vicious punch to the side of Erwin's head. After three or four more blows, Erwin lay slumped, bloodied, and almost unconscious against the door, and Otto was practically straddling the professor, who was staring in blank shock at the scene.

"Car," Luke warned.

A vehicle was pulling into the parking area. A young couple got out. Laughing, they linked arms and took the path through the trees toward the inn, oblivious to the shadow show being played out in the black sedan nearby.

"Excuse me," said the professor, a tremor in his voice, "but where is my family?"

"I don't know," said Pippi. "They should have been here fifteen minutes ago. And they didn't leave word at the hotel that they were running late."

"Maybe they did," said Luke. "Maybe something happened and they couldn't get to a phone in time."

"We have to go," said Otto. "We have to go to the boat."

"The boat's right there." Pippi pointed. "You go. I have unfinished business."

"A word in private," Luke said to her in English.

He made a point of removing the key from the ignition, and when Pippi joined him outside, he noted that the gun was still in her hand.

"There were three of them, Pippi. You don't stand a chance."

"We'll see. It's not your problem."

"But it is. You promised me: nothing that jeopardizes the children."

"They're not here."

"You don't know that."

"Give me the key," she demanded.

"No."

Her hand came up and he found himself staring down the barrel of the Browning.

"The key."

There was a gleam of something dark and dangerous in her green eyes, and he tried his best to strip the fear from his voice. "You're not thinking straight. Think of the children." A tiny tremor in her stony gaze. "Two girls and a boy. Picture them. Can you see them?"

Pippi lowered the weapon only when Professor Weintraub burst from the car. He was in a seriously agitated state now, but his English was impeccable.

"What are you doing? What is happening? Where is my family?"

Luke turned to face him. "I'm going to go and find them."

"You?" said Pippi.

"Who else? This . . . Kapitän Wilke and his cronies don't know my face."

A look of relief fell across the professor's haggard features. "Thank you."

"I can't promise anything. And if I don't come back with them, you have to leave. You can't stay, not now. We'll find another way to get them out. Agreed?"

The professor gave a single grave nod of the head.

"Good," said Luke. "Now, tell me what they look like."

CHAPTER SIXTEEN

It was a familiar sensation: the same stillness that used to descend on him when taxiing to the end of the landing strip before a
sortie. It wasn't so much a calm as a kind
of void, a vacuum, as though his entrails
had been scooped out by some unseen
hand. Approaching the port, he took the
Browning from the passenger seat and
slipped it into his jacket pocket.

It was no surprise to find the long black
sedan that had torn past them earlier now
parked in front of the Schöngarten hotel.
There was no sign of the three men, and
Luke made no obvious show of searching
for them as he drove by, although his eyes
darted left and right, scanning the sidewalks
on both sides of the street.

The concierge at the Walserhof Hotel
greeted him with a synthetic smile and a
"Guten Tag." On the wall behind him was a
bank of cubbyholes, and Luke felt his spirits

lift at the sight of a note tucked into *Zimmer 12.*

"I'm a friend of Professor Weintraub. He's staying with you. Room twelve."

"He's not here. He went out."

"I know, I'm with him in the upper town. He's waiting for an important message, and he sent me down to see if it has arrived."

"Yes, I took the call." Not even a glance behind him.

"May I?" said Luke, lifting his chin toward the cubbyholes.

"I'm sorry, sir, but I don't know you, and it wouldn't be right."

Luke fought to keep his composure. "It's important."

"As I say, sir, I really can't hand over the professor's private communications to you."

"Ah, I see what you mean," Luke replied knowingly, rounding the counter and reaching for the message.

The concierge tried to block him off. "No, sir, that's not what I meant."

But Luke had it in his hand now, and he wasn't going to relinquish it.

"Thank you."

He turned and strode across the lobby, unfolding the note as he went. It was from Ilse, the nanny, and although he wasn't acquainted with the German word *geplatz-*

ter, he knew that *Reifen* meant "tire," which was enough for him to get the gist of it. The rest of the note posed no problem: they had been delayed by half an hour.

They must have been running ahead of schedule when the incident occurred, for as he hurried down the steps of the hotel, a car passed by in front of him, traveling in the direction of the port. The driver was a woman with straight blond hair, smooth as satin, cut high off the shoulder. A young girl rode up front, her dark tresses done in plaits, and in the rear were two more children, younger, a boy and a girl. They all were just as Professor Weintraub had described them, right down to the wire-rimmed spectacles his son wore.

Luke stood watching, willing the car onward. Another fifty yards and they'd be home free, past the port and away.

That was when he saw the tall man in the dove-gray suit. He was standing stock-still among the throng of pedestrians, his eyes fixed on the approaching vehicle. As it drew even with him, he stooped to peer inside. Then suddenly, he was running in pursuit, darting past the car and placing himself in its path, raising his left hand high.

"Don't stop," Luke muttered.

But the brake lights came on. The man

pulled a gun from a shoulder holster and pointed it at the windshield.

And now Luke was running, sticking close to the pavement for the camouflage provided by other people. Fingers closing around the Browning in his jacket pocket, he arrived as the man was trying to haul Ilse out of the car. She was resisting, clinging to the steering wheel with both hands, and the children were wailing.

He slowed to a walk. "Excuse me."

As the man turned to face him, Luke struck him as hard as he could on the bridge of the nose with the butt of the Browning. The blow felled him instantly, his head thudding against the cobbles.

Luke was dimly aware of a collective gasp going up from the onlookers. Then he was reaching inside the car and trying to force Ilse across the front seat. Maybe she thought he was just another assailant, pushing at her instead of pulling, but she wouldn't give up her grip on the steering wheel.

"Ilse, I'm British. I'm here to help you."

That seemed to do it. She was shunting along when the shot rang out — not a warning, because the bullet punched a hole in the back door, right next to Luke's knee.

He spun around, dropping into a crouch. People were running in all directions now, screaming. The man with the gun was doing neither. There was something chilling in his measured pace as he strode purposefully toward the car. The moment he had a clear shot through the scattering mob, he fired again, going for the kill, the bullet hissing past Luke's head and slapping into the footwell behind him.

There was no time to take aim. Luke fired twice from the hip.

The man stumbled, recovered, and then stopped in his tracks, staring down at his chest, at the spreading bloom of blood discoloring his white shirt. There was confusion in his young eyes as he looked up at Luke. He made a feeble effort to raise his pistol before dropping to his knees and falling on his face.

The engine was still running.

"Stay down," said Luke, leaping behind the steering wheel and forcing the car into gear.

More shots rang out. The rear window disintegrated, showering the two children in the back with glass. As the car lurched away, the driver's door slammed shut from the momentum, and in the wing mirror Luke made out a third man bearing down on them from behind at a sprint. It was the driver, Kapitän Wilke, of the lantern jaw and the stubbled head. Thankfully, he had too much ground to cover, and the best he could do was to fire off several more shots, at least one of which pinged into the bodywork, before they swung out of view around the port.

"Everyone okay? No one hurt?"

He didn't realize he'd been speaking English, until Ilse translated. The children were crying but apparently unharmed.

"Good."

But it was far from good. This became clear as soon as they negotiated the first bend in the road. The car struggled to hold its line, the back end sliding away, slewing toward the verge.

"Tire," he said. They had been crippled by a lucky shot from Wilke.

"How far?" Ilse asked.

"Close."

The tire started thumping against the wheel arch. A few hundred yards farther on, it had peeled off the rim and they were running on metal.

It was impossible to keep the speed up. Their head start — enough to see them safely away — was being eaten into with every second. He had to assume that Wilke was hot on their tail. How long before the big sedan came swooping down on them from behind?

For a moment, he thought they had made it. Then, as they took the last bend before the inn, he glanced over his shoulder and saw a car swing into view at the end of the long straightaway. The margins had suddenly shrunk to seconds, possibly fractions of a second.

"The boat's there. You have to run."

He was halfway out the door even as he stopped the car in the parking lot. Scooping up the younger daughter from the backseat, he thrust her at Ilse. "Go."

"The suitcases."

"No time. Run!"

They did. And so did he — back toward the road.

The car was closing fast, and as he raised the Browning, he told himself to remain calm, to wait as long as he dared. He had counted the bullets in and out of the magazine back at the farmhouse; he had four left.

The first shattered the windshield. There was nothing to show for the second, and as Wilke's head bobbed back into view, he fired again. The sedan swerved toward the deep ditch on Luke's left. Wilke swung the wheel back the other way, but too hard. The car careened across the road and up the bank on the far side, clipping a tree and flipping over. It landed on its roof at the edge of the road with a loud *crump,* blowing the windows out and sending shards of glass skittering like a shower of diamonds across the tarmac.

He thought about using up the last bullet, but it would have been a cold-blooded execution, and he wasn't built for that sort of thing.

There were two leather suitcases in the boot of Ilse's car, large and absurdly heavy, filled to bursting. He ignored the people flooding around the side of the inn and set off as fast as he could down the dirt track. Otto saw him coming and sprinted along the jetty to relieve him of one of the cases.

The motor launch's engine was already running: a low, throaty throb that promised power and safety. Pippi was at the wheel, one hand holding the forward mooring line. Luke swung the suitcase into the boat and leaped aboard. The moment Otto had done the same, Pippi cast off and slammed the throttle lever forward.

Thrown off balance, Luke seized the back of her seat in the cockpit to steady himself.

"It's good to see you."

"You, too," he replied, drunk on a cocktail of relief and adrenaline.

"Wilke?"

"Hard to say."

A popping sound, just audible above the roar of the engine, provided the answer.

"Everyone down!" yelled Otto.

At the end of the white wake snaking off behind the boat, a lone figure was limping along the jetty, firing at them in vain. They were barely within range of a rifle, let alone a handgun.

Luke placed a hand on the wheel, obliging Pippi to hold her line. Only when she turned and fixed him with a basilisk eye did he remove it.

He hadn't noticed before now, but Erwin lay on the deck near the back of the boat, his ankles and wrists bound with rope; Professor Weintraub was sitting with his children, who were crying as he did his best to console them. Ilse slipped the catches on one of the suitcases and produced a rag doll. She smoothed its blond plaits and adjusted its bonnet before handing it to the younger girl, who smiled wanly and pressed the doll to her wet cheek.

Pippi eased off the throttle a touch and called for Otto to join them.

"We're going to cross now," she said.

"But we've never done it in daylight before."

"Which is why we need to get those

suitcases out of sight. Erwin, too."

The suitcases were tucked away in the storage area beneath the padded bench seat occupied by the Weintraubs. Luke and Otto then hefted Erwin into the compartment beneath the seat in the stern, which meant removing the anchor first. "If you make a noise," said Otto, "you'll be going over the side, attached to *this*." He dropped the anchor in Erwin's lap. "Understood?" Erwin gave a grudging nod.

A clear run across the lake on a glorious August afternoon was too much to hope for, and it wasn't long before they spotted a boat closing from the north to head them off. Otto was all for opening the throttle and going for it, but Pippi read the geometry of their intersecting paths differently. It was unlikely that Wilke had already got word to the border police yet. No, better to bluff it out. The fact that there was no hard-and-fast frontier running down the middle of the lake played in their favor: they had simply strayed a little too close to the Swiss shore on their way back to Konstanz.

Pippi conceded the wheel to Otto, then went and knelt in front of the children.

"I need you to imagine that you've just had the best day of your lives," she said. "Come on, show me; which one of you has the biggest smile?" When that didn't work, she tried a different tack.

"I'm going to tell you a story I heard from my boyfriend, and I don't want you to smile. It's very important that you don't smile, okay? One day a rabbi was walking down a street when he saw a small boy trying to reach the doorbell on a house. The boy was too short, though, so the rabbi, who was a good and kind man, crossed the street to help. He came up behind the boy and pressed the doorbell for him. 'What now, my little man?' asked the rabbi. The boy looked up at him. 'Now we run.' "

It did the trick. "That's better," said Pippi. "Enjoy yourselves. Wave if you want."

She came and sat beside Luke. He slipped an arm around her shoulders. She stiffened at first, then relaxed into the role, even laying her head on his shoulder: the happy couple on a Sunday excursion.

The patrol boat had a Nazi ensign flying above the wheelhouse, and although the gun mounted on the foredeck was unmanned, it was no less menacing for it. An officer in a gray uniform stood in the prow. He lowered his field glasses and waved his arms vigorously, crossing them above his head. When the children waved back, he yelled something and gestured several times toward the

German side of the lake. Otto raised his hand high in a sign of sudden understanding, then altered course to the northeast. As the patrol boat passed by on their port side, the officer delivered a Nazi salute.

The professor rose to his feet. "Children, I promise you, it is the last time you will ever have to do it, or say it." They stood as one and jabbed their right hands into the air. *"Heil Hitler!"* they called, along with the adults. Another wave from the officer — this time a friendly farewell.

They kept a wary eye on the patrol boat as it cruised off to the south. When they had put a good half mile or so between themselves and it, Otto turned due west on Pippi's command and opened the throttle. The patrol boat came hard about, giving several threatening blasts of its klaxon. Whether it had spotted their maneuver or had just received word over the radio was of no consequence. The launch came up on the plane, leveling out the light chop, and they were skimming toward Switzerland with an unassailable lead, squinting into the lowering sun.

Pippi turned and smiled at the professor. He gave a guarded nod of the head, his expression that of a man who would relax only when both feet were firmly planted on free soil.

■ ■ ■ ■

SWITZERLAND

■ ■ ■ ■

CHAPTER SEVENTEEN

A small wooden shack stood on stilts near the mouth of a narrow inlet. Just right of it lay a narrow strip of sandy beach with a landing stage, and fishing nets slung out to dry between tall poles.

Back from the beach, beyond the fringe of reeds, the ground climbed sharply to a grassy knoll, where three cars were parked, looking long and sleek and utterly incongruous. The men looked no less out of place, gathered at the water's edge in their jackets and ties, like a picnic party of schoolmasters contemplating a dip.

The head of this welcoming committee appeared to be a bull-necked man of average height, for he was the first to shake Professor Weintraub's hand once they all had disembarked. His Welsh accent was evident even in the formal words of greeting he offered in German: "It is an honor to welcome you and your family to Switzerland." His name was Major Kendrick, based at the British embassy in Bern. He was accompanied by three colleagues and two Swiss officials.

There was a lot more shaking of hands before some thermos flasks of tea were produced. The children were offered bars of Swiss chocolate, promptly rationed by Ilse. Luke, Pippi, and Otto hung back near the boat, smoking.

"What's going to happen to us?" asked Otto. In the heat of the unfolding events, he hadn't had a chance to digest the consequences of Erwin's betrayal. Only now were they beginning to dawn on him. "We can't go back, can we?"

"No," said Pippi.

"I have no clothes, no money, no passport . . ."

"I have money for you. I also have your passport."

"And my life? Did you bring that with you, too?"

"What life, Otto? How long before we would have been jailed, killed? How many have disappeared already?"

"You could at least have consulted me first."

"I wasn't sure whether it was you or Erwin."

Otto looked stung. "You thought it was *me*?"

"I had no way of knowing until today." She crushed her cigarette underfoot. "Otto, listen, we have done what we can, and now we will do what we can from here, from France, from England — wherever we can help." She nodded toward the gathering at the end of the landing stage. "They will help us find our feet. They owe us that much."

Luke wasn't so sure. He had seen firsthand how the British regarded those who came to them as friends and collaborators. It lay somewhere between "necessary evil" and "disposable asset." The Major Kendricks of this world weren't in the habit of rolling out the red carpet for a bunch of people-traffickers who — and there was no ignoring it — had almost scuttled a mission because of a security breach within their own ranks. Homegrown incompetence was tolerated, if only because it was so endemic, but when Johnny Foreigner messed up, well, there was no removing the stink.

"Luke will speak to them," Pippi went on.

She seemed to have forgotten that he was in no position to do any such thing. In fact, the presence of four British embassy officials was beginning to make him feel distinctly uneasy. He could see heads beginning to turn their way as details of the escape leaked out. Sure enough, it wasn't long before Major Kendrick broke ranks and came clomping toward them down the jetty.

"You're English?" he asked.

"Yes."

"Luke . . . ?"

Luke plucked a surname from the ether. "Taylor." Weak. He should have gone for something more unusual.

"Strange, Miss Keller didn't mention you in her communications with us."

"No?" He tossed the ball to Pippi. "And why not?"

"I asked Luke to help at the last moment. We're friends from university."

"I did my masters at Freiburg," said Luke. "Goethe."

"Goethe, eh?" Kendrick's deep-set dark eyes bored into him. "Ilse the nanny has high praise for you, high praise indeed." He pulled a pack of cigarettes from his pocket and tapped one free. "You have killed a man before?"

"No."

"Well, you seem to be taking it in your stride remarkably well, Mr. Taylor — for a Goethe scholar."

He had underestimated the major; he

needed to be on his guard. "I think maybe I'm in shock."

Kendrick lit the cigarette and exhaled slowly. "Not as shocked as I was when I heard just now how close we came to complete fucking disaster." The words were directed at Pippi, and the expletive suggested Military Intelligence: years of barrack-room braggadocio, then a commission, then a long slog through the ranks. Luke caught Otto's nervous glance; he hadn't understood, but he had sensed the sudden shift in the atmosphere.

"You have what you wanted," said Pippi evenly. "We're leaving now."

"Without your fee?" Kendrick patted his breast pocket. "No, you stay right here. I want a full debrief as soon as our Swiss friends have left." He turned to go, stopped, then dropped into the launch with the easy agility of a born sportsman and plucked the key from the ignition.

Ten minutes later, there were only two cars on the knoll, and Kendrick was making his way back along the landing stage with one of his embassy minions. The hang of the man's jacket suggested a holstered weapon.

Kendrick produced a smile. "Maybe I was a little harsh before. All's well that ends well. But I have to file a report, so talk me through it."

Pippi was no fool. She made no mention of the ploy to avenge herself on Kapitän Wilke, which had very nearly proved to be their undoing. She spoke only of a vague suspicion that one or the other of her colleagues might not be trustworthy, so she had taken precautions, feeding them false information about the location of the pickup as well as its timing. Unfortunately, Erwin had managed to put a call through to Friedrichshafen — not that this would have posed a problem if Ilse and the children had turned up on time. Ultimately, a punctured tire was to blame.

Major Kendrick digested her words. "I think it's time we met this Erwin."

It was the last thing Luke wanted to hear. "He's not in a fit state to make any sense."

"Well, let's take a look at him anyway, shall we?"

Luke cursed silently. A conscious Erwin could do him considerable damage. Fortunately, when they hauled Erwin from the compartment beneath the stern seat, he looked cowed, terrified, even traumatized.

"Do you speak English?" asked Kendrick.
"Yes. A bit."

"Who are you working for?" Erwin didn't

reply. "Professor Weintraub says you mentioned a name: Kapitän Wilke. Who is this Kapitän Wilke?"

"Who are you?" Erwin fired back, growing in confidence a little too quickly for Luke's liking.

"The man who can make life easier for you if you cooperate. Who is Kapitän Wilke?"

Erwin glanced at his boots before replying. "Abwehr." The German secret service, as Pippi had suspected. Erwin turned to her and said in German, "He made me do it. He said he would destroy me, my family."

"He has," replied Pippi, without emotion. "*We* were your family. Johan was your family."

"I hope you were well paid for his life," Otto spat.

Major Kendrick looked irritated by the interruption. "How long has the Abwehr been policing the Bodensee?"

"I don't know," said Erwin. "But I know other things."

"Oh?"

"About him." Erwin lifted his chin toward Luke.

"Don't you dare . . . !" Pippi hissed in German.

Luke butted in. "He'll say anything to save

his own skin."

"I'll be the judge of that, Mr. Taylor."

Erwin gave a snort. "Taylor? Is that what he said? His name is Hamilton."

So it was done. He had only one play left. "He's lying, and I've got a passport to prove it." He was reaching inside his jacket pocket for the Browning when the man at Kendrick's shoulder suddenly had a revolver out and trained on him.

"Luke Hamilton, sir."

"Yes, Hapgood, I read the dispatch from Paris."

Major Kendrick stepped forward and carefully withdrew the Browning from Luke's pocket. Weighing the weapon in his hand, he turned to Pippi. "You knew?"

"Someone is trying to kill him; he's not sure why. I believe him."

Kendrick turned his inquiring gaze on Luke.

"It's true."

"And it's a long drive back to Bern, so you can save your breath for now."

Kendrick's two other associates had obviously spotted what was unfolding on the boat, because they now came pounding down the landing stage, weapons out. Kendrick went to meet them.

"Bad mistake," said Hapgood. "Trying to

pull a gun on the major. He won't like that. Won't like it one bit."

"No, I don't suppose he will."

"Are you really one of us?"

"Air Intelligence."

"That's what we call an oxymoron in the army." Hapgood grinned at his own joke.

"That's the spirit. Should serve us well when war breaks out."

"You think there's one coming?"

"You don't?"

Luke could see Professor Weintraub and his family huddled together on the beach, watching nervously. The professor had his hand on Ilse's shoulder. It suggested more than a straightforward nanny-employer relationship. A Jew and a Gentile now free to be together. Whatever happened next, it hadn't all been in vain.

Kendrick approached. "You and you," he said, pointing at Luke and Erwin. "You're coming with us. And you two are free to go."

"Where?" asked Pippi. "Back to Germany?"

"Don't be ridiculous," said Luke. "They can't go back."

"Excuse me?"

"You might as well kill them both now and be done with it."

"They were paid to do a job." Kendrick pulled an envelope from his inside breast pocket and tossed it to Pippi. "There. *Now* they've been paid."

"They don't do it for the money and they don't do it for you. They do it for that." He pointed at the family gathered on the beach. "They've lost everything for that. The least you can do is help them get asylum with the Swiss."

"That's quite some speech," Kendrick said with an amused sneer.

"Then think of it this way: thanks to them, you got me, a big feather in your cap."

"Maybe not quite as big as you would like to think."

"I'm just saying, you can afford to be magnanimous."

Kendrick fell silent, casting a quick glance around him. "Thirteen people, two cars. It's going to be a tight squeeze."

"Not if someone goes in the boot," said Luke.

He had said it in jest, but that was exactly where Erwin ended up. Not at first, not until Kendrick asked Luke to tell his story. He wasn't comfortable doing so in the presence of Erwin, who was squeezed into the backseat along with Pippi, Otto, Hapgood, and another embassy man, Pitchforth. Kendrick pulled over and ordered an irate Erwin transferred to the boot.

"I'm all ears," said the major as both cars went on their way once more. He began to interrupt Luke almost immediately, demanding more information. What had he done before being posted to Paris? What was the exact nature of the missions he had flown in the Northern Territory? What was the command structure of his department at the Paris embassy? Had his work taken him to Germany before?

The miles flew by, and as dusk turned to night, Kendrick's cross-examination continued under the sporadic glare of oncoming headlights. Luke was as honest as he dared to be about the chain of events that had begun in Paris three nights ago, although he held back certain details, such as the exact location of his planned meeting with Borodin in Zurich. He still harbored a slim hope that he could turn the situation around in the next forty-eight hours and keep the rendezvous.

Finally, there was nothing more for him to add, and Kendrick seemed to have exhausted his store of questions. He wasn't done quite yet, though.

"Hapgood?"

"Sir?"

"What do you make of it all?"

"Intriguing, sir."

Kendrick glanced across at Luke. "Never one to go out on a limb, Hapgood. Pitchforth? Your verdict?"

"It's implausible enough to be plausible, sir."

"Very good," said Kendrick with a soft chuckle. He lit a cigarette and wound the window down an inch. "Tell me, Miss Keller, you've had dealings with this Borodin before. Does he strike you as the sort of fellow to jeopardize everything — including his life — on a matter of principle that can only be described as, well, idealistic?" It was a fair enough question, one that Luke had asked himself many times over the past few days.

Pippi hesitated. "No."

"No. So what's his real game, then? Money? Blackmail?" Another glance at Luke. "And what are we to make of the fact that he evidently lied to you? I mean, why go to the bother of fabricating a story about your being mistaken for a spy? Why not simply tell you the truth?"

"I don't know. That's why I have to be in Zurich on Tuesday." It was a direct appeal.

"I'd strongly advise against it, even if I do

decide to let you go."

"Sir?" There was a note of alarm in Hapgood's voice.

"We're talking about a man's life, Hapgood. If we send him back to Paris, we could be turning him into a sitting duck."

"You would be," said Luke.

"I'm just advising caution," said Hapgood. "For all of us."

A wry smile crept across Kendrick's face. "That's the other thing about Hapgood: he has high ambitions. Fortunately for you, some of us are cut from slightly different cloth."

Kendrick passed the remainder of the journey in silent reflection; Luke, in restless anticipation. When Bern finally loomed out of the moonless night, they found it almost entirely deserted, a slumbering ghost town.

The British embassy lay beyond tall wooden gates set in a featureless facade. Kendrick had phoned ahead from a roadside inn, and a reception committee was waiting to greet the two cars as they pulled to a halt in the courtyard.

Kendrick took immediate charge, issuing orders in a low, confidential voice. The Weintraubs were promptly whisked away by a gangling man and a uniformed nurse. Luke found himself separated from Pippi and Otto, who were also escorted up the stone steps into the building. Erwin was hauled out of the boot. Spitting fury and a few choice German expressions, he was led away by Hapgood and Pitchforth.

Two soldiers armed with rifles had been overseeing the proceedings, but only now that the crowd had thinned out to just four men did Luke sense their looming presence. They were at his shoulder, flanking him. Kendrick lit a cigarette. "Quite a day," he said to no one in particular. "Has Paris been informed?"

"Yes sir," replied one of the soldiers.

"What's their view on transport?"

"They're happy to leave the details to us, just as long we get him there in one piece."

Were they talking about Professor Weintraub? Because if they weren't, Luke had just been royally stitched up.

"I thought . . ."

"What?" said Kendrick. "That I would really send you on your way with a 'good luck' and a fare-thee-well?"

"So why all that talk?"

"Because nothing tames a desperate man like hope. I couldn't have you trying anything rash en route."

"You bastard —"

The blow from the rifle butt caught Luke

on the back of the thigh and brought him to his knees.

Kendrick came and stood over him. "Maybe you really are innocent, or maybe you fed me a big pack of lies. Either way, it's for others to decide." He ground out his cigarette and turned on his heel. "Give him something to eat; then lock him up."

CHAPTER EIGHTEEN

Petrovic was about to hang up when someone answered the telephone. "It's me," he said warily into the silence.

"I had a feeling it might be."

"Borodin called. He wants to meet in Zurich."

"Zurich?"

"To hand over Hamilton."

"Borodin spent time in Zurich."

"I didn't know that."

"Well, now you do, so be careful. What about backup?"

"He's already on his way to Geneva. I'm meeting him there."

"Just the one man?"

"If you knew him, you'd understand."

"When it's done, kill him, too."

Petrovic hesitated. "He's a good man."

"The world is full of good men. Our client doesn't want any loose ends."

"Client? I thought this was personal."

"Don't concern yourself with the details. And don't call us again until it's done."

CHAPTER NINETEEN

The room had one window, not barred, but with metal shutters that allowed nothing of the new day to penetrate. It might as well still be night. Breakfast had arrived earlier on a Bakelite tray: cold toast, already buttered, which shattered when he bit into it, and a pot of black coffee, strong and hot, now tepid.

He drained the last of it from his cup and dropped onto the bed where he had tried to fall asleep last night. Life at St. Theresa's had taught him never to walk away from an unmade bed, and the blanket was pulled tight as a drum skin, the pillow plumped for a fresh head. The moment he closed his eyes, he knew he would sleep, even with the coffee in him.

The rasp of a key in the lock hauled him back from the brink.

The guard entered. Following him were Professor Weintraub, Ilse, and the three children. Luke rose to greet them.

"They are moving us to Geneva," said the professor. He looked exhausted. "We have come to say goodbye. Children . . ."

He ushered them forward, and one by one they shook hands with Luke, thanking him in German: *"Danke, Herr Hamilton."* From Ilse he got a kiss on the cheek and a heartfelt whisper in his ear: *"Können wir nicht genug danken."*

She led the children from the room. The professor remained. "A word in private, please," he said to the guard.

"I'm sorry, sir, but my orders —"

"With the man who risked his life for my family," came the professor's firm interruption.

The guard's gaze flicked between them. "Two minutes." He withdrew, locking the door behind him.

The professor cast an eye around the room — not exactly a cell, but not much better: a basin, a bed, a coffee table, and a single chair of bentwood and wicker.

"It is like a dream for them," he said. "But know this: when we are dead and they are old, they will still remember the tall man who came back to find them, and they will tell their grandchildren his name and how they shook his hand."

"Anyone would have done it."

"Maybe, if it was their job, their duty." The professor pulled a handkerchief from his pocket and set about cleaning his spectacles. "I assumed you were one of Kendrick's men. Pippi tells me you are not."

"No, not exactly."

"And is it true what they say about you?"

"What do they say?"

"That two men in Paris are dead because of you."

Luke hesitated. "Yes, it's true. But I didn't do it."

The professor replaced his spectacles and stepped closer. "Say that again."

"What?"

"Say it."

"I didn't do it."

The professor's pale eyes held Luke's for a long moment. "Have you heard of Albert Einstein?"

"Of course."

"He was a young man when he changed the way we look at the world. One simple equation. It was more than thirty years ago, and he was working here in Bern at the time — a humble clerk in the patent office. Did you know that?"

"No."

"Everything I am, everything I do, began

here with that equation. And it begins again now. So you see, the circle is complete for me. I hope one day you can say the same thing."

The professor rapped on the door, and as it swung open, he offered Luke his hand.

"Thank you, Luke. And good luck."

He was deep asleep when Hapgood and Pitchforth came for him two hours later.

"I want to see Pippi."

"That might be possible," replied Hapgood. "After you've seen Major Kendrick."

The major's office was a grand room, large and light, with lofty stuccoed ceilings and paintings of Swiss landscapes adorning the walls. Kendrick was standing at one of the tall windows, smoking and peering down into the courtyard below.

"Leave us," he said without turning. Then, with a vague wave of his hand in the direction of the big pedestal desk: "Take a seat, Hamilton." When Kendrick finally settled into his own chair at the desk, Luke could feel the tension coming off him.

"It's a good job for you the ambassador is away at a conference in Locarno. He's a man who does things strictly by the book."

"Meaning?"

"Meaning the same cannot be said of

Professor Weintraub." Kendrick stubbed out his cigarette in the ashtray. "He's threatening to offer his services to the Americans. They'd love that. By God, they'd love it."

"The Americans?"

"He didn't say anything to you?"

"He wished me luck."

There was a manic edge to Kendrick's laugh. "Luck? Well, you're going to need a bucketload of that."

"I don't understand."

Kendrick twisted the point of an ebony letter opener into the blotter in front of him. "It's very simple. It's called blackmail. If we release you, Weintraub won't go running to the Yanks."

Luke let the news sink in. "He could be bluffing."

"Very droll, Hamilton."

"Does Pippi know?"

"Not yet, but she was the one who told Weintraub your story. None of this would have happened if we'd only kept them apart. I blame myself for that."

"Don't be too tough on yourself, Major. Everything I told you is true."

"Everything?"

"I might have fudged a few of the details."

Kendrick sat back in his chair. "I imagine I'm going to be doing a fair bit of that myself over the next couple of days, thanks to Miss Keller." He reached for the phone console and flipped a switch. "Meredith, is she here yet?"

"Yes sir."

"Send her in, please."

Pippi looked disheveled but invigorated, as though she'd just returned from a long tramp across windswept moorland. Her dark hair was a mess, but there was color in her cheeks. If she was prepared for a battle, she soon discovered she wasn't going to have to fight one. Kendrick spelled out the situation to her.

In true Pippi fashion, she took it in stride and stuck to the practical considerations. "What about Otto?"

"We'll do what we can for him. I see no reason why the Swiss shouldn't offer him asylum." Erwin was a different matter: a German citizen held against his wishes by a foreign government in a fiercely neutral nation. "We have no choice but to let him go." He glanced at his wristwatch. "In fact, he'll be boarding a train any minute now."

Galling though this was, Pippi seemed to accept it without too much trouble. "And the car?" she asked.

"What car?"

"We can't arrive in Zurich by train. It's

too dangerous."

Did she have any idea how good that one word "we" sounded to him? He hadn't banked on her keeping her side of the bargain.

"No one said anything about a car."

"It must have slipped the professor's mind."

"Don't push your luck, Miss Keller."

Pippi tossed a buff envelope onto the desk: the fee Kendrick had given her only yesterday.

He looked bemused. "You want me to sell you one from the embassy car pool?"

"It's worth more than a car."

"It's also worth more than my job." He slid the envelope back across the desk. "I can't help you, but I know someone who can."

"I have one more favor to ask," said Luke.

"Wicken four seventeen."

The expectant note in his father's voice cut right through him, and there was a waver in his own as he replied, "Pa, it's me."

"Oh, Luke, oh, dear God, my dear boy, are you all right? Lorna, it's Luke! Yes, Luke!" He heard a strangled yelp in the background. "Pick up in the hallway! Yes, the hallway! Your mother's picking up in the hallway."

Luke smiled. "Yes, I thought she might be."

"Are you all right? Are you safe?"

"I'm fine, Pa."

"I thought . . . I don't know what I thought. We didn't know what to think. But you're safe."

"Safe enough."

There was a click on the line. "Luke?" came his mother's eager voice.

"He's safe. Tell her, Luke."

"It's true, Ma, I'm all right."

"Thank God," she gasped. "Where are you?"

"It's best I don't say. And I have to be quick. Listen, I don't know what you've heard, but I'm innocent."

"Of course you are. I told him, didn't I, Lorna, that man who called from the Ministry? I told him exactly where he could park his bike."

"For goodness' sake, Ramsay, stop babbling and let the poor boy speak."

He kept it concise. Someone was trying to kill him for reasons unknown, although it quite possibly had something to do with who he was, reaching right back to his earliest days at the orphanage and beyond. There was also a strong likelihood that the murder of Sister Agnes was connected.

"It's how they found me, which means there's a good chance they know about you, too." He paused. "I'm afraid you're going to have to leave — go away somewhere, stay with friends."

"Leave?" said his father.

"They might try to get to me through you."

"We can stay with —"

"No, Ma, don't say it over the phone. And don't tell anyone where you're going — only Rip van Winkle." It was their private nickname for Solomon. "When this is all over, I'll find you."

"How long?" asked his mother.

"I can't say."

He heard her give a sudden loud sob, then choke back her upset.

"Don't worry, I'll be okay. I love you."

He had been shown into a small office for some privacy, which was no bad thing. It gave him a chance to pinch the tears from his eyes and compose himself before rejoining the others.

Otto had shown up in the meantime, and it was immediately clear that his mood had darkened overnight. He now held Pippi entirely to blame for turning him into a fugitive. Her contention that he might well be languishing in a German jail right now if she hadn't foiled the plan fell on deaf ears. He sneered at the notion of traveling with them to Zurich and asked for his cut of the fee, promptly increasing his demand to half, seeing as Erwin would no longer be getting a slice. He had a cousin married to a lawyer in Lausanne; he would beg a bed off them while his application for asylum was being processed.

When Pippi suggested that one day he would see that this was the best thing that could have happened to him, he swore at her. She remained remarkably calm in the face of his fury.

"Don't be so naive, Otto. It was always going to end badly. And if you want to forget what we did and why we did it, that's your choice." Most of the last sentence was spoken to the paneled door that Otto had slammed behind him.

Unsurprisingly, he wasn't there to see them off. Neither was Major Kendrick, though Hapgood and Pitchforth were. Pitchforth insisted on carrying Luke's jacket to the taxi waiting outside on the street. The reason for this became clear only when Luke had placed his suitcase in the boot and Pitchforth handed him back the jacket.

He felt the extra weight.

"I reloaded it," said Pitchforth under his breath.

"Thank you."

"This never happened."

"I have no idea what you're talking about."

Hapgood extended his hand and said for all to hear, "Goodbye, Mr. Hamilton. I hope our paths never have the misfortune of crossing again."

"Where do they make people like that in your country?" asked Pippi as the taxi pulled away.

"Pitchforth's okay."

"You think so?"

He flashed her a glimpse of the Browning, and she laughed: a high, almost childlike tinkle.

"That's the first time I've heard you properly laugh."

She smiled weakly. "I used to more, it's true."

The garage, a big concrete structure painted gleaming white, stood on the outskirts of the city, close to the river. On the forecourt, a couple of boys with chamois leathers were buffing up an open-top roadster.

They found Herr Knecht in his office, a small box of a room crammed into a corner of the garage. He cast a monocled eye over

Major Kendrick's letter of introduction, written on embassy paper. "As a rule, we only provide cars for guests staying at the Bellevue Palace Hotel."

"We'd be happy to take a room," said Pippi. "We're going to need somewhere to stay when we get back from our excursion."

Herr Knecht laid the letter aside. "No, I think we can make an exception, although your choice of vehicles is somewhat limited, I'm afraid." He spread his hands and raised his eyes to the heavens. "Fine weather is good for business."

It soon became clear that Herr Knecht, for all his affability, knew a thing or two about business. He demanded a hefty cash deposit and a steep daily rate (topped up with obligatory insurance) for a Citroën coupé of the type to be found all over Paris. Luke hoped the insurance was for real, for Herr Knecht's sake — it was highly unlikely they would be returning the car.

Pippi insisted on driving and retraced the route taken by their taxi driver, heading back toward the city center.

"Where are we going?"

"Shopping." She plucked at the hem of her summer dress. "This old thing is all I have."

They parked in the shadow of the cathedral and collared a well-heeled woman for advice. She looked Pippi over with eyes that said "and none too soon," and directed them to a boutique on Marktgasse. After the playful painted facades and coiling streets of Konstanz and Meersburg, there was something stolid and earnest about the architecture of Bern. The streets cutting through the old town were long and straight and flanked by buildings of a neutral, uniform gray. The sober feel was even more pronounced in Marktgasse, where the shops were set back beneath low arcades, stripping the street level of life, variety, and color.

The boutique was a large, gloomy establishment, and the assistant who approached them as they entered took them for a married couple. Pippi didn't correct her, and Luke was happy to play along: "Not that, my darling; your mother will have a heart attack."

The assistant chuckled, warming to them, or possibly calculating her commission as the garments continued to pile up: two skirts, one with a matching jacket; a patterned crepe de chine summer dress; two blouses; a cashmere sweater; a pair of leather court shoes; and a pair of low sandals (which the assistant thoroughly approved of because Pippi was quite tall

250

enough already). When the subject turned to lingerie, Luke made himself scarce, going in search of a suitcase to house Pippi's new wardrobe. By the time he returned, it had swelled to include a silk evening gown, a cream satin nightgown, a straw hat, and a navy blue swimsuit. "I like swimming," she said as she packed it away in the suitcase. She settled up with the cash she had received from Major Kendrick, and they went on their way.

"You were very patient."

Luke shrugged. "As a British taxpayer, I was curious to see where my money went."

Pippi smiled. "I earned it."

"You certainly did." They walked on a little way. "I haven't thanked you for what you did — with the professor, I mean."

"All I did was tell your story. It's him you should thank."

"Maybe I'll get a chance to one day."

They found a café in the sunshine and examined the map of Switzerland that Herr Knecht had, remarkably, thrown in for free. Pippi was firmly of the view that for caution's sake they shouldn't arrive in Zurich until shortly before the meeting with Borodin, which left them more than twenty-four hours to kill. By the most direct route, Zurich was maybe three hours away, and she suggested they loop south instead. It added fifty kilometers to the journey, but it also offered some spectacular countryside.

"I've been to Interlaken and Luzern," she said. "They are beautiful."

"It sounds good to me."

It sounded better than good: a lazy meander through the foothills of the Alps, and plenty of time to relax, recuperate, and prepare themselves for Zurich. Whatever Borodin's intentions, they had stolen a small advantage over him. He wasn't to know that Pippi would be present, too, covering Luke's back.

Pippi must have sensed his mind at work, because she said, "Try not to think about it."

"Which tells me you're thinking about it, too."

She smiled. "Well I'm not going to, not until tomorrow. In fact, we're not allowed to talk about it until breakfast tomorrow morning."

"Okay, but what *do* we talk about until then?"

Pippi caught their waiter's eye and scribbled in the air for the bill.

"The Faqir of Ipi," she said. "Tell me more about him."

CHAPTER TWENTY

Zurich Hauptbahnhof had undergone a dramatic transformation in the years that Borodin had been away. As he stepped from the train onto the platform, he paused, perplexed, taking in his surroundings. Where was the big, luminous hall where the trains came and went, and from which he had departed some twelve years ago? A low, undulating blanket of steel-and-glass arches now pressed down on the platforms. The effect was depressingly claustrophobic compared to before.

Andrej was waiting for him on the new concourse at the end of the platforms. He had changed, too. He looked smaller, shrunken, and what remained of his hair was oiled back in a few hopeful, desultory strands. The two men greeted each other with a hug that was more than cursory.

Andrej stepped back, gripping Borodin by the shoulders and surveying him. "By God, you look good, you old Croatian bastard."

"I wish I could say the same of you, you Serbian donkey-fucker."

They spoke the language shared by their two nations.

Andrej ran a hand over his bald pate. "Oh, this? I haven't lost it; it just decamped to my shoulders and my arse."

Borodin laughed. "How is Analisa?"

"She decamped, too, a few years ago. Left me for someone else."

"A younger man?"

"Older. Also uglier, if such a thing is possible."

"I'm sorry."

"You won't be when you meet Frieda. That's the woman I live with now." He picked up Borodin's suitcase. "The car's out front."

Borodin cast a parting glance around him. "I liked the old place. Why did they have to knock it down?"

"They didn't. It was too small to take the extra tracks, so they added this on. You'll see."

The old station hall, a soaring cathedral of stone and glass, lay just back from the new concourse, as magnificent as ever. The old tracks and platforms had been paved over to create a public space fringed with cafés and restaurants. *Not bad,* thought Borodin. If this was progress, he could just about live with it.

"So what brings you back to Zurich?" Andrej inquired.

"Nothing good, I'm afraid."

"Excellent. Life has been very dull since you left."

"Do you still have contacts in the police?"

"A couple. Most have retired."

"Any favors you can call in?" Borodin asked.

"For you, of course."

"I'm also going to need two taxis, with drivers who can be trusted to keep their mouths shut."

"Now I'm properly intrigued. You can tell me everything over lunch. I've booked us a table at the Kindli."

"Ah, the Kindli."

"That hasn't changed one bit since you left."

"You mean they still serve tepid soup?"

Andrej laughed. "You're right; they do."

It was a sudden impulse. Borodin held Andrej back by the arm. "I can trust you, can't I, Andrej?"

"Of course you can."

"Has anyone been in touch with you about me? Anyone at all?"

"No."

Behind the wounded look in his old friend's eyes, he detected something else. Something reassuring: concern. "Forgive me," said Borodin, "but I had to ask."

"That bad, huh?"

"I'm afraid so. And I won't be insulted if you don't want to help."

"Come on, you old fool. I'll give you my answer over a bowl of tepid soup."

CHAPTER TWENTY-ONE

The road directly south of Bern ran straight as a telegraph wire through flat and featureless countryside. Luke drove, the windows down, warm air blustering around them as he spoke.

Pippi hadn't been joking. She did indeed want to hear about the Faqir of Ipi, who had come up briefly in conversation in the car yesterday, during Major Kendrick's questioning of Luke. The *faqir* was a Pathan religious leader who had galvanized a number of the hill tribes in northern Waziristan to turn against the British, even declaring a jihad against the foreign oppressors. The first uprising, near Bannu, had been swiftly dealt with by British and Indian troops shortly before Luke was posted to 11 Squadron at Risalpur.

The faqir was no fool, though. Realizing that he couldn't hope to win by conventional methods of warfare, he had vanished with his followers into the hills, from where they made lightning raids on army outposts and the very columns of troops sent to hunt him down.

The British military adopted a policy of proscription in order to dislodge the faqir and punish those who harbored him. This meant singling out a valley known to be sympathetic to him, and bombing its villages from the air. Leaflets would be dropped a couple of days in advance, warning of the coming attacks and advising the inhabitants to vacate their homes — a practice that the faqir cleverly turned to his own advantage.

His influence extended far wider than anyone had imagined — all the way to Peshawar, in fact, and the printing press that ran off the leaflets. Having been tipped off, the faqir would hurry to the next proscribed valley and advise the tribal elders that a vision of an imminent air attack had come to him in a dream. They weren't to worry, though, for he would remain among them, and he had the power to turn the British bombs to paper.

Sure enough, the planes would appear as predicted, and harmless confetti would flutter down from the heavens. The day before the bombing began in earnest, the faqir would take leave of his hosts, claiming that the exertions of the past couple of days had depleted his magical powers to the point where he was no longer able to protect them. They would all be wise to make themselves scarce for a bit.

Amusing enough. They had laughed about it in the mess when they finally discovered what the wily old faqir was up to, and Luke laughed about it now with Pippi. The reality, however, was far more sobering. It certainly had been at the time.

You didn't need to be a genius to figure that the faqir's ruse worked only because none of the tribesmen could read the leaflets. Even the headmen were simple folk who scratched a meager living from the vertiginous slopes. They were religious, superstitious, and illiterate. In this sense, the faqir was indeed protecting his people, because without him they would never have known that death and destruction were about to rain down on their heads.

One evening in the mess, Luke had made the case for allowing the faqir to continue with his shenanigans, or they would find themselves bombing compounds and villages packed with people, chiefly women and children during the day, when the men were off working in the fields. His suggestion met with frosty silence before Captain Trevelyan asked, "Are these the same women who wouldn't think twice about slicing off your privates and stitching them into your mouth?"

"So it's said."

"So it is, Hamilton. I've seen it with my own eyes."

Others began to pipe up. They were at war. Under no circumstances could the faqir be allowed to enhance his reputation still further. The situation needed to be dealt with swiftly and firmly before the trickle became a flood. Desperate times, desperate measures.

Luke was genuinely shocked. These counterarguments, while sound enough in their logic, made no allowances for the moral dilemma he had imagined they all were experiencing at some level. Even his good friend Tommo Spurling took him to task as they strolled back from the mess to the bungalow they shared, suggesting that he keep his own counsel in the future. Yes, it could be unsavory work at times, but it wasn't as though they'd started the thing in the first place. Ultimately, the Faqir of Ipi was the one with blood on his hands.

That evening in the mess, Luke later realized, marked the beginning of the end for him, the moment when the seed of doubt already lodged in his conscience began to germinate and put down roots, fertilized by the seeming indifference of his friends and fellow officers.

The only real danger they faced on the bombing sorties came from the tribesmen who lined the ridges of the proscribed valley and took potshots at them as they swooped in low to drop their payloads. Luke now found himself welcoming the sight of the black headdresses bobbing behind the rocks — just the right side of the crest, where they knew the pilots were not allowed to fire on them — for it meant that the news had got through. When it hadn't, consolation came in another form.

Yates, the bomb aimer, who sat behind him in the Hart and who had shown such promise during their training exercises, now seemed incapable of hitting a football pitch from a hundred feet. He came close on occasions and even vaporized a donkey one time, but the people on the ground had little to fear from the silver biplane with "K-2118" emblazoned on its tail fin.

One donkey. That poor animal somehow crystalized the absurdity of proscription. What were the brass hoping to achieve? Did they seriously think that a bunch of peasant farmers could be coerced into handing over the faqir? Or was it just punishment for punishment's sake? Either way, it soon became clear that Military Intelligence had no grasp of the intricate web of alliances, counteralliances, and historic enmities that bound the various hill tribes together. Bribes were paid for information, and more often than not the informants simply disappeared with the money. Meanwhile, the faqir remained at large, forever on the move, sheltering deep in the network of caves that honeycombed the hills.

The British weren't accustomed to being given the runaround by a bearded Sufi mystic, and the frustration began to breed vindictiveness. There were rumors of maltreatment of prisoners, torture, even murder. These came to Luke's ears more often as the campaign progressed and the pilots found themselves cooperating closely with the regiments stationed at Risalpur, offering air support to the columns of ground troops that snaked through the hills in search of the elusive faqir. Assisting his own side in battle against a determined enemy far more adept at the ancient art of mountain skirmishing was something Luke had no trouble squaring with his conscience. It also seemed to bring out the best in Yates, whose aim improved immeasurably whenever they flew to the aid of the infantry.

Gradually, inexorably, the dirty tactics became more commonplace. The average Pathan's most prized possession was his rifle, usually a Lee-Enfield replica made of cheap railway steel. Ammunition was extremely scarce, and it was Captain Trevelyan's fiendish idea, after an engagement, to scatter some about, which the enemy would then recover, unaware that the .303 cartridges had been doctored to blow up in the breech when fired. As for the air force, they were instructed to start dropping delayed-action bombs — anything up to twenty-four hours — in the fields around the proscribed villages, to cause maximum disruption to the tribesmen's lives. The strafing of livestock was also encouraged.

Luke didn't share all the grim details with Pippi, nor did he speak of the creeping stain on his soul. He did voice some doubts about the wisdom of trying to bomb a proud and independent people like the Pathans into any kind of lasting submission. Mainly, though, he talked about the flying: the wild summer thermals that tossed you about like a cork on an angry sea; and the beauty of a dawn sortie, the sun rising over the Himalayas, chasing the purple shadows down the slopes.

On one memorable occasion, toward the end of his time in India, he had flown deep into the high Himalayas, on a landing-ground inspection of the garrison at Gilgit. They set off from Risalpur at dawn and within an hour were winding their way up the valley of the foaming Indus, the mountains rising ever higher around them, shrinking them, turning their craft into toy airplanes. They were among the monsters now, with their eternal snows. Nanga Parbat passed by on their right, trailing a long plume of wind-whipped ice crystals from its summit, which topped Mont Blanc's by a full two miles.

It had been a humbling experience, though not as humbling as playing polo with the locals when they finally landed in Gilgit. The first time Luke was thrown from his horse, some wag in the crowd had shouted, "It's true, they really can fly!"

Pippi laughed at the anecdote. He decided not to tell her about the scandal already breaking while he was making a fool of himself on that dusty polo field, and which would be waiting for him when he returned to Risalpur.

■ ■ ■ ■

The town of Interlaken, as its name suggested, lay between two alpine lakes. They stopped just long enough in the center for Pippi to ask directions from a shopkeeper, and ten minutes later they found themselves at a public lido on the shores of Lake Brienz.

It was a simple setup, with picnic tables scattered about in the shade of some pines, and a large expanse of grass running down to the water's edge. A swimming pontoon with diving boards was moored some distance from the shore. No doubt the place had been mobbed yesterday, but at two o'clock on a Monday afternoon, they had their pick of spots to spread out their one and only towel.

Pippi made straight for the changing cubicles. When she reemerged in her new swimsuit, a navy one-piece number made from some kind of synthetic material that hugged her long, lean figure, Luke wasn't quite sure where to look.

"Aren't you coming in?"

"I only have my undershorts."

"Then they will have to do."

He lost them on his first dive from the springboard out on the pontoon, after which

he stuck to jumping. Pale, coltish, and tireless as a child, Pippi kept hauling herself up
the steel steps for another dive. Her composure deserted her momentarily when she
graduated to the high board. Creeping out
to the end, she peered past her toes at the
drop to the bottle-green water. Then, with a
fearful little squeal, she jumped. She also
jumped the second time. After that, she
dived, and kept diving until she had mastered it.

They swam out a little farther and lay on
their backs, floating. Or rather, Pippi did.
Luke's legs kept slipping beneath the surface.

"I've never been able to float on my back."

"Everyone can."

"Not me, I'm a sinker."

She told him to extend his arms above his
head and tilt his chin toward the sky, and to
relax his legs and imagine a straight line
running from the tips of his fingers to his
heels. She made some minor adjustments to
his body position, then released him. "Ta-
dah!" she declared triumphantly.

"I'm floating! I'm not a sinker!"

They lay there together in suspension, gaz-
ing at the sky. Somehow, the setting felt
entirely appropriate to their circumstances:
a placid strip of water sandwiched between

two menacing slabs of plunging mountainside; their past, present, and future enshrined in the alpine landscape.

Back on terra firma, they let the sun dry them off. Luke fell almost at once into a deep, dreamless sleep. When he awoke, it was to see Pippi sitting cross-legged on the grass, watching him.

"How long have I . . . ?"

"An hour," she replied. "You were snoring."

"I don't snore."

"And you don't float. Is there anything else you don't do that you do do?"

He thought on it. "Yes, I never lick my plate clean when no one's looking."

She laughed. "It wasn't easy, but I left you some strudel." She nodded at a tray on the grass behind him.

"Is that tea?"

"Coffee. Cold coffee." She started to rise. "I'll get you another one."

"Don't worry, this will do." It was lukewarm, and weak.

"Tell me what happened with Kapitän Wilke."

The question caught him off guard. "I thought we weren't going to talk about it until tomorrow."

"I need to know."

"I told you already. I fired at the car. It crashed and rolled over."

"You thought he was dead?"

A dim warning bell sounded in his head. "I wasn't sure."

"You didn't check?"

The bell got louder. "Obviously not, or he wouldn't have ended up firing at us from the jetty."

"Why not?" she demanded.

"It all happened so fast."

"You should have checked."

"And what? Finished him off?"

"A man like that will kill again. You would have saved lives."

Was she really trying to make him feel bad for failing to execute Wilke in cold blood?

"Pippi, listen to me. I couldn't have done it. I'd just shot a man — no, a boy — right here in the chest." He stabbed his finger against his sternum.

"So? You've killed before."

"That was combat, from the air, at a distance. This was close up, in the middle of the street and in broad daylight."

"In self-defense."

"Yes, him or me. But it doesn't make his face go away." He hesitated. "I didn't sleep last night because of that face."

She absorbed this information impassively.

"I'm sorry it wasn't Wilke's face."

"So am I, but there it is."

It was his way of drawing a line under the conversation, but Pippi wasn't finished yet.

"I would have done it."

"Bully for you," he said, his hackles rising.

"What does that mean?"

"Look it up in a dictionary."

"I want to know what it means."

"It means you were ready to throw your life away, and now you're alive. Doesn't that count for something?"

"Not while he's alive."

"So, after Zurich, go back to Germany and finish the job."

"I plan to."

"Then you're a fool."

"You weren't there," said Pippi darkly. "I stood and watched it happen. I could have done something."

"Yes — made it worse. Got yourself killed. The others, too."

She shook her head. "No."

"For certain. And you're twice a fool if you can't see it."

"No one speaks to me like that."

"Well, maybe there's the problem."

It was a cheap shot, and he regretted it until she replied, "I was starting to like you."

"Ouch. Lucky for me I have enough

friends already."

Her face took on a sneer. "You're good at this, aren't you?"

"I've had a lot of practice."

Pippi bundled up her clothes and got to her feet.

"The question is, can you do it again?"

"What's that?"

"Kill a man close up. Because you might have to."

He held her hard gaze. "I'm not sure."

"Well, I need to be. If you can't, it changes things."

"Yes," he said. "I think I can do it again if I have to."

"Good, because we don't know what's waiting for us in Zurich."

"There's no guarantee Borodin will even show up."

"Oh, he'll be there," she said.

He watched her make off toward the changing cubicles. It was easy to resent her for breaking the code of silence she herself had imposed, souring the playful mood of the past few hours in the process, but she was entitled to be swept away by the fervor of her feelings. He had never had to stand by and watch the one he loved being kicked to death before his eyes.

270

What images haunted her while she lay in bed at night?

Chapter Twenty-Two

It occurred to Erwin only as the train was approaching the station at Kemmental. Rather than transferring to the lakeside branch line at Kreuzlingen, he could get off here and cut the corner to Seedorf on foot. It was a glorious day, and he had many hours to kill before nightfall.

He walked east from the town, passing farms and orchards before leaving the lane and striking out across the patchwork of sun-drenched pastures and cornfields. He kept to a leisurely pace and even stopped to chat with a gang of farm laborers taking a break from the harvest and the heat in the shade of a tarpaulin slung between two hay carts.

They were curious to know what he was doing out here in the middle of nowhere. And why the black eye and the split lip? Had he by any chance escaped from the asylum for the insane just over the hill at

Münsterlingen? Because if so, he was heading straight back toward it and would be wise to turn around and make off the way he'd come. He laughed along with them, ascribing the wounds inflicted by Otto to a street brawl with some Nazi fanatics back home in Konstanz. It was the same explanation they had offered for Johan's injuries when they took him to the hospital that night. The police had wanted to investigate the matter further, but Kapitän Wilke had, for obvious reasons, used his authority to ensure their story was allowed to stand unchallenged.

Rested and watered, Erwin continued on his way, up and over a densely wooded rise. Beyond, the fields dipped gently down toward Münsterlingen: a straggle of low houses dwarfed by the mental asylum, which stood austere and forbidding on a promontory jutting out into the lake. He could make out Meersburg directly across the water, and to his left, Konstanz. He lit a cigarette and surveyed the scene of yesterday's disaster, giving thanks for his good fortune.

Twenty-four hours ago, he had been lying trussed up like a pig for slaughter, in the darkness of that stinking compartment at the back of the motor launch. He wouldn't have been surprised if Pippi had followed through on Otto's threat and pitched him over the side, tied to the anchor, once the professor and his family were safely delivered. But he had seized his moment and turned the tables on them all, winning favor with the British major, trading the truth about Hamilton for a train ticket, some Swiss francs, a pack of cigarettes, and the key to the motor launch.

He had no reason to think the boat wouldn't be where they left it — the Swiss were notoriously law-abiding — but he still felt a rush of relief when, after working his way south along the shore, he came across it. The sight of it tied up at the remote landing stage brought a smile to his lips.

He fired up the motor and checked the fuel gauge. Everything was in order. Herr Salzmann would get his boat back — a little later than arranged, admittedly, but that could be smoothed over easily enough.

As he stretched out in the sunshine on the bench seat in the stern, he began to believe that his life could actually be repaired. Like a vase that had been broken and then carefully glued back together, the finished product wouldn't be perfect, but it would be presentable enough.

Pippi and Otto were accomplices to the

killing of a German official, and not just any official — an agent of the Abwehr. Returning to Germany would mean certain death for them both. He would have to explain away their sudden departure to friends and other associates, but with a little thought he could hatch a convincing story. His chief cause for concern was Kapitän Wilke, who would be wanting blood after yesterday's disaster. It would take a lot to appease him. In fact, it was probably best to avoid him for a while. Let the dust settle. Wilke was the sort of man who, when enraged, was apt to lash out at anything within reach.

CHAPTER TWENTY-THREE

The Palace Hotel in Luzern lived up to its name. Filling a long stretch of the lakeside promenade, it was six or seven floors of high Victorian pomp, with an elaborately carved facade and an entrance lobby that was a feast of swirling marble.

Pippi was set on staying there, and although Luke offered a few token words of caution about the cost, he was thinking of a hot bath and a cold beer, preferably taken together. There were no twin rooms with a lake view available, but there was a suite. The rate was staggering.

"Hang the expense," Pippi said to the concierge. "We could die tomorrow." A line intended for Luke's ears.

"Not before settling your bill, I hope," the concierge replied, his face so stony straight that they couldn't be sure he was joking.

Upstairs, they found themselves in a drawing room large enough to swallow two sofas, a dining table, and a satinwood grand piano with no trouble. The two spacious bedrooms came with en suite bathrooms done out in pale gray marble. The view from the balcony was spectacular. Across the lake, beyond the soft swell of the hills, the humped and jagged profile of a lone mountain stood out against the blue sweep of sky.

"That's Pilatus," said Pippi. "I've been up there."

"Really?"

"There's a special train that goes to the top." She had been ten years old at the time, on holiday with her parents and her brothers. "We stayed here at the Palace Hotel."

"Under happier circumstances."

"Not by much," she replied enigmatically.

She could have elaborated, and he could have pressed her to. That neither did was an indication of their current level of rapport. The drive from Interlaken had passed in strained silence, punctuated by an occasional polite exchange about the striking beauty of the scenery they were passing through. No mention had been made of their earlier argument, no apology offered, no quarter given. Each waited for the other to make the first overture, and that showed no sign of happening anytime soon.

They arranged to meet in the drawing

room at seven thirty, dressed for dinner. Then they went their separate ways, Luke to a steaming bath and a cold glass of pilsner ordered from room service. The heat and the alcohol did for him, driving him to his big bed. When the alarm clock dragged him back to wakefulness an hour later, he found a note under his door. Pippi had gone for a stroll and would meet him downstairs.

He found her seated at a table in the bar, although his eyes passed over her twice before he realized it was her.

"You look magnificent."

She smiled up at him. "Thank you."

He hadn't been there when she tried on the evening gown at the boutique, and it was immediately clear to him why she had bought it. The sapphire-blue silk was cut daringly low in front, rising to a halter neck that exposed her pale, delicate shoulders.

"What was that?" he asked, pointing to an empty glass on the table in front of her.

"A Tom Collins."

He ordered two more from the waiter.

"How was your walk?"

"I couldn't go far in this," she replied. "It reaches to the floor."

He could picture heads turning on the promenade: the admiring eyes of the men, the envious glances of the women.

"I reserved us a good table on the terrace."

Some of the tension seemed to have left her, possibly helped on its way by the cocktail. When he asked about her last trip to Luzern, she spoke with engaging frankness about that family holiday and some of the other ones, then about the cloying privilege of her upbringing, and her father's ham-fisted efforts to steer her into an early marriage with the terminally dim son of a business associate.

Their union would have put the seal on a merger that had been brewing for a number of years: her father had the factories, the other man the transport network. The notion of signing away her life to a wealthy halfwit in order to drive up business was so utterly absurd to Pippi that she never once wavered in her refusal to go along with the plan, even when her mother — usually her ally against the three overbearing men of the household — was enlisted to lean on her.

The only person to take her side was Margaret, her English nanny, whom the family had kept on past any obvious usefulness, because she had nowhere else to go.

"So that's where you get your English from."

"Margaret from Godalming," said Pippi in an impeccable Home Counties accent. "It's what my brothers and I called her, because that's how she always introduced herself."

Margaret was a well of quiet wisdom, which she dispensed from her room on the top floor. She was canny enough to know that publicly siding with Pippi would jeopardize her own precarious position, so she spoke out against Pippi's decision to study at Freiburg University (although it was Margaret herself who had suggested Freiburg over Munich, since it would allow Pippi to put some distance between herself and her family).

The cooling of relations soon deepened into a sharp frostiness when her older brother decided to inform himself about Pippi's new life in Freiburg. The first she or anyone else knew of his snooping was when he asked her over the dinner table at Christmastime if it was true she was consorting with a Jew.

"Ask Father the same question. I believe most of the people he does business with are Jews."

"By 'consorting,' I meant 'sleeping with.' "

"I know what you meant, Rolf."

The battle lines had been drawn in the shocked silence that followed the revelation.

Looking back, she could see that the schism was inevitable, not because her family was anti-Semitic — they had never shown such prejudices before — but because they were greedy. Hitler and his henchmen were set on a course that would soon see Jews struggling to hold on to their businesses. She hadn't known this at the time, but her father and brothers had. They understood that there would be rich pickings — factories and other concerns — to be snapped up on the cheap by those close to the Nazi elite.

What better way to prepare yourself for the moral dilemma ahead, to justify the gains you were set to make at the expense of the Jews, than by learning to demonize them ahead of time? It looked like racism, but it was far worse than that: avarice dressed up as racism — two ugly peas in the same rotten pod. And it left no place for an errant daughter's whimsical attachment to a Jewish student at the university she was attending.

"Whatever you think about Hitler," she said, "he is a clever man. He knew who he had to buy, and he bought them with the money of the people he hates. That is genius. That is madness. That is why we must fight him."

By now, they had moved to their table on

the front terrace, and Pippi cast an anxious glance around her at the other candlelit diners, forgetting for a moment where she was, forgetting that in Switzerland she was free to speak her mind without fear of denunciation or reprisal.

When he asked her about Johan, she shrugged and replied, "There's not much to say."

She was still talking about him when the waiter arrived to remove their entrée plates.

"My family didn't approve of our relationship, but his family were the same. I was not the right girl for him."

"Not Jewish, you mean?"

"Yes."

"You could have converted."

"We talked about it. I said I would."

"So?"

"He wouldn't let me. He was . . . a complicated man."

He certainly was. Johan had dissuaded her from following him into his faith, on the grounds that she would be consigning herself to a life of persecution, and possibly worse. At first, she had taken this noble stance at face value. With time, however, she had begun to sense that something else lay behind it. "He didn't trust my feelings for him. He thought I was just a rich girl playing a game."

"I'm sure that's not true."

"He said it to me. More than once." She adjusted the napkin on her lap, smoothing it out.

"Everybody says things they don't really mean. He was probably just testing you."

She looked up sharply. "Why? I gave him everything."

"Maybe he couldn't quite believe his luck."

"It's kind of you to try, but he didn't love me as I loved him."

"Love doesn't have to be requited to be real."

"Requited?" she asked.

"Returned. Maybe the purest kind of love is the one that stands alone, by itself."

"You don't believe that."

"And you have obviously never loved a cat."

She laughed and raised her wineglass. "Yes, I shall think of Johan as a cat."

She told him about the surly Siamese she had grown up with, and the talk then turned to pets and other animals, to the lanky hunting hounds favored by her father, and to the horses in the paddock beside the house, which she had ridden from an early age, all the way to victory in numerous jumping competitions. Listening to her wind back the years, Luke felt a mild sorrow steal over him. To picture her as a young girl, happy enough and carefree, seemed to point up the horrors that had been visited upon them both.

Their filet mignons arrived, along with a second bottle of French claret.

"Pippi . . ."

"Yes?"

"Earlier, at the lake, I said some hurtful things to you."

"Yes, you did."

"I'm sorry."

"And some things that needed to be said." She took a sip of wine. "You're right. I have to learn to let go of it, let go of Johan, live again. I don't want to die. I want to have children, and I want to lie in a bath with them and read them fairy tales."

"That's good to hear."

Pippi took the knife to her steak. "When you were being so horrid to me, you said you'd had a lot of practice. What did you mean?"

There was no way of saying it without sounding self-pitying.

"Being an orphan, a foundling, and with my coloring, at a private school for boys . . ." He paused briefly. "You learn to fight back with your tongue, and your fists if you have to."

The prejudice he had endured at St. Theresa's was tame compared to the abuse inflicted on him by a small but vicious minority of his peers at the King's School, Ely. He had managed to deflect most of it by working hard in the classroom and shining on the sports field, but the chauvinism and racism would always be there in some form or other. At university, he had come within a hairsbreadth of being sent down from Trinity for breaking the nose of another student, a boy with a double-barreled name who had called him "Heathcliff" in the college bar.

"Heathcliff?" asked Pippi.

"From the novel by Emily Brontë — *Wuthering Heights.*"

Pippi shook her head: it didn't mean anything to her.

"He's a boy with gypsy blood and ideas above his station."

"You're not so dark," said Pippi.

"Dark enough not to be a true Englishman."

No, he had learned to accept a simple fact: the privileged establishment world made available to him by his parents was not one that would ever fully accept him. He had no history, no family tales stretching back generations. He was there only by the grace and favor of the couple who had adopted him.

He no longer sought or fought for acceptance in the way that he once had. He kept his head down, his mind on the job. And he had taught himself not to rise to the gibes and the petty public humiliations.

"What sort of things?" Pippi asked.

"Oh, you know, nonsense . . ."

Like the time in the officers' mess at Risalpur when Captain Trevelyan, seated with his friends, had clicked his fingers at Luke, calling for service, before "realizing his mistake" and apologizing.

"Very funny."

"Yes, lots of snorts and snickers," said Luke. "It was Trevelyan's wife I had the affair with."

Pippi's face brightened with delight. "Oh, that's good. I like that. Tell me."

"Really? It's a pretty sordid story."

"Even better," she said, reaching for her wineglass.

CHAPTER TWENTY-FOUR

Erwin kept the revs low, even when the patrol boat was long gone and all he could make out of it was the lazy sweep of its searchlight far to the south.

The moon overhead was a slender sickle, and he was happy to cruise gently along through the deep darkness, guided by the spangle of lights that was Meersburg on the far side of the lake. When he was within a few hundred meters of shore, he flicked on the launch's running lights, opened the throttle, and altered his course toward the north.

Unsurprisingly, the small harbor at Dingelsdorf was deserted. He tied up at the jetty and dropped the key in the letter box at the harbor master's hut. He would telephone tomorrow to explain, to make his peace with Herr Salzmann. Where he would be when he made that call, he still didn't know. Maybe on the road to Metz, where his sister worked as a nurse. Or maybe he should head for Munich and lose himself there for a bit before contacting Kapitän Wilke. He had the night to decide.

The car was parked in front of the hotel where they all had eaten lunch only yesterday. Without the key, he had to use the hand crank, and his shirt was stuck to his torso by the time the engine finally fired. Most of his clothes were at the apartment in Konstanz, along with a spare revolver, but it would be too risky to spend the night there: the place was probably under surveillance. Kapitän Wilke didn't know about his uncle's sawmill in the woods, so that was where he headed, winding his way up into the hills west of Dingelsdorf, the headlights knifing the darkness.

Leaving nothing to chance, he parked the car in the woods and walked the last bit of track leading to the pasture. What little there was of the moon had sunk out of sight, and with only the dim glimmer of the stars to guide him, he made a slow, silent tour of both the barn and the farmhouse, satisfying himself that he wouldn't be surprised by any unexpected guests.

The key was where it always lived, where Otto had placed it yesterday as they were leaving: in a hole in the masonry above the wooden lintel of the kitchen window. He unlocked the door and entered.

He had just time enough to register the unexpected smell of cigarette smoke before the beam of a flashlight hit him hard in the eyes, blinding him.

"I have a gun pointed at your head."

He froze, coiled for action.

"Don't do it, Erwin."

Definitely Kapitän Wilke's voice. He saw himself running blindly through the darkness of the pasture, the flashlight picking him out and a bullet slapping into his back, pitching him forward on his face.

"Kapitän Wilke?"

"Shut the door and bolt it."

He did as instructed. The flashlight flicked to a chair at the kitchen table.

"Sit."

A match flared and an oil lamp flooded the kitchen with warm light. Kapitän Wilke was dressed casually in flannel trousers and short-sleeved shirt. He replaced the lamp's glass chimney, adjusted the wick, then switched off the flashlight.

"Schnapps?"

Erwin nodded warily. Wilke filled two small glasses and slid one across the table. "Surprised to see me?" he asked. "There's not much I don't know about you, Erwin.

I'm very thorough when it comes to the people I work with." He nodded at the glass. "Drink. You look like you could do with it. You look like you've been in a fight."

"I have."

"That's good. It suggests you tried your best."

"I did," said Erwin. "I really did, but I was outnumbered."

"They guessed it was you?"

"Pippi wasn't sure if it was Otto or me. It's why she lied to us about Friedrichshafen. I called you from Meersburg as soon as I knew, as soon as I could."

"And when were you going to call me this time? Tonight?"

"Yes."

"There's no telephone line here."

"I was just stopping to get some things before going to the apartment."

"If you say so," came the sardonic reply.

"I've only been back in the country half an hour."

Wilke waved aside his words. "You're here now. That's all that matters."

"And it wasn't easy, I can tell you."

"I really don't care. Tell me instead about the Englishman, the one you mentioned when you called from Meersburg."

"Hamilton? He knew what Pippi was up

to. He was helping her. She must have taken him into her confidence."

"What is he like?"

"Like?"

"I want to picture him. I want a sense of who he is."

"Why?"

Wilke took a slow sip of schnapps before replying. "Because I had to call my brother last night and tell him that his son was dead, shot in the chest during an operation in Meersburg."

Erwin felt a prickle of fear fan out across his shoulders. "That was your nephew? I'm sorry."

Wilke's laugh was more of a derisory snort. "Sorry? Yes, you will be if I find out there was anything you could have done to prevent it."

"There wasn't, I swear. You have to believe me."

"I don't have to believe a word of what you tell me, Erwin, but I *am* going to hear you out."

Wilke produced a bone-handled hunting knife and a coil of rope from a bag at his feet. He cut off two short lengths of rope and tossed them onto the table in front of Erwin. "Tie your ankles to the chair legs. Nice and tight. Don't try to be clever."

When it was done, he cut off another length of rope. "Put your hands behind the chair." Erwin hesitated. "You have nothing to fear as long as you are entirely honest with me."

He lashed Erwin's wrists together tightly and wound the rest of the rope around his chest, binding him fast to the chair back.

"A word of warning: I may know more than you imagine, so think very carefully before replying." Wilke perched on the table and topped up his glass with schnapps. "When did Hamilton first appear? And where did he come from?"

It was a methodical interrogation conducted by a man clearly experienced in such matters, a man who'd had time to order his thoughts and marshal his questions. Erwin played it straight. He had nothing to hide, even though he didn't have all the answers. Who could say why Borodin had spared Hamilton's life before dispatching him to Konstanz from Paris? And why had Hamilton agreed to help Pippi, despite the grave personal danger of doing so?

Wilke seemed happy enough to accept these unknowns for what they were and move on. He listened carefully to Erwin's account of events as they had unfolded in Meersburg. "Clever girl," he said eventually.

"I'm a lucky man."

"Why?"

"Don't you see? She suspected you, but it was me she was after. You were meant to make the telephone call to Friedrichshafen. She wanted me to show up. But the car with the children was late and everything changed. Her plan fell apart."

It seemed a little far-fetched to Erwin, although he kept the thought to himself. He wasn't going to say anything that might rile Wilke just as he was getting to the bit of the story that cast him in a better light. He described how, sensing that something was wrong, he had drawn a gun in the car, only to be overpowered and beaten all but unconscious by Otto. He lied about his time on the boat, crammed into that stinking compartment, terrified, certain that he was about to die, portraying it instead as an opportunity to collect his thoughts and work out his next move. On arriving in Switzerland, he had picked his moment before dropping the bombshell about Hamilton to the British major.

"Interesting," said Wilke.

"It worked. He was taken straight into custody."

"Interesting that they made such a mistake. They should have got rid of you before landing in Switzerland." Wilke's tone left Erwin in no doubt that in their position he would have done just that. "Go on."

He explained that he had been treated well at the British Embassy in Bern, and the talk had been of Hamilton being sent back to Paris to face the music.

"What did you tell them about me?"

"You?"

"I haven't figured in your story yet," said Wilke. "I'm almost insulted. They must have asked you about me. Did you tell them I am with the Abwehr?" Erwin was about to reply when Wilke suddenly raised his hand. "I have a feeling you're going to lie to me. Take a moment before you speak."

Erwin took that moment and changed his mind. "Yes, I told them."

"And what else did you say?"

"The truth: that you had approached me, threatened me."

"Not that you took almost no persuading, and that you were well paid for your services?" Wilke didn't wait for a response. "No, of course not; you were playing the victim. And it worked. That's why you're here now."

"I suppose so."

"And where is Hamilton?"

"As I said, in custody. Already on his way

back to Paris, probably."

Wilke laid his glass of schnapps aside and stepped closer. "I'm curious. I've warned you twice; I've given you every opportunity to be straight with me. So why would you want to lie?"

"I'm not lying to you," Erwin blurted indignantly.

Wilke drew on the last of his cigarette, then stamped it out. "Hamilton was released by the British. So was Miss Keller. Does that sound like custody to you?"

Fear and confusion scrambled Erwin's thoughts. "How? I mean . . . that's not possible."

"They left the embassy together in a taxi."

How could Wilke possibly know? There was only one explanation. "You have someone in their embassy?"

Wilke shrugged. "I'd be surprised if they don't have someone in ours, too."

"I swear to you I didn't know."

"Relax, Erwin. I'm inclined to believe you. It happened after you'd left for the station." Wilke loomed over him. "Do you have any idea where Hamilton might be?"

"Maybe. Yes. I might."

"That's not very convincing."

"You have to promise to let me go." He knew how foolish it sounded, even as the words spilled from his mouth.

"Look at you, Erwin. Do you seriously think you're in any position to negotiate?" Wilke took up the revolver from the table and pointed it at Erwin's left knee.

"No, don't!"

"Then be quick."

Erwin was. He explained how they had kept Hamilton tied up in the barn, and how he had followed Pippi out there and eavesdropped on a conversation between her and the Englishman. He hadn't caught all of it, but he'd clearly heard Hamilton say that he was supposed to meet Borodin in Zurich on Tuesday afternoon.

"Tomorrow?" said Wilke.

"Yes."

"Please tell me there's more."

Erwin knew he had no choice but to hand over the rest and hope for the best. "Café Glück. It's in the old town. They're meeting there at four o'clock."

"And you didn't think to tell me this before?"

"It wasn't relevant. I thought he'd been arrested by his own people."

Wilke's eyes bored into him. "If you're making this up . . ."

"It's what he said to Pippi. He could have been lying to her."

"Let's hope for your sake he wasn't. We'll know soon enough."

Wilke lifted his bag onto the table and packed away the knife and what remained of the rope.

"You're not going to leave me here like this, are you?"

"No, I'm going to gag you first," said Wilke, pulling a strip of cloth from the bag.

"No one comes here," said Erwin, a note of rising panic in his voice. "And my uncle's away for another month."

"I'll be back before then."

"But what if . . ." Erwin's voice petered out.

"What if I don't make it?" said Wilke.

"I'm just saying . . ."

"I know what you're saying, and that's enough talk for now."

Wilke moved behind him and fitted the gag, fastening it with a double knot. Then he pocketed his cigarettes and examined the bottle of schnapps. "You know, this isn't half bad." He switched on the flashlight and twisted the knob on the lamp until the flame dimmed and died. Turning, he said, "It's a good point, Erwin. Dehydration is a terrible way to die — slow and agonizing. Of course, maybe the rats will get you first." He pressed the muzzle of the revolver between Erwin's eyes. "I can spare you both possibilities right now, if you want me to."

Wide-eyed with fright, Erwin shook his head vigorously.

Wilke smiled. "I didn't think so."

CHAPTER TWENTY-FIVE

Andrej had been warned, but he still wasn't happy about being roused from his bed so early.

"Another hour," he pleaded when the bedroom door swung open. Borodin handed him a cup of tea. Andrej peered at it. "I don't drink tea."

"It's for Frieda."

"Oh."

"Ten minutes?"

Andrej grunted and closed the door.

They had worked on the plan for most of the afternoon, and then again after dinner, after Frieda had gone to bed. But it remained in the abstract, lines and scribbles on a street map. Borodin was eager to actually walk the route, to see it for himself. It had always been a habit of his, a test of sorts: if he couldn't picture the events unfolding in their proper order, then something was wrong and the whole strategy needed to be picked apart and reexamined.

They had many other preparations to make over the next few hours, but the first priority was scouting the terrain, before the city came properly to life. Unlikely though it was, there remained a slender possibility that Petrovic was already in Zurich. Bumping into him in the street before their two p.m. meeting at the restaurant would be unfortunate in the extreme.

Andrej's mood had improved a little by the time they boarded the tram, though not by much.

"I've been thinking," he growled, lighting a cigarette. "And I've concluded that it's a terrible plan."

"Do you have a better one?"

"Yes. Tell the Englishman that Petrovic is a friend of yours, a man who can be trusted; then take the money and leave."

"That's exactly what I intend to do."

"So why bother to meet up with Petrovic at the restaurant beforehand?"

"Curiosity," Borodin replied. "And there are some things I need to hear from him first . . . assurances."

"Assurances?"

"Promises."

"He could have them typed up and notarized and they wouldn't mean a damn thing."

"We'll see."

Andrej sucked on the cigarette with distaste. "You forget, my friend, I know you far too well. There's something else going on here. What is it?" His eyes narrowed. "Don't tell me you're having second thoughts."

Borodin smiled benignly.

"It's true you know me well, Andrej — maybe better than anybody. So tell me this: When have you ever known me to have second thoughts?"

They had only themselves to blame. They had vowed to turn in early, but eleven o'clock had come and gone, and by midnight so had another bottle of wine. When the maître d' informed them that the restaurant was closing, they had abandoned the terrace for the hotel bar and a quick digestif before bed: curaçao triple sec for both of them, on Pippi's suggestion.

Caught up in their conversation, it had made absolute sense at the time, but they both were paying the price now. They barely exchanged one word in the elevator as they headed downstairs for breakfast.

Throbbing heads and dry mouths accounted for much of the silence, but trepidation also played a part. Last night they had managed to stick to Pippi's original proposal and avoid any mention of what lay in store for them today. The welcome and very pleasant interlude was now over, though; it was simply a question of who would broach the subject first.

As soon as the waitress had delivered a pot of coffee to their table, Pippi leaped straight in.

"I think Major Kendrick was right. I don't think Borodin can be trusted."

What if Borodin had sniffed an opportunity that could be best played to his advantage by tucking Luke safely away in Germany for a time? Yes, he had jeopardized his own life by intervening in Paris, but this could have been a calculated risk — a route to a far larger prize. It was a bleak prognosis, but it stood up to scrutiny: pack Luke off to Germany with a bunch of lies to placate him, negotiate a deal for himself, then deliver the goods in Zurich. Pippi strongly believed they had to assume the worst.

"I thought you said you liked him."

"I do, but I'm thinking about you." She paused before adding gravely, "I don't think we should go to Zurich."

"I have to. I need answers."

"You've lived without them for twenty-five years."

"Half lived."

"Better than being dead."

He weighed her stark warning. "There's just one problem. What Borodin said to me in Paris that night, after L'Hirondelle, after he'd killed the first man and realized we were being followed by another."

"Remind me."

"If anything happened to him, I was to disappear, vanish forever, never come back. Why would he say that? He had nothing to gain from it."

"Maybe he did."

"No, you had to be there. It was a genuine warning. Someone wants me dead — God knows why — and they're not going to stop until I am. Even if I don't show up in Zurich, it won't be over. It'll never be over unless I finish it. I don't have a choice."

"You can do what Borodin said: disappear, leave everything behind."

"Could *you*?"

"I have."

He chided himself for the thoughtless question. Her family, friends, home, homeland — all gone for good. She had cut herself completely adrift.

Maybe sensing his embarrassment, she mercifully came to his support. "There's a difference. It was my choice. It wasn't forced on me. I understand."

"So do I, if you don't want to come. In fact, I don't think you should. It's not your battle."

"I made a promise to you."

"And now I'm releasing you from it."

She held his gaze. "Thank you, but no. Anyway, my plan only works with two people."

"You have a plan?"

"Of course." She smiled. "Everyone knows you have to have a plan."

They had traveled in separate carriages all the way from Geneva, glimpsing each other when they changed trains in Biel, but never communicating. On their arrival in Zurich, Petrovic set off through the crowd thronging the platform, secure in the knowledge that Jestin was shadowing him, and ready to spring into action if required.

Jestin had been an excellent choice. There was something essentially inconspicuous about the man. Short, slight, and bespectacled, he was surprisingly meek-looking for a Breton. He also carried himself with a diffidence that verged on nervousness. He didn't stride, he stepped lightly, almost daintily, as if trespassing. A stranger would have taken him for a bookkeeper or maybe a minor government official. There was certainly nothing to suggest he was one of the most notorious smugglers ever to come out of that vipers' nest known as the Port of Brest.

Nearing the front of the taxi queue, Petrovic permitted himself a casual glance behind him. Three people back was Jestin, adjusting the knot of his tie. Two rooms had been reserved for them at the same hotel, not because they required somewhere to stay — they would be gone before nightfall — but because they needed a place to talk in private, to ready themselves, and also to take delivery of the car and the two revolvers that Petrovic's contact in Basel would be bringing in a little over an hour.

As his taxi pulled away from the station, he experienced a jolt of remorse. He knew Jestin's story — had played a part in it, luring him to Paris with the promise of big money to be made. He had even met the man's charming wife, Christine, and it didn't sit happily with him that he would soon be turning her into a widow. There was nothing to be done about it, though. The Karamans had spoken.

The brothers would want the matter dealt with sooner rather than later, but it would be safer to wait until he and Jestin had disposed of Hamilton and returned to Paris. Jestin had the instincts of an alley cat. A convincing scenario would have to be constructed to put him at his ease. Petrovic pictured a staged hijacking of a lorry on a lonely road at night, the driver and his mate both armed and briefed beforehand to do the deed.

He wondered if some faceless assassin was at this very moment entertaining the same sort of thoughts about him. Could the Karamans have already signed off on his own death? He had done everything to make himself indispensable to the brothers, but he was no fool. It was a short step from indispensable to expendable. In Borodin's case, decades of loyal service had counted for nothing. Indeed, they had issued the order to kill him as casually as they might instruct a gardener to weed a flower bed.

"What if there are more than three of them?"

Wilke took his eyes off the road just long enough to glance at his elder brother, seated beside him. "It's quite possible the girl won't even be there."

"But what if she is? What if there are others, too?"

"Friedrich, we still have the element of surprise on our side. Just follow my lead."

It pained him to see Friedrich in such a state. His face, usually so animated, was a hollow-eyed mask. It wasn't just the lack of sleep after motoring through the night from Düsseldorf to Konstanz. Even his jacket seemed to hang differently from his broad-shouldered frame, as though a part of him had withered away beneath.

"There is something I need to ask of you, Friedrich. A favor."

"What?"

Wilke dropped a gear to negotiate the tight bend in the country road. "Stefan was your son, but he was in my charge when it happened."

"I've already told you, Markus, I don't hold you to blame."

"But I do. And I would like to be the one to kill the Englishman."

There was a brief silence.

"You think I'm not up to it?"

"It's not that," said Wilke. "It's not about you." This wasn't entirely true. Friedrich, a successful lawyer, was also a man of faith, and although it could hardly be described as a deep religious conviction, there was a chance he would waver at the vital moment. That could prove disastrous in a public place, where speed and timing were every-thing.

"It's about me," Wilke went on. "I was there. I watched it happen." He paused to pick the correct words. "I would find it easier to live with that memory if you allow me the honor of avenging Stefan's murder."

Friedrich turned his flat, dead gaze on the quilted slopes with their orderly scattering of farmsteads. "I have always disliked Switzerland," he said. "It's so unspeakably neat."

"Even the cows look bored," Wilke observed.

A smile twitched at the corners of Friedrich's mouth. "It's true, they do." He turned back. "Let me think about it, Markus. You'll have your answer by the time we get to Zurich."

Wilke let the subject lie. Friedrich had always had a contrary streak in him, even as a boy. The harder you pushed, the more he was likely to resist. With any luck, he would come around. It mattered to Wilke that he did, and not just for Stefan. For his own sake, too. He was consumed by a deep and urgent need to kill the man who had effectively destroyed his career.

For two years he had toiled away in and around the Bodensee, biding his time, filling his pockets and, more importantly, those of Major Goeritz, his immediate superior in Berlin. He had done everything expected of him. He had even groomed Stefan to take over from him, by way of assuring Goeritz that the stream of money would not dry up when Wilke moved to Berlin. That had always been their tacit arrangement: hard grind in the provinces followed by promotion to a post at Abwehr headquarters in the capital. The prize had lain within his reach. The arrest of a leading scientist as he was about to defect to the British would have secured it.

All gone now. He had tried and failed several times to get Goeritz on the phone — a sure sign that his superior was already distancing himself from the bloody debacle.

No, Friedrich would have to forgo the pleasure. Hamilton had to die by Wilke's hand. It was just unfortunate that circumstances would not allow him to take his time.

CHAPTER TWENTY-SIX

As Borodin approached the restaurant at the bottom of Rämistrasse, he knew he was being watched. What worried him most, though, was knowing that if Petrovic had any sense, he would make his move now, intercepting him and bundling him into a car.

The steel tip of his walking stick tapped lightly against the pavement; his right hand remained in his jacket pocket, closed around the grip of the revolver; and his ears strained for the sound of a car approaching at speed, or footsteps closing rapidly from behind.

Nothing.

Once inside the restaurant, he didn't drop his guard, but Petrovic had missed his moment. He bestowed a warm smile on the hat-check girl sitting attentively in her booth as he passed down the corridor.

The Kronenhalle had changed little since his last visit. Its somber grandeur, reinforced by the impeccable table settings and the formal wear of the staff, was still offset by the vivid splashes of color adorning its wood-paneled walls. Gottlieb and Hulda had always had a penchant for modern art, some of it provided by the artists in exchange for free meals, and he noted that they'd grown their collection over the intervening years. As the maître d' led him to the corner table he had reserved while in Paris, the only diner to show any interest in him was a skeletal woman of middle years, eating alone, picking forlornly at her salad. She seemed an improbable plant, but he didn't dismiss the possibility. Petrovic had sent a woman to kill him in Paris, had he not?

He ordered a gin fizz from the maître d' to help pass the time. Petrovic would wait a while in the hope that Hamilton might show up and the matter could be settled out on the street, without his having to hand over the remaining tranche of cash.

Lighting a cigarette, he sat back and looked around him. He recalled with unexpected fondness the many fine hours he had passed with friends and strangers in this room. Thanks to its neutrality, Zurich had always attracted a rich mix of displaced, stateless (and often degenerate) personalities. They had certainly been thick on the ground in the years immediately after the war, and the Kronenhalle had been one of their favored watering holes.

It was no bad thing, he reflected, that his life had briefly folded back on itself to a place filled with shimmerings of past happiness, because from today it would strike out on an altogether different course. There could be no returning to the places he had once known. His future lay before him, a road snaking off through an unfamiliar landscape.

It headed south, that much he knew. He had spent too long in the north. He wanted clear skies, warm seas, short winters, and the company of well- and roof-water drinkers. Naples, maybe. The offer was there, and unless Rosaria was a consummate actress, he had no reason to believe she hadn't made it in earnest. Sweet, gentle Rosaria, whose body he had bought on his last night in Paris, and who had wept the next morning when he offered to buy her a railway ticket home: tears of frustration rather than joy, because her French husband had confiscated her passport to prevent her fleeing the country.

"I'll get it for you, and anything else you want. All I need is an address."

"He's a dangerous man."

"What can I say? I've met a lot of danger-ous men in my life and I'm still here."

An hour and a half later, when he had met Rosaria at the Gare de Lyon, she had wept again — with relief this time, upon seeing her passport and the small traveling case containing the clothes and other items she had requested.

He had sent her home to Naples in style, with a first-class ticket that included her own compartment as far as Rome. "You don't have to worry," he had told her, "Xavier won't come looking for you."

"How can you be sure?"

"Trust me."

"You didn't . . . ?"

"Kill him? No, just scared him a little."

The weasely little Frenchman had bawled like a baby through his broken teeth when Borodin pulled down his trousers and held the stiletto blade to his contracting testicles. He knew the type: cheap hustler, all bark and no bite, good only for preying on the weak.

Sensing that Rosaria wasn't entirely con-vinced, he had handed her some American dollars so she could set herself up elsewhere if it would make her feel safer. In return, he had received the name of the bar in Ravello

313

that belonged to her uncle Gualtiero. He would know where she was should Borodin ever find himself in those parts.

Her last words to him had come from the open window of her compartment as the train pulled away.

"Why are you doing this?"

"Because I like you, Rosaria. Because I can."

It was more than that, though, and at some level he had known it even then. Now, sitting here in the Kronenhalle with a gin fizz in one hand and a cigarette in the other, it was more apparent to him than ever. It had been a test of sorts. He had wished to perform a good deed and see how it sat with him. Rather well, was the answer. One act of kindness could never atone for the many and various sins he had committed over the years. But the mere fact that he was even thinking in such terms suggested that deep inside him some shift had occurred, the first tremors of which he had felt while speaking to Hamilton in the Spanish pavilion.

Those reverberations had caused him to falter and had cost him dearly. He had lost almost everything short of his life. He had been stripped back to a man sitting in a Swiss restaurant with a passport in one pocket, a revolver in the other, and a sizable sum of cash stitched into his jacket lining. However matters played out later, he would not be returning to Andrej's apartment to collect his suitcase. All that he had, he carried with him. *Like a tortoise,* he thought, with a bare wisp of a smile.

It vanished when he saw Petrovic enter the restaurant and address himself to the maître d'. He was wearing a fawn summer jacket and gray flannel trousers. Borodin hadn't remarked on it before, but the peasant boy from Brgud had acquired a sense of style during his time in Paris.

They greeted each other in French, switching to their own tongue once the waiter had taken their drink order and retired.

"He's not joining us?" asked Petrovic, noting that the table was laid for two.

"Not here. Later, maybe."

"Maybe?"

"It depends what's in the case."

Petrovic placed the attaché case on the buttoned leather seat between them and slipped the catches. Borodin fished for a bundle of notes buried beneath others and discreetly flicked through it with his thumb. "If it's not all there, I'll come looking for the rest."

"I know," said Petrovic, "which is why it's all there." He closed the case and tucked it away at his feet.

Borodin could play this any number of ways, and he had lost valuable sleep last night toying with his options. Confronted with Petrovic in the flesh, he instinctively opted for honesty. It would be good, as well as educational, to turn the heat up under him, watch him sweat a bit.

"It's only fair you know: I've had no communication with Hamilton since he left Paris."

"What are you saying?"

"I told him where to be, and when. There's a possibility he won't show."

"That's unacceptable."

Borodin gave a nonchalant shrug. "It was the best I could come up with under the circumstances. You were trying to kill us both at the time, remember?"

"We had a deal," hissed Petrovic.

"Which I intend to honor. I need that money as much as you need Hamilton — well, maybe not quite as much."

"Meaning?"

"Surely you can't be that naive," said Borodin, warming to his plain-talking theme. "You're as good as dead if you don't deliver Hamilton. You may even be as good as dead already for failing to finish the job in Paris. Have you thought about that? Of

316

course you have."

The waiter returned with the bottle of white wine they had ordered. Borodin tasted it and waited till it was poured before continuing.

"You'll get what you want, but maybe not today. I need you to know that, so you don't do anything rash. It would be bad for me but worse for you, because you'll never find him without me."

Petrovic didn't reply immediately. "I understand the situation."

"That's good, because I'm not sure I do." Borodin took a sip of wine. "Look at us, Tibor: two colleagues who've rubbed along happily enough for years, not quite friends but almost, forced by the Karamans to turn against each other. Can you make sense of that?"

"It's just the way it is."

"But not the way it has to be."

Petrovic held him in his steady gaze. "Go on."

"You want to do their bidding for the rest of your life? If you take that case and walk out of here, I won't stop you."

"Run off with it?" Petrovic appeared amused by the notion. "I thought you said you needed the money."

"Not if it allows you a new start."

Petrovic snorted derisively. "You really don't know me, do you?"

"Oh I think I do. I just wanted to be sure exactly what I was dealing with."

Petrovic's face was a frozen mask. "Let's order. And then let's talk about what's going to happen when Hamilton *does* show up."

Chapter Twenty-Seven

Pippi had been gone for almost twenty minutes, and Luke was beginning to feel distinctly uneasy. Hirschenplatz was a stone's throw away. She should have been back by now.

He twisted in his pew as the main door of the church groaned open on dry hinges. An elderly woman, bent with the weight of years, crossed herself with holy water and shuffled off down the nave, toward the altar.

The church had been Pippi's idea. A man sitting alone in a parked car on a hot afternoon was likely to attract attention, and it was possible that Borodin had turned up early thinking to steal a march on them. Pippi had told Luke to stay put and be patient. It was easy enough at first, taking in the austere yet graceful majesty of the interior, before his mind had turned — inevitably, perhaps, given the spiritual nature of his surroundings — to Sister Agnes.

Bowing his head, he had shaped a silent prayer, bypassing her God and speaking directly to her, apologizing for the unwitting part he had played in her death, and appealing to her for help.

The most she had been able to offer him was a memory of the framed needlepoint sampler hanging above the fireplace in her room at the orphanage, with its line from Saint Paul's Letter to the Romans:

We glory in tribulations also: knowing that tribulation worketh patience; and patience, experience; and experience, hope.

Tribulations he had aplenty, but there was no sign yet of the benefits promised by Paul. In fact, his patience was all but used up. Another glance at his wristwatch. Clearly, something had gone wrong. He should have insisted on going in Pippi's place.

Rising to his feet, he made for the end of the pew. He was a few yards shy of the main door when it swung open and Pippi appeared, silhouetted against the sunlight. She was wearing the wide-brimmed sun hat and dark glasses they had bought before leaving Luzern — not much of a disguise, but better than nothing.

"I was getting worried."

"I found a room," she said. "It's perfect."

"I'll get the suitcases."

"No, they should stay in the car. We might have to leave quickly."

A couple without luggage meant only one thing to a hotelier, and Pippi, fearing that she would lose the room, had informed the concierge that she was traveling alone and her bags had been delayed.

"We'll find a way to get you in," she assured Luke.

In size and general appearance, the grandly named Hotel Excelsior was more of a guesthouse really, not that Luke had much opportunity to take in the details as he strolled nonchalantly across the lobby toward the stone staircase. Pippi had entered a minute earlier and now had the concierge bent over their street map, his back to the entrance.

Luke waited nervously on the second-floor landing until she joined him with the key. Number seven was a musty little box of a room, sparsely (and shabbily) furnished. What mattered, though, was the view through the French windows that gave onto their small balcony. Hirschenplatz was laid out beneath them. They had noted earlier when examining the street map that the long, narrow square had seven thorough-fares running in and out, which suggested that Borodin hadn't settled on the venue by chance. He was thinking of his getaway.

Pippi released the gauzy net curtains from their ties so that they could survey while not being observed. She then took the field glasses, also purchased in Luzern, from her bag and handed them to Luke.

Four cafés served the square: one just below them to the left; two side by side, also on the left; and another, drenched in sunlight, at the far end. Café Glück, where Luke was due to meet Borodin in just over an hour, was the farther of the two adjacent cafés. It had a mustard awning and tin tables scattered across the cobbles in front. A steady stream of pedestrians filtered through the square, many of them tourists, judging from the number of cameras hanging from straps around necks.

"I've been thinking. Let me go instead."

Pippi's words caught him off guard. "That's out of the question."

"He won't be expecting it."

"No, and there's no knowing how he'd react."

"It's a public place. What can he do to me?"

"I'd never put you in the line of fire, and that's the end of it."

Borodin insisted on paying for lunch. "Although, of course, it's really the Karamans who are paying," he added wryly. Then his tone shifted. "I need to know it's over between them and me once you have what you want."

"You know I can't promise that."

"Then tell them they had better not miss the first time, or I'll come looking for them."

"I'll pass the message on." Petrovic's smile held a tinge of sneer.

"No one is invulnerable. They know that, even if you don't. So yes, be sure to pass it on."

They had been almost absurdly polite with each other up until now, reminiscing at length about their experiences in Paris, when not addressing more pragmatic concerns, such as the yarn they should spin for Hamilton to win his trust and persuade him to leave with Petrovic. Borodin took it as a given that Petrovic would try to kill him as soon as he had his hands on Hamilton, but there was nothing to gain from broaching the subject. The endgame was almost upon them; the moves and countermoves would begin playing themselves out the moment they left the restaurant.

This had to occur at exactly ten minutes past three, because that was when the taxi arranged by Andrej would be waiting to pick them up out front.

"We have a choice," said Borodin. "It's a short walk to the funicular that climbs to the Waldhaus Dolder Hotel, or we can take a taxi."

"That's where we're meeting him?"

"There's no harm in telling you now. He knows not to show himself if I don't appear."

"You decide," said Petrovic. "It makes no difference to me whether we take the funicular or not." He finished his coffee, then excused himself and made for the toilet, as Borodin suspected he might. The information he had just received was far too valuable to sit on, and he needed to find a way to get it into the hands of his accomplices.

There would be two of them at most — Petrovic had always believed in keeping things simple — and it was safe to assume they had a car. If they happened to be on foot, the second taxi would come into play, picking them up and ensuring that it lost the first in the back streets.

As they stepped from the restaurant, the taxi appeared on cue from the side street where it had been lurking, and headed down the hill toward Pradeplatz. Borodin whistled and waved his walking stick. The driver swung a turn and pulled up in front of them.

"The Waldhaus Dolder Hotel, please."

Borodin made sure he climbed in first and settled down behind the driver, Günther, because that was where he had sat a few hours earlier, with Andrej standing in for Petrovic, when they had adjusted the wing and rearview mirrors so that Borodin would have two views back down the street without having to turn his head. What he saw reflected as the taxi made off was a car pulling up in front of the restaurant, and the driver hurrying out to recover something from the pavement: a note, no doubt, surreptitiously dropped by Petrovic. It was impossible to make out the man's face, but his lightness of foot, so at odds with his stocky physique, rang a familiar and unsettling bell. *Jestin.* Petrovic may have brought only one associate with him, but he had chosen wisely.

The taxi turned right off Rämistrasse into Stadelhoferstrasse, and although there was no sign yet of the tailing car, Borodin began to relax only when he saw Andrej at the wheel of the lorry parked up ahead. As soon as they had passed by, a fleeting look in the rearview mirror afforded a glimpse of the lorry swinging out from the pavement. Andrej was about to perform a series of torturously slow turning maneuvers that would block the street for a good while, allowing them to get clean away.

Günther picked a winding path through the residential streets of Hottingen, climbing the hill toward the hotel.

"Are we being followed?" asked Borodin.

"No, we've lost him," Günther replied.

"Then you can head for the Old Town now."

Petrovic's cold eyes flicked between them, the realization dawning that he had just been outmaneuvered.

"I'm sure Jestin will appreciate the view from the Dolder," said Borodin. "It's really quite spectacular." Petrovic glared at him. "Oh, come now, Tibor, don't look so glum. You'll get what you've come for; I just didn't want any complications." He discreetly pulled the revolver from his pocket. "Which is why I'd be happier if you hand over your weapon. Slowly, please."

The thoughts crashed over Luke like waves. What if Borodin didn't appear? What if he was now dead from the gunshot wound he'd received in Paris? Or maybe the Karamans had found him and dealt with him. Or maybe Borodin never had any intention of keeping the meeting in the first place. There were any number of reasons why today could come and go and Luke would be none the wiser about who he was.

"Stop doing that," said Pippi, on duty at the window, with the field glasses.

"What?"

"Walking around — it's annoying."

"I don't think he's coming. He's dead, I'm sure of it."

Pippi turned. "Well, he looks good for a dead man."

"It's him?"

She handed Luke the field glasses. It was indeed Borodin, and he wasn't alone. The other man was younger, well dressed, with sandy-colored hair. They settled down at one of the tables in front of the café.

"Do you recognize the other man?" said Pippi.

"No."

"Are you sure?"

"I've never seen him before."

"I still think you should let me go."

"Never." He handed her the field glasses and then the Browning. "You can watch my back."

He was reaching for the door handle when she said, "Luke . . ." Her voice had a slight tremor.

He nodded. "Don't worry, I'll be careful."

He was calm almost to the point of numbness as he made his way down the staircase. Borodin knew. Borodin carried the answers in his head. And Borodin was sitting at a table just across the square.

The man was well past him before Wilke realized who it was.

Hamilton. Yes.

He sank a little lower in his chair, peering over the top of his newspaper. The tall Englishman was walking toward the café with a sense of purpose — something between a stroll and a stride. So young Erwin had not been lying to buy himself a bit more time. He had come up with the goods. He might even have earned himself a reprieve.

Wilke reached for the cigarette smoldering in the ashtray and drew on it deeply, satisfyingly. Friedrich had relented, allowing him the honor of pulling the trigger, and was content to observe from a ringside seat. When it was done, they would disappear together in the chaotic aftermath. He knew he would feel cheated by the necessary speed of the thing, so why not sit a while and soak up the anticipation, the pleasure of observing the prey?

Besides, there was nothing to be done immediately. A policeman had drifted into view at the far end of the square: a foot soldier, the lowest of the low, there only to provide directions to disoriented tourists. It was a minor inconvenience; he would move on before long.

Borodin was stirring sugar into his coffee when Hamilton appeared at their table. He looked different. It wasn't just the sunglasses; it was the face beneath them: drawn, gaunt, haunted.

"Hello, Luke. How have you been?"

"Oh, you know, better."

He dropped into a chair and cast a wary look at Petrovic.

"This is Didier, a friend of mine from Belgium."

"He doesn't look Belgian."

"And you don't look English," Petrovic replied.

"I don't know what I am," said Hamilton, catching Borodin's eye on the oblique.

He knew. But how had he worked it out? With Pippi's assistance? It was a pleasing thought.

"What's in the case?" Hamilton demanded.

"Money, from our friend here," Petrovic replied.

"For you?"

"For us," said Petrovic. "We have to hide."

"From whom?"

"I still don't know," said Borodin. "It's more complicated than I thought."

"It's certainly a hell of a lot more complicated than you led me to believe," said Hamilton pointedly, almost aggressively.

"I had my reasons."

"I can't wait to hear them." Hamilton turned to Petrovic. "No offense, Didier, but there are some things I need to clarify before I go skipping off with you."

Petrovic shrugged. "I understand, but I am not your enemy." He offered Hamilton his hand. "I give you my word."

Borodin had to hand it to Petrovic: the line was perfectly pitched — subdued to the point of shyness, heartfelt, utterly convincing. But when he saw their hands come together — the innocent and his executioner — it struck him with the sudden force of a slap what he would do.

He just needed a moment to assimilate the enormity of the decision, to weigh its many consequences.

"Let's get you a drink," he said to Hamilton. "Then I'll explain."

He turned and waved to their solemn-eyed waiter.

Wilke had been this close to Borodin before now, but he had never actually set eyes on him. That night at the lake, he had heard him arrive in the car, heard his voice as the paintings were unloaded, then heard him drive off. He was much as Erwin had described him: still slim for a man his age, and with a full head of silver hair. As for the younger man seated to Hamilton's right, an unnerving stillness about him suggested that he moved in the same shady circles as Borodin.

The purpose of their business with Hamilton was no concern of his. It only mattered that they were here, probably armed, and therefore posed a significant threat. He hadn't warned Friedrich that Hamilton might well not be the only casualty; his brother would have balked at the notion that others unconnected with Stefan's death should also lose their lives.

It had to happen, though, and there was nothing to gain from waiting any longer. The policeman had wandered out of view, and that was good enough.

■ ■ ■

It was almost nothing — a snatch of movement at the very edge of Pippi's vision, down below and to the left. The crisp, efficient manner in which the man sitting at the table in front of the café folded his newspaper was what drew her eye.

His back had been turned to her all along, but as he swiveled in his chair and clicked his fingers to summon the waiter, she caught a brief glimpse of his jawline below the brim of his panama hat.

She felt panic grip her throat. It couldn't be. How was it possible? Kapitän Wilke? She must be imagining it.

She stood still as a statue, her eyes boring into the man, begging for another view of his face. It came as he was settling the bill with the waiter.

Snatching up her handbag and the Browning, she ran for the door.

Luke was puzzled. Borodin had fallen strangely silent since ordering a beer for him from the waiter. He didn't really want a beer, but it would come in a glass, which would serve as a far better weapon than a coffee cup should things turn nasty.

"I'm waiting," he said.

Borodin nodded a couple of times, then turned to Didier. "Tell him."

"Tell him?"

"Yes, tell him the truth. He doesn't trust me. I want him to hear it from you."

Didier shifted uncomfortably in his chair. "I don't understand."

"I'm giving you a choice. Jestin is high on the hill over there, you're alone, and there's a rifle pointed at your head."

What was he talking about? Who the hell was Jestin? And what rifle? Had Luke misunderstood, or did Borodin just turn against the man he had introduced as his friend?

"I don't believe you," said Didier.

Borodin held his coffee cup out over the cobblestones. "All I have to do is drop it, and you're dead." He feinted, as though to let the cup fall from his fingers, and Didier instinctively stretched out a hand.

"You can start by telling him who he is," said Borodin.

At that moment, the waiter swept down on them and deposited a glass of beer in front of Luke. "May I get you anything else, gentlemen?" he asked breezily.

Closing in on the café, Wilke checked his stride to allow the waiter time to move away from their table.

He saw clearly how it would happen. The others first — swift, clinical shots to the heart — then a brief word to Hamilton, loud enough for Friedrich to hear: "This is for Stefan, my nephew." He wanted the Englishman to know why.

"Kapitän Wilke?" came a well-spoken female voice from behind him. "Can that really be you?"

God in heaven! *Now?* Really? What were the odds?

Turning, he realized too late that he had been completely deceived by the warm, familiar lilt in the woman's voice.

"Tell him," said Borodin. "Tell him who he is and why you want him dead."

Before Didier could reply, two loud reports, sharp as whip cracks, echoed around the square, scattering the pigeons from the rooftops. Had a car backfired? Heads turned, searching for the source. A woman screamed, recoiling, pointing . . . at Pippi.

A man lay prone on the cobbles at her feet, and the Browning was in her hand. Luke saw the look of blank panic in her face. He also saw the policeman who had been strolling around earlier come hurrying into the square.

"Go!" Luke yelled to her. "Run!"

The words were barely out of his mouth when Borodin came suddenly to life, bringing the walking stick down on Didier's forearm. The Belgian yelped, and the small pistol he had drawn from behind his back fell from his fingers to the cobblestones. He let out another cry when Borodin dealt him two more vicious blows across the face with the cane. Didier blocked the third, seizing the end of the stick.

The triumphal look in his eye was short-lived. With a twist of his hand, Borodin withdrew the long steel blade concealed within the shaft of the cane and, in almost the same movement, thrust it at Didier's chest. Didier twisted desperately away, and the point passed clean through the muscle in his shoulder. He let out a strangled cry.

"The gun," said Borodin.

The last thing Luke saw before he lunged for the pistol on the ground was the blood glistening on the steel blade as Borodin yanked it free. The first thing he saw as his head reappeared above the tabletop was Didier fleeing, stumbling off.

Borodin rose to his feet, pulled a revolver from his pocket and took careful aim. Unable to draw a clean bead through the scattering crowd, he turned suddenly to Luke.

"If you want to live, he must die." He thrust the revolver at him. "Do it."

It was little wonder that he hesitated: a man he didn't trust, ordering him to kill a man he didn't know.

"You must," said Borodin.

The policeman was dashing toward them, his hand fumbling with the leather holster at his hip. He shouted something. The words meant nothing to Luke, but they did to Borodin, who spun around suddenly.

At a table near the café entrance, a tall man was on his feet. There was an uncertain, almost fearful look in his eyes, but the gun in his hand was pointing directly at Luke.

Borodin lunged to the left, into the line of fire, and the shot sent him staggering back into Luke's arms. Luke was dimly aware of the sword cane clattering onto the cobbles, and of the revolver in his hand, which he would never be able to aim and fire in time before the man finished the job.

A shot rang out, fired at almost point-blank range into the back of the man's head by someone hurrying from the café. The man crumpled and pitched forward, blood jetting grotesquely from the base of his skull. A summary execution, and the person responsible hadn't even broken stride in the process. Luke looked up to see him hastening away. His back was turned and the brim of his hat was pulled down over his eyes, but there was something about his bulky frame that spoke to Luke. It might have remained no more than a suspicion if the man hadn't flung a quick glance over his shoulder as he ducked into an alleyway.

It was the big American he had met on the train from Strasbourg to Konstanz. Cordell Oaks, the dairy-industry bore.

There was no time to dwell on this. Borodin was bleeding from his chest and reaching for a chair, and the policeman was almost on them, his weapon now out. Luke made a show of laying the revolver aside on a table and raising his hand in a gesture of surrender. The German words didn't come to him, so he said in English, "Don't shoot."

The policeman showed no interest in shooting. In fact, he seemed barely interested in them at all. Sweeping his pistol over the few other customers still cowering beneath their tables, he made straight for the dead man sprawled facedown near the café entrance, and picked up the pistol beside his outstretched hand.

Luke was struck with a sudden sense that finally the story would come out, now that the authorities were involved. There would be no more running scared from an un-known enemy.

"He is with me," said Borodin. "A friend."

The bullet had struck Borodin high in the chest on his left side, and a crimson stain was already spreading across his white shirt. The policeman hurried over and examined the wound, talking away in a tongue un-known to Luke. Borodin snapped a short-tempered reply, then turned to Luke. "Do you have a motorcar?"

"There, by the church." The white facade could be seen at the end of the short street across from the café.

"Get the case," Borodin ordered. "And my stick."

The policeman called to the timorous faces peering out the café windows: "This man needs to go to the hospital. Call police headquarters and tell them what has hap-pened."

Together they helped Borodin across the square.

"Who is the man Pippi shot?" Borodin asked.

"I don't know," Luke replied. The body lay only a few yards from them, but the face was turned away.

"And the man who shot me?"

"I don't know."

"What *do* you know?"

"I know that bullet was meant for me."

Borodin gave an amused grunt. "Don't worry, there will be others."

Pippi was at the wheel of the Citroën. A look of wild relief broke across her face when she spotted them approaching. She sprang from the car and pulled open the rear door.

"Hello, Pippi," said Borodin. "This is a friend of mine, Andrej."

Luke tossed the attaché case and the sword cane onto the passenger seat, then snatched the key from the ignition. "I'll get something for the bleeding." He hurried to the boot and unlocked it. Pippi joined him as he was ferreting for a shirt in his suitcase.

"Did you see?" she said. "It was Wilke."

"*Wilke?* How?"

She shook her head. "I heard the shots. I thought . . ."

Despite everything they'd been through together, it was the first time he had seen her properly shaken.

"He saved my life — again. I'll explain later. We have to go." He slammed the boot shut and handed her the keys. "You drive."

He dropped into the backseat beside Borodin, and was using his teeth to tear the shirt in two when the Citroën lurched away with a squeal of rubber on cobblestones.

"Where are we going?" Pippi asked in German.

"Where did you park the lorry?" said Borodin.

"We need to get you seen to first," Andrej replied.

"Just show her the way."

"Turn right at that junction," said Andrej, pointing.

Luke worked half of the shirt into a tight ball, pressed it to the wound in Borodin's chest, and held it there. "The man Pippi shot is a captain with the German Abwehr. I'm guessing the man who shot you was with him."

"The Abwehr?" groaned Andrej. "You didn't tell me the Abwehr were mixed up in this!"

"Because I didn't know," Borodin replied calmly.

"He was the one who stole the paintings you delivered to us," said Pippi. "The one who killed Johan."

"What paintings?" Andrej demanded. "And who is Johan?"

"Put it from your mind," said Borodin. "It's another matter altogether — a piece of bad luck, bad timing, that's all."

Andrej wasn't to be silenced, though, and

switched from German to another tongue.

"I knew it. You changed your mind, didn't you, you old fool?"

Borodin smiled weakly. "When it came to it, sending a lamb to the slaughter . . ."

"Well I hope the lamb is worth it."

"Oh, I think he is. And look at them. They make a fine couple, don't you think?"

"What, I risked my life for a piece of matchmaking by a crazy old Croat?"

"And for the large sum of money I left in the bottom drawer of your desk. It's enough to give you and Frieda a good start somewhere else, although I don't think it will be necessary. You're unrecognizable in that uniform, especially with the mustache. Even I wasn't sure it was you, at first."

"I don't want your money."

"Think of it as a wedding present."

"What?"

"She's a fine woman, Andrej. You should ask her to marry you before she realizes how much better she could do for herself."

Andrej smiled, but there was a touch of sadness in his eyes. "I've heard of a doctor out near Regensdorf. He's very discreet."

"Wrong direction. And no time. I have to get them over the border, out of the country." He reached out and squeezed Andrej's

hand. "My jacket pocket, the left one —
there's a letter. Take it. Wait a few days; then
post it for me."

By the time they pulled up beside the lorry,
Andrej had shed most of his police uniform,
revealing another layer of clothes beneath.
He forced his feet back into the long leather
boots and pushed the hems of his twill
trousers down over them. He peeled off the
two halves of his mustache, which Luke had
never once suspected of being false. He then
wished them well in German, shook
Borodin's hand, and clambered out of the
car.

"Where to now?" asked Pippi.

"South." Borodin pointed. "That way."

CHAPTER TWENTY-EIGHT

They drove in silence, alert and watchful, Borodin issuing directions to Pippi as necessary. They began to relax only when the outskirts of the city fell away and they found themselves in open countryside. It helped that the pressure on the wound was beginning to take effect. The hole in Borodin's chest was no longer leaking blood as it had been before.

Luke was steeling himself to ask the question that only the wounded man beside him could answer, when Borodin said, "Tell me everything that has happened since Paris. Every detail. It's important."

"You first," said Luke. "Who am I?"

Borodin fell silent for a moment, as if deciding whether to reply. "Your name is Vincenzo Albrizzi."

Hearing his true name spoken for the first time sent a tremor through him.

"I'm Italian?"

"Half of you. The other half is Dalmatian — from the coast of Croatia, like me."

"How did I end up in an orphanage in England?" The need to know and to know quickly had become an almost physical discomfort.

"It means nothing if I can't find a way to keep you alive. For that, I need to know everything that happened since Paris."

"Later," said Luke.

Pippi took her eyes off the road and fired a sharp look at Borodin. "Tell him," she ordered.

"I'm trying to think of a way to do that," Borodin replied.

"The beginning is as good a place as any to start," said Luke.

It was a glib statement, but it seemed to capture Borodin's imagination. "The beginning. Yes. Why not?" He paused. "It started before you were born. It started with a rock."

"A rock?"

"I don't know who threw it. Someone said it was Bartol Nicolic, but he denied it. I know this, though. If that rock had not hit your grandmother, everything would be different."

"Go on," said Luke.

It brought to mind the many times he had

sat in his father's study as a boy, listening to tales of adventure and derring-do. But this was *his* story, the story of his family, the Albrizzis, Venetians by origin, who had made the Dalmatian port of Spalato the base for their shipping business. Borodin sketched out some basic history of Dalmatia, in particular the building tensions between the Italian minority and the Croat majority in the years before the Great War of 1914.

"It was the key to everything that happened with the Karaman brothers."

"Tell me about my family, my parents. I don't want to know about the Karaman brothers."

"You should, because they are the ones who had you kidnapped. And they are the ones trying to kill you now. They are the people I work for."

"Kidnapped . . ."

It was one of the wilder theories he had flirted with during those early years of tormented speculation. Could it really be true?

"In Venice," said Borodin. "When you were a baby."

"Why?"

"I was getting to that when you interrupted me."

"Sorry," said Luke. "Tell me about the

Karaman brothers."

"No, you're right, they can wait," said Borodin. "Your father's name was Alessandro. There was a younger brother. I don't remember his name. Their father, your grandfather Vittorio — he ran the business, Albrizzi Marittima. A good business. They lived in one of the biggest houses in Spalato."

"And my mother?" Luke asked tentatively.

"Marta. Marta Urlic. Her father owned the shop where your father bought his books. He was a student then."

"Did you know her?"

"Everyone knew Marta Urlic. She was beautiful."

"Was?"

Borodin hesitated. "Maybe she still is; I don't know. It was a long time ago. You have her eyes . . . and something in the mouth."

Marta Urlic and Alessandro Albrizzi, parents to Vincenzo. This was his reality, and it felt like a dream.

"I never spoke to her, but I saw her many times with your father, walking together in town, at cafés, restaurants. Her father was not happy with the relationship. Many people were not happy. Maybe it played a part in what happened." Borodin lingered on this thought for a moment. "No, like

346

most things, it was about money and power."

It was also about an unfortunate incident that had seen the Albrizzi family drawn into the violence taking hold in Dalmatia: a big brawl down at the port between some of their Italian dock workers and a gang of Croats. Borodin hadn't been present, but the following night he had helped raise the angry mob that marched on the Albrizzis' home — a mob fired up by the Karaman brothers, small-time smugglers looking to make their mark.

Luke's grandfather had met the unruly crowd at the gates of the house and made a heartfelt appeal for calm, for cool heads, for unity.

"He had us," said Borodin. "We were silent, all of us. Then someone threw the rock."

It struck Luke's grandmother square in the face, bringing her down. Two men burst from the house and rushed to help — company men, guards from the Albrizzi warehouses, brought in for protection. At the sight of their uniforms, the beast that had been soothed with words came back to life with a sudden, snarling vengeance. The air rang with curses, and the iron gates strained against the crush. Someone called for the gates to be lifted off their hinges, and backs bent to the task.

Vittorio was making for the house, his wife in his arms, when the gates came free and crashed onto the gravel driveway. As the mob surged forward, one of the guards drew his pistol and fired. There was panic and pandemonium. Everyone scattered, vanishing into the night — all but one young man. He died later that night of the bullet wound to his neck. The guard who had fired the shot was arrested and charged with murder.

Vittorio saw that he got the very best legal defense. During the trial, witnesses were called on both sides, although the Karamans did not take the stand, having distanced themselves completely from the affair. It was later said that what swung the day were the gruesome photographs that Luke's grandmother had insisted be taken of her broken face before the surgeons and dentists went to work.

Vittorio was the only Albrizzi in court when the judge delivered his verdict of justifiable homicide on the grounds of self-defense. It wasn't known at the time, but all the other members of the family had left the country the night before on a ship bound for Venice — the last ship in the company fleet to steam away from Spalato.

Marta, Luke's mother, went with them, as did some of the household staff and a number of company employees. Albrizzi Marittima had ceased to exist in Dalmatia. The wharves and warehouses stood empty, as did the family home.

The secret exodus had been meticulously planned. It only remained for Vittorio and the guard to be driven directly from the courthouse to an airfield on the edge of town, where a plane waited to fly them to Venice.

"I don't understand," said Luke. "Why me if I wasn't even born then? Why the Karamans?"

"The boy who died that night, Toma Soric — he was a nephew of a cousin of the Karamans, or something like that, I forget." Not a close relative, but family nonetheless. And in Croatia, when it came to family, you never forgave and you never forgot.

"Retribution?" asked Luke. "An eye for an eye?"

"Yes."

"So why am I alive?"

"Because a man called Gotal could not kill a baby."

Pippi had remained silent until now. "Who could?"

"A man like Gotal," Borodin replied. "He

had a reputation. They thought he would do it, but they were wrong. He took you in the street in Venice and he carried you far away, maybe as far as he could think, and left you there."

Gotal . . . the man standing in the shadows of the orphanage driveway, ankle deep in snow, waiting for the small package he had deposited on the front steps to be discovered. Only now did the scene that Luke had forced Sister Agnes to describe to him over and over during those early years make full and proper sense. Not his father, not a distraught husband who had lost his wife in childbirth, or any of the other theories distilled in the superheated retort of his juvenile imagination. No, just a bad man who had done a good thing.

"He only made one mistake," said Borodin. Having sat on his secret for so many years, Gotal unburdened himself to the priest who took his final confession. The priest then ran directly to the Karamans with the information.

So that was what it boiled down to: a case of unfinished business brought to the Karamans' attention by a snake of a priest. The picture was almost complete, and none too soon. Borodin was weakening, drawing breaths in ever shallower drafts as he laid bare his own role in the affair. He had known nothing of the Karamans' involvement in Luke's abduction, of Gotal's change of heart, of the priest's deceit, or even of Luke's real identity — not at the beginning. He had simply been tasked with taking the life of an Englishman who worked at the Paris embassy — straightforward enough until he first set eyes on Luke and saw in his face dim echoes of long ago.

It was chilling to hear just how close he had come to completing his mission. The night before their encounter at the Spanish pavilion, he had followed Luke home through the darkened streets and been within seconds of dispatching him, before curiosity stayed his hand. Unbeknownst to Borodin, though, suspicions were growing about how long he was taking to finish the job.

"I followed you to the Spanish pavilion, and two people followed me. They saw us talk. That was enough for Petrovic."

"Who is Petrovic?"

"The head of the Paris operation. You just met him. Didier." Borodin hesitated before adding, "That's right. I came to Zurich to sell you back to them."

"But you didn't."

"No."

"Thank you," said Luke.

"You think I have done you a favor? All I have done is open the gates of hell. They will come for you, as they did for me."

He described the attempt on his life at his apartment, and how he had extracted Luke's whereabouts from the female assassin. Ironically, his only hope of survival lay in keeping alive the man he was assigned to kill. That was why he had hurried to the restaurant and intervened. That was why he had then dispatched Luke to Konstanz, to Pippi, because no one would think of searching for him there. With Luke safely beyond their reach, the Karamans would be obliged to negotiate.

"Which way now?" asked Pippi.

The wide river valley they had been traveling along for the past half hour narrowed suddenly and bifurcated in front of them, mountains rising on all sides.

Borodin pointed. "There, left."

The road sign read: CAZIS, THUSIS, ANDEER. Below it was another panel: ITALIEN.

"Italy?" said Luke.

"First a doctor for me, then Venice for you."

Borodin knew of a small pass through the mountains, open only in summer. It would be the safest place for them to cross into

Italy. With luck, the tiny border post might even be unmanned.

He let out a low groan and closed his eyes. Luke caught Pippi's concerned look in the rearview mirror.

"Why did you change your mind in Zurich?"

"You think I am not asking myself the same thing? Three times in my life I have been shot, and twice you were there." Borodin opened his eyes and smiled weakly. "No, you are not good for my health, Vincenzo Albrizzi." He coughed, and from his chest came a liquid rattle, faint but unmistakable.

"We need to get you to a doctor now, before Italy."

"You want to be arrested by the police? They can't protect you from the Karamans. Only your family can, only the Albrizzis. No, we keep moving, and you tell me everything that happened in Konstanz."

They left the twisting valley road and struck out into the mountains proper at Splügen, a picturesque jumble of wood- and stone-built houses straddling a milky torrent. They crossed the bridge and wound their way up the steep green pasture south of the village, toward the dense belt of pines. The gradient didn't ease as they entered the tree line, and the Citroën strained its way through the snake of hairpin switchbacks. The road finally began to level out, and the gloomy world of the pines gave way to a tortured, harsh, and rocky landscape.

"The border is close," said Borodin. "We need to prepare."

He pointed out a track up ahead. There was no saying where it led, not until they had cleared a steep and stony rise and saw that it petered out at a wooden chalet. Low, lopsided, and grayed with age, it backed onto a clump of pines. The shutters were closed, and there was no sign of life except for a big hawk perched on the rickety rail fence that enclosed the property. It flapped off lazily into the blue as the Citroën drew to a halt.

Borodin eased himself from the backseat and took in the view, savoring it. "Yes, this is good."

The rooftops of Splügen were just visible far below, and on the other side of the valley a mountain peak capped with summer snow seemed to tower over them, even at such a distance.

Borodin set off up the grassy rise toward the chalet. Pippi laid a hand on Luke's arm, holding him back.

"So now you know the truth."

"Do I?" he replied.

"You don't believe him?"

He hadn't meant it that way, and he struggled to find the right words. He had lived so long with the not-knowing that it had become an elemental part of him. He felt like a prisoner released from a long stint behind bars: happy to have been given his freedom, but ill-equipped to deal with it. "It's a lot to take in."

"You will," said Pippi. Her eyes flicked toward Borodin. "He's dying."

"Don't write him off yet. He's a tough old bugger."

By the time they joined Borodin, he had installed himself on a crude wooden bench beside the front door and was shrugging off his jacket. He peered inside his blood-soaked shirt with an air of mild curiosity.

"Do you have another shirt? A dark color would be good."

"I have a navy-blue one."

Borodin asked Pippi to fetch it from the car. As soon as she was out of earshot, he said, "She is strong, but she is not a killer. What she did today . . ." He trailed off briefly. "There will be a reaction."

"I'll be ready for it."

"Good, because you are all she has now."

"I know."

Borodin gripped his forearm and said with a sudden intensity, "You understand, don't you? There is only one way this will end, and you cannot do it alone."

"Then it's a good job I've got the two of you."

"No, I am staying, and Pippi is not enough. The Karamans must die. Your family is rich, powerful. They can help. You must persuade them who you are, and that won't be easy."

"What do you mean, you're staying? Staying where?"

Borodin spread his hands. "Here. I like this place."

"You need a doctor."

"I need a doctor we can trust." There was no guarantee that an Italian doctor wouldn't denounce them to the police. More crucially, though, if the Swiss border guards had been alerted about the incident in Zurich, they would be searching for a wounded man. "You are a young couple on holiday. You stayed last night in Luzern, and tonight you stay in Chiavenna."

Borodin refused to be swayed, even when Pippi reappeared and heard of his decision. At a certain point, he grew angry at their efforts to get him to reconsider. "Enough," he snapped. "I have helped you; now I am a danger to you. I know of these things; you don't, so stop talking and listen."

He spelled out their predicament with a grim succinctness. The Karamans would have assumed by now that he had revealed all to Luke, which meant Petrovic would be waiting for them in Venice. When they got there, they were to stay small, in the shadows. "You must think and you must be clever and you must trust no one."

He suggested that they drive as far as Bergamo, where they should abandon the car and take the train, though not all the way. They were to get off at Venice Mestre, the last stop on the mainland, and take a private water taxi across the lagoon to the island. Money was not a problem: the attaché case contained a small fortune. "There is also this."

He yanked at the lining of his jacket until the stitching along the hem gave way. Slim bundles of currency spilled out. He held a few back. "I have plans, too," he said.

Petrovic would have a lot of resources at his disposal, and they were to spend the money freely in order to stay ahead of him. "I know Petrovic. He will not stop until you are dead. You must kill him first." Unfortunately, Borodin's only contact in Venice had died some years ago, so there was nothing he could offer them in the way of assistance. They would have to finish the thing themselves, and it had to happen in Venice. On this he was firm. If Petrovic managed to slip away, he would be back, and Luke would know nothing of it until it was too late. "If you see him, you must kill him: no thought, no hesitation. Can you do that?"

"I'm not sure."

"Then maybe this will help," said Borodin. "Petrovic was in England. I learned it after you left Paris."

Luke frowned. "I don't understand."

"He told me it was not easy to find the orphanage. That's all he told me, all I know."

The warm breeze blowing in from the west seemed to take a sudden dip in temperature. "Sister Agnes . . ."

"Think of it," said Borodin. "Use it. Now, wash your hands; then go and find your family."

Luke glanced at his palms, stained with Borodin's blood. He headed for the stone trough nearby. The water was clear as glass and pleasantly warm after a day beneath a cloudless sky. Dusk was drawing in, the lowering sun giving ground to great slabs of shadow that crept down the mountainsides into the valleys. He looked over to see Pippi helping Borodin into the shirt. It was a touching sight. He sat slumped on the bench and she knelt before him doing up the buttons, like a mother preparing her young son for school. No place was a good place to die, but there were many worse places to draw one's last breath than here in the wild heights, far above the world, halfway to the waiting gods.

Borodin insisted on accompanying them to the car. He wished to look over the vehicle one last time, to make sure any last smudges of his blood were wiped away and that the money was well hidden beneath the backseat.

"When this is over, there is a favor you can do for me. I have a daughter, Simona. She hates me for many reasons, all of them good. I have not seen her since she was a child. I have never seen her son. They live on the island of Vis, a town called Komiza. She is married to a fisherman called Lasic. Can you remember that?"

"Viz. Komiza. Simona Lasic," said Pippi.

"The money you do not use, give to her, to them."

"When this is over, you can give it to her yourself," said Luke.

Borodin smiled weakly. "She won't take it from me. She probably won't take it from you, but you can try."

He planted a kiss on Pippi's cheek, then turned and shook Luke's hand.

"I don't how to thank you."

"I do," said Borodin. "Stay alive. Finish it." He released Luke's hand. "You should know, your family paid good money to get you back when you were taken."

"A ransom?"

"Yes, a ransom. For the Karamans, everything is a way to get rich — even revenge."

Luke struggled to see what he was driving at. "What are you saying?"

"I know what he's saying," said Pippi.

"It is good that one of you has a brain," Borodin said with a gleam of ironic mockery. "Now, go. And no more faces like that when you get to the border. Remember, you are on holiday; you are happy; you are in love."

At Pippi's suggestion, Luke drove: a woman behind the wheel was more likely to draw the eye of an overzealous border guard. There was a knock on the roof as they were pulling away, and Luke braked.

Borodin's face appeared at the driver's window.

"One more thing. Have you seen *Les Bas-Fonds*?"

"The film?"

"With Jean Gabin."

"Yes." He had taken Diana to see it at the Parisiana on Boulevard Poissonière.

"What happens to Pépel at the end? Does he die?"

"No, he goes to prison."

"Oh."

"But the girl is waiting for him when he gets out."

"Natascha."

"I don't remember her name."

"Natascha. She waited for him. That's good."

The last Luke saw of Borodin was a juddering reflection in the rearview mirror as the rutted track dipped over a brow. He was leaning awkwardly on his sword cane, his other hand held high in a gesture of farewell, and even in the radiance of the sinking sun he looked pale as ashes.

Luke glanced over at Pippi. He could tell she was teetering on the edge of tears.

"I think I know what he meant. If the Karamans are so keen to make everything pay, are they really doing this just for the principle of the thing, to finish the job?"

"Yes," she replied quietly. "That is what he meant."

CHAPTER TWENTY-NINE

Borodin eased the tip of the knife between the shutters and slipped the metal latch. The window proved to be more problematic, and he was obliged to break a pane of glass with his elbow before he could gain entry to the chalet.

Standing in the close mustiness of the darkened interior, it struck him that his life had come full circle. Here he was again, back where he had started as a sixteen-year-old runaway, breaking into houses.

There was nothing to eat in the kitchen, not even a tin of soup, although he did find a dusty bottle of schnapps in a cupboard. The liquor burned a path from the tip of his tongue to his stomach, and when he dribbled some of it on the wound, the pain was so great that his eyes watered and he cried out.

He lit a kerosene lamp, wandered through to the living room, and dropped into an armchair. He had no illusions about the severity of the wound. Everything was still functioning, but with less force, like a mantel clock in need of a wind.

He took another slug of schnapps and let his head roll back. He stared at the ceiling, at the intricate rib cage of rough-hewn beams and rafters supporting the planked roof. And when he closed his eyes, he saw a different structure, a pattern that had underpinned his actions over the past week and brought him inexorably to this place.

Why had he sent Luke south to Konstanz, to Pippi, when he could just as easily have sent him north to Garstman in Antwerp, or even to Lucille in Nantes? Both were unknown to the organization, and both would willingly have given the young Englishman safe refuge while the deal was struck with Petrovic. So why hadn't he even considered them as alternatives?

Because Konstanz and Zurich were stepping-stones to Italy, to Venice. From the moment things had turned violent in Paris — even before, at the Spanish pavilion — he was never going to trade away Luke's life. He was always going to steer him home to his family.

Why was it only now so blindingly clear to him? Did he hold himself in such low regard that the notion that he might be capable of an act of charity was too absurd even to consider? Quite possibly. Then again, maybe he was deluding himself, sensing the end and casting about for evidence of his humanity — anything to salve his soul as he shuffled toward oblivion.

He took another sip of schnapps, flattening it against his palate and inhaling the heady vapors.

No, he wasn't the type to seek some kind of private absolution. The explanation was far simpler. He had changed — a little late in life, admittedly, but it had happened. France had infected him, seduced him by slow degrees, getting beneath his skin, teaching him to look at the world and his place in it quite differently. Ten years ago, he wouldn't have hesitated. He would have done the deed regardless of any suspicions he might have about Luke's real identity.

He was glad his curiosity had gotten the better of him, for what a story it had turned out to be: a man with a history of unthinking violence sparing the life of an infant boy, who had ticked off the years in happy ignorance of his good fortune until death came visiting once more.

To have ended the thing there, betraying Gotal's uncharacteristic display of mercy, would have been like rescuing a castaway and then beating him to death for his coral necklace. It was unconscionable. No, the underdog deserved a helping hand, a chance to rewrite the final chapter.

Luke and Pippi were smart, determined, impressively calm in a crisis, but the odds were stacked high against them. He put their chances at poor to middling. Luke's disappointment at what awaited him in Venice wouldn't help matters. Should he have warned him, prepared him? He had wanted to, coming close during the drive from Zurich, and again just now, while Pippi was rummaging for the shirt in the back of the car. He hadn't been able to find the words, though.

Another slug of schnapps; another twist of the key in the clock.

He knew that if he didn't move soon, this was where they would find him: slouched in the armchair. It took a superhuman effort to force himself up and out of it.

He had to get to a phone, or at least try. It could make all the difference in the youngsters' prospects.

■ ■ ■ ■

ITALY

■ ■ ■ ■

CHAPTER THIRTY

If Pippi had had her way, they would have driven through the night, deep into Italy, leaving the frontier far behind them, and only a lack of fuel kept them from it.

Concealing their anxiety behind Cheshire-cat grins, they had passed through the border controls without too much difficulty. If anything, the Italians had been more thorough than the Swiss, demanding to know their itinerary and even poking around in the boot of the car before raising the barrier and waving them through.

There had been little in the way of celebration. They had cleared another hurdle but lost an ally in the process. No, more than an ally — the man who had brought them together, the man who had handed Luke back his life. They made the descent down the long valley below the pass in almost total silence, each alone with their thoughts, the darkness deepening around them until, by the time they reached Chiavenna, all that remained of the day was a low smear of light in the west. Borodin had suggested they spend the night in the town, but Pippi was all for pushing on, and she was clearly in no mood to discuss it further.

That had been an hour ago, the last twenty minutes of which they spent winding their way along the shore of Lake Como, jammed in between the water's edge and the sharply rising hills. With the fuel gauge needle now well into the red, Luke finally said, "If we don't stop soon, we're going to find ourselves stranded in the middle of nowhere."

"Okay," Pippi conceded. "The next town."

It was called Bellano, as was the stately old hotel, swathed in Virginia creeper, that they found down near the small port. The proprietor's wife, a woman with a no-nonsense manner, perked right up when they opted for the most expensive room available. They had just missed the last orders for dinner, but if they could be back downstairs within ten minutes, there was every chance she could persuade the chef to throw something together for them. She requested their passports for registration, then sent them upstairs with a key.

It wasn't Luke's first-ever meal in Italy —

that, presumably, had been at his mother's breast — but it felt as though it was. The veal escalope in a tuna and caper sauce threatened an unfortunate collision of tastes but turned out to be a revelation. Pippi hailed it as the best *vitello tonnato* she'd ever had — a verdict based on several trips she had made to Italy with her family over the years. They had never seen Venice, though.

"I bet you can't wait," said Luke.

Pippi had grown worryingly withdrawn over the past couple of hours, and it was good to see her smile.

"Oh, yes, Venice never disappoints. Everyone says it." She reached across the table and squeezed his hand. "I'm sorry, I do this sometimes — disappear. Johan hated it."

"Take your time. I'm not going anywhere."

"Yes you are. You're going to the car to get the gun."

"Are you sure that's necessary?"

"Borodin told me we had to have a gun with us always."

He recalled the two of them talking away intently in front of the chalet while he washed his hands in the trough. "What else did he say?"

"I'll tell you one day," came her enigmatic reply.

When Luke returned with the Browning

371

to their room upstairs, Pippi was in the bathroom, and her clothes lay neatly folded on the small divan between the French windows. The double bed, he noted, was easily large enough to accommodate them both without any awkwardness. He slid the gun beneath the mattress and wandered out onto the balcony for a cigarette.

A sickle moon cast a silver trail across the lake toward him. *This way,* it seemed to say, but it was the wrong way: westward, whereas Venice lay far behind him to the east. A tinkle of laughter drifted up from a nearby bar, bringing with it a stab of sadness. He didn't begrudge them their merriment, though he wondered whether he would ever again be able to give himself over to such unbridled jollity.

The gates of hell.

Borodin's words had struck him as melodramatic at the time, but some hard truths were buried away in them. The people set on his destruction could not be reasoned with or bought off. They were also more numerous and more experienced in such matters than he. If he was ever to be safe again, he must not only meet them on their own ground, he had to match them and then kill them — all of them. His time in the Northern Territory had taught him to think in terms of risks and probabilities. When you flew a sortie, you existed in a constant state of reckoning, weighing the factors in your favor and those against, and something told him that this particular mission held out little hope of success.

He wasn't aware of Pippi until she materialized beside him, barefoot in the cream satin nightgown she had bought in Bern.

He tilted his head at the view. "Another night, another European lake."

It was hard to believe that this time yesterday they had been overlooking the dark waters of Lake Luzern. So much had happened in the meantime; so much had changed.

"Tomorrow, the sea," she said.

She shivered in the chill night air, then plucked the cigarette from between his fingers and raised it to her lips.

"Pippi, listen, I have to go on; I don't have a choice. But you do. I know someone in Paris who can help you get far away from all this, out of Europe."

It wasn't the first time he had thought of Fernando since seeing his friend knocked unconscious by the would-be assassin in L'Hirondelle.

"You don't speak Italian," she pointed out.

"I'll get by."

"You don't want my help?"

He hesitated before replying. "I've got a bad feeling, Pippi."

"Ignore it. You have to believe. Only if you believe . . ." She trailed off. "I'm staying." She handed him back the cigarette and headed inside.

He wasn't ready for bed yet, so he ran himself a bath. Sister Agnes had always warned him that going to bed with wet hair was a sure way to a sore throat, but he let his head slide beneath the surface anyway. For a moment, it felt like a baptism, a rebirth. Vincenzo Albrizzi, the stolen boy. Did he have brothers and sisters? Would his parents know him by sight, as Borodin had? What was his grandfather's name? Vittorio? Yes. Was he still alive? And his grandmother? And what of the rest of his family — uncles, aunts, cousins? The answers lay not even a day's travel away.

When he emerged from the bathroom, he found Pippi buried beneath the covers on her side of the bed. He wound his wristwatch, turned off the bedside lamp, and slipped between the sheets. He assumed at first that she was already asleep, but it soon became clear that the deep, regular breathing was that of a person fighting back tears.

"Do you want to talk about it?"

"No," she replied. "Just hold me."

She was lying on her side, facing away from him, and when he draped an arm around her, she gripped his hand and pressed it to her midriff. They lay there in the darkness, their heads cradled by the same pillow.

"I thought I'd feel better," she said. "But I don't."

"You took a man's life. You're not supposed to feel better, never mind whatever he did to Johan."

She lay in silence a while before saying, "He was going to kill you."

"I know."

"Maybe that's why I feel bad. I didn't do it for Johan; I did it for you."

"Feel bad for Johan if you must, but not for me. I'm still breathing because of you."

She had saved his life, there was little doubt about that. Kapitän Wilke could have been there for only one reason, and there was only one way he could have known where to find them. Erwin must have told him. Erwin must have listened in on their conversation in the barn, for that was the only time Luke had mentioned Café Glück to Pippi.

Borodin was the one who had led them to this deduction while quizzing them in the car, concluding also that the tall man who had put a bullet in him had to be an accomplice of Wilke, because it simply wasn't possible that he was one of Petrovic's people. As for the person who had then dispatched that man before he could fire again, Borodin couldn't say. He had been reeling backward at the time, falling. He had heard a single shot and assumed it was Andrej who had fired.

Luke had let the matter lie, making no mention of Cordell Oaks. Now he was beginning to wonder whether his mind was playing tricks on him. What had he really seen? A gun? No, just a blur of movement, a faceless figure raising his arm as he hurried from the café. And when he had looked again a few seconds later, it was to glimpse the back of a bulky man turning into an alleyway. At the time, his brain had told him it was Cordell Oaks, but now he wasn't so sure. What earthly explanation could there be for a kind but rather dull American he'd met on a train popping up out of nowhere to save his bacon?

Whatever the truth of it, death had come for him twice in Hirschenplatz, and twice he had cheated it by the skin of his teeth. He thought about that, and he thought about the prayer he had made to Sister

376

Agnes in the church an hour before, asking
for her help and protection.

CHAPTER THIRTY-ONE

There wasn't much about the creeping curse of old age that Vittorio didn't accept with equanimity: the stiffening of the joints and sinews, the loose skin and the sagging flesh, the unreliable memory, flatulence, and fading eyesight.

What he did begrudge, though, was the loss of a solid lump of sweet, deep sleep every night. There were times when he wondered whether he'd slept at all, or simply blanked out momentarily. He had come to think of it as his body's way of telling him that time was short and he really couldn't afford to spend too many of the precious hours remaining to him dead to the world, since before long he would be, for good.

This was the reason he no longer tossed and twisted in his bed, waiting impatiently for the first sounds of the household stirring below him, choosing instead to rise and dress and creep down the staircase from his apartment on the top floor of the palazzo, past two generations of his progeny. From late November to late February, he went out into the world on foot, picking his way through the muffled, fog-shrouded thoroughfares of the city. For the rest of the year, weather permitting, he took the boat out — not Benedetto's fancy Riva (heaven forbid) or even the long, low launch he had shipped back from Spalato all those years ago, but the clinker-built skiff with the skinny Evinrude outboard, which the staff used for running simple errands.

So much of his life was prescribed — everything from board meetings to fund-raising dinners for some festival or other — that he had learned to treasure his dawn jaunts as a welcome escape from the demands of his position. Elena had once described him as a "sociable loner," and there was a good deal of truth in her observation. While he delighted in the company of his friends (and even some of his enemies), he had always had a solitary streak.

In keeping with the humble skiff, he always dressed modestly for these solitary excursions. Today he opted for baggy khaki shorts, espadrilles, a white shirt, and his old cotton fishing hat, frayed at the edges. As ever, he was curious to see where his fancy would lead him. He never settled on a course until he had cleared the stone archway of the dank boathouse in the bowels of the palazzo.

A light chop worried the surface of the Grand Canal, and he bobbed there for a moment, the motor idling. Maybe a loop north through Cannaregio? It had been a while. He could take in the Ghetto Nuovo, yes, then maybe stretch his legs in Parco Savorgnan. The large roof terrace of his apartment was thick with potted shrubs and even boasted a vine-shrouded pergola, but there was nothing quite like the feeling of real trees towering over you — an all-too-rare experience in Venice.

The first sign of life in the stirring city came as he putt-putted along Rio di Santa Fosca. A young boy hurried over the low bridge up ahead with a tin pail of milk swinging from his hand, caught between the slap he would get if he spilled any and the one he would get if he was late getting home. And for a moment, it seemed to Vittorio that an invisible hand had reached out and turned the wheel of time back several centuries.

No matter where his nose led him, no matter where he sipped his first coffee of the day, his second was always at Aldo's caffè beside the Rialto fish market. Here he sat at the small tables crowded out front, trading gossip with the fishmongers while their underlings prepared the stalls and — *shick-shick-shick* — reduced great blocks of blue ice to white chips with vicious-looking picks.

He felt honored to have been accepted by such men, for they were some of the finest he had ever encountered: sly, irreverent, quick-witted, and brimming with uncommon wisdom. No subject was off-limits, no opinion too outrageous, provided you could defend it with humor. It had taken him a while to learn the rules, to adjust himself to their speed, to accept that his role in the group was that of a whipping boy for all the injustices perpetrated against the common man by him and his kind.

Any respect they showed him had been earned over the years, except in one quarter. They had never questioned his appearance at the market six mornings a week, which suggested they knew the reason for it and had decided among themselves to stay silent on the subject.

He always left before the market opened for business, and he never left empty-handed. Today he picked out a plump, glum-looking *pesce San Pietro,* which he would fry up later for his lunch. He was expected to attend a screening at the film festival out on the Lido, followed by lunch at the Excelsior, but he knew already that he would call in sick with some affliction or other of the elderly. Hemorrhoids should do the trick; they had worked well enough for him in the past, not that he would know a hemorrhoid from a hoe handle, and not that it really mattered. Benedetto and Giovanna would be far happier mingling with the great and the good without having to worry about him.

Giovanna, he knew, had come to view him as something of an encumbrance, an irritant, over the past year, ever since he turned up in a lounge suit and open-necked shirt for a performance of Stravinsky's *Rite of Spring* at the Fenice. His defense at the time, that his flouting of convention was a conscious tribute to the rebellious spirit of the great avant-garde composer, had raised an amused chuckle from Benedetto and a deprecating grimace from Giovanna.

It was strange to find himself, at the age of seventy-seven, being treated like an errant child by his daughter-in-law — though not quite as strange as discovering that he rather relished the dynamic for the sport it offered. He would switch a couple of paintings around in the drawing room when she was out for the day, or rearrange some furniture in the library, or speak ill of her beloved Mussolini to his grandchildren over dinner, or fill the villa out at Asolo with a mob of his more disreputable friends on a weekend.

It wasn't personal: what Giovanna lacked in humor she made up for with her boundless energy and Teutonic efficiency. He supposed that the gentle needling was his way of saying that although he had taken himself off to the top floor, conceding control of the palazzo to her and Benedetto, he was still a resident with rights. He was still the head of the family.

The sun was creeping over the rooftops, and the water traffic was beginning to build, when he set off on the final leg of his journey. He aimed the skiff at the inconspicuous mouth of Rio dei Santissimi Apostoli, directly across the Grand Canal from the fish market. The narrow waterway didn't offer much in the way of sights before it finally debouched into the lagoon, and he never knew quite what to expect when he hit the open water. Experience had taught him that the short hop over to the Isola di San Michele could be deceptively perilous. A sudden wind could whip up an angry chop in a matter of moments, or a surging cross-current might build out of nowhere, rendering the Evinrude's paltry three horsepower all but useless.

After a number of close calls over the years, he had learned to forgo the pleasure of his daily pilgrimage when conditions seemed uncertain. After all, there was no urgency. It wasn't as though Elena was going anywhere. Today, though, he had nothing to fear from the lazy swell and the warm breeze cats-pawing the glassy surface. Within minutes, the high brick walls of the cemetery island were looming over him, rising foursquare from the water like the ramparts of some ancient sea fort.

Money had bought him many things, not least of all the key to one of the three tall wrought-iron doors set in the grand gateway that faced the city. As a rule, it was reserved for funerals, for the delivery of the dead, and he should really have made the tour of the island and docked in the small port beside the church. But that would have meant the distraction of other people, even at this early hour, when all he wanted was to be alone with his thoughts . . . alone with Elena. He tied up, then reached for the single white rose he had snipped from the bush on his roof terrace earlier. Clambering awkwardly over the gunwale, he set off up the wide marble steps, just as he had five years ago when following her coffin.

She lay a short distance from the gate in one of the large square plots laid out in a grid and separated from each other by dark ranks of lofty cypresses. It was a simple grave with a plain white marble top stone, and a headstone with space enough for his name when he finally joined her.

"Good morning, my darling."

He took the drooping rose — yellow yesterday — from the slender glass vase.

"It looks set to be another fine day."

He slipped the white rose into the vase and settled down on the top stone, absently brushing aside a couple of stray leaves with his fingertips.

"I bought a *pesce San Pietro* for my lunch. I think I'll have it with a tomato salad, the way we used to. The tomatoes on the terrace are particularly sweet this year. All this sun, I suppose."

Mostly, he spoke a lot of nonsense to her, though not always. She was sometimes the touchstone against which he tested his deepest concerns. He didn't believe she could hear him, but until you were dead there was no way of knowing what lay on the other side, and he was happy to natter away on the off chance she was listening.

He had done the same with his father, reduced at the end to a vacant shell of a man. Dottore Zorzi had advised him that the auditory sense was the last to fade away, and in the final weeks Vittorio had held his father's liver-spotted hand and talked about the old days and all the good times they had shared. He sometimes wondered if he hadn't bored the old boy to death.

Elena had been taken early, but she had at least been spared the cruel decline. No guttering candle flame for her, slowly drowning in its own pool of wax. Hers was snuffed out in an instant by a sudden gust. He had woken one morning to find her lying still and cold beside him in their bed. Her heart? An aneurysm in the brain? It made no difference. She was gone, and he had not permitted them to desecrate her body in search of a medical explanation that would have brought no meaningful satisfaction.

He still found it absurd that she had been taken before him: she who had shown him how to keep on living when all he had wanted to do was wither away. She had taught him that the black hole he carried within him was a part of him now and always would be. There was no point in pretending otherwise. He had to face it, as one would a wild beast that wanted you for its lunch. To run was foolish, fatal. You had to look it calmly and squarely in the eye and stare it down. Only then would it turn tail and slink off into the undergrowth.

Wise advice, as always, from Elena. By God, he missed her. Not a day passed when he wasn't at some point left breathless by her absence. He had been living half a life ever since she had been gathered from him.

"I've been thinking," he said, "about that thing I mentioned the other day. I've decided I'm going to step down, resign from the board."

Albrizzi Marittima had gone from strength to strength over the past twenty-five years, and it had taken Vittorio almost as long to accept that he had played a secondary role in the company's burgeoning fortunes. Yes, he had piloted the ship safely through the tricky shoals of the Great War, but ever since, Benedetto had been the one with the quietly commanding hand on the wheel.

Vittorio was immensely proud of his son. It was impossible to fault his instincts, or his art of subtle persuasion when it came to nudging others toward his way of thinking. As a child, he had been doggedly deter- mined but always self-deprecating, never confrontational, and he had managed to carry that same disarming mix of qualities over into adulthood.

Back in 1925, a few years after Mussolini's rise to power, Vittorio had proposed a diversification of the company's interests into the lucrative transatlantic passenger market fueled by the mass migration of Italians. Benedetto had praised his thinking before slowly, respectfully chipping away at it. He had somehow managed to get his hands on confidential papers pointing to an overinvestment by the three leading Italian companies in the field, and this at a time when the first tremors of a possible financial downturn were being felt in the United States. Moreover, he had it on good authority that Congress would soon move to limit immigration into the country.

In the first real challenge to his authority, the board of Albrizzi Marittima had persuaded Vittorio to abandon his dream and stick to what the company had always done best: shipping cargo. Thank goodness, for they would have lost their shirts on the venture.

It was around that time that Benedetto had begun making regular trips to Rome, cultivating relationships at the Ministry of Communications, which handled all matters relating to merchant shipping. Government contracts began to roll in, and in such numbers that the company barely faltered with the financial crash of 1929. The country's leading passenger carriers — NGI, Lloyd Sabaudo, and Cosulich — hadn't fared so well. Brought to their knees, they had found themselves nationalized by Mussolini.

Benedetto had grasped from the first what the rest of them had failed to see: that Il Duce was no flash in the pan. He was here to stay, and for all his strutting bombast, all his talk of mare nostrum, he fully intended to follow through on his grandiose plans to restore the nation's lost maritime glory. This would mean rich pickings for those who forged close ties with the regime.

It was a dirty business. It meant bribes and kickbacks to a variety of unsavory officials, the kind of men Vittorio's father would have refused to deal with as a matter of principle. While Vittorio accepted such practices as a necessary evil in a rapidly changing world, he had always harbored misgivings about binding the company's fortunes too tightly to those of a dictator haunted by imperialist visions.

Morally — for him, at least — there had been a hefty price to pay for the vast profits of the past few years. Albrizzi Marittima had grown rich on the back of the war against Abyssinia, supplying the Italian army with everything from boots to bullets and helping bring to life Mussolini's dream of a colony in East Africa. How many innocent Abyssinians had lost their lives in the conflict? And how many were still dying under the occupation of their homeland? Reports varied, but even the low estimates were enough to chill the blood. The same was true of the civil war in Spain, where General Franco and his Nationalists were beginning to turn the tide against the Republicans, thanks in no small part to Mussolini's material assistance, which found its way across the Mediterranean on company ships.

Vittorio had made his feelings known, and Benedetto had countered his concerns with the same seductive rhetoric employed by Mussolini in his innumerable speeches and printed articles, falling back on phrases such as "the civilizing mission of Rome" and "the universal heritage of antiquity."

There was a time some years ago when Vittorio could have made a stand, imposed his will. And if Elena had still been around to support him, he might well have done so. But that moment had passed. He was too old and too weary now to challenge his son. And to what end? No scales were suddenly going to fall from Benedetto's eyes. His friends and associates were good Fascists to a man (and woman), and he would never allow anything to jeopardize his hard-won standing among them.

Benedetto's marriage to Giovanna — a Morisini — might have opened the door, but it had taken considerably more initiative than that to earn the acceptance of those who looked down on the union as just another pairing of old money with new. Benedetto had shown humility, patience, and, most importantly, respect to the people who regarded themselves as his betters. In private, he had studied hard in all the areas that mattered to them — art, languages, literature, theater, opera, classical music, cinema — until he wore the cloak of culture as nonchalantly as they. And when he sat at their dinner tables, he let his knowledge leak out in ways that never threatened or challenged, but only entertained.

Vittorio had seen all this with his own eyes, for he had been drawn along in the slipstream of Benedetto's carefully managed metamorphosis, invited by association to the many balls, dinners, and cocktail parties that accompanied the relentless drumbeat of feast days and festivals that the city had always moved to.

Last year, they had even been allocated an annual slot in the cluttered calendar: hosting a ball the night of the Redentore, once the fireworks were over. It was the ultimate seal of approval and, for Benedetto personally, an honor matched only by the invitation from Giuseppe Volpi himself to join the committee of next year's Biennale.

It was easy to sneer, somewhat harder to face the truth: that Vittorio might have led the family back across the Adriatic to the city of their forebears, but it was Benedetto who had settled them here, stitching them into the fabric of Venetian society so deftly that almost no signs of the repair remained. The dynasty was safe, its future assured for the next generation.

It had never been in question that Salvatore would join the company after graduating from university, and in two weeks, Vittorio's eldest grandchild would do just that. It would be a first for the family: three generations of Albrizzi under one roof, both at home and at work. The occasion demanded to be marked in some way, possibly with a bonus to all the company's employees, from captain all the way down to stoker. And at the party — this being Venice, there would have to be one — Vittorio would announce his retirement, to the surprise of all (and the ill-disguised relief of Giovanna, no doubt).

"Anyway, my darling, that's what I've decided to do," said Vittorio. "My mind is made up. I think it's time. In fact, I should probably have done it well before now. Benedetto will make an excellent president; that's been clear for some years now."

He laid his palm on the marble, hoping for something, anything, but all he felt was a faint quiver of heat stored away in the stone by the young sun.

CHAPTER THIRTY-TWO

As soon as the operator had made the connection and disappeared, a voice said, "You're in Padova already?"

"We drove through the night," Petrovic replied.

Outside the soundproofed telephone booth, Jestin loitered in the main hall of the post office, smoking and looking disgruntled, which was hardly surprising: they should have been back in France by now, not traveling through Italy in quite the opposite direction.

"That's good. It means you'll be in Venice well before them." A second voice, distinguishable from the first only by its undertone of malice. Josip Karaman's younger brother, Petar, was also on the line.

"Assuming they're headed there," Petrovic countered.

"Where else are they going to go?"

"How is your shoulder?" asked Josip.

"Sore as hell."

He had bound the wound inflicted by Borodin's sword cane, but it would need cleaning and stitching up as soon as they got to Venice. Only time would heal his left eye, reduced to an ugly gash by the swelling that even now was pressing against the lens of his sunglasses.

"We've made some enquiries," said Petar. "Your story checks out."

"Not that we didn't believe you," added Josip.

"Speak for yourself."

"Ignore my brother. He's not in the best of moods."

"I can't think why," growled Petar.

"We are where we are," Josip replied with deliberation. "Let's just remain calm and take stock of the situation."

Through a contact in Zurich, they had learned since last night that there were two victims of the gunfire in Hirschenplatz, both of them German — possibly brothers, if their identity papers were anything to go by. The first had been shot twice in the heart by a young woman who then fled the scene. The second had been shot once by an unidentified man leaving the café, or possibly by a policeman. The witnesses couldn't agree on this point. It was clear, however, that the policeman had then left the square in the company of two men, one of them wounded, and had not been seen or heard of since, suggesting that he was a plant of Borodin's. Their contact was chasing down a rumor that the three men had subsequently been spotted driving off in the company of the young woman.

When Petrovic had called from Austria late last night, he all but accused them of assigning an additional team to the job, for why else had the situation in Hirschenplatz spun so violently out of control? They had assured him this wasn't the case, and Josip reiterated the point now.

"I can promise you the two Germans had nothing to do with us, and since they are both dead, we can dismiss them from the picture and stick to what we do know — or can safely surmise."

Borodin had evidently undergone a last-minute change of heart, or else he would not have exposed Hamilton to the potential danger of a meeting with Petrovic. They could assume that the Englishman was no longer in the dark about his identity. This was an unfortunate development, undeniably, but it also played in their favor, for Hamilton would feel compelled to confirm what he had discovered from Borodin. What were his alternatives? To return to his former life? A death sentence. To hide and stay hidden for good, never knowing the truth? Out of the question. No, he would show himself before long, and they would be waiting for him when he did.

"Do you have a pen?" asked Josip.

"Yes."

"Write this number down."

Petrovic uncapped the fountain pen with his teeth and scrawled the number on his forearm.

"Call it as soon as you get to Venice. He won't be happy to hear from you, but we'll do our best to appease him beforehand."

"Does he have a name?" asked Petrovic.

"Of course he has a name!"

"Petar, please . . ."

There was a weary edge to the brotherly reprimand, and a brief pause before Josip spoke once more to Petrovic.

"What you're about to hear stays with you. No one must ever know. No one."

CHAPTER THIRTY-THREE

Luke woke from his dream with a start to find Pippi standing over him, her hand on his shoulder.

"We're almost there. Venice Mestre. The station."

The train was crawling along, the sunlight slanting through the window of their compartment and splashing the seats. It was coming back to him now.

"Oh. Right."

He rose unsteadily to his feet and hauled their suitcases from the steel-and-string rack.

"Where were you?" she asked.

"Fishing . . . on Wicken Fen."

"Did you catch anything?"

"No, but I was about to."

Pippi smiled. "Sorry."

He didn't tell her that he had just hooked a car — their car, the Citroën they had abandoned on a back street behind Bergamo station a few hours ago.

They had no difficulty finding a taxi in front of the station building, and from there it was a short ride to a dock and a water taxi operated by their driver's cousin, a stout man with a silver furze of close-cropped hair and a face tanned to a deep mahogany. His name was Gregorio, and he seemed puzzled, almost offended, when Pippi didn't haggle over the fare.

A network of drab waterways trimmed with wharves and warehouses finally gave way to the lagoon and a first glimpse of Venice. It lay far off, a low mass on the horizon, identifiable at this distance only by the long and rather ungainly bridge connecting it to the mainland. Gregorio opened the throttle, and as they skimmed across the glassy surface, the city gradually began to take shape: tall towers and spires stabbing the sky, the domes of churches rising above the rooftops. Pippi abandoned Gregorio at the wheel and joined Luke on the bench seat at the back of the boat.

"He says the best hotels are full. There's a film festival happening."

"We need something more discreet anyway, somewhere off the beaten track."

"That's what I told him. He says he knows a place."

Gregorio was surprised when they exchanged the open air for the low cabin at the front of the taxi. They couldn't hope to keep their faces hidden at all times, but placing them on full display as they cruised down the Grand Canal was an unnecessary risk and best avoided. Besides, they still had a good view of the colorful pageant unfolding around them. The teeming traffic — everything from freight barges to gondolas — moved against a backdrop of ancient edifices lining the canal.

Luke had imagined an island, a city set well above the waterline, but the buildings seemed to rise directly out of the murky green waters, as though the place had been struck by a terrible flood that would never retreat. When not hurling greetings at other boatmen, Gregorio called down to them, pointing out sights, and when they passed beneath the Rialto Bridge, he let out a loud yell that echoed off the arched underside.

Not long afterward, he guided the taxi off the Grand Canal into a narrow waterway barely wide enough for two boats to pass. The laundry strung from clotheslines overhead offered some welcome splashes of color to a gloomy world that was airless, malodorous, untouched by the sun. A dog barked; a woman laughed; some thin strains of jazz came through briefly above the low thrum of the boat's engine. Luke was beginning to feel unnerved, claustrophobic, when the buildings on their left fell suddenly away to reveal a sun-drenched square.

Gregorio tied up at some steps, told them to stay put, then hurried off to check availability at the hotel (and negotiate his fee for bringing the place some trade, Pippi speculated). She declined a cigarette, and Luke lit one for himself.

"It's beautiful," she said.

Undeniably. Diners were finishing their lunch at a couple of cafés, and the marble facade of the church filling one side of the small square shone with a ghostly linen brilliance. It was flawless, all of it, and yet, he struggled to engage with the scene.

"Yes, it is," he replied.

Pippi must have sensed his hesitation. "You'll feel better when we have a room and you've heard my plan."

"Another plan?"

Pippi smiled. "Even better than the last one."

Gregorio returned triumphant and insisted on carrying their suitcases to the San Barnaba Hotel, a tall stucco building on the far side of the square. They got a warm greeting from the concierge, a young man named Foscolo, trim and spruce and absurdly handsome, who turned out to be Gregorio's nephew. Pippi explained this to Luke once a grateful Gregorio had disappeared with his generous tip and Foscolo was showing them upstairs to their room.

It was on the second floor, with two large windows overlooking the square. More than satisfied with it, Pippi disappeared back downstairs with their passports to register.

Luke splashed his face with water in the bathroom, then went in search of a hiding place for the money they had received from Borodin. The sagging mattress of the double bed was an option, if a little obvious, and it would require a knife to make an incision. He made a tour of the room, testing the floorboards with his foot, but they were nailed down solidly. The dressing table and the chest of drawers offered nothing, but the wardrobe did. A modern affair in bird's-eye maple, it had no feet, just a solid base that sat directly on the floor. He edged it away from the wall, then tilted it back, his fingers groping beneath the base till they found a hollow space. It wasn't ideal, but it would have to do.

When Pippi returned to the room, she had a map of the city in her hand. She spread it out on the bed and they took their bearings.

"We're here, Campo di San Barnaba. And this is where we're going: Campo San Polo."

"Why?"

"Because that's where the library is."

They took a water taxi. It was safer than tramping the streets, and time was against them. The driver got them as close as he could, but they had to travel the last few hundred yards on foot. As instructed by Borodin, they put some distance between each other: Luke up ahead, just another tourist in hat and sunglasses and with a camera around his neck; Pippi shadowing him. They both were armed and vigilant.

Campo San Polo was a good deal larger than San Barnaba — a vast sweep of flag-stones big enough to stage a football match. The buildings trimming the square had a neglected air that spoke of past glories unlikely ever to be revisited.

They identified the library easily enough: biblioteca was carved in large letters into the stone lintel above the entrance doors.

They knew that here they could find back issues of the main daily newspaper, the *Gazzetta di Venezia,* because Pippi had gotten Foscolo to phone ahead from the hotel. Of the two librarians on duty behind the counter, it was the man — bald, tall, thin as a pipe cleaner — who rose from his seat to attend to them. Luke's knowledge of Italian was limited to a few words and phrases, but he knew exactly what Pippi was saying, because she had spelled it out to him in the water taxi. She was an author, working on a novel set in Venice a couple of years before the war, and needed access to some newspapers of the time for her research.

She filled out a request slip for the months of December 1911 through March 1912, and they withdrew to one of the long oak desks to wait. The librarian appeared several minutes later, wheeling a steel trolley laden with four large, bound volumes.

They started with January 1912. Luke had been left on the front steps of St. Theresa's on the evening of the fourteenth, so they could assume he had been abducted in Venice shortly before that date. It seemed unlikely that Gotal would have spent any more time than absolutely necessary in the company of the small child he had decided not to kill, which probably equated to a few days' travel from Italy to England.

In reality, it had taken him five days.

"This is it," said Pippi.

The front page of the *Gazzetta* for January 9 was dominated by news of the abduction of Vincenzo Albrizzi. Luke watched in nervous anticipation as Pippi ran her finger down the columns of text. "It happened at the Rialto fish market," she said eventually. "You were taken from your pram when your nanny wasn't looking. The market was *'molto affollato'* — very crowded. Nobody saw anything. You were there, and then you weren't."

"Sshhhh."

At the adjacent desk, a middle-aged woman with a kindly face raised a finger to her lips and pointed at a sign on the wall: silenzio, it commanded in gold capitals. Pippi tilted her head in apology, then reached into her bag and took out the pad of paper she had cadged from Foscolo.

All Luke could do was watch and try to make sense of the notes she wrote in her angular German hand. By the end of January, the story had dropped off the front page, and when Pippi turned her attention to February, Luke took himself off to the lobby to smoke a cigarette. He gazed through the glass doors at the people outside, going about their lives. A young boy raced past, whipping a wooden hoop with a stick, pursued by a pack of his friends.

Pippi kept at it until the ting of a handbell announced closing time. As they were leaving, she deviated toward the counter, mur-

muring "I'll see what else I can find out. Wait here."

She quizzed the tall librarian for several minutes before rejoining Luke.

"I need a drink," she announced.

They found an unprepossessing little bar around the corner and took a table at the back, well away from the street. They both ordered beers, and Pippi also asked for a cognac. She filled Luke in on her findings: the futile search for a tall man in a gray overcoat who had been spotted near the fish market, boarding a boat with a baby in his arms; the endless pleas from the family for Vincenzo's safe return; the false sightings over the following weeks; the police lines of inquiry, which had finally petered out.

"There's something else," she said. She hadn't touched her cognac, and she now slid the glass toward him. "Drink it."

He saw the distress in her eyes, and a sudden spasm of dread gripped his insides. "What's the matter?"

"There's no good way to say this . . . Your parents are dead."

He tried to make sense of the words. "Dead?"

She nodded grimly.

"How do you know?"

"The librarian."

"Maybe he's wrong."

Pippi didn't reply immediately. "Maybe."

He reached for the brandy and took a slow sip. For as long as he could remember, he had hoped while not daring to hope, believed while doubting. Then, just as it seemed it might actually come to pass, the dream was dashed. It would never happen. He would never meet them. Never embrace them.

Pippi took his hands in hers. "I'm so sorry."

"It's okay."

"No," she said. "No, it isn't."

He watched their fingers mesh together.

"Did he say how they died?"

"Your father during the war. Your mother later. An accident."

"An accident?"

"Sailing."

"She drowned?"

"I don't know."

He threw back the rest of the brandy in one throat-singeing gulp.

"You're not alone," said Pippi. "I'm here."

"I know."

Her eyes bored into him. "But do you know *why* I'm here?"

"I can think of ten good reasons why you shouldn't be."

"Only ten?"

He gave a weak smile. "I'll be all right," he said.

"I know you will."

CHAPTER THIRTY-FOUR

Dottore Sanzogno was a short, dapper man and a creature of habit. He followed precisely the same routine when closing up the clinic at the end of every day.

He sat at his desk and smoked his first and only cigarette of the day. He then rose and crossed to the sink in the corner of his office and rinsed his hands with alcohol. Filling the zinc watering can that lived beneath the sink, he wandered through to the reception area and watered the two maidenhair ferns and the aspidistra. When he had finished, he returned to his office, checked that all the windows were closed and bolted, then gathered up his leather bag and left the room, locking the door behind him and pocketing the key.

His last act before heading home was to go over tomorrow's appointments, testing himself on the names of the animals and their owners.

This was what he was doing, seated in Ginevra's chair at the reception desk, when the doorbell rang. He ignored it at first. The bell kept ringing, though, and he rose irritably from the chair, crossed to the door, and unlocked it.

"I'm sorry, but we're closed —"

The man pushed past him, forcing him back inside and kicking the door shut with his heel.

"Excuse me —" said Dottore Sanzogno.

He received a slap across the cheek. Not hard, more shocking than anything else, just enough to silence him.

"Shut up." The man produced a gun from his jacket pocket.

"Please, I have a family."

"Then you also have a simple choice to make. You can go home to them with enough money to treat them all to gifts, or you can not go home at all."

Fluent Italian, but a thick accent. A foreigner.

"What do you want from me?"

"I have a knife wound in my shoulder. It's bad."

There was also bruising around his left eye, behind the sunglasses.

"Then you need a surgeon, not a vet. The hospital's not far."

"What I need," said the man, "is someone who can stitch me up and keep his mouth shut afterwards. Do you think you can do that?"

Dottore Sanzogno nodded. "Yes, yes, I know I can."

Petrovic rapped out the code on the door of their hotel room: three knocks, then one, then two more. A key turned in the lock, and the door swung open to reveal Jestin in his undershorts.

"Very attractive."

"I was trying to catch up on some sleep, but this heat . . ."

Petrovic locked the door behind him and shed his jacket.

"Did you kill him?" asked Jestin.

"The vet? No. We may need him again, although that now looks unlikely."

"Oh?"

Petrovic removed the sunglasses and examined his eye in the wardrobe mirror. "Borodin is dead." It felt good to observe his reflection while uttering the words.

"Are you sure?"

"It looks like he was the one who took a bullet in Zurich."

"That's great news."

It was indeed. Petrovic was only sorry that

he couldn't take any credit for it, after the humiliation of being so comprehensively outwitted. "He was found in Switzerland, near the Italian border, so Hamilton's on his own now."

"You're forgetting the others. The girl and the policeman."

"Whoever they are, they came through Borodin, which means Hamilton's problems aren't theirs. I think we can discount them."

Jestin lit a cigarette. "Isn't it about time you told me what his problems are?"

Petrovic had purposely been economical with the facts, fearing that if Jestin knew the full scale and scope of the affair, he might, rightly, begin to question his own odds of survival once he'd served his purpose.

"The details aren't important. He helped Borodin betray the organization. Our job is to find him and kill him, then go home."

Jestin blew a plume of cigarette smoke toward the ceiling. "And just how are we supposed to find him, stuck in this damned hotel room?"

"Don't worry," said Petrovic. "We'll be the first to know when he surfaces."

CHAPTER THIRTY-FIVE

The shock of hearing that his parents were dead had given way to a curious lassitude during the taxi trip back to the hotel, followed by a leaden fatigue the moment they had crossed the threshold of their room.

Luke now lay on his back across the bed while Pippi showered. He glanced at the bedside table. His cigarette had burned away untouched, to a neat trail of milky ashes. He thought about lighting another, then realized he had left both cigarettes and lighter on the dressing table. Even those few steps seemed too great an exertion, and he turned his thoughts back to the South Sea Islands.

They had been a fascination of his since childhood, when he stumbled across a traveler's account of Tahiti in an old copy of *Good Words* in his father's study. If ever there was a time to go there, to lose oneself on the far side of the planet, it was now.

Pippi appeared from the bathroom, wrapped in a towel, her wet hair combed back off her face. She came and sat beside him on the bed.

"I don't think I can go on."

"We'll talk about it over dinner," she said.

"I'm not hungry."

"Of course you are. We haven't eaten since Bergamo."

She was right: they'd had one small pastry to go with their morning coffee at the station café.

"I'll ask Foscolo if he knows a quiet place."

The humble *osteria* wasn't quiet, but it was remote, well away from the main tourist trails, deep in Dorsoduro.

A bowl of deep-fried baby squid was followed by another, then another carafe of white wine to go with the platter of various grilled fishes they had ordered as their main course. Luke felt the wine working its way through his system, loosening his limbs, his synapses, his tongue.

Having rediscovered his appetite and then his voice, he told Pippi about the vision that had come to him earlier: a life of ease in the South Seas, a bungalow among the palms just back from the beach, and a colorful boat bobbing in a turquoise bay. He knew what she would say: that if they ran now, they would always be running, always afraid, never quite free. He was wrong. Her argument was more convincing than that.

"They will use your family and your friends to find you. Even if you have not told them where you are, they will be in danger. Can you do that to them?"

He didn't reply; he didn't need to.

"Borodin was right," she continued. "We must finish it here, and for that we need your family. You have a grandfather, an uncle, nephews, nieces. They have a right to know you are alive."

"We can't just walk in there. Petrovic will be waiting for us."

"Then we find another way to contact them. I have an idea."

Luke peered at her over his wineglass. "Have you always been so capable, so logical?"

Pippi smiled and spread her hands. "I'm German."

She insisted on taking a circuitous route back to the hotel, looping through the maze of deserted streets, alleyways, and canals that lay to the south. Luke guessed what she was doing: getting to know the lay of the land in case they were forced to make a rapid escape. Night had fallen, so they broke their rule and walked together, protected by the darkness. Every so often, they stopped on a bridge to stare into the black chasm of a canal, or paused to look up at the moon-washed facade of a building — sights, Luke couldn't help thinking, that he would have known intimately if only his life had been allowed to run its natural course. This was his city, but even as he searched for a sense of his other self within it, he knew that he would always be a stranger here.

Back at the hotel, they brushed their teeth and changed for bed, and before they took their places on the bowed mattress, Pippi jammed the back of the dressing table chair beneath the door handle. Last night he had a reason to hold her. He wished he had one now. The intimacy of lying entwined together for a few precious hours had cut right through the trials of the past days.

"Do you think Borodin knew?" he asked. "About my parents?"

"It's possible."

It was the first time they had spoken of Borodin in almost twenty-four hours. They had talked around him but never actually uttered his name, almost as if doing so would curse his chances. Or maybe it was simpler than that: maybe they didn't wish

416

to be reminded how lost they were without him.

"I think he did," said Luke. "I think he knew but couldn't bring himself to say it."

"You can't blame him."

"I don't. How can I blame him for anything? He saved my life three times."

"Three?"

"Not counting the times he could have killed me in Paris but decided not to." He twisted to face her. "And then there's you in Zurich. And Gotal twenty-five years ago. I shouldn't be alive. Why am I?"

"Because you're innocent."

"That means nothing. So was Agnes."

"You're right. You're lucky." They were facing each other now, and she gently laid her hand on his cheek. "This is a precious thing and I'm going to protect it."

"Why, Pippi? Why are you still here?"

"Meersburg, of course. You went back for the children."

"I didn't know what I was doing."

"But you did it anyway. I saw you. I saw the man in the middle of you. That's why I'm here."

She shifted a little closer, so close that when she next spoke, he felt her breath on his face like a soft caress.

"If you still want to go to Tahiti when this

is over, I'll go with you."

"Really?"

"Of course."

"There's a danger we'll grow bored."

"Not with each other. And we'll get very good at swimming and fishing and sailing."

"I once read that the Tahitians ride the waves on wooden boards for fun."

"Then we'll try that, too."

The words came out as a whisper, and a moment later he felt the soft, searching pressure of her lips on his.

CHAPTER THIRTY-SIX

Luke woke to see Pippi fully clothed and seated at the dressing table, brushing her hair. She caught sight of him in the mirror and smiled.

"How do I look?"

"Overdressed. Come back to bed."

"It's late."

He groped for his wristwatch on the bedside table. "Nine thirty isn't late."

She rose to her feet and approached the bed. "We have to be at the library at eleven."

"We will be. I promise."

He reached out a hand to her. She took it but refused to be drawn down beside him.

"Have you already forgotten how good it was?"

There was a delicate, quizzical edge to her smile. "No."

Releasing his hand, she unzipped her skirt and let it fall to the floor. She undressed slowly, without embarrassment, allowing his eyes to roam over her. He had explored every curve and contour of her body, and yet he had never seen her naked before, not in the light.

"My God, you're beautiful."

She drew back the sheet and lay down beside him.

A bell was chiming midday as they hurried across Campo San Polo toward the library.

"It's your fault," said Pippi.

"I take full responsibility."

It had been an inspired idea on Pippi's part. They required a go-between, someone who could safely and discreetly approach Luke's family on their behalf. Who better than someone who sat right at the heart of the story? Bianca Rubelli, his old nanny, the unfortunate young woman who had taken him to the Rialto fish market the morning he was snatched. They knew from the newspaper reports that she had been twenty-one years old at the time, which meant she was in her midforties now, so probably still alive, and, with any luck, still living in Venice.

Pippi had put the lanky librarian onto it yesterday, and the obliging fellow had hit pay dirt. That was evident even as they entered the reading room. Spotting them approaching the counter, he gave a broad smile and waved a piece of paper above his head.

Bianca had never left the city, and although the librarian had been unable to dig up a home address for her, he had the name and address of her workplace: a laundry. He marked it for them on their map. It lay north and west of where they currently were, some fifteen minutes on foot.

Pippi led the way, with Luke following at a distance, enjoying the sight of her up ahead: the long stride, the lazy sway of hips — details that chimed with a new resonance now. He wondered whether she had given herself to him to pep him up and prepare him for battle. If so, it had worked. There was a new steel in him, even an eagerness to get the thing done, to carry the fight to the men who had robbed him of the life that was rightfully his.

The laundry filled one side of a tiny run-down square centered with a fountain so large and elaborate that it looked as if it had been placed there by mistake. They arrived as a woman was turning the sign in the laundry door from APERTO to CHIUSO. Closed. Luke hung back by the fountain and watched Pippi talk her way inside the shop. She reappeared a few minutes later.

"We just missed her. She has gone home

421

for lunch."

"Did you get the address?"

"No, because she's not going to be there. She's going to be here."

She showed him the map, her fingertip coming to rest on a building marked with a crucifix.

Although considerably larger than any of the other churches they had seen, the Basilica dei Frari was a defiantly modest building, constructed of brick. Its plain, unadorned exterior made the opulence within all the more striking. Both aisles were trimmed with a profusion of marble statues and religious paintings, not that they stopped to look as they strode down the nave. They knew exactly where they were headed, and they were eager to get there.

The Cappella dei Santi Francescani was one of several tall, narrow chapels in the transept. It stood just left of the presbytery and had an altar of its own, where a woman was kneeling. Her face was raised to the large gilt-framed painting that backed the altar. It showed the Virgin Mary seated with the infant Jesus on a tall throne surrounded by a group of men, the two most prominent of whom, filling the foreground, were clad in drab, hooded habits. Franciscan friars, presumably, like the statue set in a niche in the left-hand wall.

"Do you think it's her?"

"Yes," said Pippi. "Go."

"Not yet."

They withdrew to a row of wooden chairs directly across from the chapel, and from here they watched for a good five minutes before the woman finally moved, rising stiffly to her feet with her handbag. She crossed herself, then turned and left the chapel. She had a kind face, soft and dimpled, although there was something careworn about the two lines that bracketed her mouth.

She stopped to light a candle on the iron stand beside the chapel entrance. Fishing a coin from her purse, she dropped it in the offertory box and made off toward the main altar.

"Bianca," said Luke, on his feet now.

She turned toward him, then froze.

"Bianca?"

Her eyes widened, and her hand went to her mouth, stifling a sharp gasp. When he took a step toward her, she retreated in fear. He held up his hands in what he hoped was a placatory gesture.

She swayed like a reed in a breeze, and her eyes rolled heavenward. Luke darted forward and just managed to catch her before she hit the stone floor.

Pippi came hurrying over. She wasn't the only one to have witnessed the incident. A priest was also bearing down on Luke and the limp bundle in his arms.

It was a robing room of some kind, probably for the choir, given the number of cassocks and surplices hanging from hooks. On the priest's instructions, Luke carried Bianca to a high-backed wooden chair and placed her in it as gently as he could. She was still unconscious. Another priest, a younger man, had joined them, and he held her head to keep it from slumping forward.

They watched from a discreet distance while Bianca's pulse was checked and her cheeks patted and a cloth flapped in front of her face. She finally came to, her eyes searching the faces in front of her before coming to rest on Luke. She seized the arm of the elder priest and whispered urgently into his ear. He glanced at Luke, then patted Bianca's hand, soothing her with a few words before extricating himself from her grip.

Approaching them, he said, "Thank you. Please, you go now." He tried to usher them toward the door, but they stood their ground. "Please, go." There was a touch of anger in his voice now. "She has problems. It is not good you are here. She thinks you are someone."

"Who?" asked Luke.

"Someone from long ago, someone who is dead. Please . . ."

"Vincenzo Albrizzi?"

The priest loosened his hold on Luke's arm. "Yes. How . . . ?"

"Because I *am* Vincenzo Albrizzi."

The priest looked for the lie in Luke's eyes. *"Caro Dio,"* he mumbled, crossing himself. *"Non è possibile."*

"It's true," said Pippi. "He is."

Luke tilted his head at Bianca. "May I?"

The priest stepped silently aside. There was a clouding of doubt and fear and hope in Bianca's expression as Luke approached her.

"Vincenzo?"

He took the hands she offered him, and knelt before her. *"Sì, Bianca."*

"Ma quanto sei grande . . . e così bello . . . bello come un principe."

And now she was laughing, and crying, and taking his face in her hands and showering it with kisses. The dampness of her tears against his cheek did it for him, and he sobbed like a child. She pressed her lips

425

to his ear and filled it with words he didn't understand. When she realized this, she asked, *"Non parli Italiano?"*

The question fell just within the limits of his phrasebook Italian. *"Non parlo Italiano. Sono Inglese."*

"Inglese? Poverino. Quest'é un vero peccato."

Luke looked to Pippi for a translation.

"She is not happy that you are English. No, not happy at all." He caught the ring of amused relish in her voice.

"E un miracolo . . . un miracolo!"

The priest was hurrying away, flapping his arms like a bird.

"No, you can't tell anyone," called Luke.

The priest turned at the door. "But I must. It is a *miracolo.*"

"You can't. Please, I'm serious."

"The people who took him long ago are trying to kill him," said Pippi.

"We need your help."

The priest's eyes flicked between them. Then he locked the door and wandered over.

"My name is Father Panzini."

CHAPTER THIRTY-SEVEN

"Am I really turning into such an old curmudgeon?"

Unsurprisingly, the tomato plant that Vittorio was watering didn't reply.

It was Benedetto who had leveled the charge earlier, when Vittorio changed his mind and ducked out of the evening screening of Jean Renoir's new film. The words had been spoken in jest, with no real malice on his son's part, but both men knew that they contained a touch of truth.

There was still time to change his mind. Benedetto, Giovanna, and Salvatore would be leaving for the Lido at six o'clock. Half an hour to spruce up and make himself presentable. It could be done.

The phone trilled in the drawing room. Vittorio placed the watering can on the table and wandered inside.

"It's me, Fredo."

"I hoped it might be. I'm looking for a

reason not to waste an evening out on the Lido."

"Is that all I am to you?"

"Pretty much," said Vittorio.

"Then you're in luck. I'm inviting you to dinner — my treat."

He would at least have company tonight, very fine company indeed, but it would come at a hefty price. It always did when Fredo offered to pay.

"I'll be sure to bring my checkbook," he joked.

"There's really no need."

"You always say that, my old friend."

"Well, of course, if you happen to have it with you . . ."

It was a trattoria where they had eaten many times over the years — a large and lively place in one of the poorer corners of Dorsoduro. Vittorio arrived to find Fredo — dressed, as ever, in a simple dark robe done up with silver buttons — already installed with a bottle of white wine at a large booth table.

"Monsignor Ruspoli," he said with faux formality.

Fredo smiled up at him and offered his hand.

"I never know whether to shake it or kiss it."

"Whatever takes your fancy," Fredo replied. "The Church can be very accommodating."

"Evidently, or they'd have thrown you out long ago."

"Some have tried."

"And where are they now?"

"Oh, food for the fishes at the bottom of the lagoon."

Vittorio laughed and gripped his friend's hand. "I wouldn't put it past you, Fredo."

It was said by many that Fredo might well have become the patriarch of Venice had he only been less worldly in his tastes and more discreet about his appreciation of the finer things in life, such as his beloved opera and theater. Then there were his sermons, noted for their humanity and their humor — qualities that some deemed too frivolous for a man whose sights were set on the highest office.

Vittorio knew differently. Fredo had never wished to become patriarch, and he had played his hand to perfection. Passed over for the top job, he had been allowed by way of a consolation prize to carve out a far more appealing role for himself, one unencumbered by onerous duties and tedious

Church politics. For some twenty years now he had served as a sort of elder statesman, a roving ambassador, the patriarch's man-about-town, free to indulge his love of the arts and the high life, because those were the circles in which the real money moved.

Even Fredo's detractors grudgingly admitted that he had a rare gift when it came to extracting large donations and bequests from the wealthy. The sheer quantity of cash he brought into the Church's coffers counted for a lot. He was provided with a large ground-floor apartment on the island of San Giorgio Maggiore, as well as a budget for entertaining potential benefactors in the style they were accustomed to.

Vittorio knew how their dinner would unfold. They would discuss a wide range of subjects: everything from football (Fredo rarely missed an AC Venezia home game) to the prospects of another European war. And later, when the coffee and liqueurs hit the table, Fredo would turn the conversation to some matter or other that was troubling him, and Vittorio would ask if there was anything he could do to help. The last time he'd had dinner on Fredo, he had ended up paying for thirty orphans to go hiking in the Dolomites. The time before that, he had covered the cost of replacing the gutters on the roof of the episcopal library.

Vittorio was still on his first glass of wine, and Fredo was telling him about a woeful performance of Donizetti's *Lucrezia Borgia* he'd recently attended in Milan, when an attractive young couple settled down at the table nearest theirs. Foreigners, most likely. Too tall to be Italian. Maybe even actors, given their looks, in Venice for the film festival. Yes, there was definitely something familiar in the man's face. He seemed nervous. Maybe it was a secret tryst. They had certainly picked a restaurant well off the beaten track.

"She's young enough to be your grand-daughter," said Fredo.

"Was I staring?"

"Almost drooling. May I finish my story now?"

"I'm sorry, go on."

Vittorio kept his eyes on Fredo, but one ear on the couple. They were English, although the light guttural note to the woman's accent suggested it might not be her mother tongue. There was something halting, even awkward, in their conversation that didn't bode well for their future relationship. Fredo, meanwhile, had moved on from Donizetti and was now waxing lyrical about Bruno Vale's merits as a midfielder.

Had he met the man before, or simply seen him somewhere? Asolo, possibly, at one of the rowdy parties thrown by their neighbor Vera, the eccentric English painter whose villa seemed to be permanently packed with beautiful young things during the summer months. He tried to put the matter from his mind, but it continued to niggle away, and soon after their pasta course had arrived, he apologized to Fredo and leaned toward the couple.

"Excuse me. Hello." He had their attention now. "I'm sorry, I know your face," he said to the young man. "Have we met in Asolo?"

"Asolo?"

"In the hills near Treviso."

"I've never been there. But we have met before."

"I knew it. Where?"

"Here," said the young man. "Venice."

"I don't remember."

"Neither do I. It was twenty-five years ago."

"Were you even born twenty-five years ago?"

"Just. I left soon after, on the eighth of January, 1912."

It was a date Vittorio had done his best to expunge from his mind. Hearing it spoken by a stranger sucked the air from his lungs. He looked to Fredo for help and saw immediately, by the steady gaze, that his friend was in on it.

"What is this?" he heard himself growl in Italian.

"You should hear what he has to say," Fredo replied. "It's quite a story."

"Oh, I'm sure it is." He turned to the young man, searching for the words in English. "You think you are the first to try this? You aren't. I am a rich man."

"I don't want your money, but I do need your help."

He had to get out, leave, go far away, or he was liable to do something he regretted, even throw a punch, such was the white flame of rage rising inside him. He pushed back his chair and got to his feet.

"Please, Vittorio, sit down," said Fredo.

Vittorio pulled some notes from his wallet and scattered them on the table. "I hope one day I find it within myself to forgive you for this."

As he turned to leave, he cast a cold glance at the young man. "Vincenzo is dead."

"Tell that to the Karaman brothers, because I'm not sure they'd agree with you."

Vittorio stopped, turned back slowly.

"What do you know about the Karaman brothers?"

"Only what I've been told by a man called Borodin. He works for them."

"And where is this Borodin?"

"Switzerland, probably dead by now."

"How convenient."

"Not for him," came the defiant reply.

Vittorio was aware that people were starting to stare, and he dropped his voice almost to a whisper. "A Croatian conspiracy?"

"Yes."

"We paid a ransom for Vincenzo to two men who then disappeared. They were Sicilians, not Croatians."

"I don't know anything about that."

"No, you don't, nor does Monsignor Ruspoli here, because my son and I did not tell anyone. What we *did* do was go to Sicily, twice. The second time, they said we would be killed if we returned." He let his words sink in. "It was the Sicilians."

Luke watched helplessly as his grandfather stalked out of the restaurant. This was not what he had envisaged. From the moment Father Panzini introduced them to Monsignor Ruspoli, he had allowed himself to believe that nothing now could stand in the way of a happy reunion. Monsignor Ruspoli had intimated as much, but it seemed that even he had misjudged the situation.

The monsignor was first to break the awkward silence. "If you have lied to me —"

"We'll leave now if that's what you really think," said Luke.

The monsignor's long look was followed by a shake of the head. "Of course not. Forgive me. Please . . ." He gestured for them to join him. A waiter pounced and wordlessly moved the plates and glasses from their table to the booth.

As soon as he had retired, Pippi said, "There must be an explanation for the Sicilians. Borodin would have an answer."

Monsignor Ruspoli dropped his gaze. "I'm afraid you were right. Borodin is dead."

"How do you know?" The words caught in Luke's throat.

"The Catholic Church is everywhere. I made a telephone call after I left you at Bianca's apartment this afternoon."

The details were patchy, but it seemed Borodin had somehow found the strength to walk off the mountain. He had checked into a small hotel in Splügen, where he had made a phone call and then asked for supper to be sent to his room. The serving girl

435

had found him dead on his bed when she went upstairs with the tray.

Luke saw from the set of Pippi's jaw that she was close to tears. He took her hand and held it.

"I am sorry for you both," said Monsignor Ruspoli.

"What do we do now?" asked Luke.

"We give your grandfather time."

"That's one thing we don't have," said Pippi.

The monsignor took a sip of wine. "Do you realize what we have just done to him? I do. He is the only man in Venice I can call a true friend. I knew him as a boy when he was sent here to study, and I have known him ever since, before and after you were taken. I have seen him go to some dark places, and I have seen him come back from them. I know that every morning he goes to the Rialto fish market, and although I don't know why, I suspect it is not to think of you, but to talk and laugh with other men in that place and tell himself he can live with what happened." He paused briefly. "You cannot ask a man who has been wearing armor for twenty-five years to take it off in two minutes." He looked at Pippi. "So yes, we have no time, but we also have no choice."

CHAPTER THIRTY-EIGHT

Vittorio tilted the bottle of whiskey against the candlelight. There was enough to chase away the demons the way he used to, to silence their lies, their taunting promises that if he could only hold out a little while longer, Vincenzo would be returned and the pain would go away.

Not all of it, for Alessandro had also been taken by then: a hero's death near Gorizia in the early days of the war, with a posthumous medal to prove it. Vittorio had suspected he might not see his son again, but he had never imagined that Alessandro would throw his life away so cheaply, in a futile assault on an Austrian gun emplacement. As for Marta, she had duped them all for months with her courage and resolve, before choosing to follow her husband.

Vittorio lit a cigarette and strolled to the edge of the terrace. He took a long gulp of whiskey, savoring its fire, and turned his face toward the heavens. There was no hint of a haze, and the domed firmament was almost dirty with stars. It was good to look at the world from the viewpoint of eternity. It helped set one's private miseries in perspective, to shrink them back to proportions altogether more manageable.

How could Fredo have been so foolish, so trusting? Fredo of all people? How, for that matter, had he become involved at all? It was a shocking lapse of judgment by a man who should have known better.

Mention of the Karamans had thrown him at first, stirring up memories long since overlaid, though not forgotten. He had never actually met the brothers. One of them was once pointed out to him in the streets of Spalato: not tall, but solid as a stump, and with a prodigious mustache. He knew that they were spoken of in hushed tones, but so were many other men who worked the wrong side of the law in those days. Unremarkable both in appearance and reputation. And now?

Had he not stuck to his resolution to have nothing more to do with Dalmatia, he might know what became of the two brothers. It was a situation easily rectified. He had a number of people in Venice he could rely on to dig out the information discreetly.

He pulled himself up short. His thoughts were leading him off down a dead-end road. It had to have been the Sicilians. That much had become clear during their first trip to the island, when, under the pretense of traveling to Rome on business, he and Alessandro had headed for Palermo instead. Their contact there, a venal little rogue called Bruccoleri, had spoken of rumors, taken their money, and sent them home with a promise to be in touch soon.

Less than a month later, they were back in Sicily, near the port of Trapani this time, on their way to meet with a man who claimed to have hard knowledge of Vincenzo's abduction. Bruccoleri drove them along dusty roads, deep into the hills back from the coast. Dusk was giving way to night when they finally reached their destination, an isolated farm surrounded by olive groves. A car stood empty out front, but as they pulled up beside it, four men materialized from the shadows. It was immediately clear that something had gone badly wrong, for Bruccoleri began pleading for clemency. This earned him a slap across the face and a threat of worse to come if he didn't shut up.

They were marched across rocky ground, past twisted olive trees, until they arrived at a deep ravine. Here they were made to kneel in the dirt, one man standing behind each of them, while the fourth offered them a choice. If they left the island first thing in the morning, they would live. If they ever returned to Sicily, they would die. There would be no second chance. Moreover, if anyone else came snooping on their behalf, whether policeman or layman, a visit would be paid to Venice, and an unfortunate accident would befall one or the other of their wives.

Alessandro begged for news of Vincenzo — something, anything — but was told simply, even politely, to come to terms with his loss. When he wouldn't shut up, the man placed the muzzle of his pistol between Vittorio's eyes and asked Alessandro if he wished to lose his father as well.

With silence restored, the man then came and stood before Bruccoleri. "You are alive only because they need someone to drive them back to Palermo. Take your family and go far away. I suggest America. You have two days to arrange it."

Knowing where the answers lay — within reach yet beyond it — had been the most terrible curse. Having traveled to Sicily in secret, he and Alessandro had then been bound together in silence, for no good could possibly come of sharing their discoveries. Many years later, long after Alessandro and Marta had left them, Elena said to Vittorio, quite out of the blue, while they were reading in bed one night: "I know there is something you have never told me, and I don't want to know what it is."

"Why not?" he had asked, opening the door a crack for her.

"Because I also know you did everything you could."

But she had been wrong. If he had only been shrewder, more courageous, things might well have turned out differently.

He drained his glass and wandered back to the table for a refill.

Before tonight, he had never mentioned the Sicilians to anyone other than Alessandro. He had done so for impact, to silence the Englishman's lies, to expose him for the fraud he was and to watch his face fall.

He took a seat at the table. A moth was engaged in its death dance around the candle flame.

"It was the Sicilians."

But even as he said it, he could see how the Karaman brothers might be made to fit alongside them.

Chapter Thirty-Nine

The offer came as they were leaving the restaurant: a lift back to their hotel in Monsignor Ruspoli's motorboat. It was tied up nearby, long and sleek, its wooden decks varnished to a high shine. More befitting a man of means than a man of God, Luke couldn't help thinking as he and Pippi settled into the leather seat at the back of the cockpit. The engine came to life with a low rumble.

The monsignor didn't attempt to engage them in conversation as he guided the boat through the network of dark waterways. There was nothing more to be said. They had talked the matter to a standstill over dinner, staying late in the hope that Vittorio Albrizzi might return. Well, he hadn't, and there was no reason to believe he ever would, other than the monsignor's words of reassurance.

The desolating news of Borodin's death

pointed up the wild disparity between a stranger with nothing to gain from helping them out, and Luke's grandfather, who had nothing to lose from hearing them out. To have gotten this far only to be shunned by his own flesh and blood had emptied Luke out, leaving a dirty residue of defiance and anger.

"I've had it. I want to go," he said to Pippi.

"I understand."

"Tomorrow."

They were sitting shoulder to shoulder, hand in hand. She kissed him softly on the cheek. "Let's see."

Thank God for her soothing presence. They had spent much of the afternoon at Bianca's apartment, with Pippi acting as translator. The three of them had sat together on the sofa, Bianca in the middle, the photograph album on her lap.

"That is your father . . ."

So young. His mother, too. Both of them younger than he was now. And so happy holding him, a featureless blob of a newborn in a frilly white bonnet. His mother's dark, wide-set eyes, the same eyes that had been staring back at him from mirrors all his life; even he could see that. And something familiar in the curl of his father's smile.

Or had he been searching for signs? He

had searched for them earlier in the lean, hawklike features of Vittorio Albrizzi and detected nothing to match the quivers of familiarity stirred up by those old sepia photographs. And yet, his grandfather had surely sensed something in him. Why else had he leaned across and introduced himself? For a happy moment, the monsignor's stratagem of seating them at the next table appeared to have worked, only to backfire badly.

Luke slipped an arm around Pippi's shoulder and rummaged for comfort in the other discoveries of that day: Bianca's amazement on hearing that he had become a pilot, for he had shown an early fascination with birds — the reason, in fact, that she had taken him to the Rialto market that morning, to watch the gulls feasting on fish scraps . . . Her tears on recalling the horror of his abduction and its aftermath, the sympathy of some no consolation at all, the vilification of others hurtful but fair enough to her way of thinking, for she had failed in her simple duty of care, a victim of her own vanity, distracted by the attentions of a young man working at one of the stalls . . . His birthday, known at last — March 4, 1911, only eight days off the one assigned to him by the nuns at St. Theresa's . . . The birth itself a long and difficult one, his mother's slender build not suited to bringing children into the world . . . More tears as Bianca told of hearing the news that his father had died in battle, a tragedy doubled before the year was out by the death of his mother, a keen and competent sailor but no match for the fierce squall that had capsized her boat near the island of Poveglia, her body never recovered.

These thoughts were cut short by their arrival at Campo San Barnaba. Monsignor Ruspoli killed the motor and held the boat against the quayside while they disembarked. He suggested they stay put at the hotel in the morning — not just for safety's sake, but so he could contact them as soon as he had news.

"Have faith," he urged.

"Easily said," Luke replied.

"Think of Bianca. Three times a day she went to the Frari to pray. How many candles is that?" He paused briefly to make the calculation. "More than twenty-five thousand. But it is the last one she will remember — the one that made the difference. There is always hope."

They stood and watched him leave, waiting until the running lights had faded into the darkness.

One of the two cafés on the square was still open. Luke suggested a nightcap, but Pippi was ready for bed. They were halfway across the square when she steered him toward the café.

"Changed your mind?"

"Someone has been in our room," she replied tightly. "No, don't look."

"Are you sure?"

"Yes. I closed all the shutters. One of them is open — not much, a bit."

They took an empty table at the café, Pippi positioning herself so she had a view of the hotel frontage behind him.

"The bathroom window."

"Maybe it was the maid."

"I told her not to clean the room."

"Why?"

"Why do you think?" Pippi replied irritably.

"So we would know."

A waiter loomed over them. They both ordered coffee and lit cigarettes.

"I think we're being watched," said Pippi.

"From up there?"

"Up there, down here, I don't know."

"Let's assume you're right. It costs us nothing to be cautious."

"What do we do?" she said.

"We drink our coffee and we figure out a

446

way to test your theory."

It wasn't much of a plan, but it was the best they could come up with by the time they'd settled the bill. They strolled toward the hotel, but instead of going in, they walked on past. The far corner of the square was lost in a slab of dark shadow, and only once it had swallowed them up did they glance behind them.

Several people were milling around the square. One of them, a short and solidly built man, wasn't exactly hurrying after them, but he was heading with purpose in their direction.

"What do you think?"

Before Pippi could reply, the man raised his hand toward the hotel and gesticulated.

"Oh, Christ, you were right," said Luke. It would take a man in a hurry no more than about thirty or forty seconds to descend to the street from their room.

"How did they find us?" said Pippi.

"I don't know. Keep walking. Don't run. Not yet."

A narrow street, poorly lit, struck out from the corner of the square along the south wall of the church. Up ahead on the right was a narrow passageway, but before they reached it, they heard furtive footfalls, picking up pace, closing from behind.

"Go," said Luke, pulling the pistol from the back of his waistband.

It was a short sprint to the turning, some twenty or thirty yards, and as they rounded the corner, Luke saw with relief that the passageway was as black as a tomb. Unfortunately, the stone footbridge spanning the canal at the far end of it was illuminated, which meant they would be perfectly silhouetted against the light for anyone in pursuit.

"Faster," he called to Pippi.

"My shoes."

"No time."

They were bounding over the bridge when something rent the air beside Luke's head and slapped into the building on the far side of the canal, sending out a shower of stone chips.

No warning. No report. A silenced weapon.

The passageway beyond the bridge was also unlit, as was the small square, more of a courtyard, that lay at the end of it. "This way," Pippi hissed, slowing to slip off her shoes before tearing off into the darkness.

To flee was natural — they were the hunted, the ones with a price on their heads. But even as they lost themselves in the warren of alleyways and canals, more certain with every turn that they were no longer being followed, a creeping sense of futility came over Luke. The two things they required in order to run truly free — passports and money — lay back at the hotel, a place they could no longer go.

Borodin hadn't just foreseen it, he had spelled it out to them in no uncertain terms: they had to be ready to end the thing here in Venice, whatever it required. Luke made this point to Pippi when her seemingly tireless legs finally required a rest and they slunk into the shadows to recover their breath.

"God knows how they found us, but they'll find us again if we don't do this now."

"I don't know," Pippi whispered.

"You want to keep running in circles until we bump into them?"

"No."

"So we wait for them to come to us."

"Here?"

It was as good a place as any: a small, darkened square where three thoroughfares converged. Better still, the modest palazzo to their right was fronted by a narrow garden: two tall palms and a thicket of bushes set back beyond a low wall topped by railings.

"It's the first place I would look."

"Good," said Luke. "Let them."

The windows were shuttered and there was no sign of light within, but they still behaved as though the palazzo was occupied. Teasing open the arched iron gate, they buried themselves away in the bushes as quietly as possible.

It wasn't long before a couple passed through the square. The man said something; the woman laughed. Happy, carefree, heading home to bed, not skulking in a stranger's shrubbery, gun in hand, ready to kill if the opportunity presented itself. A few minutes later, a shadowy figure appeared near the well at the heart of the square and broke wind — not just once, but five or six times. This impressive arpeggio was followed by the momentary flaring of a match, which revealed a man lighting a cigarette, and a small dog on a leash.

The dog growled, then barked.

"Zitto," the man chided. But the animal refused to be silenced. Maybe it had spotted the momentary gleam of their eyes in the foliage when the match was struck, or maybe it simply smelled their presence. In any event, it soon became clear that they were the source of its agitation. His interest piqued, the man allowed himself to be drawn toward the palazzo, the dog straining so hard against the leash that its breathing

came in rasps.

Not good, not good at all, Luke was thinking, when shutters swung open behind them, and they found themselves bathed in a pool of electric light.

"Time to go," he said to Pippi, rising from the bushes.

There was a lot of shouting, both from the woman in the nightdress at the palazzo's second-floor window and from the man with the dog. Pippi's apologies in Italian did nothing to quell the ruckus echoing around the square as they hurried from the front garden to the alleyway that had led them here.

They had traveled almost no distance along it when Pippi gripped Luke's arm, holding him back. Sounds in the darkness up ahead: feet pounding on flagstones, people running this way, drawn by the commotion. They turned and sprinted back the way they had come, skirting the well in the middle of the square and disappearing into the mouth of another passageway.

It veered to the right, straightening out for a long stretch before depositing them by the oil-black waters of a canal. They stopped just long enough to hear the footfalls behind them, then bore left along the wide path that ran beside the canal. It was lit at intervals, and the third time Luke threw a glance over his shoulder, he saw two men, some distance back but definitely in pursuit, arms and legs pumping.

"It's them. Faster."

"I can't," gasped Pippi.

There were no turnings on the left, and the only bridge was far ahead. It was a straight foot chase out in the open, and only a matter of time before the two men started taking potshots at them.

Just shy of the bridge, the buildings on the left gave way to a church square. Another glance behind him. A quick calculation. They would have to slow to cross the bridge, presenting a target as they did.

He grasped Pippi's hand. "This way."

They cut left across the square and were racing for the opposite corner when Luke saw his opportunity. Except for one long, low building, the far side of the square was open, bordered by a canal, its bank trimmed with a tiny patch of park: grass, a few trees, and little more.

"Go," he said. "I'll meet you at Bianca's."

To her credit, Pippi didn't question him or even break stride. Luke cut into the small park beside the canal, searching for shadows. It was a near thing — a mere second or two between Pippi disappearing around the corner of the church and the two men hurtling into the square. He heard rather than saw them from his hiding place, pressed up against the wall of the building that abutted the park.

They didn't come into view until they had reached the middle of the square, where they slowed to a walk, reading the lay of the land. Luke willed them to linger. Every second they delayed played in Pippi's favor, allowing her to distance herself from the danger. The church was dimly lit, and the stucco facade threw off just enough light for him to identify the taller of the two men as Petrovic.

His heart quickened at the prospect of avenging Sister Agnes' murder. Had he been ten yards nearer the target, he might have fired and taken his chances with the other man. But they were hurrying off now toward the side of the church.

He slipped off his shoes and socks. If he was going to surprise them from behind, he needed to move in silence. He saw Petrovic stop and peer down at the canal, at the boats moored stern to prow all the way back to where Luke was hidden. What was Petrovic thinking — that they had tucked themselves away in one? A muffled command sounded, and the smaller man began working his way back along the canal, into the park.

Luke dropped into a crouch at the base of the wall, his back to the brick, fingers groping in the dirt and closing around a pebble. He wouldn't fire unless he had to, and he waited until the man was almost on top of him before tossing the stone into the grass. He struck as the man was turning toward the sound.

The pistol butt hit the side of the man's skull with a sickening thud, and he dropped like a felled ox, landing facedown in the grass. Luke recovered the pistol from his limp fingers and tucked it into the back of his waistband.

Petrovic had drifted out of sight around the side of the church, but now he returned. He gave a short whistle. Luke replied with the same.

"Let's go," Petrovic hissed in French.

Luke stayed silent.

"Jestin."

A name they had been given by Borodin: Petrovic's accomplice in Zurich. A man to be feared.

This was Luke's last thought before his feet were kicked out from under him. He hit the ground hard and found his wrist seized in an iron grip, taking the gun out of play. Another hand closed around his wind-pipe. Had Jestin been at his best, Luke might not have been able to yank the fingers from his throat and roll away. He couldn't break the grip on his wrist, though, and as he struggled to his feet, he hauled a groggy Jestin with him.

Twisting, he slammed the other man against the wall of the building and pulled free, but before he could set himself to fire, Jestin charged, seizing him in a bear hug and driving him backward, backward . . . until the ground mysteriously vanished from beneath his feet.

He was vaguely aware of the gun slipping from his fingers as they fell, and Jestin was still attached to him when they hit the water hard. Maybe it was the impact, another blow to the head, but the fight went out of Jestin momentarily — long enough for Luke to twist free. Treading water, he reached behind him, fumbling urgently for the gun in his waistband. Too urgently. He had it, and then it was gone, through his fingers and sinking away.

Jestin lashed out, landing a weak punch on his jaw, then grabbed at his hair. Luke seized him by the shoulders and forced his head beneath the surface. As he did so, he saw the figure standing on the bank, looking down at them. Hauling Jestin back to the surface, Luke swiveled to use him as a shield. Petrovic wouldn't risk firing unless he had a clean shot.

He was wrong. The man clearly put little value in the life of his accomplice, for he started firing — muted reports, silenced.

Jestin twitched and gasped and flailed as the first bullets struck his back. He clawed at Luke, for anything to hold on to; then his head jerked to the side and he fell still. Luke held him up as protection just long enough to take a lungful of air and slip beneath the surface.

He kicked out, swimming alongside the building, where Petrovic couldn't follow him. He swam until his lungs were bursting, then swam some more. He surfaced as silently as possible, sucking in air and taking his bearings. On three sides, the building enclosed an open yard that ran down to the water's edge.

A bullet slapped into the water beside his head. He sank away and struck out, his hands soon finding firm ground beneath him: a ramp running into the water from the yard. He groped his way up it, surfaced, and scrabbled ashore.

Panting, he pinched the water from his eyes and forced himself to his feet. A boat-

456

yard. Dark shapes raised on trestles. Gondolas. The heady smell of paint or varnish in the air. Some oars, too long and unwieldy to serve as weapons, leaning against a wall. The workshop doors securely padlocked. Several pairs of overalls hanging from wooden pegs. Everything neat and ordered, no convenient piles of lumber lying around. *Think.* Any moment now, Petrovic would be coming through that door in the wall, the one with the light leaking through the cracks.

Lighting. Outside. It meant a brief advantage — a second or two while his pursuer's eyes adjusted to the starlit gloom of the yard. It meant Luke had to strike immediately and decisively. Sliding one of the oars beneath the workshop door, he snapped it in two, leaving himself with a club some four feet long. He then removed the overalls from the wooden pegs — all but one pair, which he rehung by the shoulders before bundling up another pair into a ball that would do for a head. Even if his makeshift scarecrow in the shadows didn't fool Petrovic, it might be enough to draw his eye, to distract him just long enough.

Though he was anticipating it, the bullet that blew out the door lock still caught him by surprise. Petrovic entered the yard warily, then spun and fired twice at the overalls. Stepping from the shadows, Luke brought the club down on the gun hand. The weapon clattered to the ground, and as Petrovic instinctively lunged for it, Luke swung again, going for the left shoulder, where Borodin had run him through with the sword cane.

Petrovic bellowed and rolled away, fleeing on hands and knees, unable to stand for all the blows raining down on him. Blind, raging, Luke broke off only to kick out, going for the ribs.

Petrovic made a few feeble attempts to seize the club or get to his feet, but it was useless. He ended up at the water's edge, spent, hunched in a ball. "Please. Stop."

Luke swung the club. "Did Sister Agnes ask you to stop?" Another blow. "Did she?" Another. "Did she?" Three more blows in quick succession — two across the shoulders, one to the head. "How does it feel?" Another blow to the head.

Petrovic now lay limp and unresisting at his feet. Luke backed away and sank to his knees, heart thumping wildly. He had yet to shed a tear for Sister Agnes, but they came now. He wept for what she had been and for what he had become because of her. He also wept for what men like Petrovic had turned him into, and for what he was about to do, and for what Agnes would think of him if she was up there somewhere looking down on him.

He dragged the sodden sleeve of his jacket across his eyes and rose to his feet. He had kicked the gun away when the beating began, and he found it eventually, wedged between the wall and a wooden barrel. Steeling himself for the task, he recalled Borodin's words of warning: that Petrovic would never stop, that he would keep on coming, no matter what.

But Petrovic was no longer there, not where he had been just moments before, in the shallows at the top of the ramp, prone and motionless.

Luke waded down the ramp until the water was at his chest, but all he saw were a few whorls and eddies breaking the silvered surface of the canal.

It was only as he neared the hotel that Luke realized he was limping. The toes of his right foot were stiffening up, sprained, or possibly broken, by the barefoot kicking in the boatyard. He had recovered his shoes from the park, and with his jacket slung over his shoulder, and his hand in his pocket, closed around the gun, he hoped he cut an inconspicuous figure as he strode into Campo San Barnaba.

In front of the café, a waiter was stacking chairs near a table of diehards looking to stretch the night out. Foscolo had warned them that they might have to ring the bell if they got back late, but the hotel door was unlocked. The lobby was deserted, and there was an empty space where their key should have been on the rack behind the counter. There was no way of knowing whether Petrovic had been the man in their room — the man Jestin had waved at while crossing the square. Although it seemed likely, Luke nonetheless crept cautiously up the staircase.

He waited at the door of their room, listening for sounds of movement inside. Satisfied, he eased the door open a crack and flicked on the electric light. He waited again before finally entering, and what he saw made him recoil.

He knew immediately from the pale yellow shirt that the man sprawled facedown on the floor at the end of the bed was Foscolo. He closed the door behind him, skirted the body, and checked the bathroom. Foscolo's throat had been slit. The pool of blood lacquering the floorboards suggested there was no hope of finding a pulse, but he checked all the same. Foscolo's wrist felt cool beneath his fingertips.

What had happened? There was no point in speculating. He needed to get what he had come for and get out. The room had been thoroughly searched. Drawers were open, clothes scattered about the place. The wardrobe had been moved, suggesting someone had searched beneath it. It was a good job he had thought better of it as a hiding place. The ceiling light was an opaque bowl of dark-green glass, suspended by three lengths of chain, and he could just make out the shadows of the money and their passports.

He stripped off his damp clothes, dried himself with a towel from the bathroom, and got dressed. He packed a suitcase with a change of clothes for each of them, shoes for Pippi, their toiletry bags, the field glasses, and the camera.

Stopping on the way out, he crouched and laid a hand on Foscolo's head.

"I'm sorry."

So many dead. Some innocent, some not so innocent, but all of them dead because of him. He was the wellspring from which so much blood had flowed. Would Gotal have spared him twenty-five years ago had he known what the true cost of his compassion would be?

He stole silently down the staircase and was descending the final flight to the lobby when he heard someone enter the hotel. He backtracked, withdrawing to the shadows of the landing. From here, he had a partial view of the reception counter. A man approached it, but it was only as he leaned over the counter, reaching for the register, that Luke caught sight of his face. There was no mistaking him, not this time. It was Cordell Oaks, the American.

Luke backed away from the banister, retreating along the corridor that led to the first-floor rooms. Halfway along was a tall wooden linen press, and he slipped behind it, turning the suitcase on end so it didn't protrude. The blood was pulsing so loudly in his ears that he had to strain to hear the footsteps. They paused briefly on the landing before carrying on up the staircase.

Thirty seconds later, he was hurrying across Campo San Barnaba. He didn't look back until he reached the relative safety of the footbridge beyond the church. The light in their room was on.

CHAPTER FORTY

Vittorio hadn't slept for three hours straight in years. Then again, it was years since he had put away half a bottle of whiskey in one sitting.

He had woken in the early hours of the morning to find himself sprawled on the sofa, an empty glass still in his hand, and had lain there in the darkness with his headache for another hour, replaying the events of the evening. After a hot bath and two cups of tarry black coffee, he had dressed, snipped a rose from a bush on his terrace, and crept silently from the top of the palazzo to the boathouse at its very bottom. Not since Elena had left him so suddenly had he needed her more than he did now.

It was a good hour until sunrise, and the skiff rose and fell on an unseen swell as soon as he was clear of the canal. The effect was so calming, so hypnotic, that he slowed to a crawl, savoring the lazy pulse beneath him and the creeping twilight above. The dark, shapeless mass of Isola di San Michele lay before him like a ship of the dead, and he knew in that moment that he would not be landing there.

"Forgive me, my darling," he said, "but I think I've just made the biggest mistake of my life."

He twisted the throttle and turned the skiff to the south.

The monastery of San Giorgio Maggiore had long been a sorry neighbor to Palladio's magnificent church. A military garrison for much of the past century, it now stood abandoned and boarded up, its stonework crumbling, its gardens and cloistered court-yards overgrown.

On Fredo's initiative, one small section of it had been renovated, and this was where he now lived, in a large ground-floor apartment giving onto what had once been the monks' vegetable garden. His dream was to see the whole complex restored to its former glory before he died. But there were some within the patriarch's inner circle for whom it was not a priority, and the best he had been able to do was stop the rot by seeing that the roofs were kept in good repair.

Vittorio tied up next to Fredo's sleek black motor launch in the tiny harbor sandwiched between the back of the monastery and the expanse of overgrown woodland that made up the rest of the island. From here, it was a short walk to the monsignor's front door.

He was reaching for the knocker a third time when the door swung open. Fredo stood before him in his nightshirt, tousled and bleary-eyed.

"I thought it might be you," he said wearily.

"The Karamans used the Sicilians as bagmen, couriers, to throw us off the scent."

"It seems likely."

"Is he here, Fredo?"

"No."

"But you know where he is?" He could hear the note of desperation in his own voice.

"Yes, don't worry." Fredo drew him inside and closed the door. "I'll get Mother Ignatia to put some clothes on and make us coffee."

Mother Ignatia was a woman of colossal faith and calamitous appearance.

"Don't make me laugh," said Vittorio.

Fredo laid a hand on his shoulder, guiding him toward the living room. "Why not? You should be happy. You will be when you hear what I have to tell you."

"Do you really think it's him?"

"I'm sure of it."

"What have I done, Fredo?"

"Nothing that can't be rectified, you old fool."

Luke woke with a start, eyes wide in fear. Someone was standing over him, reaching for him . . .

Pippi, in her satin nightdress.

Cold panic giving way to relief. Light now bleeding through the slats of the shutters in Bianca's living room. The gun lay beside him on the sofa, which he had turned so that it faced the front door.

"I'm sorry, I fell asleep."

"I'm sure you're wrong," said Pippi.

"But what if I'm not?"

Apart from Bianca, who was well above suspicion, Monsignor Ruspoli was the only person who had known they were staying at the Hotel San Barnaba. They had told him in this very room, soon after meeting him for the first time. It seemed implausible that they had somehow fallen into the clutches of a senior Venetian prelate with connections to the Karaman brothers, but Luke felt entitled to indulge his paranoia. After encountering Cordell Oaks at the hotel,

466

anything was possible.

He hadn't mentioned Oaks to Pippi. There was nothing to gain from adding to her fear and confusion. All that mattered now was getting through the night and leaving the city with their lives.

Pippi settled down beside him on the sofa, tucking her feet beneath her and laying her head against his shoulder. He planted a kiss on her forehead.

"Go back to bed."

"No, I want be with you."

"That's nice."

"And I don't want you shooting Bianca's brother when he gets here."

Fredo suggested that they take the skiff in tow behind his launch.

"It'll slow us down."

"Not by much."

"I just want to get there, Fredo. Can we please just hurry?"

Fredo obliged. They flew across the channel north of the island, the launch finally coming off the plane only as they entered the mouth of the Grand Canal. Vittorio felt almost intoxicated with anticipation as they turned into Rio de San Barnaba. He sobered up fast when he saw a police launch and a water ambulance docked beside the *campo.*

467

"Dear God," he muttered.

His worst fears were confirmed even before they had tied up. A small crowd was gathered in front of the Hotel San Barnaba.

"Wait here," said Fredo.

"I can't."

"I'm telling you to stay."

He did, watching in dumb horror as Fredo crossed the square and addressed himself to a *carabiniere* keeping a small crowd of the curious at bay. A body came out of the hotel, on a stretcher carried by two medics. It was covered from head to toe by a blanket, which meant only one thing.

"No . . ." groaned Vittorio.

Before he knew it, he had scrambled ashore and was hurrying toward the hotel. He saw Fredo step forward and fold back the blanket; he saw him make the sign of the cross over the corpse; and he saw some in the crowd take their lead from the monsignor and cross themselves. Fredo covered the face, then turned and caught Vittorio's eye.

Was that a shake of the head? What did it mean? No, he's not alive?

Fredo caught him by the elbow and steered him away, back toward the boat. "It's not him."

Had he heard right?

"Are you sure?"

"It's the concierge. He was murdered, his throat slit."

To celebrate such news was inappropriate, and Vittorio's elation was tempered with a twinge of guilt. "Is there any sign of them?"

"No, but I have an idea where they might be."

"Where?"

"If we're not too late."

The last time Vittorio had seen Bianca, she was a young woman. The person who opened the door to them had dark hair threaded with deep, gray lines around her mouth, and eyes as hard as gemstones.

"Bianca, this is —"

"I know who it is, Monsignor."

"And do you know why we're here?"

She didn't reply to the question. Instead, she turned her unforgiving gaze on Vittorio and asked, "Where were you when he needed you?"

"I know, I know . . ."

"Where were you when *I* needed you?"

Vittorio felt his cheeks flush at the memory. He had not only accused Bianca to her face of colluding in Vincenzo's abduction, he had then denounced her to the police, who had taken her into custody and questioned her for several days.

"Bianca, God requires us to forgive."

"Oh, I forgave him a long time ago, Monsignor. I just needed to say it."

"Are they here?" asked Fredo.

"You just missed them. You'll have to hurry."

CHAPTER FORTY-ONE

"Why are you smiling?" Pippi asked.

Bianca's brother Araldo was at the wheel of the boat, and they were standing beside him, the wind in their faces, squinting at the low shoreline on the far side of the lagoon.

"I was thinking . . . we didn't just fail; we're now fugitives from justice in four European countries."

"But not in Tahiti."

It had started as a fantasy, a solace, something to cling to. No longer. In a few minutes, they would come ashore in a remote spot and find a car waiting for them, and also a man — a friend of Araldo — ready to drive them wherever they wished to go. They had yet to decide. Far from Venice as quickly as possible, that much was certain. Maybe south to Bologna, then a train to Livorno, followed by a boat to Spain, where the chaos of the civil war, the flood of foreigners coming and going, lent itself to losing oneself. From there it was a short hop to Portugal, to Lisbon, to the Atlantic and everything beyond it.

Luke turned and took one last look at Venice, the floating city of his birth, receding behind them . . . and something not receding. A boat was flying across the lagoon, set on the same course as theirs.

"Pippi, look." She turned and took in the view. "It's probably nothing."

Pippi wasn't so sure. *"Araldo, più rapido,"* she said. Araldo threw a quick glance over his shoulder and pushed the throttle lever forward as far as it would go.

It made little difference. The boat continued to gain on them. Luke spun around, taking in the approaching shoreline. "We're not going to make it."

"No," Pippi concurred.

She threw open the suitcase and fished out her gun. As soon as Araldo saw the weapon, he started to panic. Pippi snapped at him in Italian, but the poor man was almost in tears. Pippi grabbed the field glasses from the suitcase and trained them on the boat. "I can't see," she said, trying to focus. "Oh, God, it's Monsignor Ruspoli."

Luke took Petrovic's silenced pistol from his pocket. Three cartridges. He had counted them in and out of the magazine last night at Bianca's apartment.

"There's someone with him."

Pippi's pistol held six. Nine total. Enough to give them a fighting chance.

"It's Vittorio."

"My grandfather? Are you sure?"

"Yes, it's him."

It took a bit of persuading to get Araldo to ease off the throttle and bring them to a halt. The monsignor's launch overshot them, carving a long turn before drawing up alongside. Nothing was said until Luke had helped his grandfather clamber aboard.

"Fredo has told me everything. Is it really you?"

"I don't know," Luke replied.

Vittorio smiled. "I do." He reached for Luke and they clung to each other. "I'm sorry, I'm so sorry, forgive me." He choked back a sob. "Come home."

"I can't. They'll find us again. How *did* they find us?"

"I don't know. *Ma ci si può giocare in due.*" Vittorio turned. "How do you say in English, Fredo?"

"Two can play at that game."

CHAPTER FORTY-TWO

Benedetto, Giovanna, and the children were leaving for the villa at Asolo that evening for a couple of weeks, and when Vittorio returned to the palazzo he found it a hive of activity. Giovanna was at the heart of the commotion, snapping orders — the general marshaling her small troop of staff. There were beds to be stripped, rooms to be cleaned, clothes to be ironed and packed. Benedetto was off at the Lido, getting one final dose of the film festival before the break, but even if his son had been present, Vittorio would have said nothing to him of Vincenzo.

Vincenzo? Luke? Did it matter? No, the only thing that mattered for now was his safety, and there was still a way to go before that could be ensured. It meant acting with speed and ruthlessness, well outside the law, and he didn't wish Benedetto to be guilty, even by association, of the dark deeds that needed to be done.

Alone in his apartment on the top floor of the palazzo, he sat with this thought for a good while, following it through. By the time he finally rose from the chair on the terrace, he had accepted, with regret, that Vincenzo would never be able to take his rightful place in the family — not publicly, at least. How could his miraculous reappearance after twenty-five years be explained? With the truth? The truth would condemn him in Germany, where he had shot and killed an official; he was party to two more killings in Zurich; and here in Venice, a murdered man had been discovered in his hotel room. Through no fault of his own, simply to stay alive, he had left a trail of bodies across Europe. Could he really just show up in Italy and hope to be forgiven?

There was another vital consideration, and it was this that ultimately sealed the matter in Vittorio's mind. For it to be truly over, it wasn't enough that the Karamans die; they had to die in a manner that left no connection between Vincenzo and their deaths, or someone might come looking to avenge them. Yes, his big, beautiful grandson was back, and although he wanted to scream the joyous news through the streets of the city, only immediate family and a handful of friends could ever be allowed to know it.

His first priority was personnel. He needed men who could be trusted to act without hesitation and keep their silence afterward. There was never any doubt who he would contact first.

"Giorgio, it's Vittorio Albrizzi."

"*Dottore,* what a pleasure it is to hear from you."

"How's the haulage business?"

"Better than ever, but don't tell anyone, or the drivers will ask for a raise."

Almost thirty years had passed since the two of them left the courthouse in Spalato and boarded the plane back to Italy. Giorgio had fully expected to spend a good deal of his life in jail for murder after firing on the mob that had threatened to overrun the Albrizzis' residence. "I'll never forget that you stayed and fought for me," Giorgio had said at the time, and many times since. Vittorio had given him the money to buy his first truck, and he had been honored when asked to be godfather to Giorgio and Laura's first child, Grazia.

Giorgio was the one to cut the pleasantries short. "Come on, Dottore, out with it. What's on your mind?"

"It's . . . delicate."

476

"I may look like a brute, but I can do delicate."

"Do you remember our last day together in Dalmatia?"

"Only every morning when I wake and give thanks for another day of freedom put between me and it."

"It's not over, Giorgio. It never went away."

There was a heavy silence at the other end of the line. Then: "Sounds like we should meet."

"Yes, that would be good."

"Just name the time and the place, Dottore."

Vittorio thought about telephoning Croatia but decided it could wait. Another ten minutes was neither here nor there in the grand scheme of things. Best to call in another favor first. He asked the operator to put him through to the Questura.

By law, all foreigners had to submit their passport to the hotel or *pensione* where they were staying. The details were then recorded and passed on to the Questura, the local police headquarters. There was every chance that the Karamans' henchman, Petrovic, was in the system, an arcane and bureaucratic world shut off to the masses — unless you happened to have someone on the inside. Some years ago, Vittorio had used his influence to secure a promotion for the son of a friend. Carlo Gasperi's steely ambition had done the rest, and he now held a senior position in the Questore's office, where reaching him meant getting past his private secretary.

"I'm afraid Signore Gasperi is in a meeting, sir."

A lie. She would have known that already without having to check.

"Please tell him it's a matter of the utmost urgency. I'll hold."

Carlo finally came on the line. "Signore Albrizzi," he said, his tone guarded, even cold.

"I'll come straight to the point, Carlo. I need a favor."

"I assume you're joking."

"Why would I be joking?"

Carlo lowered his voice. "You haven't heard what happened at San Barnaba?"

A lifetime in business had taught Vittorio that there were times to feign ignorance, and times to feign knowledge.

"That was unfortunate, I grant you."

"Unfortunate?" snorted Carlo. "I can think of other words."

"I don't doubt it." Vittorio felt his mouth moving, heard the words issuing from it, and felt a cold dread in his heart.

"I owe you a lot, Signore Albrizzi; I'm the first to admit it. But please don't contact me again. And you can tell Benedetto the same."

Vittorio closed his eyes, exhaled, then said, "Don't hang up, Carlo."

"This conversation is over."

"Listen to me very carefully. You are complicit in a murder."

"All I did was —"

"Be quiet and listen. There is a café in front of the church of San Niccolò da Tolentino. Be there in half an hour. Do not speak to anyone else in the meantime — no one at all. If you don't show up, I will destroy you. Have no illusions about that. However, I can also protect you. Your life will go on just as before, and this will become no more than a bad memory. Do you understand me?"

"Yes," came the feeble reply.

"Half an hour. Don't be late."

With a trembling hand, Vittorio replaced the receiver on the cradle. He could have told Carlo twenty minutes, but he needed a bit more time to gather himself.

Benedetto? Surely not. It wasn't possible. But he saw the why of it, saw how it fit with everything else, and felt the euphoria of the past few hours seeping away.

The last time Luke drowsed with the sun on his face had been while lying beside a lake in Switzerland. It felt like a lifetime ago, but as he traced the road back in his mind — to Lake Como by way of Bergamo, then over the Alps to Zurich and Luzern — he calculated that only four days had elapsed, almost to the hour, since Pippi insisted they stop for a swim at Interlaken.

They had been ignorant then, and now they had the answers. They had killed and they had watched men die. They had fought each other, consoled each other, and slept together as lovers. Jubilation, terror, hope, despair, laughter, revulsion . . . Was there any emotion they hadn't experienced together in that time?

And now this: an uneasy calm. The eye of the storm, or the end of it, as his grandfather had promised them? Before leaving them in the care of Monsignor Ruspoli, Vittorio had given them his solemn promise that he would see them safe for all of time. A tour of the abandoned and sadly dilapidated monastery where the monsignor lived had been followed by a light lunch of cold roast duck, salad, and chilled red wine, and from the table on the terrace it had been a short stroll to the bench at the end of the garden, where Luke now hovered on the fringes of sleep, not quite able to give himself over to it.

Male voices. His hand groped for the gun in his jacket pocket as his eyes struggled to focus. His grandfather had returned, and there was someone with him.

"This is Giorgio."

Giorgio was a powerfully built man with a heavy brow and hair growing up his throat. He gripped Luke's hand and said something in Italian that earned him a laugh all around.

"He's happy," Pippi explained. "The last time you met, you cried when you saw him."

They had bad news: Petrovic was alive. He had checked out of his hotel room this morning. His whereabouts were currently unknown, but there was every chance they would have another fix on him by tomorrow at the latest, assuming he was still in Venice.

"How did you find him?" asked Luke.

"The same way they found you: the Questura."

Before Luke could ask what he meant, Monsignor Ruspoli said with surprise, "They have someone in the Questura?"

"No, but they have someone who does."

Vittorio faltered before adding, "Bene-detto."

Luke had received a family history lesson yesterday from Bianca, and there had been more talk of his relatives over lunch with the monsignor. "My uncle?"

"Yes."

The monsignor was clearly pained by the news. "Why?" he demanded.

"I will tell you when I have talked to him."

For now, the most likely explanation seemed to be that the Karamans, on discovering that Luke was still alive, had sought to capitalize on the information, peddling it to the man who stood to lose the most from it — along with a promise to nip the problem in the bud. As theories went, it fit with Borodin's final words of caution to Luke and Pippi: that the Karamans always sought a way to make a situation pay.

"What are you going to do?" asked Monsignor Ruspoli.

"With Benedetto? Why, use him, of course."

"And then?"

"And then we'll see."

Luke saw the vacant look of sorrow in his grandfather's eyes. "I'm sorry," he said.

"After everything you have been through, you think of me?"

"His father's son," said the monsignor.

"Yes, just like Alessandro."

As he was leaving with Giorgio, Vittorio took Luke aside.

"I know you want to help, but you and Pippi must stay here with Fredo and let me finish it. There are some bad things to be done. I am an old man; I don't have to live with my conscience for long. You have your whole life."

CHAPTER FORTY-THREE

Vittorio waited until the family were about to board the launch before making his move.

"Stay with me tonight," he said to Benedetto. "You can join them in Asolo tomorrow."

"You know I can't, Papa. Giovanna —"

"Giovanna won't mind when she hears why. I've made a decision. I'm stepping down."

"Stepping down?"

"Retiring. From the company. That's right. Albrizzi Marittima is yours."

Benedetto appeared genuinely stunned. *"Mine?"*

"To do with as you see fit, without your old father throwing his weight around."

"Are you sure?"

Vittorio contrived an ironic smile. "Well, I might change my mind if you can't spare me one little evening to talk it through."

He watched from a distance as Benedetto

broke the news to Giovanna, and he thought for a moment that she might actually let out a yelp of joy. Collecting herself, she hurried over and gave Vittorio the first hug he had received from her in years.

"You'll still be living with us, I hope."

It was the last thing she hoped for, and it cost Vittorio nothing to boost her pleasure still further. "Please don't be offended, but I thought I might take a small place of my own. I'm not getting any younger, and all those stairs up to the top floor . . ."

"I'm not offended, Papa."

So, not just a hug; he was "Papa" again.

With the staff all gone, it fell to Vittorio to open the bottle of vintage champagne he had placed on ice earlier.

"I've booked us a table at Harry's Bar," he said, filling two flutes. "Your favorite table."

Benedetto beat him to the toast: "To the best father any man could ever hope to have."

They clinked glasses.

"How does it feel?" asked Vittorio. "You now have everything you always wanted."

"I only want what you want, Papa."

"Benedetto, please, you're allowed to be happy for yourself. It's only human."

"Okay, yes, I'm happy," he beamed.

"That's good, because I want you to hold the prize, to feel it in your hands, feel the weight of it, before I ask the question."

"What question?"

Vittorio took a sip of champagne and bestowed a kindly smile on his son. "Do you have a telephone number for the Karaman brothers?"

"Who?"

Impressive. Barely a tremor in his eyes.

"You heard me. Do you have a number for the Karamans, or do they call you?"

"I'm sorry, I don't know what you're talking about."

Vittorio laid his glass aside and lit a cigarette, letting Benedetto stew. "I'm going to allow you two more denials. After the third, I can't help you."

"Help me with what?"

"That counts as one. I'm talking about Vincenzo. I'm talking about Petrovic."

"Petrovic? I've never heard that name before."

"You can have that one on me. It's possible you don't know his name. Petrovic works for the Karamans. He is the man you told about the Hotel San Barnaba."

"Papa, I really don't know what you're talking about."

"And you've just used up your second denial." Seeing that Benedetto was about to reply, Vittorio raised his hand. "No, think very carefully before you speak again. You're wondering if I am bluffing. I am not. I know about Gasperi at the Questura. I know you gave him a name: Luke Hamilton. Where did you get that name, Benedetto? Who told you about him?"

Benedetto made to pour himself some more champagne, then changed his mind. Abandoning his glass, he sat down on the divan, head in his hands.

"Look at me, Benedetto. I said *look at me.*" Benedetto finally looked up, his face creased with shame and anguish. "How much did you pay the Karamans?"

"What they asked for."

"Tell me. I want to know how much your nephew's life was worth to you."

"Four hundred thousand lire."

"Company money?"

"Not all of it."

"What were the terms of payment?"

"Does it matter?"

"It does to me," replied Vittorio.

"Half up front, the rest on completion."

"Completion . . . It sounds so innocuous. Do you have any idea how many other

487

people have been 'completed' because of you?"

"No."

"Do you want to know?"

Benedetto bowed and shook his head. "No."

Vittorio had told himself he wouldn't lose his temper, but he hurled his flute into the fireplace, where it shattered across the tiled hearth. "At least ten, from what I've been told, and it's not over yet!"

Drawn by the noise, Giorgio came hurrying into the drawing room with two men at his shoulder. Vittorio nodded at them and they retired warily.

"What's he doing here?" asked Benedetto.

"You'll see."

"None of this would have happened if it wasn't for him. If he hadn't fired at the crowd."

"Don't you dare seek an excuse for your actions. You should have come to me when the Karamans approached you." Vittorio crushed out his cigarette in the ashtray.

"What are you going to do?" Benedetto asked in a quavering voice.

"Bury it — along with the Karamans. And you're going to help me. You won't be joining your family in Asolo anytime soon."

"What do I tell Giovanna?"

"That something has come up, that you can't get away. Or you can tell her the truth if you like: that I've decided to sell the company."

"Sell it? You can't."

"I think you'll find I can. We have a number of suitors, as you know, and I don't like the direction you've taken it in."

"We're doing better than ever," Benedetto whined.

"For how long? I don't have the same blind faith in Mussolini that you and your friends do. There's a war coming, and something tells me we're going to be on the wrong side of it this time. What do you think Albrizzi Marittima is going to be worth after that?"

"It's a mistake."

"I've made my decision. If you fight it, you'll fight from prison."

Benedetto seemed to weigh the threat. "And if I don't fight it?"

"You'll receive a portion of the proceeds from the sale — less than you would like, but more than you deserve — enough to get started, though not in Italy, not even in Europe. Far away. You will present your departure as your own decision, one taken in anger against a father who sold your life's work out from under you — a father you never wish to see or speak to again."

Benedetto nodded several times. "Is this what you want?"

"No, I want my only son back. I want it to be like it was before, but that's not possible." Vittorio took a moment to steady himself. "Back to my first question: Do you have a telephone number for the Karamans?"

"Yes."

"Good, because you're going to call them and tell them exactly what I tell you to say."

CHAPTER FORTY-FOUR

Petrovic knew the symptoms because he had broken ribs in the past. Every intake of breath was a dagger in his chest. The aspirins had taken the edge off the bruising around his shoulders, back, and thighs, but he was going to need something stronger for the ribs.

Curled up on the mattress, groaning, it was hard to think of himself as a lucky man, but he knew he was. He had come within seconds of death last night. Hamilton had been ready to kill him, and if he had broken off, it could only be to look for the gun to finish the job. Summoning every last scrap of strength, Petrovic had slithered into the water and swum silently away, around the corner into a narrow canal. He had hidden in the dark, tight space between two moored boats, shivering and listening, before finally hauling himself over a gunwale, too battered and exhausted to do anything but lie beneath a piece of tarpaulin until daybreak.

His clothes had all but dried off in the morning sunshine during the walk back to the hotel, and he had checked out immediately, decamping by water taxi to another hotel — one closer to the station, closer to the car. The Karamans had been surprisingly sanguine about last night's debacle, possibly because he had come so tantalizingly close to completing the mission. Watching Hamilton and Jestin thrashing around in the water, he had assumed it was as good as done. Two birds with one stone: Hamilton dead and Jestin silenced. How had he gone from that to writhing on a bed, with at least two broken ribs?

The pain was getting worse. He needed to get to a pharmacy before the shops closed. A bottle or two of cough syrup should do the trick — something with an opiate in it. He was dressing himself with difficulty when the phone rang.

It was Josip Karaman.

"Albrizzi just called. He heard what happened at the hotel. He's happy as a king."

It didn't make sense. "I don't understand."

"There's no sign of Hamilton. He thinks you have dealt with the problem."

"I will," said Petrovic. "You have my word."

"I don't want your word. I want you to call Albrizzi and arrange to pick up the last payment. He has the cash ready."

"And Hamilton?" he asked.

"Long gone by now, if he has any sense."

"I'm not finished with him yet."

"You think *we* are?" said Josip. "You'll have your fun when we find him. For now, the money comes first. You'll drive it to Monfalcone, then head back to Paris. We need you to put our house in order there. The vultures are already circling."

The ringing phone cut through the nervous silence in the drawing room.

"Remember, you're delighted with the outcome," said Vittorio. "Don't forget to thank him."

Benedetto tapped the ash from the end of his cigarette and rose to his feet. "I know what I'm doing."

Of course he did, Vittorio mused. He had shown himself to be a master of deceit.

Benedetto crossed the room and raised the receiver to his ear.

"Albrizzi," he said.

A couple of hours ago, Petrovic reflected,

he wouldn't have been able to climb into the boat, let alone row the damn thing. Two bottles of foul-tasting cough syrup had worked wonders. He felt almost nothing — just a dull throb in his side, and a giddy sense of well-being. Emboldened, he even toyed with the thought of keeping the money for himself. Where would he go? And how long would it be before the Karamans tracked him down? No, he would take his chances with Monfalcone, and take precautions when he got there.

When he reached the Grand Canal, he guided the rowing boat to the left, counting off the palazzos as he passed them. There it was: a pinprick of light — the lantern Albrizzi had said he would hang in the boat-house. He stopped briefly to place his pistol in his lap as he maneuvered past the wooden pilings and beneath the arch. The lantern cast a dim, eerie light around the vaulted space, and the water lapped lazily against the narrow quay where the big launch was moored. He waited, allowing his eyes to adjust fully before clambering out of the boat. Then he waited some more. No hurry. Better to be safe.

He almost felt sorry for Albrizzi. If he thought this was the end of it, he was sorely mistaken. He would be doing business with the Karamans for the rest of his days. Now that they had a hold over him, his ships would be running their contraband before he knew it. That was where they made the real money: ensnaring wealthy, respectable, influential types like Albrizzi and folding them into the organization.

He pulled the flashlight from his jacket pocket and ran it over the launch, firing the beam through the windows of the low cabin. A leather bag sat on the table, exactly where Albrizzi had said it would be. He stepped warily aboard, avoiding the coil of heavy chain on the rear deck, and peered into the cabin before entering. He was reaching for the bag when something hit him so hard across the shins that he fell on his face before he could put his hands down.

There was a brief moment of dazed consciousness, the metallic taste of blood in his mouth, then nothing.

The sound of a motor. The slight pitch and roll of a boat. He breathed in and gagged. Blood in his throat. From his nose. He tried to reach for it, but his hands were bound fast to his side. No, not bound, exactly. He was wrapped in chain, cocooned like a chrysalis, lying on the deck.

"Help!" he shouted in Italian. "Help!"

"No one can hear you," said a voice in the language of his youth.

A man at the wheel of the boat, no more than a dark mass.

"Who are you?" he asked, the terrible reality beginning to dawn on him. The whole thing had been a setup by the Karamans in order to get rid of him. Why else was this man speaking Serbo-Croat? "You work for them, don't you? You work for the Karamans."

The man chuckled at the thought. "No, but I'll be seeing them very soon, and I'll be sure to convey your respects."

Petrovic struggled, but it was useless under the crushing weight of the chain. He couldn't even roll onto his side.

"Wriggle all you like, little worm; you're not going anywhere."

"Where are you taking me?"

"Here," said the man, cutting the boat's motor. The sudden silence was disturbing.

"Where are we?"

"Out beyond the lagoon, beyond the Lido."

"The sea?"

"You're a smart one, aren't you?"

The man seized him by the shoulders and hauled him across the deck.

"What are you doing?"

"Finishing what I started."

"What does that mean?"

"Work it out for yourself."

He found himself hoisted up until his head was hanging over the side of the boat. "No, don't, please, I beg you!"

"How did you think you would die? Peacefully in your sleep? A heart attack while gardening?" The man put his mouth close to Petrovic's ear. "You beat a nun to death, and now you're going to pay for it."

Petrovic felt his feet being raised, and he began to sob. "For the love of God, don't! I have money. I have a lot of money. It's yours."

"What, no apology?"

"I'm sorry. They made me do it to her. I didn't want to do it."

"Do you even know her name?"

"Her name? No. Yes." Hamilton had mentioned it last night. What was it? "Wait. Yes —"

"Her name was Agnes."

He's just trying to scare me. He'll haul me back out. That was his first thought as his head plunged beneath the surface.

The speed of his descent was what struck him next. Then the drop in temperature, the black cold closing around him, calling to him.

He opened his mouth and screamed back at it in anger.

CHAPTER FORTY-FIVE

They were finishing breakfast on the terrace when Vittorio appeared, alone and unannounced. Monsignor Ruspoli soon made himself scarce.

"He knows what I am going to say, and he does not want to hear it. Petrovic is dead."

So, it was done, as Borodin had insisted it must be. Pippi poured a cup of black coffee and slid it across the table toward Vittorio.

"Thank you, *cara.*"

"No, thank *you,*" she replied.

"Things are moving quickly. It is time for you to leave Italy."

"How?" asked Luke. "They'll be looking for us at the border."

"They won't find you. You will fly from Trieste on a private plane. No one will check your passports. It has been arranged."

"You can do that?" asked Luke.

"Transport is my business."

"Where are we going?" Pippi asked.

"Paris." Vittorio turned to Luke. "You have to make things right with your own people. I have spoken to a man I know in London, in the Foreign Office. He will help you from his end."

Luke glanced at Pippi. "There's something we need to do first — a promise we made to Borodin. I'd like to keep it if possible."

"Tell me," said Vittorio. "I'll see what we can do."

Monsignor Ruspoli accompanied them through the grounds of the monastery to the harbor. He brushed aside Luke's and Pippi's thanks, then hugged them both, wished them well, and shooed them on their way.

Luke was standing beside his grandfather as the launch nosed out of the harbor.

"Benedetto wants to meet you," said Vittorio.

"Why?"

"To apologize."

"I don't want his apology."

"I told him you would say that. I also told him I would give you this."

He produced a letter from the breast pocket of his jacket and handed it to Luke. A single word was written in a neat cursive hand on the envelope: *Vincenzo.* Luke was tempted to toss it over the side, but he folded it and slipped it into his hip pocket.

CROATIA

CHAPTER FORTY-SIX

The shadows cast by the smattering of clouds high above them spotted the blue-green waters of the Adriatic far below, like lily pads on a pond.

It was Giorgio's second time in an airplane. The first had been almost thirty years ago: the flight from Spalato to Venice with Luke's grandfather. He had hated the experience then, and he hated it more now. He sat rigidly upright in the leather seat, his big hands throttling the armrests with every creak, groan, and lurch of the aircraft.

The letter had been in Luke's pocket since morning, awaiting its fate. He opened it now and read the two pages of densely packed handwriting. When he had finished, he handed it to Pippi, seated just in front of him.

"It's better than nothing," she said when she was done.

"You think?"

"You don't?"

"I think they're just words, from a man who got caught."

Vittorio returned to his seat from the cockpit. "I told the captain you are a pilot. He is happy for you to . . ." He gestured toward the cockpit.

"It's a bit bigger than I'm used to." The seaplane was, in fact, considerably larger than any aircraft he had ever flown.

"But the principle is the same, no? It would give me great pleasure for my grandson to fly me home to Dalmatia."

Luke rose from his seat. "Just don't ask me to land the thing."

The first officer vacated his seat. Luke took a moment to familiarize himself with the controls; then the captain took his hands from the wheel, and the seaplane was his. Compared to the nimble little Hawker Harts of India, it handled like a pregnant sow, bleeding speed in even a gentle turn, but it felt good to be flying again. More than good.

The rugged Croatian coastline was littered with islands of all shapes and sizes, from long strips of sea-girt woodland to mere pinpricks of rock. Vis lay near the southern end of this sprawling archipelago, and on the captain's instructions Luke descended

to three thousand feet. He leveled off, then made way for the first officer.

They came in low over the sea, heading for the large bay at the western end of the island — a giant bite taken out of the wooded hills. The captain overflew the waters he intended to land on, checking for boats before banking steeply over the headland to the north and coming around for their final approach.

Giorgio let out a strangled cry when the hull of the aircraft hit the water, but soon he was beaming with relief and applauding the captain for not killing them. The town of Komiža was small, not much more than a stone jetty, a fortified watchtower, and a cluster of attractive stone houses topped with red clay tiles. A gaily painted fishing boat came out to meet the seaplane. Pippi was the first to be helped aboard, Luke the last. The man who assisted them was tall and ruggedly handsome. He looked at Luke, shaking his head as if in disbelief, before smothering him in a big bear hug.

"This is your mother's brother," said Vittorio. "Your uncle Baltazar."

"Why didn't you say?"

Vittorio shrugged. "I wanted it to be a surprise."

A pack of skinny, bronzed children aban-

doned their sport of leaping off the jetty and collected on the quayside to greet them as they docked. It was unlikely that any of them had ever seen a flying boat before. They had questions, and Baltazar had a question for them in return. They stabbed their fingers at the mouth of an alleyway, then insisted on following. Baltazar's efforts to get rid of them got results only when he took a fistful of change from his pocket and flung the coins out into the harbor.

The house was a humble two-story affair with a postage-stamp lawn out front. Vittorio knocked on the door. It was opened by a young woman with a child on her hip and a guarded look in her eye. Luke searched her face unsuccessfully for signs of Borodin, and it took a fair degree of persuasion on Vittorio's part before she finally relented and invited them in. Giorgio and Baltazar remained outside.

The discussion that took place around the pine table in the kitchen was lost on Luke and Pippi, not that they required a working knowledge of Serbo-Croat to grasp that Simona Lasic was unmoved by Vittorio's words. When he took the leather bag from Luke and revealed its contents to her, she shook her head and said something.

"She doesn't want bad money in her

house," explained Vittorio.

It was a life-changing sum. She must have really hated him.

"Maybe her husband will think differently."

"She says it is her decision."

"Tell her the money has been washed clean by her father's actions." Vittorio translated, but Simona said nothing. "I don't know what sort of man he used to be, but I know what he became at the end."

This time she replied.

"She is not interested," said Vittorio.

"He gave his life for me, a stranger, so you see, I have to tell her what he was really like, whether she wants me to or not."

Vittorio translated. Simona's eyes swung around and locked on to Luke's.

"Please. For me," he said softly.

Vittorio offered no translation, and none was needed.

Simona nodded her assent.

They stepped from the house to see Giorgio and Baltazar backed up against a wall, showing their empty pockets to a mob of dripping kids.

"*Sono degli animali,*" called Giorgio, earning himself a kick in the shin from a young girl clearly versed in Italian. He spread his

arms wide, growling like a bear, and the children fled, screaming in delighted terror.

"An interesting woman," said Vittorio as they strolled back to the harbor.

"Infuriating," said Luke.

"Extraordinary," said Pippi.

Simona had listened closely and dispassionately to Luke, and when he had finished the story, she reached for the leather bag, holding it briefly in her lap before sliding it back across the table to Luke.

"She accepts the gift from her father," Vittorio had explained. "And she now offers it to you."

"I don't want it."

"It's not for you. She asks that you give it to the orphanage."

"Saint Theresa's?"

"Yes. And she would like us to leave now before her husband gets home."

The fishing boat delivered them back to the seaplane. The captain offered his hand and helped Pippi through the door. Luke followed. No one else made a move to do the same.

"I will see you both very soon," said Vittorio.

"You're staying?" Luke could guess what it meant.

"Everything is arranged. You will be in Paris by tomorrow evening."

Baltazar stepped forward, pulling a ring from his finger and handing it to Luke with some words that meant nothing to him.

"It belonged to your mother's father," Vittorio explained as the fishing boat drifted away.

"Thank you, Baltazar."

Baltazar offered a mock salute. Giorgio followed suit. Vittorio just smiled and raised his hand.

Luke didn't examine the ring until they were in their seats and taxiing toward the takeoff point. It was a solid gold signet ring engraved with a trefoil knot symbol: an unending loop, eternal.

The engines roared, the seaplane began to pick up speed, and Pippi and Luke reached for each other's hand across the gangway.

CHAPTER FORTY-SEVEN

A swim before breakfast was an old habit for Josip and Petar Karaman. As boys, they had taken their early morning dip in the sluggish summer waters of the Cetina River. As men, it was in the large tiled swimming pool they had sunk into the orchard beside the big farmhouse they bought and then built onto so that it could accommodate both their families. Fifty years ago, they had eaten breakfast in a dirt-floored room; now it was at a table beneath the rose arbor where Pavel was smoking a cigarette and absently pointing his gun at imaginary targets.

"Still no news from Petrovic?" asked Petar.

"You think it slipped my mind to tell you?"

"I don't need you to tell me what I already know. He has taken the money and disappeared with it."

They turned and set off back down the pool, side by side, in a leisurely breaststroke.

"Petrovic is as loyal as a beaten dog," said Josip.

"You have always had too much faith in him."

"Until a week ago, he hadn't put a foot wrong."

"So, you admit that he has now. Borodin made a fool of him in Zurich."

"And how well do you think *we* would have fared against the old fox? No, we have been played for fools, too, right from the beginning. It's strange. He may be dead, but I can still sense him, out there somewhere."

"Don't change the subject."

"I'm not. You have always been stronger and crueler than me, Petar, but I have always been that bit smarter. And I'm telling you, something is happening here that we don't know about. I need to speak to Albrizzi again, to hear his voice."

"Why?"

"Isn't it obvious?"

"Not to me."

From the house came the distant tinkle of breaking crockery.

"What was that?" asked Josip. "Our breakfast. I've said it before, Hana is getting too old. Her feet are going."

"Pavel."

513

"Boss?"

"Don't just sit there. Go and see. Help. Something."

"Yes, boss." Pavel holstered his gun and made for the house.

"Tell me," said Petar, "why do you need to speak to Albrizzi?"

"Because if I'm right about Petrovic's loyalty, Albrizzi's silence can mean only one thing."

"He has betrayed us."

"Exactly."

"He wouldn't dare. He knows what would happen."

"Then someone has gotten to him," said Josip.

"Who? Hamilton?"

"No, I don't see it."

"Albrizzi senior?"

"That sad old geriatric?"

"Who, then?"

"That's as far as I've gotten with my thinking."

They swam in silence for almost an entire length before Petar said, "I still think Petrovic has taken the money for himself."

"Maybe you're right, but we would be wise to lie low for a bit, until we know for sure."

"We could join the others out on the island."

Their families wouldn't be back from Olib for another week.

"I was thinking Zagreb," said Josip. "The house there is a fortress."

Their breakfast had finally arrived. An old man came shuffling along the path from the house, stooped by the weight of the big tray in his hands.

"Who is that?" asked Josip.

"This place is becoming like a nursing home. The gardener is so old he barely has the strength to prune a rosebush."

"You — who are you?" called Josip.

The old man kept coming, smiling benignly.

"My name is Vittorio Albrizzi."

Two men stepped from the trees at the far end of the pool. Josip saw the guns in their hands and felt a cold knot of fear congeal in his belly.

Vittorio placed the tray on a low table beside the pool.

"Good morning, gentlemen."

They were almost indistinguishable, both of them so hirsute that they looked like seals at play. One of them made for the side of the pool.

515

Vittorio pulled the gun from the pocket of his flannel trousers. "Touch it and I'll shoot you both."

The seal went back to treading water.

"You know why I am here. You have destroyed my family. You took my grandson, his father, his mother, and now you have taken my other son from me."

"That's nonsense. Your son was a war hero."

"Alessandro lost the will to live because of you. He tossed his life away. His wife, Marta — you remember Marta — soon did the same."

"That was a sailing accident."

"Was it? Did you read the letter she left for me? No, you didn't, because I burned it immediately."

"Pavel! Bartol!"

"Don't bother," said Vittorio. "Accept that your lives have narrowed down to a fine point." He took a carving knife from the tray and held it up for them to see. "*This* point."

He tossed the knife into the pool. The long blade flashed silver like a darting fish as it sank to the bottom.

"It's very simple. Only one of you will walk up those steps there. The man who does has my word I will not kill him."

"Why should we believe you?"

"Because you don't have a choice. Because I'll shoot you both like fish in a barrel if I have to."

"Kurvin sine!" one of them spat. *"Jebi se."*

"Save your breath; you're going to need it."

The brothers eyed each other warily as they began to tire from the effort of staying afloat.

"Not like this, Josip."

"No, he can shoot us both. You hear that? You can —"

He broke off as the other one dived for the bottom of the pool. And then they both were gone.

It was quick. A flurry of arms as they surfaced . . . a flash of steel . . . several cries . . . blood beginning to stain the water . . . the fight going out of one of them . . . the knife thrusting, finishing the job . . . a body, inert, facedown in the water . . . the other brother swimming through the crimson cloud for the steps at the end of the pool.

Vittorio and Baltazar were there to greet him. He was heaving from the exertion, and his hooded eyes held a look of pure, distilled hatred.

"Which one are you?" Vittorio asked.

"Petar."

"The younger one. The sadist."

Baltazar raised his pistol.

"You gave your word!"

"And I intend to honor it," said Vittorio. "But what Baltazar here chooses to do is entirely his own business. He is Marta's brother."

"This isn't over," growled Petar Karaman. "My son will find you."

Vittorio took a step toward him. "Well done, you have just killed your son. How does it feel — first your brother and now your son?"

"Go to hell!"

"Where do you think I've been for the past twenty-five years?"

He expected obscenities, or maybe a plea for mercy, but all he heard as he headed for the house was a single shot and the splash of a body hitting the water.

He didn't look back.

The son would be allowed to live, because the son would hear from the cook and the men who had been overpowered that their attackers had been Romanian, as indeed the three men currently in control of the house all were. By now they may even have let slip the name that would steer suspicions toward an old enemy of the Karamans in Bucharest.

It was information that Baltazar had dug up. As for what might happen after that, Vittorio neither knew nor cared.

■ ■ ■ ■

FRANCE

■ ■ ■ ■

CHAPTER FORTY-EIGHT

It wasn't Luke's first visit to the Ministère des Affaires Étrangères. His work in the Air Intelligence Department had brought him a number of times to the palatial building on Quai d'Orsay for meetings with his French counterparts. The first-floor offices lacked the overbearing opulence of the ground-floor reception rooms, but they still oozed a nonchalant grandeur that seemed to have infected their occupants.

Reynaud — he had offered them no other names or titles — sat at his desk, his back to the tall windows overlooking the manicured gardens at the rear of the building.

"It is an interesting story," he conceded in his heavily accented English. "If it is true."

Higginbotham uncrossed his legs and smoothed his trousers with his palms. "I don't see why you should question our account of events. We have nothing to hide from you, Monsieur Reynaud."

Luke had known Higginbotham for all of three hours, two of which he had spent at the British Embassy, being debriefed by the coldly competent diplomat and his silent, watchful colleague from London, Armstrong.

"As you know," said Reynaud, "Monsieur Hamilton was involved in an attack on a minister of the French government."

"Hardly an attack. Monsieur Balthus was relieved of his motor vehicle . . . while in the company of a woman who was not his wife, I believe."

"How do you know this?"

Higginbotham ignored the question. "I really can't see that it's in Monsieur Balthus' interest to pursue the matter further. Besides, we have evidence that Mr. Hamilton here was an innocent and unwilling party, not just to the hijacking of the car, but to all the unfortunate events that occurred that night."

"Evidence?"

"In the form of a handwritten confession." Higginbotham produced a letter from his briefcase. "This was received by the British Embassy a few days ago." He rose and handed it to Reynaud. "As you can see from the postmark, it was sent from Zurich. It's from Borodin, the man known to your lot

as Bernard Fautrier."

It was the first that Luke had heard of any such letter. Higginbotham caught his inquiring look. "I didn't want to get your hopes up," he said quietly as he sat back down.

Reynaud pulled a number of sheets from the envelope and examined them.

"It's rather long, I'm afraid. He didn't hold back on the details. We also have several witnesses waiting outside who can corroborate much of what —"

Reynaud raised a hand. "Yes, yes, let me read it."

He smoked as he read, flapping irritably at the air around him as though someone else were to blame for the annoying fug of smoke. They sat and waited patiently, and Luke wondered if the bronze bust of Napoleon on Reynaud's desk had been placed there on purpose as a taunt to the English visitors.

"How do I know this is real?" said Reynaud eventually, laying the pages aside.

"If you feel the need to confirm its authenticity, I'm sure an expert graphologist could offer an opinion based on a handwriting sample taken from Borodin's apartment. I should also add that Mr. Hamilton is here today entirely of his own volition. He has chosen not to invoke his diplomatic im-

munity to the charges currently standing against him."

"So far."

"I see no reason from our side why it should come to that. It would be most unfortunate for anything to sour the long and happy relationship between our two nations at a time such as this. You and I both know what is coming. We also know that England and France will stand together as allies against a common enemy, even if we don't yet know the face, or faces, of that enemy. Cooperation is surely the order of the day, Monsieur Reynaud."

Luke felt comforted having Higginbotham in his corner. Who could hold out against such relentless eloquence? It just kept coming at you in waves.

Reynaud removed his spectacles. *"La coopération est fondée sur la reciprocité."*

"Indeed it is, Monsieur Reynaud." Higginbotham turned to Luke. "You can leave us now." He accompanied Luke to the door. "We're almost there. A bit of reciprocity, and everything in the garden will be lovely — the bananas'll be right over the fence."

Higginbotham had evidently been posted to the tropics at some time or other.

It was a long walk along a parquet corridor to the seating area where Pippi, Fer-

nando, and Diana were waiting. They all rose expectantly to their feet as Luke approached.

"Borodin wrote a letter explaining everything."

Pippi hugged him.

"Is that good?" asked Fernando.

"Very good."

"You mean I don't have to save you? I wanted to save you."

Diana laughed, and Luke thought, *Oh, dear. Poor Diana.* Their brief affair earlier in the year had been conducted in complete secrecy; now was the first time that Diana had been exposed to Fernando's roguish charms.

"I shall have to buy you lunch instead, all of you," said Fernando.

"I really should be getting back to the embassy if I'm no longer required."

"But you *are* required, Diana. In my country, it is a great offense to reject food that has been offered to you."

"Then it's a good job we're in France," Diana replied with the faintest curve of a smile.

Fernando spread his hands in a gesture of surrender. "Okay, you win. No lunch. Dinner it is."

Pippi laughed.

Oh, God, not her too.

They were searching for a taxi on Quai d'Orsay when Luke spotted him. He was standing in the shade of a tree, smoking a cigarette. He raised a hand, the palm displayed in a simple gesture of peaceful greeting.

"Wait for me," said Luke.

He approached with caution, eyes scanning the faces of the pedestrians around him, searching for signs, anomalies.

"Mr. Hamilton."

"Mr. Oaks."

"All sorted with our French friends?" Cordell Oaks nodded at the ministry building. Everything about him seemed different: the voice, the look in his eye, the way he held himself. Where was the grave, thoughtful, pleasant-mannered American Luke had first met?

"Who are you?"

"Hell, I'm not sure I rightly know anymore. But you have nothing to fear from me." Oaks tapped the ash from his cigarette. "I owed Borodin a favor — several, in fact."

"Oh?"

"He asked me to keep an eye on you."

"That's not possible. We were on the same train from Strasbourg."

528

"Same train from Paris, too."

Luke shook his head. "No."

"You say so; I know so. I got a call telling me to be at the Gare de l'Est in half an hour."

It fit. Borodin could have phoned Oaks when he left the bar early, before Diana showed up with Luke's passport and the suitcase.

"Works, huh?" said Oaks. "Not much else did." He had lost sight of Luke in Konstanz, then picked him up again in Zurich.

"So that *was* you at the Café Glück?"

"Too late to do anything for Borodin."

"But not for me."

"No offense, but I shot that bastard for Borodin. I wasn't thinking of you, not then." Not until Borodin had called him from the hotel in Splügen and told him the whole story. "He made me promise to stay on the case, even left some cash for me at the chalet. I picked up your trail again at Bergamo station."

"That explains it."

"What's that?"

"I saw you at the hotel in Venice."

"You were there?" asked Oaks.

"Leaving as you were arriving."

"My job was to get you out if things turned hairy."

"We'd still be running now if we'd left with you then."

Oaks looked intrigued. "Your folks came out all right?"

Luke nodded. There was no point in confusing the issue with talk of Benedetto's treachery.

"The Karaman brothers . . . ?"

"No longer with us."

"That's too bad." Oaks grinned, dropping his cigarette at his feet and grinding it into the pavement. "Borodin won. It cost him dear, but he won. Hang on to that. I know I'm going to."

"I will."

Oaks glanced past him. "You should go. Your friends are waiting."

Luke offered his hand. "Thank you."

"You ever need anything, you call the US embassy here and ask for the Department of Fiscal Relations."

"Not milk?"

Oaks laughed. "Have my brother-in-law to thank for that. Mr. Cream Cheese, dullest man in the known world. You got off light: there's a load more where that stuff came from."

As soon as the door of Reynaud's office had closed behind them, Armstrong said to Hig-

ginbotham, "Am I dreaming, or did you really just do that?"

"You heard the man: 'Cooperation is founded on reciprocity.' "

"Reciprocity? You traded a French mole in the Colonial Office for a minor official in the Air Intelligence Department of the Paris embassy!"

"After everything Hamilton has been through? Have you no heart?"

"I know for a fact *you* don't, so I'm asking myself what you're really up to."

"It's called knocking the ball into the long grass," said Higginbotham. "It's called orders from on high."

That piqued Armstrong's interest. "How high?"

"Vansittart."

"Vansittart? What does he care about a man like Hamilton?"

"Theirs not to reason why; theirs but to do and die."

"To hell with Tennyson."

"I couldn't agree more. I find his poetry so achingly portentous. But if I *were* to reason why, I would say this: Hamilton is a doer, and he didn't die. Think about it for a moment. The fellow has been hunted from one end of Europe to the other, and he's still alive. Not only that, he also found time

to serve his country along the way."

"You mean Professor Weintraub?"

"Weintraub would never have left Germany without his children. Thanks to Hamilton, we have him."

"It was brave, I grant you."

"More than brave. It required him to kill a man and keep his head afterwards. How many are made for that sort of thing? You? Me?"

"I think I can see where you're heading with this," said Armstrong after a moment.

"And I haven't even started on the girl."

"The winsome Miss Keller . . ."

"Quite a team, the two of them. Vansittart certainly thinks so — enough, at least, for the possibilities to be explored."

They were descending the main staircase when Armstrong said, "I'm actually quite a fan of Tennyson."

"That is because, like all misanthropes, you have a great sentimental streak in you."

■ ■ ■ ■

ENGLAND

■ ■ ■ ■

CHAPTER FORTY-NINE

On his mother's orders, Luke had mowed the lawn and was now weeding the borders. Hearing the sound of a car approaching down the driveway, he was struck by the pleasant realization that a mere three weeks ago, the crunch of tires on gravel would have set his heart racing and had him hurrying to the corner of the house, hoe in hand, to see who it was.

He was getting there more slowly than Pippi, but he wasn't so far behind her. She had embraced her new life with enthusiasm, possibly because it was the only one available to her. She was an exile now. There was no prospect of her returning to Germany anytime soon, if ever. For Luke, though, home came with its complications. There were echoes, not all of them good.

Hardest of all had been their first visit to St. Theresa's, and the guilt he had carried with him to the foot of Sister Agnes' grave.

There was no avoiding the painful truth: she had been killed because of him. If he had never entered her world as an infant, she would still be alive today. The sense of blame was so overwhelming that he had thought for a moment he might lie to Mother Hilda, distancing himself from Agnes' murder. He could have invented an excuse for his failure to attend her funeral, and the money that Simona had asked him to give to the orphanage could easily have found its way into the coffers by means of an anonymous bequest. But finding himself in Mother Hilda's office, the very room where Agnes had forfeited her life, he had opted to come clean about his involvement in the tragedy. He had also requested Mother Hilda's discretion.

"My grandfather in Italy has done his best to bury the story for reasons of our safety, to avoid further repercussions. But I can promise you that the man responsible for what happened in this room has been brought to justice."

Mother Hilda had parsed the true meaning of his words. "Then that is enough. I see no reason to share what you have told me with the detective in charge of the investigation. He shall have to keep tearing his hair out."

"Thank you."

"No, thank *you*, Luke. For your honesty and for this extraordinary gift. As you know, there are many wonders we can perform with this money."

"It's from Simona."

"Yes, but also from Borodin. He sounds like a remarkable person."

"He was," Pippi had concurred.

It was then that Mother Hilda had offered a slightly curious interpretation of events. "I think maybe that the pure spirit of Agnes, on being released, found a new home for itself in this man Borodin."

It didn't fit with any tenets of Christian theology that Luke had ever come across, but he still thought of those words and drew comfort from them.

There had been better times since: trips to Ely and Cambridge, punting on the Cam, a picnic in Grantchester Meadows with his parents, a weekend by the sea in Southwold, and for Pippi, long jaunts through the fens on a frisky piebald mare that Solomon had found for her to ride.

An agreeable limbo, but limbo nonetheless. For Luke, the days seemed to be growing longer, even as they grew shorter. His status was still unclear, his future within the Royal Air Force yet to be determined. He

continued to receive his salary, but there had been no definite news from London.

"Luke, Luke . . . !" Pippi hurried from the house, bounded across the terrace, and skipped down the stone steps. "This just arrived by messenger. Pippi Keller is dead."

She handed him a pristine passport. The photo inside was of Pippi, but the name read *Emily Sutton.*

"What do you think?" she asked.

"I think I want to kiss you, Emily Sutton."

When he reached for her lips, she recoiled in feigned modesty. "But we have only just met."

They laughed, then kissed.

"You know who I have to show this to, don't you?"

"I can't wait," said Luke.

Solomon was filleting a fish for his lunch when they showed up.

"It's true," chimed Pippi. "Look. I am British like you."

Solomon rinsed his hands in a bowl, dried them on a stained towel, then took the passport from her.

"All this proves is, the world's so twisted, if it ate a nail it'd shit a corkscrew."

"Solomon!" she gasped. "There's a lady present!" It was a phrase she had picked up

from Luke. Solomon enjoyed trying to shock her; it was part of their game.

Solomon glanced again at the passport. "You're no more an Emily than I is."

"You'll get used to it."

"Don't got much choice, do I?"

When Luke told him to save some space for dinner, Solomon grumbled, "More damned Continentals."

Solomon had never made any bones about his low opinion of foreigners, and although his words had a playful edge — especially since Luke now fell within their unsavory ranks — the prejudice was also bred in the bone. Solomon was descended from men who had gone out at night to slit the throats of the Dutch engineers brought in to drain the fens and destroy an ancient way of life.

"Just my grandfather and my uncle," said Luke. "Are you sure you can cope? You're going to be outnumbered, four to three."

Solomon gave an amused snort. "What, you think four of you lot is worth three of us?"

The train was due to arrive at Cambridge station shortly before six o'clock, and Luke and Pippi were on the point of leaving when the telephone rang.

"Luke, it's a Mr. Higginbotham for you,"

his father called.

Higginbotham sounded in a good mood. "I just wanted to check that the passport had arrived."

"This morning. I really don't know how to thank you."

"No need. She more than earned it. The other documentation is being prepared. She should be fully naturalized within the week."

"You changed her name, I see."

"It made sense."

"Sense?"

"For her. She shot and killed a man in Zurich, remember?" Luke heard Higginbotham light a cigarette. "Listen, there's another matter that has come to my ears. I thought you should know. The RAF are talking about an honorable discharge for you."

Luke felt his heart sink.

"They want to wash their hands of me?"

"They're struggling to see where you might . . . well, fit. In the light of everything that has happened, I mean."

"I see."

"I don't. I think they're bloody fools, but there it is."

More than talk, then. A fait accompli.

"Thank you for warning me."

"Maybe we can have lunch at my club

when you're next in London."

"I'd like that."

"There are a couple of people I want you to meet. Oh, and bring Miss Keller with you." Higginbotham grunted. "My mistake — Miss *Sutton*. I can show her the seat of her new government, or maybe a tour of the House of Commons isn't quite her thing."

"No, I'm sure she'd enjoy that."

"Next week is good for me, assuming you have nothing better to do."

So Higginbotham wasn't entirely without humor.

"Whitehall three five seven. Can you remember that?"

"It's a sequence of prime numbers," said Luke.

"Is it? So it is. Interesting. I wonder who has two three five."

"Call it and see."

Higginbotham chuckled. "I might just do that. One never knows. The world can turn on such things."

They took the slow road to Cambridge, through Burwell and Swaffham Prior, the sinking sun striking the black-soiled fens at an angle and throwing off a limpid purple light.

"He's up to something," said Luke.

"Higginbotham? Maybe he just likes us and wants to help."

"It's good to trust others, but better not to."

"Who said that?" Pippi asked.

"Borodin, to me, in Paris." Luke drove on in reflective silence. "I never even asked him his name."

"He told me at the end, at the chalet. Ivan."

"Ivan Borodin. You asked him?"

"He wanted me to know."

"Why?"

"He had his reason."

"Am I allowed to hear it?"

"Maybe one day."

Luke glanced over at her. "I'll get it out of you."

"Then you don't know me."

"I know you're ticklish. You'll cough it up."

Pippi laughed. "Okay, but he was the one who said it, not me." She leaned over and whispered in his ear.

"He really said that?"

"He really did."

Luke took a moment to consider his response.

"But what if it's a girl?" he asked.

Pippi laid her hand gently on his thigh,

although her eyes remained fixed on the straight road ahead.

"Ivana, I suppose."

ABOUT THE AUTHOR

Mark Mills graduated from Cambridge University in 1986. He has lived in both Italy and France, and has written for the screen. His first novel, AMAGANSETT, won the 2004 Crime Writers' Association Award for Best Novel by a debut author. His second, THE SAVAGE GARDEN, was a Richard and Judy Summer Read and a number one bestseller. Under the name Mark B. Mills, he has written the comic novel, WAITING FOR DOGGO. He lives near Oxford with his wife and two children.